Kip sat on the computer for company. Yesterday for Pennsylvania, his sister had returned to Atlanta with Barry, and after their all-too-pleasant afternoon together two days ago, he refused to allow himself to call Anna. Without his family around he found the house uncomfortably empty. He'd grown up with his brothers and sister around him and all the companionship and hustle-bustle a large family entailed. He missed it. In California he lived alone, but chasing bad guys didn't give him much home time, and if he did have extra time, he usually stopped in on his shipping business, not so much to oversee it, but to touch base with his very competent manager. He thought he'd gotten used to the solitary life, but after a few weeks at Marsh Winds he realized how much he missed all the family, all the laughter and fun.

He leaned back against the cushion of his wicker chair and listened to the sounds of the old plantation house—the patter of acorns on the tin roof, the rustle of palm fronds and oak leaves in the wind, the birds singing away over the harsh squawks of a few marsh hens—all sounds he loved, but he missed the sounds of Dylan's daughter bustling through the house or interrupting him to attend a tea party she'd set up or show him something she'd made. He missed the sound of Maribel and his sister chatting as they worked with his mother in the kitchen, and he couldn't help but remember back to another time when it was his Marie who'd been the helper, his son who'd been there wanting to play ball. Being here these past weeks had brought back all the old feelings for the family he'd moved away from and his family that was dead.

He drew in a deep breath and stretched out his legs.

And then there was Anna. Once he'd promised to always love her, to protect her and never hurt her. He'd broken all his promises. A relationship with her would necessitate commitment, marriage. He couldn't afford that. Never again. *Anna, Anna, send me away. I don't want to hurt you again.*

He wasn't the monster she suspected him of being. He didn't murder her sister or burn her house, but he wasn't simply the guy she'd fallen for in high school either. He'd seen things, done things that could turn a man inside-out if he dwelled on them. The constant cloud of danger that hung over him wasn't the kind of life he wanted to share with a woman.

He needed her out of his life so he could regain his balance and concentrate on the case. On the other hand, he needed to find her sister's killer. Ironically, in order for him to find the killer he needed to know everything Anna knew. That necessitated he spend time with her. Technically, he thought with a tightening of his jaw, he was what one would describe as being caught between a rock and a hard place.

The kiss had been a mistake. The kiss had only rekindled memories best left forgotten and made him want more. He needed to back off, keep the relationship impersonal. A picnic at Ft. Pulaski—what had he been thinking of?

Hell, he was already in too deep.

Winds of Fire

Ann Merritt

Highland Press Publishing
Florida

Winds of Fire

Copyright ©2014 Ann Merritt
Cover Copyright ©2014 Amber Wentworth

Produced in the United States of America. All rights reserved. No part of this book may be reproduced or transmitted in any form or by any means, electronic or mechanical, including photocopying, recording, or by an information storage and retrieval system—except by a reviewer who may quote brief passages in a review to be printed in a magazine, newspaper, or on the Web—without permission in writing from the publisher.

For information, please contact
Highland Press Publishing,
PO Box 2292, High Springs, FL 32655.
www.highlandpress.org

All characters in this book have no existence outside the imagination of the author and have no relation whatsoever to anyone bearing the same name or names, save actual historical figures. They are not even distantly inspired by any individual known or unknown to the author, and all incidents are pure invention.

ISBN: 978-0-9895262-8-0

Highland Press Publishing
http://highlandpress.org

Romantic Suspense

Dedication

This book is dedicated to the memory of my late husband, **MacAllister Merritt**. He was my best friend and my confidant.

To **Leanne Burroughs**, my editor, for providing me the opportunity to pursue my love of writing. Many thanks, Leanne.

As well, I want to thank the brave men and women who serve in the **United States Armed Forces**. Without their constant vigil and selfless sacrifices America would not be the wonderful country it is today. Without their courage and dedication we would not live in Freedom. Thank you. God Bless you.

Chapter One

Anna Hanley was in her kitchen boiling an afternoon's catch of crabs. On the adjoining burner a second pot simmered with a solitary hotdog. The evening was hot for November, muggy and peaceful. Along the coast of Tybee Island a sleepy blue haze of dusk had settled across the sky.

The house was antebellum, originally built for a summer retreat, and had been in Anna's family for more than a century. Since her parents' untimely deaths three years earlier, the house belonged to Anna. Last year she upgraded the kitchen with modern appliances, repainted the walls to a cheerful yellow, and installed white cottage shutters in the many windows. A few months ago she sanded down the cabinets and coated them with white paint, rubbing the seams and edges to maintain the distressed look. Now each time she entered the room she delighted in the fresh, sunny feeling she got.

The oversized pine table in front of the brick fireplace at the room's center turned the kitchen into a hub of family activity for all the summers Anna could remember. Tonight one end of the table was full of treasures Anna and her sister Holly had found at yesterday's garage sales. The other end was set for supper with three straw mats and a roll of paper towel placed within easy reach. On one of the chairs sat a red, yellow, and gold plastic booster seat.

In the distance a foghorn sounded as a cargo vessel made its way down the Savannah River to port and drew Anna to an open window. Bracing her hands on the windowsill, she lifted her chin and breathed deeply. The scent of the sea was as much a part of her as the old wooden walls of her home. With the tide poised to start coming in, the breeze was slight and overly warm and did little to disperse the heat that blushed her face. Still, she was loath to close the windows and crank up the air conditioning friends had convinced her to install, preferring instead the moist warmth lingering from a day of sunshine. She gave herself to it, savoring the warmth, the feel of isolation, the peace that descended over the island in the off-season.

From the front room where her sister and her sister's son Danny sat in front of the TV and "Curious George," she heard a burst of laughter and smiled as she squeezed fresh lemon into the chunks of butter melting in a saucepan. It was good to have her sister and nephew here and the laughter of a child in the house again.

The smile quickly faded. Her sister was having marital problems and had come from Fort Worth, Texas for a couple weeks while she tried to sort out her future. Before Holly returned, Anna hoped she would be more forthcoming about what was afoot. Anna hadn't pried and wouldn't, but the tidbits of information Holly had dropped left Anna with growing concerns about the state of her sister's marriage.

Anna sighed and was about to check on the crab when a movement outside the window caught her attention. As she watched, a shadow separated itself from the dark of a tree and ran toward the beachside of the house. Too big to be a dog or even a child, the shadow moved with a stealth that led her to believe it was a man or woman not wishing to be seen.

She was still trying to assimilate what she'd seen when a loud crash resounded from the front room, followed immediately by the tinkle of broken glass and Holly's shout of alarm. Anna jerked upright and turned toward the sounds, listening for her sister to reprimand Danny, the scolding words poised on her own lips. But after the first shout there was nothing.

Silence came into the room. With it came a quivery feeling that settled in Anna's core. The birds stopped singing; the big pot filled with crabs ceased to bubble. It was as though the world had come to a stop.

The ding of the microwave gave Anna a start. The mac and cheese she was reheating to go with Danny's hotdog were ready, but she didn't move toward it. Frozen, she held her breath.

Then her nephew began to wail.

Anna let out a sigh of relief. Something had broken. Not a big deal. Kids will be kids. It could have been the glass lamp she'd filled with shells had been bumped from the end-table. Perhaps the crystal vase at the end of the hall filled with the fresh mums had been knocked over. Maybe Danny had thrown his tennis ball, and it had gone awry, hitting the window or the glass of one of the framed watercolors.

She snatched up a broom and dustpan from the closet near the back door and started toward the living room then stopped midstride. Was that gasoline she smelled? She sniffed the air, mentally searching for reasons why the scent of gasoline would be present in her kitchen—fumes from a neighbor's gas-powered weed-eater, exhaust from a rusted muffler coming through the open window—but the silence belied those possibilities, and she quickly dismissed them.

A moment later she detected the scent of smoke. Her eyes widened with alarm. It seemed incredulous yet the thought came with such force she couldn't ignore it. The house was on fire. Someone had used gasoline to torch her home.

"Holly! I smell smoke! Are you all right?"

As were most of the old homes and many of the new ones on Tybee Island, Anna's house was made of wood, old wood that had been baked in the sun. The house was a fire-trap, and Anna knew it. But with so much love and happy memories tied up in the only home she'd ever known, she liked it just the way it always had been. In the event of a fire she feared it would be only a matter of minutes before the old wood would be ablaze. Her stomach clenched.

"Holly! Answer me!"

The broom and dustpan clattered to the floor as she hurried to the sink for the fire extinguisher the insurance agent had insisted she install. It wasn't there, and she remembered she'd moved it to the pantry where it better fit. She jerked open the door, grabbed it, and ran. At the end of the hallway connecting the front room to the kitchen a puff of smoke, just a wispy one, so wraithlike that at first she thought she imagined it, twisted toward the ceiling. She bolted down the hallway, the extinguisher in front of her like a gun. Past the door to the butler's pantry with its glass-paned cabinets filled with ancestors' glassware, past the entrance to the large dining room where priceless paintings hung, she ran toward the cheerful tune coming from the TV, her heart pounding.

At the end of the hallway clouds of smoke billowed from the living room. She was stunned the blaze could have erupted so fast. How was she supposed to make the extinguisher work? She studied it a moment before pulling out the clip. The trigger was hard to compress. Finally she got it to budge, and the stream of white foam came out but without much force. Dang, she was probably doing it wrong.

"Holly! Holly! Are you and Danny still in here?" She shouted and sprayed the foam in front of her. She tried to remain calm but heard the desperation in her voice. "Speak to me! Where are you?"

Nothing but the crackle of the fire and the drone of the TV answered her.

Her eyes burned. Was it possible Holly ran upstairs before the fire started? Had she and Danny already fled out the front door? She prayed it was so, but her mind screamed *No*. Immediately following the breaking of glass, she'd heard her sister's scream and Danny's cry. Something was terribly wrong.

The last time she'd seen Holly she'd been sitting by the window reading. Anna made her way toward the window, the extinguisher dribbling out its foam, her tennis shoes crunching over shards of glass. The sting in her eyes was so painful it was impossible to keep them open, so she closed them and went by memory. She bumped into the chair suddenly, nearly falling into it. She forced her eyes open. In the thick smoke, at first Anna couldn't make out her sister in the over-stuffed chair. Then she did and wished she hadn't. Holly's head was slumped to her chest, and she wasn't moving. Anna dropped the extinguisher, grabbed her sister's shoulders, and shook.

"Holly, get up, wake up! The house is on fire."

She slapped her sister's cheeks. No response. On the end table beside her sister there was usually a phone. She groped for it, found it and dialed 911. She held the phone to her ear. Nothing! The line was dead.

Behind her Danny coughed and choked. Then he began to cry. "My eyes hurt..."

"I'll be right there, sweetheart."

Praise God, at least Danny was alive. Anna couldn't ignore his crying. She whirled toward the sound, remembering he usually sat on the sofa to watch TV, then turned back to her sister and made one last effort to rouse her, slapping her face

Winds of Fire

harder this time. She thought maybe she heard a groan, but it could have been the fire. She wasn't sure.

"Dammit, Holly! Get up! *Get up*! Please! You've got to get out of here. The house is on fire."

Her actions were to no avail. She realized she had no choice but to leave her sister for the moment. She had to take her nephew out of harm's way. It would be what her sister wanted.

"I'm coming, Danny."

She tried the phone one last time. *No dial tone.* She tossed the worthless thing to the floor. So much for it being a lifeline. Then coughing and bending double to stay under the bulk of the smoke, she ran blindly across the room, moving from memory alone.

The choking sobs led her to her nephew. She scrubbed at her eyes, forced them open, and saw the child had placed the sofa cushions into some sort of garage and hiding place. His eyes just showed above the cushion wall and were red and pouring tears. When she bent over to pick him up, his skinny little arms were wrapped around his chest. In each of his hands he clutched a car. And Anna couldn't hold back her tears as she grabbed her nephew and pulled him against her.

"Here I am, honey." Flames now erupted near the beachside of the room and were devouring the hemp rug she so loved. No, she couldn't think of things. She had to focus on Danny. The way to the front door looked to be blocked by fire. She couldn't believe the flames had gotten so far so fast. She hugged her nephew to her, trying to alleviate both his and her fears. "I'll take care of you, sweetheart."

She hitched his little bottom on her hip and thanked God he was still alive. With him held close against her body to protect him from the heat and any falling debris, she cradled his head against her breast, and ran. Her head throbbed, her knees were weak, but she ran like a fullback, darting this way and that, bumping into the coffee table and chair, dodging the scattered cushions in her way. She had to hurry and get Danny to safety so she could and get back to get her sister out. *Please God, help her.*

Through the short hall, she ran back into the kitchen and out the back door to a nearby jetty where the sand was piled up damp and the fire couldn't reach. She rocked him a little and kissed his head.

"It's all right, sweetheart," she crooned to her nephew once again, but in truth nothing was right. She wondered if it ever would be again. "Hush, little one, don't cry any more..."

His gulping sobs broke her heart. He was shaking so much, but she certainly couldn't fault him for that. She was as well. In truth, she couldn't tell where his shaking ended and hers began. But she had to leave him. She had to. She had to get back to her sister. Precious minutes were ticking away. She tried to put him onto the sand, but he held her fast. She pried his little fingers from her arms and her shirt and forced him to the ground. Every second she waited with him could be the last for his mother.

"No, Danny, don't get up." She forced her voice to sound stern. She couldn't be worrying about him right now. What a ridiculous thing to think! But she had to focus on what was happening. And what she still needed to do. "Sit down and wait right where you are." She reinforced her terms again, making her voice slightly harsher. The last thing she wanted was scare him, but if she didn't return to the house soon—without him—there'd be no way to safely rescue her sister. No! *Please God! Please keep my family safe.*

She turned her attention back to her nephew. "Please do that, honey, so I can try and get your mommy. You be a big boy, sweetie. Don't go anywhere. Do you understand?"

He began to sob harder than before, but he didn't get up. It was like a knife in her heart to leave him. "I'll be right back." She prayed it was true as she ran toward the burning house. *God, please don't let him stray.* She didn't look back.

In the seconds it took her to reach her house, she remembered the hose. She turned it on full force and grabbed it and pulled it through the back door. The kitchen was filling with smoke, but no flames were there yet—just smoke, oceans of smoke. But soon as she stepped from the connecting hall into the living room she was met with a wall of heat and smoke so intense not even the water pouring from the hose protected her.

She reeled back, firing the water into the smoke and fire.

Through the swirling black clouds of smoke, Anna detected movement. She spun toward the shadow in hopes her sister might be trying to escape through the front door. "Holly? That you?"

Immediately she saw her error. The figure outlined against the waning light from the front window was clearly a man, and he was clothed in something dark like he wanted to melt into the night. The front door swung open, and the figure disappeared, leaving the door open behind him. Smoke and flames rushed toward the new air.

He was *inside!* Horrified, she had no time to dwell on it.

Remarkably the lights were still on, the TV talking about the man with the yellow hat coming to rescue George from one of his misadventures. None of it registered with her, only that the entire room was choked with smoke. Like a breathing monster, smoke sucked up the oxygen and puffed out the open windows, down the hall and up the stairs. It was asphyxiating her, but her sister was in there and could still be alive. At least she prayed her sister was alive. Anna doused her head and shoulders with water and fell to her knees, beginning to crawl with the hose spurting water ahead of her.

There Holly was! Sprawled on the floor. Anna was certain she'd left her sitting in the chair. The notion kicked her with a fresh spurt of hope that her sister was alive and had tried to escape. On the floor beside Holly, shattered glass from the window gave gruesome evidence of a homemade bomb that had been tossed inside. Anna grabbed a pillow and batted at the flames that rose from the rug beside her sister, then froze in disbelief.

Revealed in the bright light coming from the lamp was something that hadn't been there earlier. A nasty gash on her sister's neck. Anna reeled back in shock. God, in Heaven, what was going on? What kind of monster had come inside her house and done that to her sister? Why? Anna choked in a breath, aimed the water at her sister, and pulled hard on the hose. It jerked free from her hands. The hose had run short.

She let it lay where it dropped and used the cushion to smack at the flames that had ignited the rug. Then she tried to lift her, but Holly weighed a good thirty pounds more than she did. Desperate, she tried to rouse her once again, quickly realized it was a waste of time. Holly was limp, her eyes glassy and open. Anna feared her sister would never again hug her child. But she couldn't just leave her to burn. There was always the chance that even with the gash she could be saved. This was her big sister, her confidante, her rival, and her best friend. Holly had supported her in everything Anna had done. Gasping for breath, Anna dragged Holly to the water gushing from the hose and began to pull her from the room.

Eyes streaming, Anna wondered how much longer she could manage to breathe. She thought of little Danny on the beach all alone and terrified. She couldn't give up. She simply couldn't.

The prudent thing to do was run from the house and save herself. Yet looking into her sister's lifeless eyes, she knew she'd never live with herself if she did that. Squatting down in front of Holly, Anna found strength she didn't know she had. She grabbed her sister's ankles and pulled with all her might.

As she passed into the hallway, by habit she glanced at the wall mirror and what she saw through the smoke caused her heart to stop beating. The hulking shadow of a large man was peering through the front window. Anna gasped and hurried her steps. Had he seen her? Did he understand she was heading out through the back door? Would he be waiting there to block her way?

She *had* to get out of the house!

Her strength was nearly gone. She dragged Holly across the floor, and began to crawl backward toward the door once again, but much slower this time. Each step might be her last.

She bumped into a chair and realized she was at the kitchen table, not fifteen feet from the door and life-giving air. She renewed her efforts, slithering across the wooden planks. She was coughing, gagging, but she couldn't stop. Her eyes were blind. Her throat burned. Her lungs ached. She couldn't catch a breath.

With resolve she clamped her mouth shut and drew on the last of her strength, inching toward the door. She had to have enough to get them both onto the back stoop. If only…

It was no use. Her hands slipped from her sister's ankles; her head dropped to the floor.

Chapter Two

Kip McTeer stood at the open doorway with the smoke billowing into his face and tried to locate the woman he'd seen run inside. For several seconds he stood, struggling for breath, without seeing her. Then his gaze landed on the length of hose twisted across the floor. He followed it to a spot on the far side of a table. There not fifteen feet away from him were two bodies.

He covered his face with his arm and ran to them. The first woman he reached was still alive. He scooped her into his arms and grimaced at the sudden sharp pain in his chest. He staggered and very nearly dropped her, then hissed an oath and ran from the house.

The child remained sitting in the sand, his mouth down turned and trembling, his soot-blackened face streaked with tears, but he'd stopped crying. Before he left the woman beside the boy, he glanced at her, and his gut clenched. He forgot to breathe. Anna... *Damn.*

For a moment he couldn't move. Anna... The last of the daylight caught in her long, straight, blonde hair, reminding him of her at seventeen and the nights they'd spent on the dunes together. In another lifetime, he had loved Anna Hanley with all his heart. His jaw tightened as he turned away.

He ran back inside the house a second time and came out with the second woman. Holly. Her throat had been slit, and she was beyond any earthly help. He left her body on a sand dune a few feet from the house and returned to Anna and her boy.

When he bent over her to bring her back into his arms, she glared up at him through red and swollen eyes. Kip was grateful to see no recognition in her gaze, but the anger there startled him. It was just as well, he thought with a wistful smile. It made things easier that way.

This time when he hauled her into his arms, he steeled himself. Still, shots of pain radiated from his arm and side. He closed his eyes. It took several deep breaths before he could overcome the pain and hoist her son up over his other shoulder. He stood that way for several moments. When he could catch his breath again, he walked with them straight into the sea without giving the fire a backward glance or his pain further consideration. There he ducked down below the water's surface.

Soon as he judged every smoldering ember was thoroughly doused, he rose again and walked toward the sand. Immediately the boy began to wail at the top of his lungs.

"Bastard!" Anna uttered a whispered gasp and sputtered for air. His mouth twitched. So much for her knighting him with thanks and eternal gratitude for his efforts.

She began to gag and then to cough. Setting her on the sand, he rubbed her back, then gently patted it as he kneeled beside her. If she'd been touched by the flames, the places would burn like hell from the salt water. But at least he was assured nothing burned on her now.

Night hovered over the shoreline, descending across the sky like a warm blanket. Only a thin haze of daylight remained. In the shallow waters close to the shore where the seagulls swarmed and a breeze blew, he sat cross-legged with Anna and her boy in his arms and settled down to wait. It was quiet here, and he could almost imagine he was walking along this beach on a warm, moonlit night like he'd done hand-in-hand with her many times before. Except that if his presence were known on this beach at this time, it wouldn't bode well for him.

Her coughing didn't stop, and it was obvious it was causing her significant pain. He drew her head closer under his chin, and tried to calm her. "Shhhh, shhh, don't try to take in all the air at once. Breathe slowly." He wasn't certain what more he could do for her.

It seemed he waited a long time with her while the tide lapped at his back, long enough for a gibbous moon to come up over the horizon and float over the water and into the sky, long enough for a few stray sandpipers to wade past, long enough for him to slip the top half of his wet-suit down around his waist and tuck it neatly inside the pants. Beneath the suit he was heavily bandaged under a navy blue T-shirt that sported no logos nor proclaimed any affiliation or place of vacation. The label had been cut from the shirt as it had been from his dive suit and the scant clothing he wore beneath. He pulled the shirt over the bulge of his wetsuit, adding the appearance of weight to his flat belly, and ignored the blood that seeped from his chest.

He had a mobile phone in the waterproof pack he'd hidden in the dunes, but he'd not used the phone to dial 911, and it wasn't his intent to do so now though he was sad to see Anna's home ablaze. A mobile phone could be traced. Though the homes adjacent to hers appeared to be vacant, he'd noticed other houses further down the beach were lighted. Earlier, as he'd walked through the shadows of the sea oats, runners and others who strolled in a more leisurely fashion traversed the beach. Someone, he reasoned, would see the blaze and make the call. The hour wasn't late.

After her initial outburst, Anna remained unresponsive in his arms, her breathing labored, her coughing deep and full of phlegm. She needed oxygen and in a hurry. He found himself growing impatient to hear the sound of sirens.

The boy had ceased his crying and surprised Kip by falling asleep in his arms, his blond head a precious weight on his shoulder, his even breathing a warm tickle on Kip's neck. It reminded him of a time when he had a son. His jaw tensed.

When the little boy tightened his skinny arms around Kip's neck, before he could stop himself he pressed his mouth into the child's wet hair and closed his eyes. Those memories were in the past and best forgotten. He drew in a deep breath, straightened and turned his head away—from Anna, from the boy, from the memories.

Anna moaned but didn't open her eyes again. He thought she was becoming chilled and carried her and the boy away from the water into the lee of the sand dunes near the remnants of a campfire. While he waited in the sand with her head in his lap, he rubbed a piece of charred wood onto his face, taking particular care to cover the one inch scar that ran from his eye across his right cheek. The scar was an identifying feature, and he wanted none.

He thought of his cell phone again and dismissed it.

After that he silently watched the smoke come from the house. The house had been a pretty one, two stories tall with a wrap-around porch and a guesthouse/garage connected to the main house by a covered walkway and porch, surrounded by live oaks gnarled and bent by the winds. A widow's walk was on the roof. As a child he'd conjured images of a woman standing against the railing with her hair and gown blowing in the wind as she watched for her special someone to return from the sea.

At last he heard the distant wail of sirens and breathed a sigh of relief. Moments later lights flashed and he heard the gravel crunch as police and fire vehicles speeded down the narrow roads of Tybee's south beach. As he watched a flash leapt from behind one of the windows. Anna had done a good job in slowing the fire, but it wasn't yet dead.

He waited until he heard the voices of the firefighters and the sounds of their pumps before he retrieved a navy-blue baseball cap from the waist of his diving suit and put it on. He pulled the bill low over his face. With Anna and her son secure in his arms, he headed for the flashing police lights.

A small group of onlookers had already gathered on the beach in front of the house. He crossed into the woods of a neighboring house to avoid them and the bright lights of the ambulance. At the rear of the house a few people who'd heard the sirens were arriving from the street. Several local police officers immediately started to rope them off. The first EMS attendant he spotted was standing beside the opened back doors of his vehicle.

He took his time and approached the attendant from behind, deliberately stepping on a twig at the last instance.

The medic swiftly turned to face him.

"This woman and the boy need medical assistance. They were caught in the fire," he said from the shadows of the EMS vehicle.

"How bad?"

"Smoke inhalation, mostly, as far as I can tell." He released the child into the medic's arms then laid Anna on the stretcher another EMS wheeled forward. "The woman was in there a long time. She's been coughing since I found her. I've also noticed a few burns on her hands and knees. Right now she needs oxygen."

Winds of Fire

"We're equipped for that. I'll see she gets taken care of right away. I'll start an IV on her, too." The attendant looked young but seemed to know his business. "Any more of them in there?"

"I'm guessing not. She brought the boy out first then went back in to try and bring out another woman. That woman didn't make it. Her body's on the south side of the house. You can't miss it." He looked at the smoking house. "I cannot imagine there's anyone alive in there now."

The EMS followed Kip's gaze and nodded agreement.

A uniformed policeman approached. It was time to make his exit. He turned and began to walk away.

"Just a minute," the cop called after him. "You next-of-kin?"

He paused and half turned, taking care that his face was in the shadows. "Never saw them before, officer." It was true—sort of. He'd never seen the boy before. And Anna, a lifetime had passed since he'd last laid eyes on her.

"You see what happened here tonight?" The cop had a round face with a neatly trimmed moustache and was carrying twenty pounds too much on his large frame.

"Only that a lot of smoke was coming from the house and that the woman left the boy on the beach and went in and didn't come out." Kip deliberately clipped his words in a good imitation of a New Englander.

"You're not from around here, are you, boy?" The cop spoke with a lazy southern drawl that belied the sharp intelligence in his eyes.

Kip shook his head.

"What's your name?"

He gave them the first name that came into his head. "Jay Smith."

"Well, stick around, Jay. That fellow over there with the pad and pen talking to the other people—he'll want your name and telephone number in case we need to question you later."

"Yes, officer, glad to be of help." He headed in the direction the policeman indicated until the officer's attention was diverted, then he cut into the trees and kept right on walking.

A good hundred yards from the fire Kip made a sharp turn toward the shore and quickened his pace. He jerked his black dive suit up over his chest and slid his arms inside the sleeves, then he tucked his cap out-of-sight in his pants. His only stop before he headed back into the water was to pick up his fins, diving tanks, and the rest of the gear he'd hidden behind a sand dune.

He hoped the lack of light and the dark blue T-shirt had prevented the ambulance attendant and the cop from noticing he was wearing a diving suit from his waist down and that his shirt was soaked with blood. Nothing he could do about it now.

He needed to hurry. His small boat was anchored near the mouth of the Savannah River a good hundred yards off shore, and he was a long way from having recovered his strength. The seepage of blood on his chest reminded him that before he could make his next appointment, he'd have to apply first aid. Though he hadn't found out what he set out to look for this night, the foray had produced much more than he'd expected. His lips tightened. He hated to think what would have happened to Anna if he'd decided to wait another day or two to recover before he took his look around her place.

Anna Hanley. The last time he'd seen her had been in the airport, when he kissed her good-bye with promises to love her always before getting on a plane headed to Colorado Springs for his freshman year at the Air Force Academy. He remembered her tremulous smile and the little wave she gave him when he turned halfway down the boarding ramp and how his heart ached. Two weeks later, after a teary phone call, Anna flew across the ocean to Italy for her junior year abroad. Never had he thought twelve years would pass before he saw her again. And never could he have imagined their next meeting would be like this.

On the many long nights he spent in faraway places, he sometimes envisioned returning to Savannah, to the sandy beaches where the scent of the ocean filled his nostrils and the warmth of the sun reached into him like a soothing balm. Early on Anna had been a part of those dreams. But in the summer after his junior year, while Anna toured Europe with some friends, Kip met Marie, a dark-haired beauty and world class skier. Six weeks later she told him she was pregnant. They married the following month in a quiet ceremony at her parent's home.

Upon graduation Kip entered the Air Force Office of Special Investigations (OSI), and he, Marie, and their son Patrick moved to the agency headquarters at Andrews Air force Base in Maryland for his training. Four years later, while the three of them vacationed in England, Marie and Patrick were murdered. The official investigation failed to identify or capture the culprits. Knowing the bomb had actually been meant for him, Kip knew he could never rest until he did all he could to bring the perpetrators to justice.

Anna flung her head to the side in anguish and watched the man who threw a firebomb through the window of her house then returned to slash her sister's throat walk away.

"Stop him..." But her words were strained, weak. She glanced toward the ambulance attendant to see if he'd heard, but he was absorbed in his efforts to connect some tubes to a tank.

"That's the man who killed my sister..." she attempted to say as the EMS lowered a mask over her face. She clawed at it and tried to make him listen. But someone took her hands away.

"Hold still now, miss," the attendant said kindly.

"Stop him." She struggled to speak the words from behind the oxygen mask, though they came out more like a fit of coughing.

"The oxygen is for your own good. Leave it in place, ma'am. It will make you feel better," the EMS said, misunderstanding.

Frustrated and angry in equal portions, she tried to pluck the attendant's sleeve to alert him to the man's escape and discovered someone held her wrists fast while he bound them to the gurney. She lurched to the side to better keep track of the arsonist, the killer, for she knew in her heart that her sister was dead. The man was walking casually away, not so quickly as to draw attention, but with a definite mission to disappear. He looked oddly out-of-place with his shoulders down and his head bent away from the smoking house. She tried to draw breath to speak again, but the effort only deepened the coughing.

"Settle down, miss," a new voice told her. "Your son is over there with Lorraine. She'll take good care of him. He's going to be just fine."

Danny. Danny was okay. She tossed her head from side to side in an effort to locate him. There. He was a few feet away from her, looking content in the arms of a woman who wore a shirt that identified her as EMS. Danny was fine. Oh, Holly, Holly...don't be dead. You have a wonderful son that needs you. Stay alive. But Holly was dead. She knew it in her heart.

"The police and the fire department will take care of everything from here on out. You just need to relax."

Relax. How could she relax when no one would listen to her, and the perpetrator was getting away? And sirens were blaring everywhere around her. The sirens were making her head hurt. There were more sirens than for just one fire truck and an ambulance. She wondered how bad the fire had gotten. Was she going to lose her house? Why couldn't she stop her coughing? Why couldn't she make them understand that the man who started the fire was getting away? She struggled against the bindings securing her wrists.

"Take it easy there, miss. We'll have you in the hospital in no time."

They rolled her gurney into the ambulance, and the lights began to flash. The EMS who'd been with Holly's son climbed inside with Danny and sat on a seat beside her. Danny was licking a sucker she must have given him. Anna endeavored to smile reassuringly at him from under the mask, then squeezed her eyes shut.

Her sister most probably had been murdered, and the police had just let the perpetrator get away. The thought made her shiver. Someone immediately put a hand on her arm. Someone else laid a blanket over her. *Thank you.*

She tried to stop her shivering but couldn't. Even through her skin burned where the heat had scorched it and her lungs burned, she was still cold. Deep down cold. The nightmare of what had happened, of the hulking person in black who'd done what that man did wouldn't let go of her. It didn't just terrify her to realize such evil existed, it angered her. The anger was inside her, and it was making her tense. If only she could stop coughing. She tried to hold her breath and stop the coughing.

"Breathe...breathe..." Those were his words, the killer's words, echoed now by the EMS attendant. She remembered the man in black saying that but thought it was when he tried to drown her. She compressed her lips. Why, for Heaven's Sake, was she lying on this gurney while her home and all her possessions were going up in flames and thinking of him?

The ambulance doors closed. It eased forward, and the sirens and the cacophony of the firemen and police and the gushing water receded into the distance. But she could still smell the smoke, the pungent, acrid stink of the smoke. She doubted she'd ever forget it.

The attendant said, "You'll only feel a prick..." A needle went into her arm, then, mercifully she drifted away...

Remembering...just before the blackness overcame her an angel had appeared in the doorway. Barely visible through the smoke, his black silhouette, stretched tall and lean in the open doorway. His feet were splayed, his hands braced on the doorframe as if looking for something, someone, and rising from his broad back were the gossamer wings of an angel.

Only now she knew the angel wasn't an angel at all. He was a man, and he'd been dressed all in black. He was the man who'd started the fire. He was the man who'd thrown his bomb through the window and then come inside to be certain his victims didn't escape. And she was unable to stop him from walking away.

Chapter 3

Thanks to the early settlers of Savannah, the city was laid out in squares, each square unique with fountains and monuments to fallen heroes and walkways shaded by live oaks. As it had been in bygone years, the squares were surrounded by stately homes and churches, many predating the Civil War. On the east end of Monterey Square adjacent to Forsythe Park stood an unpretentious brick building known as the Oglethorpe Club. In 1870 the club had been founded by eight gentlemen as a social club, and as were many of the private clubs in Savannah, the Oglethorpe Club's membership was limited to men. But unlike in earlier years, when the look of a skirt in their hallowed halls would have sent the steward to immediately put a stop to such blasphemy, women were often seen at their affairs. Tonight was no exception.

Promptly at seven, the first couple arrived for cocktails and heavy hors d'oeuvres. The governor and his wife entered fifteen minutes later and were greeted by several members who'd positioned themselves at the door for just that purpose.

Dylan McTeer, a tall, dark-haired man with movie-star good-looks, shook the governor's hand, then his wife's. "Good evening, Governor, Mrs. Wesley. Delighted you could join us at our little affair."

Beside Dylan stood a petite woman with short-cropped auburn hair. Dylan put his arm around her back and eased her forward. "You remember my wife Maribel."

"Of course we do." The governor took her hand in both of his and flashed his perfect set of caps that helped win him many elections. "It's a pleasure to see you again, Maribel. And congratulations on your husband's promotion."

"Yes, sir, it's a fine opportunity for him, but I have to admit I'm not looking forward to moving out of Savannah."

"I guess I shouldn't be surprised you've already heard I was kicked upstairs," Dylan said. "I only got the word myself a couple of days ago."

"Harry keeps his finger on the pulse of Georgia," Mildred Wesley said with a smile. Millie was closing in on sixty-five but looked fifteen years younger. Whenever she could manage a few weeks out of the public's spotlight she'd had a lift here and a tuck there, and she wasn't ashamed to admit it. But her charm was genuine, her family Georgian for four generations, and the citizens of Georgia loved her.

The governor barked a short laugh and glanced at his wife. "I wish I could keep up with everything. What Millie means is that I try to, and I've got lots of good help around me. But as you well know, International Paper is an important part of Georgia's economy. I'm expecting it will be good for us with you being up in Wilmington making decisions. We're proud of you, Dylan. Our sincerest congratulations."

"I ditto Harry's feelings," Millie said, "and let me add that when Harry got wind your name had been put forward for the position, he sent in a glowing recommendation. I know it glowed, because I read it, and—" she gave her husband a conspiratorial grin—"and I even upgraded some of the glow."

"Thanks." Without seeming to, Dylan ushered the governor and his wife out of the front foyer where it was becoming crowded with new arrivals.

The adjourning room they entered, while not large, was originally constructed in 1857 before the advent of air-conditioning, so the ceilings were exceptionally high, giving the room the feeling of grandeur. The three floor-to-ceiling windows that punctuated two sides of the room were hung with heavy red velvet drapes that had been closed for the evening. The drapes and the intricate mahogany ceiling and chair-rail moldings gave the room a dark and staid appearance.

The owner and operator of the Pirate's House and other Savannah fine dining establishments met them halfway into the room and pulled the governor into conversation with several others who were waiting to speak with him. Before she was caught up in the throng with her husband, Millie slowed her step and put a hand on Dylan's arm.

"What's that brother of yours up to these days? The last time I saw him was nearly six years ago at the funeral for his wife and son. I heard he got out of the Air Force and is running his company out in California, but how's he doing?"

"Kip was doing just fine until several weeks ago when he was in some sort of motorcycle accident, doing God knows what. I guess he got hurt pretty bad. He spent nearly a week in the hospital in California despite his protests. I imagine they virtually restrained him to keep him in there that long. Mom actually flew out to put in her two cents face-to-face. With the doctors firmly behind her she insisted Kip take a leave from work and fly to Savannah so she could keep an eye on his recovery." Dylan smiled. "And you know my mother—she can be a force to be reckoned with when she's on a mission. Kip flew in two days ago with the promise to stay awhile. To be honest with you, I think he must have had some business in Savannah or he wouldn't have given in so easily. Anyway, he's up and about now, and seems to be doing well enough. We're expecting him to arrive here any minute."

"Splendid. Be sure to send him over so I can ask him when he plans on getting married again and providing his mama with some more grandkids." Millie chuckled. "No, I promise I won't do that. My own three children have taught me enough that I know to keep that question locked up."

"Mrs. Wesley…" A heavy-set woman with graying hair held out her hand, and turning to the group that had gathered around her with a friendly smile, Millie shook her hand. Dylan stepped back to give way to the newcomers. "Can I get you something to drink?"

"A glass of Chardonnay would be nice, thank-you." Mildred turned to the women who waited to claim her attention.

When Dylan turned, he saw that his mother was sashaying across the room in his direction with a broad smile on her face and the aplomb of a queen. There was no doubt that Sarah McTeer was a handsome woman, even at sixty-five. Her snow-white hair was expertly cut in a short casual style that suited her whether dressed in the elegant attire as she wore now or the old jeans she preferred around the house. A diamond broach sparkled from a gold chain over her simple white, high-necked silk blouse. Matching earrings were clipped to her ears, jewelry that spoke of heritage and grace as assuredly as did the slender woman that approached him.

"Looking good." Dylan bent over to give her a little squeeze.

"You don't look so bad yourself. Your father and I produced some handsome kids, if I have to say so myself." She tapped his cheek with two fingers as she met his gaze. "I've been looking for your brother. Have you seen him yet?"

Dylan nodded toward the hallway and took a swallow of his drink. "Just came in. He's over there by the front door." He noted his brother's hair, a thick, dark brown that closely resembled the color of a hawk's feathers, was in need of cutting. His features were bold, more rugged than his own. Still, the resemblance between them was strong.

"Oh, good, I'm glad he made it."

Sarah reached for a plate. Across the table a tall, white-haired gentleman smiled at her. "Hello, Sarah, I was hoping you would be here tonight."

Sarah smiled back. "Evan... I thought you weren't due in from Florida until tomorrow."

"Hello, Dr. Schroeder. Good to see you." Dylan shook the older man's hand before he reached for a chilled jumbo shrimp and added cocktail sauce.

"I'm glad to see you, too." Dr. Schroeder gave his attention back to Dylan's mother. "You're right, Sarah. I wasn't expecting to return today. There was a change of plans. I started to call then decided to surprise you. I arrived about an hour ago."

"How are your granddaughters?" Sarah plopped a plump, juicy fried oyster into her mouth.

"Beautiful, fun—right now they're into volleyball. I went to their tournament. Dallas' team got eliminated in the quarter-finals so they weren't to play tomorrow. That's why I'm here. We needed your cheering."

Sarah laughed, acknowledging her enthusiastic support of her own grandchildren's teams.

Kip McTeer walked through the second floor entry of the Oglethorpe Club to a bevy of welcoming handshakes and warm greetings. He was a recent addition to the club, though he wasn't a new member. Upon the death of his father ten years ago, the plantation known as Marsh Winds had passed to him, and while Kip had been in Savannah to settle his father's affairs, several of his father's friends had approached him to join the club. Though Kip lived in California where he carried on his great-grandfather's building supply business, he hoped one day to return to Savannah—to his roots.

Well versed in his ancestral history since birth, he'd always known his great-great grandfather had arrived in Savannah from Scotland in 1740, seven years after the worthy General James Edward Oglethorpe himself had arrived. When the offer of membership into Oglethorpe Club was proffered, Kip readily accepted, making sure to visit Savannah and his mother and siblings as often as he could. In Savannah he found a gracious charm that he encountered nowhere else in his world-wide travels. And despite that years sometimes stretched between visits, because of his ancestral lineage McTeer was eagerly accepted by 'old' Savannah.

Tonight a large round table was set in the center of the rich-mahogany-paneled room and covered in gleaming white linen. Displayed on the table were simple but sumptuous morsels of tender filet mignon mounded on large platters. Fresh oysters on the half-shell and fried oysters served with various sauces of butter and cocktail variety had been set in strategic places between trays of cheeses and fruits and finger-sized freshly baked buttermilk biscuits.

Though it had been close to a year since he last placed a step in this staid room, old friends and acquaintances immediately made him feel right at home. It didn't surprise him that news of his accident had made the rounds quickly. Kip fielded their good wishes and queries with grace, but truth be told, after tonight's foray to pull Anna out of her burning home, he was feeling a little off his game. After his shower when he went to redress his wounds, he'd noticed the flesh around his chest wound was raw and puffy and black and puckered at the edges. Blood was seeping from it at a slow but steady rate. He taped some gauze pads over it then rewrapped the ace in hopes that the blood wouldn't reach through the layers to his shirt. Now as he felt the wetness, he was glad for the sling that held his arm over the area.

Out of the corner of his eye, Kip watched Dr. Evan Schroeder move around the food table to where his mother was putting a few oysters and some cocktail sauce on her plate. Sarah slid a glance to him then leaned in to kiss his cheek. The doctor responded by lacing his fingers between his mother's and holding her hand, and there was warmth around Dr. Schroeder's mouth, and affection in his eyes. Kip had known Evan Schroeder all his life and thought him a compassionate and friendly man, an exceptional doctor, but this was his first inkling that his mother held feelings for him. A half smile formed on his lips. He needed to get home more often.

Sarah dabbed her lips with a linen napkin then turned toward the entryway where Kip looked ruggedly handsome in a dark suit and red tie, with his dark hair. Across the length of the crowded, noisy room, their gazes met—his dark and filled with the mysteries of his life, hers bright with the worry and the love she felt for him. He winked at her, and she couldn't help grinning back at him. Though she'd never say so, she thought he looked peaked beneath his tan and that his smile was a little too forced, his eyes glassy like his fever had returned. In the worse way she wanted to make all the aches and disappointments in his life go away.

His arm was in a sling though he'd regained most of the use of it, and under the soft blue dress shirt he wore a bandage wrapped around his midsection. A motorcycle accident, he told her, but when he'd still been sedated, she'd seen the nurse change the dressing on his side. To her the wound looked more like he'd been the recipient of several bullets and filled her with concern. She shivered to think her son was still getting shot at, but if she wanted him to stay in her life, and she did, she'd better keep his secrets.

But dear God how she wished she could take the sadness from his eyes.

Across the table Sarah noticed Dylan's wife talking quietly with some friends. When Dylan had announced he was going to marry the plain little girl from town, she'd worried that she wouldn't be her charming and extroverted son's best match. But Maribel soon won her over, and now Sarah secretly hoped Kip would find someone of similar nature.

Kip McTeer had come along at a time when Sarah's husband Neal had been stationed with the Air Force in

Germany. Shortly before Kip's birth Sarah had flown back to Savannah and stayed at Marsh Winds, Neal's family home, instead of her family's more modest home across the river on Isle of Hope.

"One day Marsh Winds will belong to our son," Neal had said to her. "I want him to love it and Savannah as I do." She hadn't argued, and now with Neal in his grave these past ten years the stately plantation she called home actually belonged to her son, passed on to him as it had been for generations to the oldest surviving McTeer son.

"Sarah, I've been looking for you." Millie Wesley came to her side and took her arm. "I might have known you'd be at the food. I declare, I never will understand why you don't ever gain any weight."

"Millie. How wonderful to see you." Sarah pecked the air beside her dear friend's cheek and embraced her with genuine warmth. "It's been too long."

"I completely agree," Millie said then mildly rebuked, a privilege afforded to old and dear friends. "If you'd accepted any of the many invitations I've sent your way, it wouldn't have been such a long time."

Sarah smiled sheepishly. "I know, I know, but I just hate driving in that Atlanta traffic."

"Then I'll see to it you're picked up at the airport and driven wherever you want."

Sarah chuckled. "I'll hold you to that, Millie." Sarah linked her arm through Evan's. "You've met Evan Schroeder, haven't you?"

"Dr. Schroeder? I'm afraid I know him from his reputation only. I'm pleased to get the chance to meet you in person. Your book on your adventures sailing around with *Doctors Without Borders* has made quite a hit. The governor read it and quite enjoyed it as much as I did. I understand it made the New York Times best seller list."

"I was only doing what hundreds of others do every year. I just wrote it down. The reward was far greater for me than those we were fortunate enough to be able to help," Evan said. "Now if you two lovely ladies will excuse me, I see my son over there, and there are a few things I need to talk to him about."

Soon as he was out of hearing range, Millie lowered her voice. "You ought to snap up that man. Not only is he intelligent, he's famous, and he's handsome."

Sarah watched Evan move through the crowd, stopping here and there when his friends greeted him, and she felt a warm flush move up her cheeks. "He is all those things," she said to Millie and changed the subject. "But before you get dragged away I wanted to say you're looking wonderful. Being the governor's wife seems to suit you just fine."

"It does have its advantages," Millie said.

Sarah smiled. She knew all about being a politician's wife. Her husband had been a U.S. Senator for twelve years before he decided not to run again.

"And"— Millie leaned in closer to Sarah's ear—"I had a little work done around my eyes a couple of months ago."

Kip watched his mother chat with the governor's wife for a few minutes before he walked over and gave both women a kiss on the cheek. "Mother, Mrs. Wesley."

"Honestly, Kip, you and your sister need to start calling me Millie."

"Mama taught us to be respectful. And now that you're our esteemed Governor's wife, I thought I should be even more so." He grinned.

"Kristopher McTeer, stop it right now. You're going to make me feel old. I've known you since you were just a thought in your mama's head. But I haven't seen you in a coon's age, and I want to hear all about you. What happened to your arm?"

"I was going down hill a little too fast on my motorcycle, and I ran into some gravel when I tried to brake on a turn. I lost control, spun out, landed against a tree, and banged myself up. That's about it. I'm surprised Barry didn't tell you. I saw him a few weeks ago. He came to see me while I was in the hospital."

"Never mentioned it. That son of mine—I'm going to have to give him a good whooping when I see him."

Kip laughed, but he was seeing his friend rappelling down the cliff in his efforts to rescue him, and the laugh was cut short. "He's looking fit, been doing some climbing in the Rocky Mountains."

"He didn't mention that either. But he did say he'd be coming to Atlanta soon."

Kip knew that and something not even Barry knew. In the next day or two Barry Wesley would be receiving some information before he was dispatched to Savannah. Unbeknown to either set of parents, he and his long-time friend had been working together off and on for many years. Kip showed no evidence of what he knew but professed to be pleasantly surprised and left it at that. For Kip, deceiving his family and friends had always been the difficult part of his job.

Kip looked past the governor's wife to a man talking with junior state Senator Louis Norton and tried to place him. Taking his time, he added fresh shrimp to his plate then cocktail sauce. The man was maybe seven inches over five feet and fit. His complexion was ruddy, his dark hair sprinkled with gray, wavy, and cropped close to his head. There was no doubt he'd seen the man or a photograph of him.

"That man in the Armani suit beside Senator Norton—he looks familiar," Kip said to his mother when Millie Wesley's attention was drawn away. "Recognize him?"

"Can't say that I do."

"Can't say you do what?" Dylan came up to his mother's side. He pecked the air beside her cheek and stole one of her fried oysters, eliciting a teasing frown from her.

Kip said, "That man across the room in the group talking with Norton—he's a dead-ringer for California Senator Marshall Quinlan. Do you know him?"

"Not personally, but I think he *is* the senator."

Kip forked a slab of filet mignon into his mouth and chewed. It was melt-in-your-mouth tender. "What's he doing here?"

"I heard he had business in Atlanta. Norton must have invited him. And I've just given you the sum total of my knowledge of him. Shall we join them?"

"You boys go on." Sarah waved them off. "I've already spoken with Louis, and I see Ester Porter and her husband have just arrived."

Kip took another bite of the tenderloin, wishing it would replenish his waning strength and followed Dylan, thinking the smile Norton wore probably had a great deal to do with getting him elected to office. It was wide and genuine.

Norton spied the brothers before they crossed the room. "Dylan, Kip." Norton held out a hand to each. "Good to see you both again. Let me introduce you to Senator Marshall Quinlan. Kip, you probably recognize him. He's the senator from your adopted state."

With his full head of black, wavy hair, sprinkled with gray, Quinlan was of obvious middle Eastern descent and more handsome in person than on television. There was fire in the dark gaze he bestowed on both him and his brother as they shook the senator's hand.

Not really feeling like himself, Kip clasped his forehead with his thumb and forefinger and allowed himself to massage his temples for a few seconds. After a few minutes of giving lip-service to the conversation, he excused himself.

Chapter 4

A dim light from the corridor kept the hospital room from being completely dark. Kip stared at the sack of solution hanging on a hook above his bed and the intravenous tube that snaked down to his arm, an all too familiar sight. He shut his eyes a moment, ruminating over the range of last night's events that led to the hospital bed and the IV.

An hour into the reception at the Oglethorpe House Kip realized that blood had seeped through his bandage and stained his shirt. He figured the sutures on his chest had torn the rest of the way out, so he made his excuses and headed for the exit. His mother waylaid him at the door and begged a lift.

He had no sooner backed the car onto Bull St. when she turned to him. "Now I want you to drive straight to Memorial Hospital, and I want no words out of you."

Kip looked over at his mother. "What's wrong? Are you having an attack of some sort?"

"No. There's nothing wrong with me. It's you. You're bleeding badly and need to be tended to."

"Oh, that. I was going home to change the bandage."

"I'm much more worried about the fever. You're burning up." To emphasize her point she reached over and touched his forehead. "You want me to drive?"

"No, I'm fine." Kip had to smile. To his mom, once a little kid, always a little kid. Maybe he could have persuaded one of his brothers or his sister that the blood was nothing to worry about, that he just needed a fresh dressing, but not his mother. She was far too perceptive. He was just light-headed enough not to put up much of an argument. Anyway, the stitches needed to be removed or replaced, the dressing, too, and better to be done by a professional, so he drove himself to the hospital while his mother used her cell to call her friend Dr. Evan Schroeder, who was still at the reception, and asked him to meet them at the hospital.

"No, I'm fine. It's Kip. Sorry I couldn't warn you, but he left suddenly, and I needed to catch him before he got away. I think you should take a look at him. If you don't mind, I'll let him explain. Yes, a room would be good. Thanks. We'll be there in fifteen minutes."

A nurse met them at the front door. While his mother parked the car, the nurse bypassed the chaos of the emergency room and escorted him directly to an examination room where she promptly stuck a thermometer in his mouth. She'd just finished taking his blood pressure when Evan Schroeder came through the door wearing his rimless glasses and a white lab robe. He gave Kip a warm greeting.

A few moments later he'd cleaned the wound sufficiently to assess the damage. "Does your mother know you were shot, Kip?"

Kip looked down at the red streaks that radiated from the wound. He didn't remember seeing them before this evening. "I've told her I was hurt in a motorcycle accident. I'm not sure she believes me, but I'd like to keep the shooting part under wraps, if you will."

"Of course. This is quite an incision. I take it the bullet caused some internal damage."

"Some..."

Dr. Schroeder's eyebrows shot up but he kept his attention on the wound as he plucked the torn stitches from Kip's skin. "The sutures all have been yanked loose, son. Whatever you did to pull them out, may I suggest you refrain from doing it in the near future?"

Kip chuckled. "Yes, sir."

"I'm going to clean it out and stitch you up again, but I'm afraid the area around the bullet's entrance is showing signs of infection, and you're running a fever of 103 degrees, enough to concern me. I'm going to have to keep you here overnight for observation and get you on some antibiotics."

Kip swore under his breath.

"I know it wasn't what you were expecting, Kip. But I've known you since you were a kid, and believe me, whatever it is you need to get done, it probably isn't worth your life. Now am I going to have order you hog-tied to keep you here tonight?"

Kip relented and managed a smile. "No need for that."

That was last night. This morning he was feeling much better and thought it was due to the fever having receded.

Kip knew it was a chance he shouldn't take, but he couldn't get Anna out of his mind. He needed to know for himself that she was all right. Before anyone came into the room, he dialed the front desk of the hospital from his bed.

"I'd like to find out how Anna Hanley is doing. There was a fire in her home last night. I believe EMS took her to Memorial."

"I'll connect you to her room." In a few minutes the operator came back on the line. "I'm sorry, sir, but Miss Hanley cannot take any phone calls at this time."

"But she's all right?"

"I couldn't say, sir. Someone in her room picked up the line and said she couldn't take any calls. That's all I know."

"What's her room number?"

The operator gave it to him, and he hung up.

Caught in the quagmire of her memories, Anna rolled her head from side to side on her hospital bed. Despite all her efforts, she couldn't shut out the images of her sister's dead eyes, the bloody gash on her neck, or the bottle shattered on the floor, all gruesome evidence the fire had been deliberately set, her sister murdered. Nor could she remove from her senses the choking stench of smoke and gasoline and the terror of seeing the man dressed in black running from her living room. A terrible sense of loss and fear rose from her gut and swelled into her chest to cut off her breath. Tears came suddenly and rolled from her eyes onto her pillow.

After a while she must have slept, for it seemed like no time passed when she had the sensation of someone staring at her. She blinked, expecting to see a nurse. Instead, a man stood inside the door mere feet from her bed. She opened her mouth to scream. The inrush of breath hit a wall of phlegm, tickled her swollen throat, and caused her to cough. Once she started to cough she couldn't stop. She fought for her breath.

Steps sounded in the hallway.

A light came into the room, and a nurse came in. "Are you all right?"

A hoarse croak came out of her mouth. She sprung up into a sitting position, suddenly deathly afraid all over again. "Over there," she croaked. "The man over there in the doorway. He...he killed my s-sister."

The nurse whipped her head around toward the doorway like she was feeling some of Anna's fear then shook her head. "There's no one there. You must have had a bad dream."

When the nurse moved aside and Anna could see the doorway again, she saw it was empty. She had been so certain. She started to shiver.

The nurse's hands took hold of her shoulders, pushing her back down with insistence.

She looked around her. The corners of her room were dark. Outside her window it was dark. Was the nurse right? Had she been dreaming?

She rolled to her right to check the time, missed her bedside clock. "What time is it?" Her voice came out hoarse, and she tried to clear her throat. It hurt, so she stopped.

The nurse switched on the light and checked her watch. "Six twenty in the morning."

Anna recoiled from the sudden light, blinked, and once again saw the dark silhouette of a man standing just inside the doorway. He was clad in surgical scrubs but she was sure he was the same man she'd seen earlier. Terrified, Anna fought against the nurse's hands. The contest was unequal. The nurse outweighed her two fold. In seconds Anna was flat on her back.

"Check the hall again," Anna croaked, surprised when the nurse did. Anna heard her converse with a man in the hallway.

"There's no one there, dear," the nurse said in a tone that dripped with the excessive patience one used when talking to the mentally impaired. "One of the patients poked his head in a minute ago. He was looking for his room, realized he had the wrong one, and left. He said he didn't see anyone else in the hall."

The nurse's assurances did little to calm Anna. She was afraid, shivery afraid. She supposed it would take her a long time before the fear would go away. She closed her eyes and turned her head toward the window while the nurse took her blood pressure. "The little boy who was with me last night. Where is he? Is he all right?"

"I don't rightly know, miss. I just came on duty at five. You'll have to ask the doctor about your son."

She didn't bother to correct her about Danny being her son.

The nurse picked up her things. "Are you feeling up to some breakfast?"

Anna thought she could eat, but she wasn't sure. Her throat felt raw, burned, like she had strep throat or something, but she nodded anyway and hoped they would bring her something smooth like yogurt or ice cream.

The nurse left then poked her head back into the room. "Oh, I almost forgot. A gentleman phoned your room while you were asleep. He didn't leave his name."

Anna thought of Dennis Sadler, until recently a lawyer with a prestigious Savannah firm. Several months ago Dennis took leave from the practice to return to school and pursue his dream of becoming a professor of literature at a university. Before he left town he'd asked her to marry him, and she accepted. One of her friends could have found out about the accident and called Dennis to let him know of the fire. Naturally he'd be concerned, but why wouldn't he have left his name?

She glanced back at the doorway. Thinking of the man she thought she saw there earlier, she quivered, and pulled the covers up over her face. The man who killed her sister surely was brazen enough to call the hospital and find out which room she was in, in order to come and finish the job half done. She hugged the pillow, felt the rough muslin sheet so unlike her soft cotton ones at home, and wished she could be safe and warm in her own bed in her own house and far away from the nightmare of the past dozen hours.

Then it hit her that the home she remembered didn't exist anymore.

Over his doctor's objections and with a promise to get some bed rest, Kip left the hospital before lunch. Over sandwiches and soup with his mother at lunch-time, Kip was surprised when she handed the morning's paper to him. "Did you see this article about the fire at Tybee last night? Anna Hanley's house burned."

"Anna? Hopefully she wasn't hurt."

"The paper says she was admitted to the hospital to be treated for smoke inhalation but expected to be all right. I'm sorry to say her sister died. It's written up on the front page. Here, take a look."

Maribel, Kip's brother's wife, came into the room behind her daughter and headed for the coffeepot. "Did I hear you say someone died?"

"Anna Hanley's sister. She was killed in a fire at Anna's home last night," Sarah reached into the cupboard and handed Maribel a mug.

"That's terrible. But Anna's alright?"

"According to the paper she is, but what a terrible thing. I wonder how bad the damage is to her house. I'll have to bring her over some vegetable soup this afternoon and invite her to stay here if she wants."

Kip winced, though a part of him would be glad to have her close enough so he could look after her. And if she was out of what was left of her house, it would be much easier for him to go in and make the search through her sister's things he'd hoped to do before the fire.

"The news may not have made the Atlanta papers," he said. "Robyn will want to know. Maybe you should call her."

Though Robyn was coming to Marsh Winds at the end of the week for the going away party his mother planned for Dylan and Maribel before they headed to Delaware for Dylan's new position, Kip wasn't surprised when his mother walked right over to the phone and dialed her daughter. Kip knew her well. While she didn't want to interfere in her children's lives, she was always looking for an excuse to give them a call.

She cupped her hand over the receiver and gave him a frown. "Remember your promise to the doctor, Kip. Soon as you've finished, why don't you head up to bed so you don't end up back in the hospital?"

Kip knew she was right. It was like all the wind had been taken from his sails. The simple act of standing on his own two feet was an effort, so he didn't argue. He thought of calling Barry and asking him to come down now, but he was doing some important leg-work in Atlanta. Unfortunately, the search of Anna Hanley's house couldn't wait past tonight, if indeed he wasn't already too late and the police hadn't combed through the remains before him and taken anything of interest.

Kip felt restless. He was worried about Anna. His visit to her hospital room had been a disaster. It had been a foolish notion in the first place and nearly exposed him. Though she couldn't have seen his face, she appeared terrified of him. Obviously she thought he was the man who set her house on fire and murdered Holly. He'd barely had time to slip behind the door before the nurse came charging down the hallway and into the room.

He of all people knew better. It was as if he were eighteen and smitten all over again, taking foolish chances. If he was going to have any hope of searching the house tonight he needed to conserve his energy and develop a less risky strategy.

Chapter 5

Hobart Goddard was spending Friday evening with his wife and mother-in-law, watching a movie in his Landings home in Savannah, some girl flick about true love and all that sentimental garbage that bored him. He was struggling to stay awake.

At seventy-three Mabel Osgood was overweight by a good twenty-five pounds and no longer the beauty she'd been in her youth. But she was rich. Her square face and jowls gave her a hang-dog appearance which some mistook for stupidity. Hobart Goddard had made that error once years ago. It had cost him a high-powered job with a prestigious brokerage house in New York and his good reputation. It very nearly sent him to jail.

He had pilfered millions from Mabel's account, covering himself well, he thought, with bogus figures and misleading fees, but to his surprise, unlike most women of her station, she watched every move of her money and understood the stock business as well as he did. She reported him to his superiors.

On the morning when the accusations hit the papers and the scandal was about to erupt into a conflagration, Mabel Osgood came to his office without her lawyers and shut the door. She had all her facts about him, and she had the facts straight. There was no doubt in Hobart's mind that she could put him into prison for a long time. But Hobart wasn't easily intimidated. After Mabel had finished with her accusations, he'd risen from his chair without speaking and turned his back on her to look out his window at the steel and concrete high-rise across the street.

When he'd turned back to face Mabel Osgood, he'd braced his hands on the back of his chair, ready for a fight. But it turned out that Mrs. Osgood hadn't come merely to rip him apart. It turned out that certain facets of his personality had attracted her attention. He was unprincipled, dishonorable, hard-core, and without shame, and that very much appealed to Mabel Osgood. But she was smart enough to realize those traits were found among many of the lowlifes she dealt with in her various businesses outside the brokerage house. What Hobart Goddard had that made him stand out from the others was his intelligence. It was because of this that she'd come to his office that morning. She wanted to offer him a job. The job would entail doing almost precisely the same things as what he'd been doing with one major difference. The huge sums of money he dealt with would come from bogus firms. Mob money and slush funds for powerful people.

Hobart had had no trouble agreeing to her terms.

And in all the thirty years since their bargain had been struck, the charges dropped, and Goddard Financial formed, he'd never regretted it. He glanced at his wife's mother now, found her looking at him as though she read his thoughts. His mouth twitched, and he inclined his head and kept right on looking. She'd long since been an attractive woman in the traditional sense. Perhaps because of that she'd kept her body clothed in the best money could buy. Her thinning hair was well cut in a short layered style, dyed brown. Her breasts were stuffed into an uplifting bra that gave them the appearance of being firm, and numerous trips to the plastic surgeon had lifted the jowls around her mouth and tightened the sagging skin of her neck. For seventy-three she didn't look too bad.

Over the years he'd grown to respect Mabel's powerful, even ruthless, business acumen. Once money may have been Mabel's primary objective or maybe it had been for the power, but by the time Hobart met her she already had a controlling hold over her business dealings and was what Hobart thought of as 'filthy rich.' Twenty-five years after Hobart opened his investment agency, Mabel surprised him by announcing her retirement.

"I'm tired of New York winters," she said one evening when they were gathered around the dinner table. "I want to move to a place where it's warmer. I want to travel and enjoy my money while I'm still young." At the time Mabel was sixty-four, New York was experiencing a particularly brutal winter, and Hobart was in the process of moving his primary residence to Savannah with his main office to be in Atlanta to avoid New York's excessive taxes which entailed moving Mabel's only daughter and grandchild with him.

Preferring the excitement of metropolitan life of Atlanta to Savannah, Mabel had bought a home in Marietta on the outskirts of the city. Her retirement lasted a year before she grew bored enough to quit and go back to work in the city as Senator Louis Norton's private secretary. What she did for the good senator, Hobart didn't ask.

Despite that she was fourteen years his senior, Hobart sometimes thought that in many ways Mabel would have been a better match for him than her daughter. In almost every way Harriet was the opposite of her mother. The beauty she'd shown as a young woman grew into fat in her thirties, and long before that, shortly after their two sons were born, he'd realized what he'd earlier taken for her cute and flirtatious ways covered an inane immaturity. Not once had she shown him evidence of her mother's acumen.

The slam of the front door cut into Hobart's musing and brought his gaze around toward the hallway where his youngest son had come in on a rush of cold air, a canvas tote slung over one shoulder.

"Hello, ladies. Pa." Carl paused only long enough to give his mother and grandmother pecks on their cheeks.

Hobart watched him start up the steps before he rose and turned back to the women. "Can I get anyone something more to drink?"

"A touch more wine would be lovely, Hobart," Mabel said. "Whatever you have opened will do."

"A diet coke for me, darling, and can you bring in more chips to go with this dip?" Harriet didn't take her eyes from the movie-sized screen.

Hobart was still in the kitchen when Carl stepped inside the room, his handsome face looking worn as though he hadn't slept much. His dark, shoulder-length hair stuck a couple of inches out from under a black knit hat that had been pulled down low. The drab green anorak he wore was beaded with rain and dripped on the floor. He reached into the refrigerator and helped himself to a long-neck beer.

"Well, I'm off." Carl twisted off the cap.

"What do you mean *off*?" Hobart placed a can of soda onto the table. "You just got the hell in! Fall break started a week ago. Your mother's been wondering where you were, and your grandmother's here. You can't spare the time to come in and sit with them a while? Where the hell you going at this time of night anyway?"

"I'm meeting a few friends for some beers," Carl said reasonably. "We're celebrating. I got a job. That's why I couldn't get home before this."

"And it kept you too busy to call? What kind of job?" Hobart wasn't convinced.

"The kind that pays." Carl smiled. He dug his hand into his pocket and pulled it out again with a fist full of neatly folded bills. "And you better believe these aren't ones. And there's more where this came from."

Hobart gave the money a cursory glance with a sour taste in his mouth then turned to pour the can of coke into Harriet's glass. "I wouldn't go flashing that all over town. So why didn't you tell me about the job?"

"I wasn't sure I had it. Then it lasted longer than I thought it would. After that I was too busy to call. I thought the job would make you happy."

"I'd be happier if you finished your degree and came to work for me at the firm. I thought we'd agreed you'd go back to school and get your degree without further delays. Investment planning is a good steady job."

"A boring job, you mean."

"Managing money isn't boring, damn it, and you've only got one semester left. Southern isn't going to put up with your flip attitude forever, you know."

"I know. Don't worry. I plan to go back in the spring." He returned the bills to his pocket and brought his hand out again with a box of matches. He struck one.

The light flashed in the corner of Hobart's eye, and he swung his head around. Carl seemed not to notice his father's glare as father and son watched the flame burn down until the heat forced Carl to shake it out.

Immediately, Carl flipped the burned match on the counter, stuck a cigarette into his mouth, and lit another match. He touched the flame to the end of the cigarette then watched it burn. The heat of the flame glittered in his eyes, and Hobart felt like his son had just lit his own fuse. The anger in him began to burn. Smoking was a recently acquired habit of Carl's. Hobart had forbidden him to smoke in the house. Carl knew it and normally refrained from the practice in Hobart's presence.

"I've told you not to do that. Put the damn cigarette out," Hobart said between tight lips. He didn't miss the amusement that leapt to his son's eyes. Something had changed in Carl these last months he'd been away, and Hobart had an uncomfortable feeling he wasn't going to like it.

Carl put the matches back in his pocket and stubbed out the cigarette on the bottom of his boot. Hobart felt his blood pressure begin to rise. He was taking pills for it, but in his line of work there were pressures coming from all sides.

He didn't need problems from his son as well.

Hobart felt uneasy as he watched his son walk into the entertainment room and listened to him speak with his mother and grandmother. A moment later the front door opened and closed. He glanced out the window, troubled. Hobart only knew of one kind of job that paid the amount of cash his son just displayed. The kind that paid under-the-table.

In the streetlights he could see that the rain was coming down hard, and he wished Carl hadn't taken the opened beer into the car with him. But Carl was twenty-eight years old, and for years Hobart's control over him had been nonexistent. He thought of his oldest son Buddy, murdered in his prison bed seven years ago. Unconsciously his fingers tightened to fists. The person who put him behind bars had still gone unpunished.

Before returning to the movie, Hobart stopped at the bar and poured himself a large scotch. He took a deep swallow and topped it off and jotted something down on a piece of paper before he carried it in with his drink and the others for the ladies. When all were served, he returned to where Mabel sat and handed her the folded piece of paper, whispering close to her ear. "If it hasn't already been done, I'd appreciate if you could see that this is taken care of immediately."

Without waiting for a response he sat back down in his recliner, relishing the soft feel of the fine leather. He tilted back his chair and raised the foot rest with a sense of relief, knowing she would see it was done. Over the years since its inception, to give credence to Goddard Financial's legitimacy the firm had taken on other clients and other brokers. The new clients were all rich, the brokers ignorant of Hobart Goddard's clandestine dealings. The arrangement was one to Hobart's liking, except for one small thing. His margin for error with his underworld clients was nil, nada, nothing. No matter the swing of the stock market, they expected to make money.

To compensate for the market fluctuations, Hobart had taken precautions. In the times when returns were good, funds from his legitimate clients had been siphoned off and deposited into an account bearing his name. His safety net, he called it. And when times permitted it, he used the money freely for his own means, a yacht, a home in the Virgin Islands, a numbered account in Switzerland, but when the market was bad, he was careful, very careful to use it to give dividends to his clandestine clients. Since Mabel Osgood had caught him with his hand in the till, he'd learned a few tricks, and no one, not even Mabel knew about this personal account.

What the mob and unsavory politicians did with the money Hobart made for them, who they had on their payroll, whether they used it to finance terrorists, run campaigns, or simply to live in style, never concerned Hobart.

Anna was in her hospital bed toying with a tray of tasteless liquids she'd been informed was lunch, when Holly's husband Stanley called. At the sound of the telephone ringing, several of Anna's friends who were visiting moved over to the window where a dinner tray and dresser where loaded with flowers from well-wishers.

"I just got the news about Holly," he said, "I can't believe she's gone. It's so unexpected...a terrible thing."

She supposed the police must have called him. It took several attempts before Anna could speak over the tears constricting her throat. "Yes...devastating..." Her sister, her best friend and confidante, was gone. It was more than she could bear.

Stanley remarked about Anna's close call and enquired about how she was doing. At length, he brought the conversation around to his son. She took a deep breath and told him Danny was fine.

"Would it be possible for you to take care of him until I can get there for Holly's funeral?"

"I planned on it," she said in a voice she didn't recognize as her own. "Earlier a friend took Danny to her house. Her youngest son is the same age as Danny, and she's willing to keep him until I'm released. Her husband is a pediatric surgeon right here at Memorial. I think you'll agree Danny's in good hands."

"I knew I could count on you. But it sounds like your throat's hurting, so maybe it'd be better if I call back tomorrow."

"Probably, but I'm feeling much better than last night. I'm to be released this afternoon. And oh, Stanley, I'm glad you're coming. I was afraid you might not."

"Then Holly told you we were splitting."

"She did, but I know it would mean a lot to her that you come to her service. We'll talk about what you want me to arrange when you call tomorrow. And oh, call on my cell phone. The other is down, of course."

A few minutes after she'd disconnected, Dennis was on the line and full of apologies for not having called earlier. "Darling...I just heard. I tried your cell, but of course, it's probably still at the house. I'm sorry I can't be with you, but I'm glad I caught you. Are you all right?"

He sounded nervous. She glanced at the gauze that wrapped the palm and thumb of her left hand, the hand she'd used to propel herself in and out of the room while her right was occupied either dragging the hose or her sister, and thought of the other gauze wraps on her arms and legs. Beneath the wraps the skin still burned, but she didn't want to worry him. "I'm doing fine, just a few minor burns; mostly it just hurts to talk."

"I'm glad you're all right," he said, and she waited for him to say he was on his way, but what he said was, "You get my flowers?"

She tried to pick out the flowers he'd sent from the host of others sitting on the dinner tray and dresser along the wall and couldn't. "Yes, thank you."

"You were very brave, Anna."

Anna thought about Holly's lifeless face and sagged back against the pillows, closing her eyes against the sudden surge of tears. She didn't feel brave, just terribly sad. With effort she swallowed back the lump of hurt that swelled in her throat. All of a sudden she didn't feel like talking. "I can't talk anymore... my throat hurts."

"I understand, darling. It sounds painful. I have a class anyway. I'll call you tonight just to let you know I'm thinking of you," Dennis said, considerate as always. Immediately she felt contrite for not understanding how important his classes were to him, but then Mary Katherine was back at her bedside with a cheery smile and a tall paper cup with a curled straw.

"Thought this might soothe your sore throat." She put it in Anna's hand. "It's a vanilla ice cream soda, just like you always told me you'd have with your mother when you were a kid. They sell them at the cafeteria. Can you imagine?"

"Oh, Mary Katherine, how did you ever remember that?"

"It's the sort of thing you would do for us. Actually I can't take credit. It's from Robyn. I phoned her on the way to the hospital, and as soon as she knew you were doing fine, she insisted I get you one from her. I told her it was hard for you to talk, so she said she'll wait until tomorrow to phone. Go ahead and try it."

Anna did and laughed and immediately felt better. Thank God for her friends.

By afternoon the room had cleared, and aside from the pain in her throat which didn't particularly bother her as long as she didn't converse, Anna saw no reason to remain in the hospital. In fact, she was chaffing to leave.

When the doctor arrived at three o'clock, she was able to convince him she was well enough to be discharged. With the use of Mary Katherine's car, upon leaving the hospital Anna drove straight to her home on Tybee Island. By then under the cloudy skies, the light of day was already waning, and her mind was roiling with unanswered questions.

Chapter 6

Since 1920, when Highway 80 had been completed, Anna's family had lived on Tybee year round, but many of the homes on the island were summer residences only and empty. Who had called the Fire Department? What was left of her house? Had the firemen been able to save the surrounding oaks and palms? Mary Katherine said the place wasn't a total loss, but what did that mean?

When she pulled into her drive with the questions bombarding her mind, the sky was leaden and low, so burdened with the impending rain that in places it seemed to meld with the sea. In the grey hue the house took on a brooding appearance. Anna looked at it and shuddered beneath her borrowed jacket.

She cut the engine and stepped onto the crushed oyster shell drive, breathed in a shaky breath. The familiar scent of sea and sand was overridden by the stink of burned timbers. She sighed and placed a hand over her eyes, clasping a thumb and forefinger to her temples against the headache she'd failed to mention to the doctor. Just behind her lids hovered the image of her sister's dead face. Would she ever be able to look at her house again without seeing Holly laying lifeless on the floor?

With a lift of her chin, she sucked in a deep breath, and with determination turned her mind to the good news. The house still stood. From her position on the driveway it didn't look to be noticeably damaged. On closer inspection, however, she saw the evidence all around, the melted end of the hose at the bottom of the back steps, the singed palmetto palm fronds, and of course, she couldn't miss the gaudy yellow tape that roped off the house as a crime scene.

Ignoring the yellow tape, she stepped over it and took the path on the south side of the house that wound between palmetto palms and a tangle of underbrush around a gnarled and misshapen live oak, moving toward the beach along the same way she'd run with Danny. The passageway was a quagmire of mud trampled by heavy boots, but she was relieved to see the live oak showed no discernible damage.

Around the corner of the house the smell of smoke grew stronger, oppressive. Her steps slowed. As she approached the front, she searched for the familiar white pillars of the covered porch that wound around the front of the house, facing the beach. Her steps stopped altogether.

A good portion of the porch was gone. Charred and misshapen timbers had taken its place. The wall that once enclosed the living room and supported the second floor balcony outside her bedroom was a charred skeleton. Furniture inside the living room had morphed into unrecognizable black bumps in the smoldering ashes.

A trio of men were sifting through the ruins, one in a police uniform. Anna didn't acknowledge them but lifted her bandaged hand to cover her nose and mouth against the stink and turned away. Little good it did. Her throat closed, and she coughed then gagged, struggling to pull in a full breath.

Overcome, she walked down the beach, away from the house to the place where she'd left Danny that night. Was it only yesterday? Fog rolled toward the shore; the wind came at her from the sea, blowing in the tide and her hair from her face. Her gaze dipped to the sand, and she remembered the feel of Danny's little hands clawing at her shirt to keep her from leaving him there. She saw the terror on his tear-stained face, the pleading in eyes, heard his crying, but in the end he stayed where she left him. And because of it he was alive today. Anna closed her eyes, glad to have this first chance to see her wounded home alone but anxious to hold her nephew again.

The first few drops of rain blew against her cheeks and mingled with the tears already there. She lifted her face to the wind, relishing its moist caress, overwhelmed by the sudden turn her life had taken. Her sister was dead. *Oh God, Holly was dead!* Most likely murdered. Her family home was devastated by fire, the man she'd promised to marry hadn't made the five and a half hour drive from Dahlonega to be beside her, and there was her sister's son who'd be leaving her as soon as his father could take him away. The precious little boy would be without his mother now, and after Stanley took him to Ft. Worth, there was no knowing when she'd ever see him again.

Three years ago her parents had been killed in a private plane crash while on their way home from a vacation in Canada. The news had devastated her. She was barely two years out of college and suddenly alone. Then Holly showed up with her infant son in her arms, and she wasn't alone anymore. They had hugged and cried and somehow gotten through the tragedy together as only sisters could.

At the back of the house Anna slowed to stare at the wooden planks nailed onto the kitchen door in the form of an X. Slowly, a sickening ache in the pit of her stomach, she wrapped her arms around her waist and climbed the four steps to peek inside. She wasn't sure what she expected, but she was surprised to see that except for the soot and watermarks everything looked pretty much the same as before. The crab pot was still on the stove, and it crossed her mind that in a few days it would stink worse than the burn. On the counter by her house phone was her purse. It looked to be unscarred, and she desperately wanted it.

Slowly, she walked down the steps again and turned toward the garage where her car and her sister's rental were locked inside, recalling the call Holly received on her cell the night before her death. She had taken the phone into the yard to have her conversation in private which wasn't like her. Anna had assumed the call was from her husband concerning their pending separation and therefore personal. She'd thought nothing more of it. Now she was thinking a lot about it and wondering where Holly's cell phone was. She'd like to find out who made that last call. Had the fire destroyed Holly's purse and cell phone, or had the police found and confiscated them, or had the murderer lifted one or both of them from where she often left them beside her chair?

With the intention of sneaking inside to have a look around, Anna hurried her steps down the brick path through the modest gardens to the walkway connecting the main house to the garage and the apartment above the garage. Ten years ago when her grandmother moved permanently to the garage apartment, the walkway had been enclosed against the weather. Her grandmother had suggested a screened porch be built above the walkway at the same time, and Anna's parents liked the idea of the screened sitting room so well, they expanded the original concept to widen it to ten feet. For easy access to and from the kitchen, a stairwell was also added near the side door of the kitchen. As well, a sliding glass 'walk-through' dissected the passageway, connecting the little walled garden to the beachfront.

The porch was one of Anna's favorite spots in the house. Her one regret was that it didn't connect to the bedroom it butted up to. The need for that fourth bedroom no longer seemed important, and it was on her 'To do' list to open up the connection as soon as she could and convert the room into a game and television room.

Pleased to see that the enclosed passageway and porch above looked unscathed, she headed for it, only to come up short when she noticed a man stood in the overhang by the back entrance. He was wearing a black rain jacket with no hat and appeared to be guarding the door. She was pretty sure he hadn't been there when she drove up. The thought of retrieving her hide-a-key in the back and racing him through the passageway to the kitchen in order to retrieve her purse crossed her mind before she dismissed it as ludicrous and held out her hand.

"Hi, I'm Anna Hanley," she said in her damaged voice. "This is my house, and I thought I'd go inside and get some of my things. My cell phone is on the counter just inside the kitchen."

"Detective Joe Brady, Ms. Hanley—" he looked up with assessing eyes—"and I'm afraid I can't let you go inside just yet. It's still too dangerous, and..."

"...and you want to investigate," she said, unable to quite bite back her disappointment.

"Yes." Detective Brady smiled, making creases in his jowly face. He appeared to be in his early fifties with a thick body and streaks of gray in his black hair. "At the very least we believe arson took place here."

"I understand. So when do you think I might get inside to look around?"

"My guess is that it could be another couple days."

She opened her mouth to protest. He held a pudgy hand up to waylay her, and she shut it.

"I know it's inconvenient, miss, but you've got to look at it from our perspective. Parts of the building may be unsound.

Something still could collapse, and it's our job to see that no one else gets hurt. Come with me for a moment and let me show you something." He walked back around to the beachside of the house to where the other three men appeared to be sifting through the rubble looking for clues. One man was holding a partially melted bottle inverted over a stick. Both men wore gloves. She thought she recognized the bottle as the one that had come through the window and started the fire.

She didn't believe the fire or her sister's murder were random acts, and from the looks of it, the fire marshals appeared to be working under the same assumption. Good.

After introducing her to the other men, Detective Brady turned back to her, "Look here."

She looked where he pointed to the funnels of smoke that rose from the rubble here and there like miniature volcanoes.

"Those are hotspots and could still ignite."

A gust of wind and a creaking sound. All four men plus Anna looked up.

"See what I mean?" the detective said. "I'd be negligent if I let you go inside."

"Then I don't suppose I can sweet-talk you or one of your men to escort me up the back stairs to get some clothing."

"Not a chance, miss. No one is going upstairs until we're assured the top floor can support us. Right now it's unstable, and we can't make it safer until the fire is completely out. And the police will want to log all the calls and contacts on your cell for their records."

"All right." She gave in. "What about the apartment over the garage? I was hoping I could stay there until I can get the house rebuilt."

"You're welcome to stay there. The fire never got that far. Your sister was staying in the house and not in the apartment?"

"That's right." Anna remembered that Holly had retreated up there with her cell phone for a few hours a couple times.

"I'll make sure we check the apartment out before we leave today so we won't have to disturb you tomorrow. Is the lock keyed the same as the house?"

"No, but my keys are in my purse inside the kitchen."

"How did you manage to drive over here without your car keys?" he said without missing a beat. She couldn't help smiling.

"A friend's car and keys. But there's a hide-a key to the house so I can get inside through the back. That is, if you'll allow it. If you won't let me get my purse, maybe one of your officers can go in through the back door and retrieve it—that's all I ask. It's only a few feet from the door. You can check it all out, whatever—but I sure would like it..." She knew she was begging, but she didn't care. "Let me show you where it is."

"Sorry, ma'am. No can do. Tomorrow maybe. We need to check out the tracks in the kitchen before any of us can walk through. Will that hide-a-key let you get into that carriage apartment?"

"I hope so. If I can go through the door you were standing in front of and on through the passageway, I should be able to go up the stairs to the carriage house. But if I locked the door from the inside and went out through the garage, I'm sunk. If you have no objections, I'll get the key and give it a try."

He had none, so Anna excused herself, retrieved her key from where it was nailed under the roof of a bird house in her garden, and returned to where a man in the police uniform had joined Detective Brady. Brady introduced the uniform as Officer Ned Teuton. The man was a good fifteen years younger than Detective Brady, six inches taller, with brown hair cropped close to his head.

Anna handed Det. Brady the key, and he in turn gave it to Officer Teuton. "Check this out for me, Ned."

Anna watched the policeman until he disappeared inside the door that connected the utility room to the kitchen and passageway. "Mind if I go with him?"

"Help yourself."

She thanked him and hurried after Officer Teuton, knowing she wouldn't wait days before she searched for her sister's briefcase of papers and her computer. For the little she'd seen from outside the yellow tape, she determined the room where her sister had stayed looked to be intact. If the stairwell wasn't destroyed, she thought she could get up there and back if she was careful. Of course the briefcase and notebook could have been downstairs with her sister and not have survived the fire.

The police officer opened the door and held it for her. He was sharp-eyed with a ready smile that put her at ease. She led him inside, up the steps and across the sitting porch, hoping she'd not locked the apartment from the inside. He gave the handle a turn. She held her breath then let it out again when it swung open.

"There you are, ma'am, a warm and dry place for the night." He flipped the switch, and amazingly, the lights came to life.

"Is someone watching the place to keep looters away?" she asked.

"As much as we can, ma'am. Unfortunately we don't have the staff to keep someone here 24-7 for very long. We'll be round the clock tonight, probably tomorrow, too, but I'd suggest you get a moving company to cart off anything worth salvaging soon as the house is safe enough to go inside."

Before she left, Anna took a moment to go into the garage, retrieve her garage door opener, and check to see if by some unlikely chance she left a set of keys in her car. No such luck. Not in her sister's rental either.

Outside again, she heard waves crash behind her as they broke against the shore, and though she couldn't see them from the house, she turned toward the sound. She closed her eyes and breathed in a quivery breath before she turned and got into her car. This was her place, her home, and she was determined to bring it back to life as best she could.

Ten minutes later she was at Mary Katherine's house, hugging Danny. The two of them stayed long enough to join the family for a dinner of lasagna and fresh salad and for Anna to call her insurance company to report the fire. Afterward, insisting that she and Danny would be all right in the carriage apartment with the police stationed right outside, Anna persuaded Mary Katherine to drive her back. On the way they stopped at the grocery for some staples for breakfast and lunch.

"Hopefully, I'll get my purse and my cell back early tomorrow," Anna said, thanking Mary Katherine for all she'd done.

As it turned out, a uniformed policeman who hadn't been there earlier met her when she got out of the car. He was about 5' 11" with a ruddy face, sandy-colored hair, and deep-set blue eyes. "Det. Brady thought you'd like to have this." He held out her purse. She very nearly kissed him.

After many years of sleeping in the same room in her house, Anna expected the carriage house apartment would feel strange that first night after she and Danny moved in, but from the start the rooms had been welcoming almost as though her grandmother's spirit was still there, and after a few hours of hearing the familiar beach sounds, she'd settled right in.

The closets and dressers had been emptied of her grandmother's personal items, but many of her grandmother's things were still there. The paintings she'd collected in a lifetime of travels and moved from the main house to make room for her daughter's own collection of artwork adorned the walls, warm, familiar. A collection of antique dolls was displayed in a tall display case beside a case of miniature model ships constructed by her grandfather. A three-story doll house made by her great-grandfather for her mother was filled with antique doll furniture.

The apartment was equipped with an efficiency kitchen and full bath, but there was only one bedroom. The pastel blues and pale yellows of the feminine room gave it an airy effect in daylight, but tonight the bank of windows overlooking the ocean were curtained and closed, and to Anna the room seemed overly somber. The Oriental rug covering the hardwood floor was old, a muted pattern of rose and Cornelian blue that Anna loved. It had been in her grandmother's bedroom for as long as she could remember.

She tucked Danny in on the roll-away she'd retrieved from the back of the closet, flicked off the bedside lamp, and headed for the door.

His sweet little voice came from the dark and brought her back into the room. "Will mommy be back tomorrow?" Her heart nearly broke.

She sat heavily on the edge of her grandmother's four-poster, too shaken to let him see the tears that sprung to her eyes. She had to swallow twice before she could speak at all. "No, Sweetheart." Her voice broke, and she worked to clear her throat. "But tomorrow you and I will stop at the library and get some books for us to read."

She was so sore she had to hold onto the bed to bring herself to her feet. Gingerly, she bent down to Danny and kissed his brow, smoothing back his blond waves. "Then we'll go to the store and buy you some new clothes and maybe a toy. How does that sound?"

"Fine." He rolled onto his side against his pillow. "Do you think my teddy might be okay?"

"I do think so. Hopefully we can get him for you tomorrow, too. Now you go on to sleep, and we'll talk more in the morning." He had been so good. She couldn't believe how good he'd been. She hadn't planned to, but when he asked her, she'd told him about his mother over a bowl of cookies and cream ice cream, his favorite. In her heart she feared he didn't truly understand that his mommy wasn't just gone for today and tomorrow but for always. Even she couldn't comprehend it.

A beam of light from the hallway illuminated a picture on her grandmother's marble-topped dressing table. Her father had taken the photo on Christmas a few months before her grandmother passed away at the age of ninety-two. It was a photograph of her, Holly, their mother and grandmother, three generations of Hanleys. She picked it up and carried it with her into the kitchen. With the exception of her all the women of the Hanley family were dead.

Oh, Holly, Holly, what am I to do? Who killed you? Why?

After the fire marshal's warnings about it being too dangerous, Anna had second thoughts about going upstairs to her sister's room to search her things. God forbid, the stairs collapsed or the floor caved, and she fell and hurt herself. She might not be able to return to Danny before he awakened. How afraid he would be. But if she was going to search at all, it had to be tonight. Tomorrow the police would be scouring everything.

Chapter 7

The afternoon storm moved out to sea that night, and the sky filled with stars. It was the kind of night Kip often dreamed of when far from home. As he had on the previous night Kip once again maneuvered his childhood dinghy across the river toward Tybee beach. A gentle breeze flapped the sail; the ocean lapped against the hull, and the marsh grass along the shore whispered its own refrain. Closing his eyes, he listened to nature's music and breathed in the fragrance of the brine. For a precious few moments he was a boy again, sailing the rivers with his brothers and his dog; the sun was on his face, and the world was a simple place where the bad guys were only on TV.

How he loved the natural elements of life, the wind, the rain, the mountains and valleys alike, the sun, the trees, the scent of the earth as God had created it. Often he thought he could carve a life for himself in the harshest wilderness, and there were many times in his life that he'd been forced to test that theory. Sometimes it would have been easier to just stay there in God's country, but he always returned. There were needs in his soul to finish whatever job he'd set out to do. The need was in him now.

Though he had much to lose if the authorities picked him up, tonight wasn't one of those times when he sensed danger was near. Leaving the house unnoticed hadn't been difficult. He knew every creak in the old stairway, and once outside it was easy to skirt the house and walk through the trees to where the skiff was tied at the dock. Trying to keep his weak condition from showing in his face during the evening meal with his family had been a good deal harder.

Throughout the day he'd felt their awareness of him like a pack of mother hens hovered over a sick child, but he'd done his best not to let them know how debilitated he was, drained both physically and mentally. The family wouldn't understand the search of Anna's house was something that couldn't wait. They wouldn't understand the promise he'd made to Marie and his son to bring their murderer to justice. As well there was no time for his superior officer Colonel Harrison to get someone here to fill in this job for him. Bad guys out there needed to be tracked down. Only he could get to Anna's house in such short order, so he put his weakness out of his mind.

Besides all that, he had a gut feeling Anna was in grave danger.

His skiff was small, not twelve feet in length, and hardly seaworthy, but Kip didn't have far to travel. Had anyone been peering out a window at 2:00 a.m. when Kip left his house, he might have noticed his silhouette in the starlight. But no one was looking.

No doubt the police would be at the Hanley house guarding their crime scene tonight, and they would pose a problem for him. If the structure of the house had been judged unstable, he reasoned the police might not yet have searched the upstairs. He fervently hoped that was the case, for if they had, his trip would be wasted.

Twenty feet off the Tybee shore he threw out his anchor, stripped off his jacket and loafers to leave in the boat, and slipped on some neoprene boots with heat-resistant soles. The water was cold, but not as cold as the air, and he swam to shore with his wounded arm held close to his chest so as not to dislodge the new stitches. It made the swimming slow and difficult, but he was a strong swimmer, and the distance was short. Soon his feet touched bottom.

He walked along the beach to where Anna's house stood dark against the backdrop of stars, like a massive rock with a large crater scarring its face. One quarter was gone, burned, gutted to charred timber, but the shell remained like a ghostly reminder of what had once been. And what could be again. Anna's quick thinking and use of the hose had saved much of the structure.

As he neared the house, Kip looked for a light, found none, not even in the carriage house where rumor was that Anna Hanley planned to sleep. He expected a guard somewhere nearby, perhaps in a car for the night was cold enough to want to avoid the penetrating wind. Like a shadow he moved through the dunes and on to the house until he located the guards in the back drive. There were two of them inside a marked patrol car, and they looked to be awake. As they were parked on the inland side of the house, he thought they were assuming their mere presence would deter any would-be looters, but undoubtedly they would make irregular walkabouts, too. He would be on the lookout for them.

Once inside the house he was struck by the warmth and realized that parts of the place were still smoldering. He opened the small waterproof pack he'd strapped to his waist and withdrew night goggles and fastened them over his eyes, and then some rubber gloves, a computer memory stick, and a small camera. If his luck held, it would be all he needed. He pulled on the gloves and made his way through the charred ruins to the front stairs, careful to avoid places where he sensed the heat.

Vague starlight was coming into the front room, but as he neared the center of the house, it disappeared. Without his night goggles he would have found it difficult to find the stairs. The walls in the front hallway were discolored with soot and water stains but otherwise appeared to have been largely missed by the flames. On the other hand, there was a groan over his head whenever the wind gusted. It told him the structure was unsound, and that worried him. He decided to take his chances and headed for the steps. Slowly, one step at a time, he climbed toward the landing above.

On the fourth step a creak froze him against the wall. He waited for close to two minutes before he started up again, even slower this time, keeping his steps away from the center of the worn wooden treads. There were fifteen steps in all, and it took him several minutes to reach the top. Now he was at a disadvantage. He had no idea which room Holly used, so he walked down the short hallway and glanced into all four of the rooms until he located a suitcase visible in an open closet. It was in the last room he checked. Like the other front room this one was large and had four windows that overlooked the ocean and two that looked out to the side. The room reeked from the fire and from being soaked. Everything was covered with a film of black soot. He was careful to touch as little as possible, but he saw that he was leaving tracks.

It didn't take him long to locate a briefcase on the floor, resting against a wooden rocker. He found it unlocked, withdrew the computer, placed it on the bed, and knelt on the floor in front of it. His luck held, for the computer had been left on, so no password was needed. In seconds he was inside. Once there he worked efficiently, rapidly loading the files onto his memory stick. He placed the stick in a pocket inside his wetsuit, replaced the computer into the briefcase, and checked his watch. Six minutes had passed.

The next part would take more time. He paused and listened for the cops, but aside from a gust from the wind every now and again, the night was quiet. There were several legal pads and a file of newspaper articles as well as a pile of loose papers still in the briefcase. It would be easy to take them all, but he wanted to leave no trace of having been here, other than his tracks, he thought with a wry grin as he started with the legal pads and began to photograph as quickly as he could.

He'd gotten about a quarter of the way through one pad when he saw a flash of light. He was surprised he hadn't heard a car door shut, but someone was walking inside with a flashlight.

With all her clothes except the ones on her back in her house when it burned, Anna scoured closets and attic of the carriage apartment for something to better protect her feet than the flip-flops Mary Katherine had loaned her. The search produced some thick-soled hunting boots that had once belonged to her father and were several sizes too large. Walking in them was awkward, and she felt like a small child trying to walk in a grownup's shoes as she stole from the apartment.

Once she stepped into the remains of her front living room she switched on her flashlight. The light was weak. She slid the switch forward to make sure she had it on full beam. It was. Still, the light didn't reach to the right and left of her and that made her feel uneasy. It was like she was walking through a tunnel, and she realized that the tunnel was growing narrower. The batteries were dying.

The only batteries she knew about were in the kitchen drawer, and she headed that way. For fear of arousing the policemen camped outside, she groped her way through the house in the dark only to discover there were no D size batteries to be had. She retraced her steps, clinging to the charred walls for guidance.

When she passed into the burned-out front hall, she had the frightening sensation she wasn't alone. Her heart began to beat more rapidly. She made a full circle, directing the flashlight beam into the dark surrounding her. Unfortunately, the light was too feeble to extend more than a few feet. Nothing appeared to move, nothing but a few lingering plumes of smoke, but she wasn't reassured. It would be easy for a man to hide in amongst the charred and broken beams. Her pathetic light would never expose him.

A creak. She froze, clutching the wall. The sound seemed to come from over her head. She glanced at the ceiling in indecision then looked to her right and left and behind her. It was pitch dark, and she couldn't make out much.

She didn't want to believe that someone else was in the house. Maybe the sound had come from the wind. She waited for the sound to repeat itself. It didn't. She waited a full minute more and heard nothing except the wind and the creak of the upstairs itself, sounding like it was in danger of collapsing. She began to think she'd misheard the creak. Probably a gust of wind had caused a limb to rub against the house. Maybe a stray dog or cat or raccoon had wondered in, but there was no mistaking the instability of the house so maybe it had been just the house groaning. She sighed and compressed her lips. She was already halfway to her sister's room so she might just as well go on and finish the job.

She started up the steps as quickly as she could in her father's boots.

Working swiftly Kip returned everything to the briefcase and placed the bag against the rocker where he'd found it. Someone was mounting the stairs with little attempt at stealth. Out of habit when he entered a strange room, Kip had established the best methods of escape, but in this room the options were few. The only door in and out led directly to the hall at the top of the steps. That route wasn't feasible unless he wanted to collide with the newcomer. He looked out the closest side window. Directly below him was the roof of the wrap-around porch, but on his way in he'd noticed it had been badly damaged in the fire. It might not hold his weight. Also, all the windows were shut. In an old house like this, windows often stuck. Leaving through the door or windows weren't good choices. The only viable alternative was to hide.

A split second before a flashlight beamed into the room he ducked into the closet and drew his gun. Inside, there were just enough clothes to conceal him. Not trusting the old hinges not to squeak, he left the door ajar, exactly as he found it, and had a good view of the doorway.

A cough, muffled.

Anna, he thought seconds before she appeared in the doorway. The stench from the fire in the house was still strong enough to trigger reflex coughing, especially in someone who'd sustained smoke damage to her membranes as she had. Though he wished she had postponed her search until morning, Kip had to admire the gumption it took for her to return to her sister's room in the dead of night and after what she'd just been through. It also meant she was looking for more than her own personal items, and his curiosity increased. Just how much did Miss Anna Hanley know about her sister's activities?

Sooner or later the light she was using though dim would attract the attention of the police on the other side of the house.

A few steps inside the doorway she stopped and looked around. As soon as she saw the briefcase she went right to it, picked it up, and slung the long strap over her shoulder. After another brief survey of the room, she moved out of his sight. Seconds later she reappeared with a red notebook and walked out.

He waited until he heard her descending the steps before he came out of the closet. Then he waited a few seconds more pondering his next course of action. Should he follow her, reclaim the briefcase and notebook, finish his job, and therefore blow his cover, or plan on a visit to her garage apartment at a later time when she was gone?

He had determined on the latter when a yelp followed immediately by a thump took the decision out of his hands.

Anna decided she'd had enough. Pleased with her find, she was anxious to be out of the house as quickly as possible. She headed back down the stairs. Without giving it a second thought she skipped the last step like she so often did when she was in a hurry. Unfortunately she'd forgotten about the boots.

Overlarge as they were, the heel of her left one stuck on an exposed nail in the tread. Her boot stayed there while the rest of her flew over the step. She reached for a wall that was no longer there, and landed awkwardly on all fours. Hot cinders found her hands and knees, singed them. She couldn't restrain a breathy yelp as she yanked her hands back and shot to her feet.

Remembering belatedly she was where she had no business being, Anna replaced her boot, snatched up her flashlight and her sister's briefcase, and prepared to make a run for the carriage house. It wasn't to be.

A hand grabbed her jacket and jerked her backward. The next thing she knew she was back in the cinders on her hands and knees. She rolled to face her assailant and lashed out at him with a foot. The boot was heavy and connected. The man grunted an oath and stepped back, but he wasn't deterred.

"Help!" She slapped the flashlight at the assailant's hands and arms.

With her voice no more than a feeble whisper, she didn't believe the police would hear. She didn't believe anyone would be coming to rescue her tonight. She'd thought she might have trouble with the police, but she hadn't expected to be attacked. She had underestimated the man who'd killed Holly. Because of it she would likely end up dead like her sister.

Everything was happening so fast. In seconds it would all be over. If she was to live, she had to save herself. She screamed at her assailant until no sound at all would pass through her damaged throat. Before he regained his feet to tackle her once again, she hurled her flashlight at his head. Unfortunately, he was ready for the move and deflected it mid-flight. Coming on like a ninja and dressed all in black, he pushed her backward until she came up against the one wall that remained in the hallway. Before she could regain her balance something solid came down hard against the side of her head, and her legs turned to jelly.

Kip abandoned any thought of stealth and charged into the hallway, pulling his gun from the holster inside his wetsuit as he did. He hadn't thought it would be necessary to have it, but he was a cautious man.

A bullet whipped by him and he dropped to the floor, looking down the steps. A man was running, and he had a good head start. Kip took aim, fired at the assailant's gun arm then leapt up and ran forward, jumping down the rest of the steps. But the man had already disappeared around the house. His tracks led into the dunes, and Kip knew he would have a car hidden somewhere. On foot it would be impossible to catch him. Meanwhile Anna was hurt.

He tucked his goggles into his pack and walked back into the shadows of the house to where Anna was lying on the floor, one of her boots half off her foot, the briefcase she'd been carrying nowhere in sight. He bent down beside her slowly.

His head was spinning again. She was coming to, and he touched his hand to her face. She turned away.

"Where are you hurt?"

She didn't look at him, didn't speak. Keeping his back to the little light from the stars so that his face was in shadows, he placed his hand at her cheek and moved her head around so she was forced to face him. Black camouflage paint was smeared over his face and when they came face-to-face again as they inevitably would, he wasn't particularly worried she'd be able to recognize him.

He gripped her arm just above the elbow and helped her to sit. Her face had taken on a pallor that told him she'd received quite a blow, and on her cheek the glint of a tear caught in the starlight. Her forehead was bleeding a little, but it looked to be superficial. He picked up her boot and put it back on her foot. She winced, and he thought maybe her ankle had been twisted in the fall. If that was all that had been injured, she was lucky.

"Let me help you get out of here," he said.

For a long time she just stared at him, and he could feel her nervousness, sense her confusion.

"I can do that without any help from the likes of you." Her tone was defiant, but her voice was rough like dry sandpaper over hardwood, and her mouth quivered. "You already have my sister's briefcase, so why don't you just go back to your hole or wherever you came from? What more do you want?"

"I don't have the briefcase, and right now I want to get you out of here before either of us catches on fire. Then I'll go back to my hole," he said, amused. He placed his arm around her back and pulled her to her feet. "Do you think you can walk?"

Kip was sweating. He could feel the beads on his forehead and knew the fever was causing it. He should be back in his house sleeping and not searching for information in the dead of night in a house still smoldering from a recent fire. And he knew he was in no condition to be lifting young damsels in distress either, but it was looking more and more like he was going to have no choice in that matter either.

"I can walk." Again, that defiance was in her voice.

To prove it she took a step and would have landed in the ashes once again if he hadn't caught her. She fell against his chest, and before he could pull away, his face was in her hair, and the sweet fresh scent of flowers filled his senses. For a dizzying moment his hand came up and hovered over her head, and he yearned to cradle her against him.

Footsteps sounded on the paving stones at the side of the house and brought him to his senses. He swore under his breath. The police had at last been aroused.

He lowered her to her feet. "The police will be here in a moment, so I'll be taking my leave now."

He backed up a few steps when her voice brought him to a stop again.

"I thought I heard gunshots. Why didn't you shoot me?"

He didn't answer for a moment, surprised by her question. "Because I wasn't aiming at you," he said honestly. Then he turned and ran.

It must have been the fever, he thought later as he maneuvered his skiff back toward Marsh Winds that caused his body to react in such a way to Anna Hanley.

Chapter 8

By the time Kip reached the shores of Marsh Winds, dawn was on the horizon and his fever was nasty. A wave of nausea hit him, and he doubled over, waiting until it passed. His limbs were heavy as he staggered to a tree. He leaned there until he thought he could make the long walk across the lawn. Still, if it hadn't been for his mother's habit of rising early, he might have gotten away with the clandestine foray. As it was, she must have spied him through the kitchen windows, for she was at the back door waiting for him.

But when she opened it, it was Harlie, his black tri-colored Australian shepherd, who charged through first, nearly knocking his mother over in the process. She stepped back to give Kip entry and folded her arms around her waist.

He kept a hand braced on the doorframe while he bent to pet his dog. "Morning, Mom." He decided the easiest way through this was to bluff.

"Good morning, son. Your dog woke me up hours ago with her pacing and whining. She was looking for you."

He'd considered taking Harlie as far as the skiff and tying her up, but he didn't want to take a chance she'd follow him, so he'd left her closed in his bedroom, hoping she'd settle down and sleep. "I'm sorry she woke you. I couldn't sleep…" It was the first thing that came into his fogged brain.

"So you put on your wetsuit and went for a swim."

He'd forgotten he was wearing his wetsuit. He shrugged. "If you'll excuse me, I believe I'll head on up to bed."

"You need any help getting up the stairs?"

He straightened his shoulders. "No."

"Fine, but you smell like smoke. You better wash it off if you don't want the others to know where you've been. And that blood that's on your shirt, too…don't leave it where your sister can find it. She's coming home today."

He glanced at her, but she was already turning away. Then she stopped and retraced her steps. "You want some help redressing the bandage?"

"No, I can do that."

"Had a lot of practice, have you?" She shook her head.

"I'm afraid so," he said, and he was smiling now.

She stretched up to put a kiss on his cheek. "I thought you were through with all that sort of stuff. Well, I'm just glad you made it home. Goodnight, son. Get some sleep."

Kip refrained from comment and focused his concentration on walking as he headed for the stairs. A few minutes later in front of his bathroom mirror, he took a good look at himself. His wetsuit was torn at the elbow. Blood was dripping from his T-shirt where it hung out from the waist of his wetsuit. Though he'd tried to remove it, traces of black makeup still clung around his eyes and nose. His face was flush, his eyes hot with fever, and his left cheek was smeared with blood. His shoulder and back felt stiff and sore from his dive to the floor, his limbs heavy and unresponsive. His hands were scraped. He couldn't remember where the scrapes had come from, but he thought the blood might be from the cut on Anna's head.

As he scrubbed away the blood he thought about her. Both encounters with Anna had been under adverse circumstances and brief. He didn't know her at all since high school, hadn't had a normal conversation with her in twelve years, and yet both times he'd encountered her he'd felt drawn to her. It was like time had held still, and it disturbed him.

By the time he staggered onto his bed, daylight was seeping through the edges of his window-blinds. When lunchtime came and went without his appearance, his mother arrived at his room. His head was pounding, and his mouth was parched. The last thing he remembered was when he swung his legs over the side of the bed to try and stand. After that he remembered nothing until he came to in his brother's SUV, shivering and shaking with an ice pack strapped over his head. He reached up to remove the ice.

"Leave it," Dylan ordered. "You're burning with fever."

"I'm freezing is what I am." Kip pushed the ice pack off his head with a shaky hand.

Dylan, his normally cautious and conservative brother, hissed an oath and laid a hand on his horn. He kept it there as he sprinted around the cars ahead of him. Kip glanced at him and then at the speedometer. Victory Drive was a 35 mph zone, and Dylan was doing 55mph through traffic.

"You got a death wish or something?"

Dylan looked over at him and said nothing, but Kip could see the worry in his face.

"Hey, I'm fine, Dylan."

"You damn well are not. You passed out, Kip. When the deuce have you ever passed out before?"

Kip could think of a few times, like last month when he was shot on the top of the mountain in Colorado. That time he'd tumbled down the cliff where his friend and colleague Barry Wesley had found him more dead than alive two days later. That incident led to all his current problems, he thought, but he kept his thoughts to himself.

Six minutes later when Dylan plowed his SUV through the parking lot and brought it to a screeching stop at the emergency room entrance of Memorial Hospital without incident, Kip had to hand it to Dylan. He was one hell of a good driver. The cop who'd been blaring his siren behind Dylan for the last five miles wasn't as impressed.

The next two nights were spent at the hospital receiving a regiment of intensive antibiotics and repair work on the stitches, followed by a stern lecture from Dr. Schroeder on the need for rest.

Now, four days later, he was home alone and restless to be done with the ensuing forced days of recovery and inaction. The rest of the family, including his sister Robyn, who'd flown in from Atlanta for the day, had left to attend Holly Everett's funeral. He'd been given orders to stay put and concentrate on getting well.

Soon as their cars were out of sight on the driveway, he dialed a yellow cab, grabbed a case with some equipment, and went to the front steps to wait.

When the cab dropped him back at Marsh Winds less than an hour later, the house was still empty. He took a short walk around the back yard, mentally promised himself he'd widen the walk tomorrow and maybe even do some running and walking in intervals, increasing the distance as he built his stamina. But as he lay back down on his bed and picked up his laptop he was wise enough to recognize the heavy feeling in his body was because he was still a long way from having regained his full strength.

Chapter 9

In the quiet confines of Bonaventure Cemetery four days after her clandestine raid to her home in the middle of the night, Anna sat under a canopy on a folding chair with her sister's son on her lap and her fiancé Dennis Fowler beside her. She wiped a crooked finger under her eyes. The day couldn't have been lovelier, the temperature a balmy seventy-two degrees, the humidity low, the sun brilliant in a cornflower blue sky. But all Anna could think was her sister would never again experience a day such as this one. She dipped her cheek against Danny's soft blond hair, and let her attention wander past the open grave and casket, past the centuries-old grave markers, to the Wilmington River as it made its way to the sea, letting the feel of the antiquity in the ancient cemetery, its history, all the lives of those who had passed on before Holly, settle over her. After a moment she managed to breathe again.

After the service at historic St. John's church in downtown Savannah and the reception put on by the women of the church that followed, Anna, Stanley, and Danny, rode to the gravesite in Dennis's Honda for an interment reserved for family and close friends. Father. James, keeping to his promise that he would keep his words brief, was closing the service with a final prayer. Anna turned her attention back to him. The heart-wrenching day was almost over. For Anna it couldn't come too soon. With no family to lean on, the brave front she'd managed to uphold all day was fraying at the edges.

The few remaining mourners came to express their final condolences. She placed Danny on his feet with a little pat to his fanny and rose to accept Kip's sister's hug.

Robyn McTeer spoke close to her ear. "Kip sends his condolences. He intended to come, but Mother threatened to put him back in the hospital if he disobeyed the doctors' orders again."

When the ceremony started, it crossed Anna's mind to wonder if Kip might stop by, but in light of what Robyn told her about the complications he was having from his motorcycle accident, she hadn't expected him. It was probably just as well. Right now she wasn't sure she was strong enough to see him face-to-face.

Twelve years.

"He's all right, isn't he?"

Robyn nodded. "Yes and no. He's been sick with a serious infection. But don't tell him that. He considers it just a trivial setback. I believe he thinks he's Superman."

Anna smiled despite herself. "That's the Kip I remember. Tell him I said hello."

Dennis and Father James stood at her side as she watched Robyn and the other McTeers get into their cars, the last to depart. Dennis put his arm around her back and gave her a squeeze. Gratefully, Anna leaned into him.

"I know you're exhausted, darling, but I'd say everything went well, including this fine day. Don't you agree?"

Anna closed her eyes and offered her face to the sun. She would have preferred the day to have been cold and rainy, a far more appropriate testament to the misery in her heart. "Yes, I suppose so."

Holly's husband came up behind her and touched her arm. "Excuse me, Anna, but I have to leave shortly. I have a plane to catch, and I wonder if I might have a word with you before I go."

"Of course."

"I'll keep an eye on Danny and leave you two alone," Dennis offered. Giving Anna a peck on the cheek, he walked out from under the canopy with the minister.

Anna watched Danny run on ahead of them. "This is a beautiful place," she said with a sigh, then turned to Stanley. She noticed that the stress of the day had taken a toll on him. His movie star good looks showed signs that he hadn't slept much since his estranged wife's death. No doubt he was feeling guilty for all the heartache he'd caused her. Or was it more sinister than that? She had always perceived that Stanley for all his handsome features was a weak man.

"I've already packed Danny's things," she said, "not that there was much, but we got a couple puzzles he seems fond of and some clothes. You might as well take them with you.

Anyway, it won't take long for him to be ready to leave. What time's your flight?"

Stanley shifted his weight on his crutches, and Anna sensed his unease. "Around four. Thanks for taking care of all the arrangements for me."

Suddenly Anna realized this wasn't going to be a casual conversation. The old adage her mother had often voiced came into her mind. *When it rains it pours...* Her mouth tightened. What new revelation was he about to drop on her?

When he didn't immediately say anything more, she started toward some seats. "It's already been a long day. You want to sit?"

He nodded and followed awkwardly on his crutches.

"I'm sorry about your broken ankle."

"A silly accident," he said with a dismissive wave of his hand. "I should have paid more attention to what I was doing. It'd been raining. I was in a hurry, and I slipped down the back steps at the house."

She picked a seat under the canopy, and he flipped a chair around to sit across from her. "Where are you staying, Anna? Have you got a place to stay?"

"In the carriage house. I found a cot for Danny."

He went on to explain how sorry he was that Holly had been murdered, his shock that it had happened, and touched on his version of the estrangement between Holly and him. Anna listened without comment. He wound down with, "So how's Danny getting along?"

"He seems to be coping fairly well, but he doesn't really understand that he won't see her again, you know. It's going to take a lot of time for him to adjust."

"I know." His gaze pinned on his shoe. It looked shiny and stiff, like the leather was new. The leg of the pants to his dress suit had been unstitched to his knee and cleverly pinned to accommodate his cast. He picked imaginary lint from the cloth then scrubbed a hand over his mouth.

She knew she should feel sympathy for Stanley for whatever was on his mind was giving him obvious discomfort. Instead, she found herself growing impatient with his stalling and his obsequious smile. She was anxious to put the day and her sister's husband behind her. But more than that, she realized she was dreading saying her good-byes to Danny. Over the past few days they'd become very close, and she desperately hoped Stanley would see fit to allow the little fellow to visit her on a regular basis. For that reason alone she smiled at him.

"Is there anything else I can help you with, Stan?" she said in her throaty voice.

"Well, actually there is..." he said and dropped his bombshell. "I'm hoping you might be able to help me find a reputable adoption agency."

For a moment she was too stunned to speak.

"What?" she said on an exhalation of breath. "Did you just say you wanted to find an adoption agency?"

"Yeah, I've been thinking I'd put the kid up for adoption."

"By 'the kid', do you mean Danny?" She couldn't believe he'd just said that. "You want to put Danny up for adoption? Your son?"

"Yes," he said, hesitant. "You do know the boy isn't mine, don't you?"

"What? No, what do you mean he isn't yours? Are you telling me you aren't Danny's father?" Anna realized her mouth was open and snapped it shut.

"Let me explain." He told her he'd been sterile since he was a teen and had the mumps. "I thought she would have told you by now. Holly never confided in you about the boy?"

"No, none of it. Did Holly *know* you weren't Danny's father?"

"Yes. I told her after Danny was born. At the time she'd been seeing another man."

Anna's fingers bit into her arms. Beneath her black silk suit, her pulse was racing. "I find that hard to believe. Anyway, Danny's four. That was a long time ago. He thinks of you as his father as does everyone else."

A black and white cab pulled to a stop directly in front of the grave site and drew Anna's attention. The windows were rolled down, and Anna was bothered by the thought that she'd seen the cab earlier parked at a different gravesite. In the shadows she couldn't make out who was sitting in the back seat, but she couldn't miss the flash of sunlight reflected off the telephoto lens protruding from the window.

"Someone you know?" Stanley asked, following the direction of her gaze.

"Maybe, I can't see the face in the shadows. But whoever it is, I believe he just snapped a picture of us."

The car began to move slowly away. Anna shrugged, turning back to Stanley, and discovered she had the beginnings of another headache. "Do you know who Danny's father is?"

Stanley shook his head. "Holly never told me his name, only that she met him when she was on assignment in England. He was someone prominent, a tycoon in the import-export business, a playboy with a wife who stayed with him for his money. They had a brief fling, and the affair was over by the time she found out she was pregnant. She never told him about the child, and she adamantly refused to divulge his name to me. That's how she told it to me anyway. I thought you might know the guy's name."

"No, I don't."

At the far end of the tent two men began to pack up chairs. Her lips drawn tight, Anna shot to her feet. Stanley Everett had to be the world's number one creep. One didn't just give away a child. The strength of the anger she felt toward him surprised her. To give herself a moment to calm down, she paced a few yards away then came back and stopped directly in front of him. She skewered him with a glare that spoke her anger clearly.

Stanley looked pained. "What would I do with a child, Anna? I'm rarely home. I'd hoped you understand why I can't keep him."

"Well, I don't understand. I don't understand at all." His whiny tone irritated her. She opened her mouth to tell him that there were a lot of single fathers in this world who did just fine but realized there was no point in it and closed her mouth. Stanley was a creep and a loser and always had been.

"No need to search for adoptive parents. I'll keep Danny. I'll adopt him. Leave him and get out of my sight before I smash one of those crutches across your face. And see to it the proper documentation is drawn up by a lawyer and sent to me immediately." She looked at his handsome face, at the sheen of sweat that beaded his upper lip, and couldn't think of anything more to say so turned and walked away.

Bewildered at all the new facts that were suddenly coming to light, Anna stopped at the guest register someone had left on a chair and picked it up. Holly not only had been murdered, but she had a lover and a son that wasn't her husband's. Inside, she seethed, but when she greeted Father James and Dennis, she managed a smile and said brightly, "Change of plans. Danny's coming home with me."

"I thought Danny was flying back with Stanley this afternoon," Dennis said as soon as the three of them were alone in the car.

"I'll explain when we get to the apartment."

When they arrived, she asked him to wait and took Danny upstairs to the apartment, where his suitcase was packed and ready beside the door. She sat him at the table and gave him some juice and a cookie she made for him the day before. "I'll be right back, honey. I need to talk to Dennis for a moment."

Dennis was outside the car, pacing, obviously in a hurry to get started on the long drive back to Auburn. "What's this all about?"

She told him, concluding with, "So I'm going to adopt him."

She supposed she shouldn't have sprung her plans on him in such a sudden manner, but she didn't seriously consider he would object.

In his quiet, curve ball approach, Dennis made it abundantly clear that he did object. "I thought we'd have children of our own one day down the road, but I'm not sure I can take on someone else's child, especially while I'm in school and trying to write a book. You should have consulted me before making such an important decision."

He was right. She should have consulted him. But, overwhelmed by the stress of the day, of the week, she didn't react well.

They had their first fight. She gave him back his ring.

He drove off angry, and she spent a sleepless night, worrying about Danny and hoping he hadn't overheard any of their conversation.

Chapter 10

The old pelican flew out past the island to where the sea and the Savannah River met and melded. Three smaller birds followed. It was a blue, windy day, the twelfth of November, less than two weeks after the fire in Anna's house. Kip McTeer stood at the end of the pier with a long-necked beer and watched the pelican until the smaller birds peeled off, and the pelican disappeared around the bend near Magnolia Point.

He smiled, listening to the exaggerated grunts and groans from his brother Dylan and Barry Wesley as they banged the tables and chairs on the lawn. Barry had arrived from Atlanta by car earlier that morning with his sister Robyn. She'd flown into Savannah five days earlier to attend Holly Everett's funeral and then flown back to Atlanta the following day.

Kip's mother had put the men to work setting up for tonight's oyster roast, while Kip had been ordered to rest. When he turned and headed back down the pier without hurry, there was no trace of a smile on his face, but he couldn't keep the twinkle of mirth from his eyes, understanding well that all the grunting and groaning was solely for his benefit.

In the shade of one of the live oaks that had graced the grounds for centuries, Kip stopped, leaned a shoulder against the trunk, and stared at the house that had been his family's home since one hundred years before the Civil War. Since the war, little had changed with the old plantation house and the acres surrounding it, or so he'd been told. A few updates here and there—the kitchen had grown toward the river to accommodate new appliances. Several new bathrooms, closets, and air conditioning had been added. But the oyster-shell frame remained much the same as it had been during the Civil War, as did the large screened back porch where the family still gathered for iced drinks and conversation in the cool of the evening. And as long as he was the owner, he planned to keep it that way.

For several more moments he watched the two men struggle to move an over-sized oak table that had been a fixture around the plantation house all his life and probably a great deal longer. A man of action, the urge to add his muscle to the lift was strong. He shoved his hands in his pockets and forced himself to look away to the slowly moving river, to soak in the peace it offered him.

The table banged down on the brick patio. Dylan cursed and Kip's attention turned back to his brother and Barry. The table was too much for the two men.

"Here, girls, let me help you with that." He came across the grass with his long stride.

"Wondered how long it would take you to disobey doctor's orders." Dylan leaned on one end of the massive table and breathed heavily.

"Just long enough to hear Mom drive off." Kip's mouth twitched, almost a smile. "What she doesn't know won't hurt her."

"Don't do this." Dylan frowned at him, but Kip paid him no heed and stepped up beside Dylan at the end of the table. He put a restraining hand on Kip's arm. "If you want to help, move a few chairs. I know what Dr. Schroeder told you. He called the house and read us all the riot act, and frankly I don't have time or the constitution to make that kind of trip to the hospital again. Barry and I can take care of this albatross. Truth is we ought to chop the wretched thing into firewood and do all our backs a favor. It's probably a hundred years old."

"Probably older n' that." Kip liked the looks of the knots and the dark grain in the wood of the oversized table. "Just like this place. Too bad Lawton couldn't be here tonight—we could use him about now."

"Medical College of Georgia seemed to think his exams were more important than an oyster roast for his brother," Dylan quipped.

"I know. He phoned while I was in the hospital, then again last night, but I miss seeing him." Kip took hold of one end of the table, "Ready... We lift on three..."

For the next hour Kip helped carry all the tables and benches and chairs from the carriage house to the yard.

Winds of Fire

"Grandma's coming," Dylan's five-year old daughter Wendy shouted from her look-out position near the driveway then ran around to the front of the house at full speed.

But Kip had already heard the car. By the time his mother came out the back door from the porch to see how things were going, Kip was lying in the hammock on the porch with a magazine on his chest and his eyes closed. She stared at him for several long moments, frowning.

"You look a little sweaty, darling," she said sweetly. "You sure your fever hasn't come back?"

"Quite sure." Kip tried to look like she'd just awakened him.

She stared at him for several more seconds. "Darn you, Kip McTeer, you've been moving the furniture, haven't you? Don't try to tell me you haven't. You've got dirt all over your hands and that magazine is a bridal magazine Robyn brought for Anna. When are you ever going to learn to take care of yourself, son? If you were just a little bit smaller I'd turn you over my knee and give you a whopping spanking."

Kip couldn't hold back the smile that vision created.

"Well—" Sarah straightened her shoulders—"it was almost worth it to see you smile. It's too rare these days, son. Now go on upstairs, take a shower, and repair whatever damage you've caused to yourself. I don't even want to know. I don't want to see you again until everyone starts arriving around 5:30."

Before she returned into the house Sara turned to Dylan and directed a frown at him and then another at Barry.

"Why you looking at me that way?" Dylan said. "I don't pull Kip's strings."

Defeated there, she swung back to Barry who lifted his hands, palms up, all innocence, but then he spoiled it all by laughing.

Sarah knew when she was beaten. "Anyway, thanks for setting this all up. It looks great. Dylan, darling, one more favor to ask. Do you mind dropping by the bakery to pick up the cornbread and desserts. I promised we'd get them by before 4:00, and it's almost that."

"Glad to, I'm on it right now." Dylan put his arm around his mother's shoulder and led her toward the house. "And, Mom, Kip's a big boy. Stop worrying."

Soon as Sarah McTeer and Dylan disappeared into the house, Barry pulled a chair up beside the hammock and sat. "Your mom's right, you know, you do look a little worse for wear," Barry said quietly.

Kip nodded and pushed himself out of the hammock. "Before I take that shower, why don't we take a stroll along the river? I need a little exercise."

"I'm thinking that's the last thing you need, buddy, but sure, I'll walk with you."

The men walked in silence to the water's edge where they turned left down a path overgrown with scrub oaks, waxed myrtle, and palmetto palms. Harlie, who had no intention of being left behind any time her master was on the move, trotted behind. When they reached a live oak that some hundred years ago had been blown over in a storm, Kip motioned for his friend to sit on the thick trunk that looked to have been used for just that purpose by many before them.

Before he sat beside him, Kip broke off a length of wild waxed myrtle and brought it to his nose. The scent was one of his favorites. He looked at the river and the seagulls skimming the water, but he was remembering six weeks ago when he stood alone on the ridge of a mountain, drinking coffee from his battered tin cup. That morning the smell of the previous night's storm had filled his nostrils and a hawk had been riding the thermals. The temperature had been cold, he remembered, bitterly cold for August, but the panoramic view of the sunrise had been riveting.

Three hundred million dollars in US currency, old bills scheduled for destruction, had been hijacked. Kip had followed the responder to the Rockies and was waiting for the others in his team who'd been delayed by weather.

The whole incident had all gone down in a few seconds. A tiny flash in the sun. He saw it out of the corner of his eye and dove for the ground an instant too late. The jolt of pain shot through his chest and threw him sideways. He rolled for the cover of a rock, but halfway there his pack got hung up on a branch wedged between the rocks and held him fast. He drew his Glock and fired.

The next bullet tore into his arm. His gun hand dropped.

"Forget it, McTeer, there's no way out." The voice came from close behind him, the voice of a stranger. They knew him. Had been hunting him. But who were they?

He lifted his hand again and coolly spouted fire while he worked to loosen his pack. The pack came free suddenly, and he found himself falling, rolling, bouncing painfully over rock, down, down the side of a cliff. Surging waves of pain went over him and through him. Then he was in free-fall. He clawed at the rock face and shrubs to slow his descent before he slammed to a sudden stop on a narrow out-cropping of rock. If not for Barry Wesley and the others in his team, he would have been a dead man.

"Good to see you up and about, buddy." Cutting into his reverie, Barry gave him a friendly punch. "When I left you in the hospital in California, I had my doubts."

"Yeah, well, you took your sweet time getting to me up there on that mountain," Kip said in mock disgust.

Barry joined his chuckle. "Yeah, well, next time maybe you can find a better place to get shot. I'm not that fond of rock climbing. And now it looks as though you're about to get yourself in another heap of trouble."

Kip sobered. "So how much do you know about what's going on down here?"

"Not a hell of a lot. I figured you'd fill me in soon as I got here. On the drive from Atlanta your sister did tell me about the fire at Anna Hanley's house and that her sister Holly Everett was killed. I recognized the name from the initial report. I assume this Holly is the same woman you were checking out."

Kip nodded. "Stanley Everett's wife."

Barry let his breath out in a whistle. "So are you thinking that the fire and her death are connected to the hijacking and missing 300 million?"

Kip rubbed his hand across his jaw. "Not necessarily. My gut tells me the fire was started to cover for Holly's murder, but whether any of it's connected to the hijacking is too early to tell. It could just be someone wanted to keep Holly Everett from delving any deeper into the gambling ring she was investigating. Or it could be something else entirely."

Barry digested the information a moment then shot Kip a teasing grin. "And Holly's sister—is she the girl you practically eloped with before you left for college?"

Kip nodded then quickly lifted his shoulders and looked out at a passing ship before the flood of memories took over his mind. "That was a lifetime ago. We were just kids. We both had plans. Two weeks after I left for the Academy Anna went abroad for a year that turned into fifteen months. For all I know, she's married. Until I found out differently, I thought the boy she pulled out of the fire was hers."

"From Robyn's description of Anna, she's not a woman easily forgotten."

Kip smiled, recalling the impact she'd had on him when he'd held her in his arms on the beach and then again in the ashes of her house. When he volunteered for the assignment in Savannah, he didn't reckon on his reaction to Anna.

"Robyn told me Anna graduated valedictorian from St. Vincent's. Smart enough to lay out a master plan of such a massive robbery then destroy the evidence?"

"Undoubtedly."

"Do you suspect Anna had something to do with her sister's death?"

Kip shook his head emphatically. "Not at all. In fact, I believe if I hadn't decided to have a look around that night, Anna might have died along with her sister. I was well down the beach from the house when I saw the smoke. On the beach maybe fifty feet from the house a boy was crying. I had started toward him when I noticed a woman run into the burning house. I wasn't sure the woman was Anna until I got closer and recognized the house. When she didn't come back out..." Kip lifted and dropped his shoulders, but the action didn't quite mask the intensity of the feeling that had burned through him when he realized the woman was Anna.

Barry filled in some blanks. "Then it was you who went in after her. Why aren't I surprised? Robyn mentioned someone pulled Anna out of the fire and that the police are looking for him. I should have known it was you. She didn't recognize you?"

"Apparently not. She was in a pretty bad way. Her eyes were tearing from the smoke, and I tried to keep my face in the

Winds of Fire

shadows. Anyway, it's been twelve years since she last saw me. I'm sure she's forgotten all about me." He hoped she had. "The problem is I can't be sure. Worse yet, if she recognized me, I'm sure she thinks I set the fire. Likely she's told as much to the police. To further complicate matters she and Robyn are best friends. Robyn asked that she be invited to Dylan's party tonight. I just wanted to warn you."

Barry laughed. "I shouldn't laugh," Barry said, laughing harder. "If she identifies you as her sister's killer..." Barry didn't finish his thought, and his expression sobered.

"It gets worse..." Kip said with a sardonic grin. "I went back to Anna's house the night after the fire to look for Holly's notes. Anna showed up shortly after me apparently with the same idea."

"She sounds like one gutsy lady."

"I'll have to give her that. Unfortunately, someone else was there as well. He was wearing a ski mask. And he was packing."

"Is that why you were in the hospital again?"

"No, he wasn't wearing night goggles and his aim was off. I was in the hospital because my wounds got infected."

Barry's mouth tightened, and he shook his head. "Not surprising. Those SOBs on the mountain pumped you pretty full of lead. Frankly I didn't think you'd make it out alive."

"I didn't think so either." Kip watched a fluffy white cloud march across the lugubrious sky. "You never gave up. Thanks..."

Barry held up a hand and looked him straight in the eye. "No thanks necessary. It was no more than you would have done and have done for me on more than one occasion. Glad I could return the favor. So let's nail the bastards." Barry broke the somber mood. "Did you find anything of value in Holly's room?"

Kip propped his back against a branch of the tree and folded a leg on the trunk. "I got her computer data onto a stick before Anna interrupted my search. There's probably more on the hard drive, but the intruder got the computer and a load of newspaper articles that were in Holly's briefcase. The gunshots attracted the cops who were guarding the place, and I had to make a hasty retreat."

"Knowing you, you've probably read every word on that stick."

"Enforced bed rest will give you time to do that. But except for Stanley Everett's name showing up on the list of gamblers his wife compiled, there wasn't much. I've spoken with Col. Harrison and expressed him a copy of the stick. He's got Larson working on it, checking names and cross checking them with the names of the passengers on Flight 2651. No hits yet, but I've got my fingers crossed."

"If anyone can find out connections, Joe can. What about CK Barnard of seat 6A?"

"Looks like the name's fictitious, his ID forged."

"What about the newspaper where Holly worked? Anything show up there?"

"Harrison has a team digging there as we speak, but it appears Holly's office computer was wiped clean before she left."

"Sounds suspicious. Why would someone wipe clean her computer unless she had something to hide?"

Kip nodded. "Exactly." Kip reached down to scratch his dog under her chin. "Did the colonel fill you in on Stanley's little jaunt to Chicago on the week-end of the hijacking?"

"To visit the sick brother who died when he was ten? Yes. You'd think he could come up with a better story than that."

Kip laughed. "You'd think. It's confirmed he was on a plane bound for Chicago, but once he landed there he disappeared. Surveillance cameras have no record of him boarding flight 2651 or any other plane for that matter; none of the cabbies have records of a passenger fitting Stanley's description leaving O'Hara Airport after his plane arrived either. Someone could have met him, of course, but why the elaborate cover story when it could so easily be renounced?"

"A woman, maybe?" Barry said. "He could be having an affair."

Kip leaned back against the branch. He hated to acknowledge the throbbing in his chest and arm. A hot shower was growing in appeal. "That could have accounted for the fictitious story. But why not tell his co-workers he was going to see a friend?"

"It doesn't sound like this Stanley Everett is the sharpest knife in the drawer."

"Maybe that's what he wants us to think. You got the photos I emailed you from Holly's funeral?"

Barry looked up. "I thought you were at home in bed."

Kip gave him a sheepish grin. "Most of the time. I couldn't pass up the opportunity to observe ol' Stanley up close and personal, so I arranged for a cab and took a few pictures. Don't worry; I was in bed when the family returned. That first one is a copy of the one on file at the bureau. You can see that he's slim with regular features, but the photo doesn't do him justice. As you know, I have an excellent telephoto lens. Stanley is a good looking man, attractive to women, I hear."

"He's also a fellow who likes to have a good time, spend a lot of money. I saw in your photos that he has a broken leg. What's the story on that?"

"An ankle actually. According to Stanley, he slipped on his back steps. His alibi for the night of the fire at Anna's house is rock solid."

"Your sister told me Stanley left town without his kid. She said Anna has the boy."

"So Mom told me," Kip said.

"You think Stan's thinking of running?"

"Could be, but he won't get very far. The police have him under surveillance."

Barry rose from the tree and walked closer to the river. The cargo ship had passed from sight; another was coming on in the distance. "Think Stanley's our man?"

"I think he's our connection to the man." He picked up a stick and threw it down the path, and watched Harlie run after it. "There's something that's bothering me about the device that set off the explosion in Anna's house. I could well be grasping at straws, but in the police report Colonel Harrison forwarded to me, the IED is meticulously detailed. A bottle rocket was attached to make it look like the work of an amateur and ensure the window broke, but the device itself was quite sophisticated and unlikely to be made by an amateur.

"It appears to be eerily similar to the one that killed Marie and Patrick. I know the notion is far-fetched. At this juncture I can't imagine how a bombing in Savannah, a hijacking in

Chicago and disappearance of 300 million, and my wife's and son's deaths in London could be connected. But I need to see what's left of the device they found to satisfy my own curiosity."

Barry frowned. "I trust your instincts. Anything I can do to help?"

"You remember Nick Howell from OSI training?"

"Who could forget him? Why?"

"When he retired from the service a few years back, he took a job with the police department here in Savannah. I called him this morning. He's agreed to let me take a look at the IED. I'm meeting him tonight at ten."

"Why not wait until tomorrow? You're already beat."

Kip didn't answer for a moment then looked at Barry. "I can't say I know what's going down, but I figure the clock's ticking."

Barry's dark eyes narrowed with understanding. "And you think Anna's life's in danger?"

Kip nodded, and there was an odd hollowness inside him. "She may have been an intended target all along. There are too many loose ends in this case for me to rest easy. Maybe Nick can help me tie up a few and see that Anna and Danny are kept under surveillance until we get the bad guys behind bars."

"You know that'll be the end of your cover."

"After tonight's encounter with Anna and Danny, I figure it's going to be busted anyway." Kip pushed himself to his feet. "We better head back."

Chapter 11

Kip slipped into some jeans and moved to the open bedroom window, leaning an elbow against the window frame, not really seeing the guests arrive but remembering the feel of the wind of a summer long ago as he stood at this same window. Yesterday's wind was warm, full of dreams and ambitions, full of love for Anna Hanley. Today the wind bit with November's chill, and Anna Hanley was someone else's sweetheart.

This morning he'd awakened thinking of her, remembering the plans they'd made. That he thought of Anna at all beyond a professional assessment didn't settle well with him. That he'd thought of her every day since their encounters was down-right disturbing.

Since the death of his wife and son, Kip had kept his affairs brief. The business he was in was dangerous. He did it for love of his country and because he didn't much care if he lived or died. And for the most part he did it alone. Any other way was too risky. But in Anna Hanley's eyes he'd seen something remembered that called to him and left him feeling unsettled.

Stepping back, Kip raked his fingers through his hair. If it were up to him, he'd pack up tonight right after the party, but he'd been given an assignment to find out more about the blue-eyed beauty he'd once promised to love forever and her murdered sister. He would stick with the case until it was solved or he was reassigned.

A light rap on his door drew his attention.

"Kip, you all right?" It was Robyn's voice.

"Fine, I'll be down in a couple of minutes."

She poked her head inside the door anyway. "Good. Several people are coming just to see you again." She stepped into the room but held onto the door knob and took a deep breath. He heard it and knew she was going to hit him with something he didn't want to hear. He waited for it. He didn't have to wait long. Robyn rarely spent time on idle chit-chat.

"Since Marie died," she said, "life seems to have left you behind. She's been gone six years, Kip, and never once have you brought home any girl."

"That doesn't mean I don't have droves of women waiting for me back in California." He bent over to retrieve a long-sleeve tee and to hide his smile. "There are plenty of women in my life."

"Anna's coming."

"So you told me. You tell her I was going to be here?"

Robyn's blush answered the question before she shook her head.

"Coward," he said. "Anyway, I thought you told me Anna's engaged."

"She was, but she isn't any more. She and Dennis broke up after Holly's funeral."

That was news he hadn't heard.

"So if there are so many women," Robyn changed the subject back to one more to her liking, "why is it none has ever called to see how you were, Kip?"

"There have been a few calls on my cell," he said with a wry grin.

She went on as if he hadn't spoken. "Of course, knowing you, you probably haven't told any of them where you are or even that you were so seriously hurt. Don't you ever think about getting married again and having kids?"

His face sobered. "Sometimes. I did it once you remember, but—"

"But now you're afraid to take the risk again."

"Something like that."

"Cell phone, eh? Anyway, I've worked hard to convince Anna to come tonight. I know you two haven't spoken in years, but I want you to be on your best behavior with her. She's had a rough time recently. She doesn't deserve all that's happened to her, so don't make it any harder on her. She's a very nice girl," she said and walked out the door before he could further comment.

Nice, he mused. There were a whole lot of better words other than nice to describe Anna Hanley. Beautiful, sexy, brave, and independent were a few that came to mind.

Anna was surprised how easy it was for her to fall into the roll of mother, though with the sudden addition of a four and a half year old to her life on top of everything else, Anna felt as though she was living in a whirlpool. There were things a child, even such a precious one as Danny, needed, and she had a great deal to learn.

Anna was thinking of her new responsibilities as a mother when she parked her Jeep beneath one of the oaks that lined the drive of Marsh Winds and stepped out. The smell of smoke struck her immediately. One hand on the car door for support, the other over her mouth and nose, she closed her eyes. Though she could see no smoke, her eyes stung with it, her throat burned from it. She reminded herself it was just the fire for the oysters and nothing to worry about, but the fear constricting her lungs kept her from drawing a full breath.

"What's the matter?" Danny's voice came out reedy, and his little mouth quivered like he was about to cry. She reprimanded herself for conveying her trepidation to him and summoned a smile and a cheery voice.

"Nothing's the matter, sweetheart." She opened the back door for him, but a few moments later when she headed toward the house with Danny in tow, her legs were still shaky.

Anna hadn't planned to attend the oyster roast. After all that was going on these past few days, topped off with a long afternoon answering questions at the police department, she was worn out. The oyster roast had slipped from her mind. She just wanted to get away from the firefighters, the police, and curious friends and neighbors who meant well. She looked forward to a hot shower, a light supper, followed by bed with a good book. When Robyn phoned at five o'clock to remind her of the party, Anna at first made excuses.

Robyn had been insistent. "It'll be good for you and for Danny to get away from the house...it's a small gathering, mostly family...you have to eat anyway...there'll be lots of food and other children for Danny to play with..."

Though there was little Anna wouldn't do for her friend Robyn, the reason she was walking toward the back yard of Marsh Winds right now wasn't because of her friendship with her but because Robyn was right about Danny. A party with children would be fun for him.

And perhaps she did need to make an effort to start seeing friends again, partly because of the other thing—the disturbing something she hadn't breathed a word about to anyone. She was having strange fantasies about the arsonist. She kept remembering how on both of her encounters with him he'd taken her in his arms and held her close, like he cared. No matter how hard she tried to get the comforting feel of his arms around her out of her mind, she couldn't. And most alarmingly, thinking about him brought on an inexplicable and inappropriate surge of desire. What was wrong with her? Perhaps Robyn was right. A casual evening with friends was just what she needed. Or a psychiatrist. By the time she turned the corner around the house, Anna realized she was looking forward to seeing everyone.

Danny tugged Anna's hand, and she smiled down at him. She was glad to see that no trace of his earlier apprehension showed on his face. In fact, his brown eyes were so wide with excitement and something so adorably mischievous that Anna's heart swelled. She'd made the right decision about bringing him.

Looking at him, she couldn't fathom why Stanley Everett would give him up, and yet he'd overnighted the signed preliminary papers yesterday. Still, she found herself lying awake last night thinking of all the things that could go wrong and prevent her from adopting Danny. There were so many loose ends. If Stanley wasn't the boy's father, who was? What was to prevent that individual from claiming his child? Some part of her hoped Stanley was right, and Danny's biological father didn't know he had a child.

As she and Danny rounded the corner of the house a ball flew out of nowhere and headed straight for Anna. Had she not had the presence of mind to reach out and pluck it from the air, it would have smacked into her head. The ball, she noticed when she caught it, was a tennis ball, soggy and devoid of much of its felt.

"Good catch," Robyn said, coming up behind her.

Before Anna could turn toward her friend, a dog, a tri-colored Australian Shepherd, came bounding up after the ball and skidded to a stop at her feet, panting, tongue lolling from the side of her mouth, eager to claim the ball. Anna gave the dog a rub and handed over the ball then watched the dog race across the grounds and come to a sit in front of a man who was standing with a shovel beside the fire. He was a tall man and wore a navy blue sweatshirt with the remnants of a few gold letters stitched on front that once had proclaimed it to be from Michigan. Under the sweatshirt the tails of a white shirt hung over his jeans, accentuating his narrow hips and muscular frame. The jeans were faded, the knees worn to threads.

Kip. She couldn't breathe.

Chapter 12

He leaned against the shovel and stared at her across the flames, irreverent, dark...sexy, just like she remembered him.

The wave of attraction she felt surprised her, annoyed her.

He bent over to retrieve the ball from the dog and handed it to a little girl who was standing beside him then pointed in a direction away from the fire. This time the child's throw veered to the right, toward the water. In a blur of black and brown, the shepherd bounded after the ball, catching it in flight.

He blatantly continued to study her as the shepherd trotted to him with the ball. He didn't smile. Nor did she.

"I'm so glad you and Danny are here," Robyn said at Anna's side.

Anna swung around to face her friend. "Robyn, you didn't tell me Kip was going to be here."

Robyn gave her a hug. "I told you he was staying with us while he recovered from a motorcycle accident."

Anna swallowed a sigh. She supposed she did know, but with so many other things going on it had slipped her mind. She just hadn't expected the intensity of her feelings at seeing him to be so strong. "I remember he always wanted to be in the Special Forces. I heard he got his wish. He still doing that sort of stuff?"

"No. I don't know. He says he's retired from OSI. I stopped asking about it years ago. But a couple of weeks ago he nearly died. When Mom heard, she went to California to see him in the hospital. He was in a bad way, and she insisted he come back home to recover so she could keep an eye on him. With the doctor's help she managed to get her way. Since he came back, he's had to return to the hospital twice."

"He looks to be doing okay now. I'm glad."

"I think he is, but you never know with Kip. He could be on his deathbed and get up to offer to help a little old lady across the street."

Anna smiled. She remembered that about him.

Robyn bent to Danny. "Hi there, young man. You must be Danny. I'm very glad you came."

Danny smiled but put his arm around Anna's leg and held on. This was something new, Anna thought, relieved to have something else to think about.

"Normally he's not shy," Anna said, and very nearly added, I don't know what's come over him, but of course she did.

"Understandable." Robyn looked down at Danny. "A few of the children are playing dodge-ball. Would you like to play?"

Danny shook his head, and Anna corrected, "No, ma'am."

"No, ma'am," Danny repeated, but he didn't let go of her leg.

"You're sounding like a mother already, Anna."

A man came up beside Robyn and stood at her shoulder with a friendly expression on his face. He had medium brown hair, and wore a worn denim jacket unbuttoned over an Air Force Academy T-shirt. The jacket did little to conceal his powerful build. Robyn turned to him, her face brightening with pleasure.

"I don't believe you've met Barry Wesley. Barry attended the Air Force Academy with Kip, but he grew up in Atlanta."

That Barry Wesley, Anna thought. The governor's son. She held out her hand.

He shook it and smiled into her eyes. "I've been looking forward to meeting you, Ms. Hanley. On the drive down to Savannah Robyn regaled me with stories of your high school years spent at St. Vincent's together, in particular your accomplishments as a tennis player. I believe she mentioned something about a state championship. I played tennis in high school, too, but I can't lay claim to any such honor."

Robyn had mentioned Barry on several occasions as well, and Anna could see why. Not only did he look like he could protect her in a dark alley, his manners were those you would expect of the governor's son.

After a few moments of polite conversation Barry excused himself and headed toward the fire. Robyn touched Danny's back. "Come on, I'll show you around. This way, Danny. There are some juice boxes in the cooler right over here."

Robyn dropped her empty beer bottle into a box at the end of the table. "Glass goes here—we're recycling." She looked around. "Now where could that brother of mine have gotten to? I want you two to say hello before one of you gets away. I guess I should just look for Harlie. She's never very far away from him." She chuckled, looking back at Anna. "It's hard to believe you two haven't crossed paths since high school, but I guess it's possible."

She stopped at a red cooler filled with juice boxes and turned to Danny. "We have red ones and purple ones. What would you like?"

"Purple..."

"Purple, please," Anna corrected again and Danny dutifully added the please.

"Ah, there's Kip tending the fire...come on." Robyn caught Anna's arm and pulled her in the direction of the bonfire where the men were shoveling the cooked oysters onto a newspaper-covered table.

Anna watched Kip across the yard with his dog sitting at his feet like a shadow. That sweatshirt he was wearing—Anna remembered it from football practice at nineteen, a purchase from a long ago recruiting visit to the Ann Arbor campus. Just like him not to throw anything away. She tucked a lock of hair behind her ear, knowing it would be a mistake to relive those days, even in her mind. She was a different person than she'd been then. So was he.

People were taking turns coming up to him to exchange small talk while he shoveled. Everyone seemed anxious to have a word with him, and judging by their smiles and hugs, he seemed at ease with them all, genuinely glad to see them. The little girl he was playing with earlier was nowhere in sight. Her place had been taken by an attractive brunette Anna didn't recognize. The brunette must be Harlie, the girl Robyn mentioned as always being at his side.

Robyn waved and caught his eye. He acknowledged it with a nod and leaned his shovel up against the wheelbarrow as he spoke to the woman. After Robyn's comments about them being inseparable, Anna was surprised to see him heading their way without the woman. His smile grew slowly, revealing his white, even teeth, and was charged with the same hefty dose of masculine appeal she'd never forgotten.

Unlike his light-haired brothers, Kip's hair was dark brown. His features were bold and rugged, more rugged than she remembered. Anna came to a stop in front of him, and his dark blue gaze settled on her, relaxed, friendly, like they bumped into each other regularly. But behind the casual façade she sensed an intensity that hadn't been there before. He'd become a tough man, a man who missed very little of what was going on around him.

Kip studied Anna a moment more before he held his hand out to her. "Hello, Anna." The voice was deep, languid. He hadn't shaved in maybe two days, and she doubted his hair had seen a comb since his shower.

Anna took a breath. "Hello, Kip." She mimicked him and placed her hand in his. His was a large hand, warm, and it closed around hers with an earthy sexuality that had her quickly taking her hand back and stepping away from him.

He shrugged, amusement creeping into his eyes, and then he turned to Danny and squatted in front of him. He held five fingers up to him for a high-five. "Hello, Danny, I'm Kip."

When Danny didn't immediately extend his hand, Anna touched his back to nudge him forward. He slapped five fingers against Kip's, then surprised her by moving between Kip's knees and putting his arms around his neck. He held on tight, and Anna was taken-aback. Even if her gaze hadn't been zeroed in on the two of them, she couldn't have avoided seeing the wave of emotion that rocked Kip McTeer. His eyes slammed shut, and his mouth hardened. With the slightest of hesitations he drew the boy off his feet and into his embrace, burying his face in the child's hair, and for a few breathtaking moments, he stayed that way.

Suddenly Anna remembered hearing that Kip's first wife and son had been killed in a terrorist blast when the three of them had been traveling in England. She frowned. Then Kip eased the child from his embrace and sat him upon his knee.

When he spoke to Danny, his voice was rough with emotion he couldn't quite conceal. "I don't believe you've met Harlie, my dog."

Anna found herself smiling. So Harlie was a dog, not the brunette.

"Come here, Harlie," he said. "Sit." When the dog obeyed, Kip instructed Danny to hold out his hand which Danny did, and the dog put her paw on the child's hand.

"Wow! That's cool." Danny's grin broadened, irresistible. "Can I pet her?"

"You bet. She'll be disappointed if you don't."

Danny slid from Kip's knee and accepted Harlie's wet welcome then he did something that caused Anna's heartbeat to falter. He leaned his head against the dog's fur, looked back at Kip, and said, "Mommy got hurt, and she had to go to live with God."

Kip McTeer's blue eyes darkened, and something terribly sad came over his face. He looked to Danny. "I know you miss her, son, but your mommy will be safe in Heaven with God."

Anna had the feeling that Kip was talking to himself as well.

"Anna's going to be my mommy now," Danny said, and Anna wondered what Kip would say.

He glanced up at her, and she tried not to squirm.

"Now that's a lucky thing for you, Danny. Miss Anna is a very special person, indeed."

Kip drew a breath, and changed the subject. "What Harlie loves to do most is chase balls. What do you think, Danny? Should you and I throw some for her?"

At the sound of her name Harlie's ears perked up, and her short tail began to wag.

Danny turned to Anna. "Is it all right? Can I throw balls for Harlie?"

"*May* I throw balls, not *can* I..." Anna corrected without thinking and felt the color rise to her cheeks. "Danny, I'm sure Mr. McTeer has better things to do..."

"Not at all." Kip focused his deep blue eyes on Anna.

She stared into them and breathed out. And suddenly she felt as if she were on the edge of a bottomless pit. She knew where she'd seen those eyes, not twelve years ago when they'd said good-bye at the airport but recently. Last week. Into her mind flashed the image of the man reflected in her hall mirror, a man who was dressed all in black like some commando and running away from the scene of his crime, a man who was trained to know all about explosives and stealth.

Those eyes belonged to the man who murdered her sister and set her house on fire. *No, Kip, not you...* Suddenly it was like an anvil had dropped on her chest, closing it off. Too quickly she tried to fill her lungs. Unable to, she coughed instead and turned away, struggling for air. The doctor had warned her the fire had caused the formation of chemicals that caused injury to the normal lining of her respiratory tract and mucous membranes. He explained it would take time to heal and she should expect this sort of thing. Even though she understood why it was happening, it was a helpless feeling not being able to breathe. But not as helpless as looking into the eyes of her high school sweetheart and knowing he was the same man who'd murdered her sister.

"Anna," Robyn said. "You all right?"

She wasn't all right, but Anna nodded. Still, the coughing wouldn't stop, and tears rushed from her eyes. And then his hand was on her back, rubbing, patting, with gentle insistence. She cringed back but his hand prevented her from moving far.

"Easy there..." he said.

He was so close she could smell the fresh scent of soap on his skin and in his hair. The night her sister died he smelled of the sea. He was the man who stood at the threshold of her kitchen door with smoke billowing all around him like he was like some demon from hell or an angel. He had lifted her from the floor and carried her to where the air was fresh and sweet. Once they had promised to love each other forever. Now he had murdered her sister. Yet had saved her life. On the beach she felt comfort in his arms and shame that she felt that comfort. She needed to hate him.

But the feelings she had for him were unclear. The notion that Kip McTeer had killed Holly seemed preposterous. And yet, if he didn't murder her sister, why did he leave the scene without identifying himself to the police or to her? If he had nothing to hide, why did he maintain his silence when the newspaper, radio, and television stations were broadcasting daily that the police were still searching for the man who'd carried her to them then disappeared?

She hesitated and breathed.

His brow creased, and she had the sensation he knew precisely what she was thinking. He always could do that. What if she were wrong about him? To accuse her best friend's brother of murder would cause irreparable damage to her friendship with Robyn. Robyn adored her brother, and to date no evidence proved his guilt. The description of the man they searched for—heavy-set, average height—didn't fit. The police had turned up no leads—not even a footprint—that pointed to him. Perhaps she was wrong about him murdering her sister, but she knew she was right about one thing. He was the man who plucked her from the rubble of her burning house and held her in his arms and gave her comfort when she so desperately needed it.

She breathed in, and the air came easier now. He took his hand away from her back, and she missed it, the warmth, the reassurance. "I'm so sorry." Her voice came as a hoarse whisper. "My throat's still sore. I must have swallowed wrong."

She stared at him, uncertain. Under her scrutiny, he didn't flinch. Whatever his feelings were, he held them under tight rein. She sighed at her own confusion and looked away, deciding that before she confronted him she'd ask subtle questions and gather more information, such as what his alibi was on the night of the murder.

"On second thought," he said, pulling her gaze back to him. But his words were directed not to her but to Danny. "It's getting too dark to throw the ball for Harlie. Why don't we save it for another day? Besides, aren't those hotdogs I smell roasting on the grill? I don't know about you, but I'm getting hungry."

"Me, too." Without another word Danny placed his hand in Kip's.

"No need for you to worry about him, Anna," Kip said quietly, glancing back at her and seeming once again to read her mind. A sad smile lifted the corner of his mouth. "He'll be safe with me."

Before she could think to respond, he walked with Danny and his dog toward the picnic tables. And the sun moved lower in the sky, sending out streaks of orange light that were too much like tongues of flame. And the breeze picked up the scent of smoke and oysters steaming on a large metal plate over the fire and blew it to her. And regret that her sister's life was ended too soon tugged at Anna's heart.

And the many shades of night spread over the river in unhurried increments.

Chapter 13

Barry caught Kip's arm and stopped him in front of the grill. "So do you think Anna recognized you?"

Kip nodded. "Without a doubt, but she isn't positive I killed her sister or set her house on fire." He handed Danny a hotdog in a bun on a paper plate and pointed him toward the condiments and chips. He watched him until he reached the table and was out of hearing range before he spoke quietly to Barry. "There's no doubt in the little fellow's mind I was the one who sat with him on the beach. He knew right away, but then he wasn't in as bad shape as his aunt was and got a good look at me. I'm fortunate he didn't say something that gave it all away."

"It'll happen, sooner or later." Barry grabbed a hotdog off the grill, blew on it, and took a bite.

"I'm hoping it won't happen until after we have a good lead as to who the real killer is. But I'm not betting on that." Kip reached down to grab a bottle of beer from a large washtub filled with ice. He twisted off the cap and started walking away from the table.

Barry fell in beside him. "Speaking of Anna, I heard the fiancé balked at adopting her sister's kid, and she dumped him. To hear Robyn talk, he wasn't right for her, but then I think she harbors plans for you and Anna to get back together."

Kip drew in a breath and blew it out again. "Not a chance. Though a date with Anna now would certainly make for an interesting evening. I can see it play out over a candlelight dinner. She leans over her plate and whispers, 'Oh, by the way, did you murder my sister?'"

Barry laughed, then sobered. "Seriously, if it weren't for that itty-bitty snag and the fact that guys already appear to be lining up ahead of you, including that fellow over there who's talking with her right now, you could do worse. But then she'd be sure to discover what a hard-headed fellow you are and that you're prone to be in the way of passing bullets, and all would be lost. Too bad. From all I hear, Anna's a top-notch girl."

For a moment Kip remained silent and glanced over to where Anna was indeed talking with a tall, lanky man Kip recognized as Dylan's longtime friend Joe McKinley. Joe had gone to Benedictine Academy with Dylan and was now the golf pro at the Savannah Golf Club and according to his mother, newly divorced. Whatever Joe said to Anna brought a smile to her face, and a corner of Kip's mouth twitched with regret.

He glanced over at Danny who had discovered the dessert table and was piling his plate with brownies and cookies. He thought to go over there and slow him down a bit, but Anna was watching, too, and beat him to it. She whispered something into Danny's ear, and he watched the two of them put a few of the sweets back on the serving plates.

He noticed her fingers were long and slender, the nails neatly trimmed, but she'd stopped wearing the bright pink polish he remembered. She still wore her hair in a ponytail, and several strands had blown free and waved like fine silk on both sides of her face. He decided he noticed too many things about Anna Hanley and headed on over to the fire to help Dylan.

Barry brought Kip to a stop with a hand on his forearm. His voice was quiet, intense. "You look like hell, buddy."

"Thanks for the ego booster." Kip affected a South Georgia country drawl. "And after I'd gone and gussied myself up for Dylan's party." He flashed a smile, but it disappeared almost as quickly as it came, and his eyes didn't deny that he'd overdone it with his afternoon of lifting.

"Someone should hog-tie you in bed until you're completely healed."

His gaze met Barry's. "I've spent too damn much time flat on my back as it is. You and I both know there's no time for that. When I returned to my room earlier, I found an email from Colonel Harrison. He thinks the hijacking and murder of Anna's sister are being directed from somewhere high up and what we see is just the tip of the iceberg. He expects whatever is going down is going to happen soon. It's already been close to two weeks since the hijacking, and leads are disappearing. Command is worried, so I'm worried, and you should be, too."

"I am, but I'm more worried about you. The sorry fact is that no matter how many crooks and murderers and terrorists we expose, the corruption in Washington isn't going to disappear. No use killing yourself over it."

"I know, Barry, and I appreciate your concern. We'll talk more about this later. Right now it looks like the second wave of oysters are about ready to be served. Let's head on over there and help Dylan shovel them onto the tables. Then I intend to partake."

Kip picked up a shovel, and Dylan put a restraining hand on his arm. "You better lay off that lifting for a few more days, Kip. You've already overdone it today."

"Mom tell you to say that?"

"She might have," Dylan said, noncommittal, "but I think she's right this once." Then he grinned. "We're all sick and tired of you lying flat on your back with IVs stuck into you."

Kip chuckled. "So I've been told more than once, but I can assure you you're no more tired of it than I am." The mirth died in his throat. "Okay, okay, if you insist, I'll be a good-natured fellow and let you and Barry do the heavy work. I'll just grab myself a glove and a knife and make myself comfortable. It's too damn long since I've been to a family oyster roast, and I'm looking forward to this. But I have to admit I wish the occasion were different. I hate that you'll be leaving the roost. Mom's going to miss having you in town and seeing her only grandkids."

"I'm going to miss being here, too. I intend to come back for good soon as I can. But if you..." he started and stopped, looking into Kip's eyes, and his mouth suddenly curved into a grin.

Kip held up his hand and stared at him a moment. Then he chuckled. "What is this, a family conspiracy? Now I know you've been talking to mom or Robyn or both. Let me finish the thought for you. I should marry again, come back to Marsh Winds, and settle down to raise a passel of kids, right?"

Dylan had the grace to look abashed. "It's time you put the past behind you," he said, but he looked defeated.

"Well, the past isn't behind me, Dylan. I don't know if it ever can be, not until the ones responsible for their deaths are dead or behind bars, and I don't see that happening any time soon." Kip started to walk away, but his gaze fell on Anna, her face lit up with warmth and caring as she watched her sister's son, and instead he turned back to his brother and put his hand on his brother's arm. He gave him a light squeeze. "I'm working on it..."

Before he headed to the table Kip satisfied himself that Danny had found a place at a table filled with children and seemed to be getting to know Dylan's daughter. To the earthy tones of Johnny Cash and *I Walk the Line* coming over a loud speaker, Kip found a spot at the oyster table and squeezed in. Moments later Anna, Joe the golf pro, and his sister claimed places at the opposite end.

As Anna sank to the bench, she looked his way. Her gaze narrowed, and he saw the distrust in her big blue eyes before she picked up her knife and glove and went to work on an oyster. He watched her ease the oyster from its shell with practiced skill, dip it into the cocktail sauce, and pop it into her mouth.

Once again he felt that tug of desire. He pushed it away, wondering if she felt the same tug he did. Probably not, he decided. She was too caught up in the death of her sister and the misconception that he had a part in her murder. Just as well. He had no business even entertaining thoughts of her. As Marie and Patrick's murder so aptly illustrated, the life he'd chosen for himself left no room for a woman.

Kip awoke to a mournful sky and a dense fog outside his window. A cold breeze was coming through his open window, and over his head his ceiling fan whirred. After the oyster roast, followed by a meeting with Nick Howell at the police department, he'd stayed up half the night going over and over Holly Everett's computer files. Either he was missing something, or there was nothing there for him to find.

He rolled over and looked at the red numbers on his digital clock, surprised to see it was already 8:00 AM. He stared out the window at the fog, wishing for the vigor to rouse himself from his warm bed, but he didn't have the energy to move. It had been a long night, an unproductive one that resulted in little sleep and a decision that didn't settle well with him.

No matter how much he reminded himself he didn't want to get involved with Anna Hanley again, if he wanted to make any progress in this case, he had no other choice. He needed to talk with her. He needed to find out if she knew what was in her sister's papers or if the disjointed notes on her computer made more sense to her than they did to him. He needed to know more about Anna's sister's husband Stanley Everett and what made him tick. And he'd have to take risks to make it happen.

After three more stolen hours of sleep and a long, hot shower, Kip trotted down the front stairway around 11:30, feeling almost human, and found the house empty. A note on the breakfast table informed him that everyone had gone to church and would be attending a late brunch at Cleary's should he care to join them. If not, there was coffee warming in the pot and plenty of food in the frig.

Kip pictured the boxes, packed and ready for pick-up, that were stacked in the front parlor and debated the prospect of joining his family. He was tempted. Tomorrow the transport company was scheduled to pick up Dylan's family's personal things. The day after that Dylan and his family would set off for Wilmington, Delaware, driving both their cars. Though Dylan had recently purchased some riverfront property close to Marsh Winds and assured his mother he would bring his family back to Savannah as soon as he could and build, the return wouldn't be for years.

Last night after several toasts were made to Dylan and his family on their new venture, Dylan and Maribel rose and announced that the baby they were expecting was to be a boy. And to applause, they promised they would make every effort to be at Marsh Winds for his birth in April. Kip was sincerely pleased for his brother and his wife, but though he controlled his own grief last night, today in the bleak light of day, his own anguish at the loss of the son he'd adored rocked him. He sank into the chair at the breakfast table, stunned by the magnitude of the ache in the pit of his soul. In short order the ache was followed by a rage that made him erupt from the chair. He stormed across the room and back again, then out through the back door. By the time he reached the end of the pier the anger had left him, and the dull feeling of emptiness he lived with each day had come in.

He pinched the bridge of his nose, but to his dismay tears spilled from his eyes. Three years ago when they told him his wife and son had died in a fire in the flat where he'd been staying in London, England, it was the worst day of his life, but he hadn't cried. At their memorial service back in San Francisco, he'd been so choked with grief that he couldn't breathe, but he hadn't cried. So why the tears now, three years later? Soon as the thought passed into his mind the answer hit him. Anna's little boy...Danny was almost the same age as own son was when he was murdered. Yesterday the grief and need he felt in the child's hug had nearly undone him.

Days after he'd laid the remains of his wife and son to rest, he learned the London fire had been caused not by faulty wiring as had first been suspected, but had been set off by an IED. At the time it had gone off he'd been in a meeting with British Secret Intelligence service, hot on the trail of a local terrorist group, and there was no doubt in his mind then or now: the explosion and resulting fire had been meant to kill him. Patrick and Marie were collateral damage.

Breathing hard, he sank down to the rough planking of the pier, hugged his knees to his chest, feeling an invisible band tighten in his chest. The wind, cold and heavy with fog, blew its chill into him and through him, and he began to shake. Harlie nudged her nose under his arm until he glanced down to stare into her big black eyes. He swallowed then drew in a shaky breath, swiping at the tears. "Ah, Harlie, you're a good girl..."

Harlie licked the tears from his chin then settled down with her head on his lap and went to sleep. He stayed with his arm around her looking into the fog, and he had no awareness of the passing time or that it had started to rain, only that a knot of emptiness burned inside him. A seagull swooped past him to perch on a nearby piling, drawing his attention, and they watched each other until the bird flew off with a noisy cry and disappeared in the clouds.

Realizing he was soaked to the skin and shivering, Kip pushed himself to his feet and walked with his dog beside him back down the long pier to the house and his second hot shower of the morning. A glance at his watch told him he was too late to join the family so he fixed himself a breakfast of scrambled eggs, leftover shrimp, and grits, and washed it down with two cups of strong, black coffee.

Half an hour later Kip drove his mother's dark blue SUV from the house with Harlie riding in the front seat. He was feeling considerably better. Tybee Island wasn't far from Marsh Winds, about seven miles down a two-lane causeway that ran across the Wilmington River and through the marsh. A light drizzle was still falling, just enough to keep his windshield wipers on and destroy any tracks he and Barry might hope to find on the beach when they got together later that day. The fog had receded some, and the thin light coming through it revealed an eerie world painted in hues of gray and white and dark brown. Everything looked different, almost surreal, like it was a place he'd only seen in his dreams though he'd driven that way hundreds of times.

He noticed things he'd forgotten in the years since he'd lived away from Savannah—how the tide meandered through the marsh grass like it was spilled from a jug; how the mud banks where fiddler crabs had taken refuge appeared pockmarked; how the delicate white egrets that walked the flats in search of food left their signature prints behind in the mud. It was a beautiful part of the world, and he'd seen enough of the world to know how to compare.

Kip drove the narrow Tybee streets from memory, passing houses built in the 1800s sitting alongside new ones. Most of the homes were packed close together on small lots and had their first floors a story above ground-level in case of flooding. Anna's home, was one of the oldest homes on Tybee. It had belonged to her family almost as long as Marsh Winds had belonged to the McTeers, a good hundred years before Tybee became a tourist town and real estate prices skyrocketed. Hence, the grounds around her house were a rare several acres that bordered both the ocean on one side and the river on the other.

At the familiar oyster-shell drive he turned in. On both sides of the drive, tangles of Indian Hawthorn struggled to grow beneath wind-blown oaks and wayward arms of wax myrtles in need of trimming. From this side of the house, except for the yellow police ribbon and the lingering stench of burned debris, it was hard to see signs of the fire.

Anna's ancient Jeep was parked in one half of the two-car garage. Kip pulled in behind her and cut his engine. Off to the garage apartment side of the house, on the banks of a sand dune in the shade of a thatch of Sea Oats sat a yellow bucket and a faded red shovel, and beside that were a half dozen matchbox cars lined up on roads that had been scooped in the sand.

The sight was so like remembered forts made in the sand by his own son he shut his eyes and sat awhile, his hand on the door handle, his breathing labored. He pulled in a deep breath and was cracking the windows for Harlie when his cell phone vibrated.

He checked the ID before he spoke into the receiver. "Yes?"

"Hey, Wolf." Only two men called him wolf to his face, Barry Wesley and Nick Howell. Barry had a deep southern drawl. Nick was from the Bronx. Nick wasn't one to waste any time on niceties. "I thought you'd be interested in a call that just came in from Senator Norton's secretary, Mabel Osgood. She's been calling the department almost daily on the senator's behalf to get updates on the Holly Everett case. A few minutes ago she asked if you were on the case."

"I wonder what gave her that idea. What'd you tell her?"

"I told her I'd never heard of you. I got a feeling she didn't buy it."

"You never were much of a liar. It's a good thing you never went undercover."

"My wife tells me the same thing. The name Mabel Osgood ring any bells?"

Kip rubbed his hand over his chin. "Not a one. Incidentally, I'm outside Anna's house right now, and I don't see a black and white parked anywhere around."

"Robbery at a Seven-Eleven a few blocks from there. I'll see that they get back there soon as they can. I've got a nasty feeling about this case."

"There's some sort of network out there. Whoever's running it is ruthless. Wish I knew what the hell they're after. Keep in touch." Kip disconnected, but he shared Nick's nasty feeling that something unpleasant was about to explode. Whatever it was, he prayed Anna wasn't involved in it.

Chapter 14

At her kitchen table Anna rubbed a hand over her burning eyes and leaned back in her chair, stretching out her legs and arching back her head. She hadn't slept well. Her dreams had been a series of disjointed memories of her and Kip mixed in with images of her sister and the fire, and troubling. Last night's charged atmosphere of coming face-to face with him at the oyster roast had followed her to bed, and this morning it left her with a headache and an underlying feeing of discomfort and confusion.

Was Kip actually guilty of setting her house on fire and murdering her sister? It seemed unlikely the man she'd known most of her life and fallen in love with was capable of such vicious acts. But in his capacity as US Air Force Special Forces agent, Kip had lived and fought in the harshest of places. He was no longer the same man she'd known in high school.

With a sigh Anna reached for her coffee and drank. Over the lip of the cup her gaze settled on the roll-top desk that once belonged to her grandfather's grandfather and now served as a stand for her television. It was one of her favorite pieces in the small apartment. Across from it a loveseat was covered in an ugly brown and gold plaid that went out in the sixties and desperately needed to be replaced. Beside the sofa a glass lamp was filled with shells she and her sister had collected with her grandmother. A painting of dunes and sea oats that once had been in her parent's bedroom now hung over a narrow Mahogany table with legs delicately carved in the Queen Anne style. On the floor in the center of the room, Danny's coloring book and crayons purchased at Walmart a few days ago lay discarded in his haste for breakfast.

Everything in the tiny apartment was steeped with memories of her family. With the exception of Danny, all of the people who made those memories were gone. Anna pulled in a deep breath, just catching herself before it became a sob, and forced herself to turn her attention back to the papers scattered across her table.

The rain had almost stopped at one o'clock when Anna heard the sound of a car coming down her drive. The sound caused a jolt of fear. Then she remembered Robyn had promised to drop by. She pushed 'save' on her computer and got up to look out the window. Expecting to see Robyn's red PT Cruiser, she was surprised to find an unfamiliar dark blue Mercedes SUV pulling up beside her garage and out of sight. Moments later a car door slammed.

Then she remembered Robyn had driven from Atlanta with Barry and would necessarily be in a different car. But the police car that had been keeping watch over her house—why wasn't it parked where it usually was? She pulled back from the window. The side door to the garage was open, deliberately left that way so Robyn could come on up. She looked at the door leading to the steps into the garage. Had she locked it? Normally, she didn't lock her doors except at night. She was pretty sure she hadn't locked it. The realization hurried her forward.

She was halfway across the room, when a knock seemed to explode in the quiet. For a second she stared at the door then dashed back to the kitchen table and her purse. Her cell phone was inside, and it took her a few seconds to find it. She opened the screen and typed the 9.

You're overreacting, being ridiculous, she told herself.

"I know you're home, Anna. I can hear you." The deep voice sent a rush of memories down her spine and her back a step. Not Robyn but Kip.

"May I come in?"

"I'm busy right now."

The doorknob turned, unlatched with a click, and she stood rooted while he pushed the door open and stepped onto the threshold. "I'm sorry, Anna, but I need to talk to you." He shoved his sunglasses to the top of his head and came into the room.

He was wearing the same ragged jeans as last night and a dark brown leather flight jacket that showed evidence of heavy wear. His hair was damp from the rain, his feet in mud-crusted Birkenstock sandals, and she couldn't squelch the immediate wave of attraction. She told herself the increased heart rate meant nothing. He was simply a sexy guy she'd loved a long time ago.

"You should keep your doors locked." He gave her a sardonic grin and reached behind him to close the door.

"Get out, and I'll be sure to lock it."

His grin widened then fell away when his gaze fell on the phone in her hand. "If you intended to use that, you shouldn't have hesitated. It could be a fatal error."

He stepped up to her and removed the cell from her fingers. She grabbed for his hand and came up empty. "Too late, Anna. Better I keep this for a while. After we've talked, I'll return it. Is Danny here?"

In an instant her sudden anger changed to fear. Her gaze swung up to collide with his. "Why? He's all right, isn't he?" To her own ears her voice sounded nervous, high-pitched.

"You would know that better than I. I just wanted to know if he was here, because we can talk more freely if he isn't."

"I have no intentions of talking with you, so please go away."

He slipped the phone into his pocket and dug around until he came up with a computer stick. He held it out. "Maybe this will change your mind. It's a copy of the contents of your sister's computer. Other than the murderer and the copy I gave the police, I am the only one who has it. May I sit down?"

"No you may not. But you can tell me why I should believe *you* aren't the person who murdered my sister. You were at the murder scene and you were there again searching my house." She hurled the words at him. "There's no reason I should look any further for my sister's murderer than at you."

He grabbed her forearms and swung her so she faced him, giving her a little shake. "All right let's start there. If you truly believed I murdered your sister, you'd have exposed me last night at Dylan's party. So, did you report me to the police?"

She hesitated then shook her head. "I should have, but no, I haven't, out of respect for my friendship with Robyn...and because I knew you used to be special operations for the Air Force, and whatever else you have or haven't done...you saved my life. I planned to talk to your sister about it when she comes over this afternoon, and then decide whether to call the police."

"You might be lying, but my gut tells me you aren't. Now look at me, Anna. There are things I cannot tell you about myself and my life right now, but I didn't murder your sister or burn your house." Having said that he smiled, looking visibly relaxed.

Maybe it was the smile, a small lift at one side of his mouth in a self-deprecating way that was almost sad. Maybe it was because of their past relationship, but she realized she believed him. "All right, but I'd still like to know what you were doing on the beach the night of the fire and wearing a wetsuit."

For a moment before it fled, amusement twinkled in his eyes. "Still want all your ducks in a row, don't you, Hanley? I figure that's what makes you such a good investigative reporter."

"I'm surprised you've had time to read any of my articles."

"I might as well confess before Robyn tells you. She's been emailing me copies of them for years." His gaze, with its piercing blue settled on her, a one-sided smile curving his mouth. "I think she had ulterior motives. Anyway, for what it's worth I think they're very good. You have a good insight into people and a way with words."

"Just like you, McTeer, to change the subject. What were you doing outside my house on the night of the fire?" She wasn't about to tell him how often Robyn spoke of him and how pleased she was that he liked what she had written.

"I sailed from Marsh Winds in our dinghy, anchored it off shore then swam to the beach. I could lie and tell you I was on the beach for a walk on a lovely evening," he said, his tone quiet, "but I wasn't—and that's all I can tell you. Believe me, I was as surprised at the course of that night's events as you were."

But he had an agenda.

"Now you're back because you want to find Holly's killer?"

For a second his eyes closed. If she hadn't been staring at him, she might have missed it. When he opened them again, any friendliness there before had evaporated into desolation. It shivered through her like a chill. "Something like that, yes," he said, and left it at that.

Anna wrapped her arms around her middle and curiosity opened her mouth, but his expression told her he would entertain no more queries on the matter, so she closed it again. In her mind there was no doubt whatever the connection between Kip McTeer and Holly's murderer, it was powerful.

He pulled in a breath and spoke through unyielding lips. "I thought we could strike a bargain. I'll load the information from your sister's computer onto yours, and in exchange you can tell me what you found in the notebook you're studying. Or, if you prefer, I can take the notebook and the papers from your table and leave right now without sharing what I have."

"You have a lot of gall," she said on an out rush of irritation, but she knew he had her.

On the day after Holly's funeral, Anna had gone into her office at the Savannah Morning News and had a talk with her boss. He was more than willing to give her some time off, but instead Anna had convinced him to allow her to investigate the case for a feature story with photographs and all. Who would be better qualified to make it a personal piece, she told him, and he'd agreed.

So Anna was more than anxious to get a look at what was on her sister's computer. Besides, the hard set of Kip's mouth told her he wasn't about to be browbeaten into leaving so she capitulated and swung around to her left, toward the efficiency kitchen that was tucked into the corner of the room, leaving him with the choice to follow or not.

He walked past her and glanced into the solitary bedroom and bathroom before he paused at a photograph she'd taken of a blue heron in the marsh grass. She had managed to capture the bird at the moment it took to the air. "I like it. Is it one of yours?"

She nodded, and he came back, stopping at the table beside her, one hand on the back of a wooden chair. "How's Danny managing?"

She took a breath. "As well as can be expected, I suppose. He asks a lot about when his mom will be back. I try to explain, but it's hard for him to grasp. I try to keep him busy."

He nodded, his jaw tightening. "It's got to be hard. Where is he? I didn't see him playing outside."

"He went over to a friend's house to play with her son."

"All right then, shall we sit?"

Her gaze skidded to the table. Every inch was cluttered with the notes she'd found in the binder the arsonist had somehow left behind. Not large, the table was made of oak and like so many of the pieces in the apartment had once belonged to her grandmother. Four chairs sat around it. On each was a ruffle-trimmed cushion covered with a muted floral pattern, but the one Anna had recently vacated also had a pillow for her back. He left that one and took the one next to it, turning it around so he could straddle it and rest an arm on the chair-back.

His other arm, he kept close to his chest, like it hurt him or he was protecting an injury. She remembered the motorcycle accident and noticed the skin beneath his eyes was bruised. The ripple of tenderness that washed through her was unexpected. She tamped it down, gripped her hands on her chair back, tense, but no longer as annoyed as she'd been moments ago.

She glanced at the microwave clock. "I don't have time to go over this right now. I need to go to the store before I pick up Danny at noon," she said reasonably.

"Call your friend and tell her you'll be a few minutes late. It's imperative I see what information you have. Believe me, Anna, as much as I'd prefer not to involve you further, it appears I have no alternative."

She drew a deep breath, almost a sigh, came around the chair and sat, leaning back. She cleared her throat. "All right, give me back my cell, and I'll call while you load the information on my computer."

She held out her hand. He stood and placed it onto her palm then shrugged out of his jacket. Tossing it over an empty chair back, he flipped his chair the right way around, sat beside her, and leaned forward as his fingers worked the keys to upload the stick.

"The most recent entries are all about a gambling ring in the Ft. Worth area," he said when she'd finished her call. After typing in some instructions, he opened a file and began to scroll down a list. "Look at these names and tell me if any looks familiar."

"At first glance the info looks like the same as I found in her notebook." She gathered the papers within her reach, tapped them into a stack, and shuffled through them until she found the one she wanted. The list was only about fifteen names long.

She studied, glancing back and forth between the computer screen and the paper in silence for a few seconds. Then she pushed a strand of hair from her face. "Frank Skinner and Leonard Omari look vaguely familiar. Long shots but I recall meeting a Frank and a man Stanley introduced as 'Lenny' at a party last year."

He tapped the information onto his iPad, and she looked at him, at his closed face, at his faded blue T-shirt with YMCA CAMP COUNSELOR printed in bold letters across his chest. The shirt looked to have gone through a hundred washings and had to be at least fifteen years old, if he'd worn it when he was a counselor. Beneath the thin fabric she noticed the faint outline of bandages wrapped around his chest and that his biceps stretched the sleeves taut. Whatever he'd been doing these past ten years, he'd been keeping in shape. Uncomfortable with the direction her thoughts were heading, she turned away.

Seconds later he said, "Those names are someplace to start. I'll do some checks on them tonight." He reached over her to break off a piece of her glazed doughnut. "You didn't used to get stuff like this."

"Once in a while it doesn't hurt. Danny and I couldn't resist the fresh baked sign flashing in the window when we drove by last night."

"You never could."

"You have a good memory, and they were worth every calorie."

He laughed and stuffed the rest of the piece into his mouth.

"Did you know your sister was writing about a local gambling ring?"

She bit off a sigh and took a sip from her cold coffee. "Yes, we usually discussed our work. But unfortunately we didn't get into the details."

"But you knew that Stanley gambled?"

Anna shook her head, her mouth tightening. "Not at first, but I figured it out. She let a few things slip, and when he phoned her I couldn't help but pick up some of the tension between them. Even when she took the phone outside the house to talk, the windows were open, and parts of the conversations traveled inside. I believe it was part of the reason for their divorce. It didn't take a crack detective to get the picture."

Kip opened a file and pointed to a six-digit number. "Take a look at this—it's what Stanley owed."

"Whew. Stanley didn't have that kind of money. I wonder where he got it."

"When we find that out, everything else will begin to slip into place. Whoever set up Stanley's credit also very likely made certain he lost."

"You think the outcome of the games was fixed?"

He nodded then rocked his chair back on two legs and clasped his hands behind his head. "I think someone wanted something from Stanley, and this was a sure way to get it."

The notion seemed far-fetched. She snickered. "What did Stanley have that anyone could want that bad?"

"Information. Don't forget that he works at the Bureau of Engraving and Printing where U.S. currency is printed."

Chapter 15

Anna wished she weren't so attracted to Kip McTeer. Her life was already too complicated. He glanced at her, caught her staring, and his mouth twitched in the semblance of a smile as if he were privy to her thoughts. No question, Anna thought as she rose and moved to the kitchen to put some distance between her and Kip, seeing him again was a problem.

Some years back the newspaper had written a story about Kip and his service in Iraq and Afghanistan. A local American hero, the paper said. The accompanying photo had been of him at the White House receiving a decoration from the president. Several months after the article came out, she read his wife and son had been killed in England. The article had been brief and short on details, and Anna remembered wondering what had happened and hoping he would come home to Savannah. He never did.

Now he was here, and she wished he weren't. According to Robyn, after his wife had been killed, Kip retired from the OSI in order to run the shipping business in California. Supposedly, the business had been in the family since shortly after the Civil War. But it was evident to her Kip was deeply involved in this investigation. Why? What had really brought him back to Marsh Winds after so many years?

She took two bottled waters from the efficiency refrigerator under the counter and put one on the table in front of him. "I wonder if Holly figured out who was bilking Stanley," she said, because she had to say something to break the tension filling in the room.

"If she did, I have yet to find it in her notes. But I have some ideas on that. We'll get to those later." He rocked forward and shifted the computer screen. "Come here and take a look at this."

She did, and a whiff of the fresh, clean scent of him came to her. She had to force herself to concentrate on the computer screen. "Telephone numbers. Where'd you find them?"

"In a locked folder titled 'numbers', but there were only these two. Do you recognize either of them?"

She shook her head. "Not offhand, but this one is an Atlanta area code. Before Holly married Stanley, she spent a couple years in Atlanta working for the *Atlanta Constitution*. She met Stanley in Atlanta at a political fundraiser. Said he was picking up overtime as a security guard. Shortly after they married he got the job in Ft. Worth."

"The last time the folder was opened before I opened it last night was over five years ago." He showed her the date.

She did some calculating. "That would be about the time Holly and Stanley got married."

He nodded. "And about the time she would have found out she was pregnant."

Obviously, he'd done some calculating, too.

"I haven't tried either of the numbers. Why don't you try one now?"

She dialed the number and waited. On the third ring an answering machine picked up. "Goddard Financial. Our hours are..."

"Goddard Financial," she repeated for his benefit then held the phone away from her ear while the message droned on. "Odd...why would Holly feel it necessary to put the telephone number of Goddard Financial in a locked file, when anyone could look it up in the telephone book? Besides the office in Atlanta, Goddard has an office on Broughton St. here in Savannah, and there's probably a third in Chicago. Hobart Goddard's son Carl went to grade school with Holly until the family relocated to Chicago. Carl was in Holly's class."

"Interestingly, I ran into Hobart Goddard at the Oglethorpe House on the night of the fire. Is it possible your sister could have dated Carl before she married Stanley?"

"If she did, she never mentioned it to me, and I think it'd be something she would say since we both knew him. Personally, I haven't seen Carl in a number of years, but I heard he's back in town. Someone told me he got an accounting degree at Georgia

State and planned to join his father's firm. I'll check with the local Goddard Financial Monday and see what I can find out."

"I don't suppose you have an Atlanta phone book handy?"

She shook her head, seeing where he was going.

"What about a Savannah directory?"

"Maybe an old one." She went into the kitchen, pulled open a couple of drawers, and held one up in triumph. "A mere ten years old." She laughed and handed it over to him. "You check. I'll call Atlanta information." A minute later she closed the phone and handed him the number she'd jotted down.

All the numbers were different.

"As employees of Goddard Financial both Carl and his father would have access to a great deal of money and theoretically could have set up Stanley."

"You're catching on." He grinned.

She told herself it was the prospect of getting closer to finding Holly's murderer that quickened her heartbeat, not the dimples that framed his cheeks.

She dialed the second number he'd found in the locked file and a recording picked up saying the number was no longer in service. She dialed it twice more and got the same results. "This number's no longer in service."

"Not surprising. Sometimes those numbers can be traced. I'll see what I can do at my end. I'll make a search on the computer before we give up." He typed in Carl Goddard and Goddard financial, but none of the phone numbers matched the one no longer in service, and the information he found wasn't of particular interest. After that he asked her a few more questions, sounding very much like the questions the police had asked.

She sank back into her seat with a sigh, one she tried to conceal with a little cough and pushed her hair back from her face. Suddenly the reality of the past days' events felt like a crushing weight on her. She shuddered and tried to get hold of her emotions. "I'm finding out there's quite a bit I didn't know about my sister. She was a private person. We sometimes talked about our cases, but only in superficial terms. I keep thinking if only I had probed more, maybe she'd be alive today." Her voice broke.

He looked up from the computer, and she noticed a flare of intense emotion in his gaze. "Don't beat yourself up about something you can't change, Anna. It was her decision to keep the information to herself, not yours. If she sensed any danger, she probably wanted to protect you from it."

Anna took a swallow of water to conceal her turbulence then folded her arms around her middle as if that simple act would keep her emotions from bursting free. Her gaze dropped to the computer screen that had gone bank. She stared at it, struggling to expel the sudden overwhelming sense of loss. *I have to be strong. For Danny, I must be strong.* But after a lifetime of having her sister no farther away than a telephone call, it was hard for Anna to imagine the future without her.

Somehow his hand wound up on her arm, drawing her away from her thoughts as if he understood she would welcome his reassurance. She looked at him, and his steady gaze captured hers. There was a tension pulling at his mouth, and whatever had recently robbed him of his health showed in the shadows under his eyes.

He took his hand away and ran it through his hair, but she could still feel the warmth where it had rested.

At length Anna shrugged and straightened her back. "After you left I found my sister's notebook at the bottom of the steps. The police caught me with it, so I had no choice but to hand it over."

He laughed. "Me they would have hauled in."

Silently, she agreed. "When you were nineteen you wouldn't have left me to face them alone."

His jaw tightened. "I'm not nineteen anymore, Anna. It would be a mistake for you to think I'm the same person you knew in high school."

"I'm not thinking anything about you at all, Kip McTeer. I'm not the one who came barging into your house." She shot to her feet. He grabbed her elbow and swung her back to her seat, drawing her closer to him until their gazes held. There was something hard in his eyes, something vulnerable, too. She pulled in a deep breath, aching to kiss him, and pulled her arm free.

"Listen, Kip, obviously your OSI training has involved you in this sort of thing before, but you're under no obligation to try and find Holly's murderer."

He gave her a hard smile. "That's where you're wrong, Anna. Besides, I've been stuck flat on my back with a lot of time to think about it." He twisted the cap off his bottle and drank the rest of the water without coming up for air. Then his eyes flicked toward her. "How'd you get the notebook?"

"I asked for it. A couple of days ago I persuaded Detective Brady to give me these copies. I just finished reading them late last night."

"And...?

"I have to believe Holly's investigation got too close to someone."

He leaned back in his chair, balancing on the two back legs. "So what's your impression of Stanley?"

She took a few swallows of her water and glanced a sideways smile at him. "I didn't say I thought the someone was Stanley." But she'd been thinking exactly that. "But you asked, so I'll tell you straight. I've always thought of Stanley as a good-looking good-for-nothing. I think he has the mentality of a jock who never matured past high school, the disposition, too. I imagine he thinks he's some kind of hotshot in bed and irresistible to women, particularly since he's a cop, and he may well be all those things. But he's weak. He's way down the food chain from my sister. And I'll bet you a dollar he married her for her money. How's that for an opinion?"

He laughed, rocking his chair forward. "So I guess I don't need to ask what kind of marriage she had."

"An unhappy one, especially of late. My sister and I were close, but she didn't drag me into her problems. Just for the record, I never expressed my opinions of her husband to her either, but my guess is that if I had, she would have agreed. That said, in his way I think Stanley still cared for her. Also, though he logically fits the bill, I don't think he was capable of murdering her."

Kip nodded his head once. "You never know what's hidden inside a man, what drives him. I never met Stanley, so I can't speculate on what he's capable of, but from all accounts, I agree that he appears to be a weak man. I think he's our link.

Someone may be jerking his strings. Why do you think she married him?"

"If you asked me three weeks ago, I'd have said she must have cared for him. He is a handsome man, some might say sexy. I never asked. I figured she was pregnant before they married—she was already showing, but I never guessed the baby wasn't Stanley's until he told me at the funeral. And I don't know who Danny's biological father might be which I suppose is your next question. I expect Holly wanted it that way."

"What do you know of Stanley's family?"

"Very little except he was raised by a single mother. Everett is his mother's maiden name. He attended a small college in Illinois, spent a couple years as a ski instructor in Colorado before he went to the police academy in Springfield. He met Holly when he was working security in Atlanta. As I said, the Ft. Worth job came after they were married."

"Do you know if he knew who is father was?"

"I think he did. I think he reacquainted himself with his father after his mother died. Sorry, but I don't recall his father's name. I think Holly mentioned it once because he's someone fairly well known, but I don't remember who he was."

"You'll have to ask Stanley."

"I intend to."

He said nothing but turned and stared out the window, and she thought he wasn't thinking about Stanley Everett, the high school jock. Between them the silence stretched, and into it came the sound of waves crashing against the sand, of birds singing, and the scent of damp earth.

Once again she noticed the outline of the bandages wrapped around his chest and wondered if the motorcycle accident story he dished out was true. There was much more to him than he let on, and for the second time in her life she found herself being drawn to him like a moth is drawn to a flame.

"Holly had already made up her mind to divorce Stanley before she came for this last visit. She was looking for a reason not to, but I couldn't give her one. It didn't surprise me when she told me she was going to file divorce papers on him. A couple of nights after she arrived, she set up an appointment with a lawyer. The appointment was scheduled for the day after her murder."

She took a quick breath and put more distance between them, but she could still smell the soap he'd bathed in, spicy, masculine.

A gust of wind came through the window, caught some papers, and scattered them to the floor. She leaned over to retrieve them. When she looked up, she grew still. The sunlight that had been struggling to come out for the past few hours had pierced the clouds, casting the shadow of a perfect cross over the varnished wood tabletop. For several long moments she watched the cross until the clouds shifted and moved, morphing the cross back into the crossbars of the windowpane.

"On the day before she was killed," she said, her gaze still fixed on the brightening sunlight coming through the window, "we lay on blankets on the beach just like we did in high school, trying to soak up the rays. Danny was building a fort in the sand beside us. The temperature was pretty cold, but the sun was bright so we managed to stay warm in our shirts and jeans. It was like we were kids again. Holly and I talked and laughed. Never once did she let on she might be in danger. I can't believe someone would murder..." Her words caught in her throat.

Her sorrow swelled up suddenly. The tears took her by surprise. She swiped at them with the back of her hand. "I'm sorry. Right now every little thing seems to make me cry..."

He fixed his gaze on her, and she felt the heat like a caress on her face. "Sometimes it's better to cry than to hold it all in," he said, and she wondered what made him cry. She'd cried and cried when he'd phoned to tell her he was marrying Marie.

He reached for her hand, and his thumb rubbed the spot where she normally wore her engagement ring. Then he glanced at her, his eyebrows raised in query. "Robyn told me you'd broken it off at the funeral."

She looked away, pulling in a deep breath, knowing he was trying to divert her from her grief, knowing she didn't have to confide anything to him, but also knowing in her heart he was part of the reason the ring was gone. Her mouth almost smiled when she turned back to him. "It seems Stanley isn't the only one who doesn't want to be a father. I won't abandon Danny. End of story." Except that it wasn't the end, of course.

A mockingbird began to carry on outside the window, and a moment passed in silence as they both listened. Anna started to pull back her hand, but he stopped her by enfolding it in his as though he sensed her need. Her gaze dropped to their joined fingers, and she felt the strength in his hand, in him, remembering a time when he'd meant everything to her, and she didn't pull away.

"I'm sure it isn't the right time or place to say this, but when I left for the Air Force Academy, I made you a lot of promises I didn't keep. I let you down, and I'm sorry. Someday, maybe I'll be free to tell you about it," he said, his voice low, his dark brows knit. "And now all this happening...it's been a rough week for you."

"Umhumm." She couldn't bring words over the lump in her throat. She looked at him, this man she'd loved since she'd been a kid, this man who by some quirk of fate returned to Savannah in time to pull her from her burning house, at the hard cut of his jaw and the caring in his eyes. Her mouth quivered, and tears welled in her eyes.

He opened his arms and pulled her against his chest. It surprised her to realize how much she wanted it. On her own for so long, she needed to feel support. He said nothing but smoothed his hand over her hair like he would a child, holding her against him like he had that first night when he pulled her from the fire. In time her breathing revved down.

Outside the window a dog began to bark. His dog?

She made herself pull away and gave him a wavering smile.

He stared at her with haunted eyes and didn't return her smile. His finger brushed a trail along her jaw then swept a stray lock from her forehead.

She reached up a hand and touched the stubble on his cheek. A jolt rushed through her, and she pulled her hand back.

"Anna..."

He lowered his head. Her face lifted. His mouth came down on hers, a light brush but charged nonetheless.

She pulled away and swallowed around the emotion lumped in her throat.

He was breathing heavily through his nose. He brushed a finger across her lips. "It'll be okay." But considering the circumstances, she couldn't imagine how it would.

On the table the cell phone began to vibrate, and it took her a moment to register what it was. She reached for it and read the ID.

"Robyn." She moved away from him with a little smile.

"Just like a little sister..." he said, and she saw he was smiling, too, as she brought the phone to her ear. He rose and walked to the window and stood with his back to her.

"Anna, hi. How are you doing?"

"Fine, thanks, reading, working on the computer. You still coming out?"

"That's why I called. Would you kill me if I didn't come today? Barry's staying in town for a few more days. Now that the sun's come out, we thought we'd take advantage of the day and head to Ft. Pulaski to ride the McQueens rails trail on bikes. Mom has a few extra bikes at the house for him to borrow one."

"Sounds like a great idea."

"We were thinking maybe you and Danny would like to join us? We planned to ask Kip, too, but it's better if he takes it easy for a another week or so. Anyway, he's swiped Mom's car and disappeared. But you and Danny should come. Danny would enjoy seeing the cannons at the fort."

"I know he would. Right now, he's visiting a friend, though I'm about to pick him up. I'll see if his friend can come along. Either way, it sounds like a grand idea. We'll meet you at the fort in about an hour."

"Great, I'm glad you're going to join us. We'll be leaving the house in about five minutes, and we've got sandwiches. Want us to pack some for you?"

"Thanks, but I've got some stuff. We'll make our own."

"Call when you're fifteen minutes away. Come to think of it, I'm not sure there's cell service out there, but we'll be on the lookout for you. We'll meet you in the picnic area. That way we can have lunch before we go into the fort."

"Wonderful. We'll see you there shortly, and thanks for thinking of us." Anna put the phone in her pocket and reached for her water.

Kip hitched a hip on the windowsill, one long leg crossed over the other, his hands deep into his pockets, and looked at her expectantly.

She took a couple of swallows of her water and stood. "Robyn and Barry are going bike riding along the McQueens Island rails trail. They want Danny and me to join them for a picnic."

"If you haven't got a problem with it, I'd like to tag along. Last time I was at Pulaski was when you and I walked over to Cockspur Lighthouse and got caught in the high tide."

Anna pulled out a loaf of whole wheat bread. "It's a public place. Just don't get any ideas. This isn't a date—it's more a detective-research-sort-of-thing."

The corners of his eyes crinkled with his smile as he reached for the peanut butter jar and the knife she'd laid on the counter and began to spread it on the bread.

Chapter 16

As Kip drove the back streets of Tybee Island with Anna beside him, he stole a glance at her—the straight nose, the pale hair, and high cheekbones. She looked fit and even more beautiful than he remembered. But he didn't fool himself. She wasn't the same teenager who'd fallen for him in high school. She'd traveled the world with her camera and her pen, covering human interest stories for her paper and free-lancing for magazines.

Her book of photography from her winter spent with the Aleut natives in Alaska lay on his coffee table in his LA apartment. Not that he needed her book to rekindle his memories of her. She had been his first love, and he'd never loved any woman as he'd loved her.

His grip tightened on the steering wheel. Looking at her made him think of things he had no business thinking of—family, children—things they had planned together so long ago, things that for him were never to be. He regretted his hasty offer to picnic with her at the fort. Being near her threw him off balance, made him forget who he was and what he did for a living. He turned away.

He needed the investigation finished, and he needed to know she would be safe. Then he would leave, and they'd both get on with their lives.

Located on Cockspur Island between the north and south channels of the Savannah River, Ft. Pulaski is midway between Tybee Island and Whitemarsh Island. Before the road was built in 1920 the only ways to reach the fort and the beaches of Tybee Island were by boat or the rail line. As they drove by the portion of the old rail line that had been converted into a six mile gravel trail, Kip pointed it out to Danny and told him a bit of the history of Robert E. Lee and the fort Lee had designed as a young man.

"More than a hundred and fifty years ago, when the North and the South were at war, Robert E. Lee was a famous general for the South."

"So how come the fort is called Pulaski? Why isn't it Lee?" Danny asked.

Kip chuckled. "Good question, but since I wasn't around back then, I can only speculate it was because Lee wasn't famous when he designed it."

Anna added, "General Pulaski was famous long before Robert E. Lee was even born. He fought in a much earlier war and saved the life of our first president."

Kip parked Anna's jeep in the half-filled parking lot and turned around to look at Danny. "The park ranger at the gate said there'll be a cannon firing this afternoon at three. Would you like to see it?"

"Yes, sir."

With a green grocery bag filled with water, PB&J sandwiches, and grapes slung over his arm, Kip walked with Anna and Danny onto the pine-covered path toward the picnic area. Overhead, a small plane flew east toward the sea, momentarily drowning out the wind's whisper through the tops of the pines. The path was wide enough for the three of them to walk side-by-side, but when Harlie, seeing her chance to run, raced ahead, Danny took off behind her, leaving Anna and Kip alone.

"It smells good out here." Kip smiled to himself, filling his lungs with the fresh scent. "I'd forgotten how beautiful Ft. Pulaski is."

There was a lot he'd forgotten, he brooded, mostly about the simpler things in life like the picnics, the walks hand-in-hand with someone you cared about. Normally he ate, slept and breathed the cloak and dagger intrigue of his life. Now as he walked with the warmth of the sun filtering through the pines onto his head, it was hard to think of it. Instead, he found himself struggling to erase from his mind how neatly Anna fit into his arms and the way she looked moments ago as she lifted Danny from the car and gave the child a little kiss on his cheek like she couldn't help herself.

He very nearly reached for her hand before he stopped himself and shoved his hand in his pocket. Good thing, too, he thought moments later when Robyn and Barry rode around the corner on their bikes. He was surprised to see Dylan and Maribel behind them with their daughter Wendy riding at the end of the column on a pink bike.

Dylan stopped his bike inches in front of Kip. "Hey, didn't expect to see you here."

Kip grinned. "Air Force gave me a lifetime free pass."

"We're last minute additions, too. We're all sick of packing. Besides, it's too beautiful a day to waste staying inside," Dylan said. "And I got to thinking, right now in Delaware it's about forty degrees for a high. We're going to miss days like this." He angled his head toward the path. "This way. We left our lunches on the table about a hundred yards down."

As they took their places at the picnic table with a barrage of familial banter, Kip was struck by how easily Anna fit in. While they ate, the afternoon sun seeped in through the pines, warming them. Half an hour later, when all that was left of the sandwiches were crumbs, Kip suddenly realized he was enjoying himself, really relaxing for the first time in years. For the moment, the theft of the three hundred million and Anna's sister's murder seemed far away.

After lunch they all trooped over to the fort for the demonstrations and the cannon firing, then they took the three-quarter mile walk along the open marshes beside the Savannah River to take a look at Cockspur Island Lighthouse. The lighthouse, small in comparison to most, was built between 1837 and 1839 on an islet comprised of oyster shells and marsh grass and was a treasure to Savannah locals and history buffs alike.

Kip came up behind Danny and his niece and put a hand each on each. "The lighthouse was built to guide ships up the shallow South Channel of the Savannah River."

"Why doesn't it have a light?" Wendy asked.

"Because it's day time, silly," Danny answered before Dylan or Maribel could.

"That's partly right, Danny." Kip squatted between the two children. "But it's only part of the story. When it was built long ago, ships weren't as big as they are today. The big freighters of today need deeper water to come into Savannah, so they began to use the North Channel instead of the South Channel. When that happened, the little lighthouse wasn't needed any more. The light was put out almost a hundred years ago."

"Can we go and see it?" Danny tugged on Kip's hand.

Kip looked at Dylan, and Dylan shook his head. "Not today, kids. The tide's on its way in. Shortly, water will cover the path. The best way to get to Cockspur Island is by boat. We'll have to save that for another day."

"Oh, look, kids." Anna pointed into a marshy area along the river. "There's an alligator over there, hiding in the grass."

Shortly after that the day came to an end. Kip drove Anna and Danny back to her house, pleased to see a police car stationed outside. He hated to see the relaxing day come to an end but resisted inviting the two of them to have supper with him and headed back to Marsh Winds.

At her desk outside the door to Senator Louis Norton's Atlanta office, Mabel Osgood stacked some papers, restacked them, then took a bottle of antacid tablets from her purse, popped two into her mouth, and chewed. She liked being the senator's private secretary; liked the power it offered her, the prestige, and the information that passed across her desk. But two weeks ago she'd discovered something that made her worry that her days of working for him were numbered. Senator Norton had been acquainted with Mrs. Holly Everett.

On the face of it, the news was hardly a revelation. In his line of business, the senator made a point of meeting as many people as he could, and his wife's family owned a summer house on Tybee Beach. But ever since the senator read in the newspaper that Holly Everett had died in a fire at her sister's home, he'd been visibly upset. Unlike himself, on the day the news made the papers he'd called off an important budget meeting with the governor to make some calls of inquiry instead of asking Mabel to make the calls on his behalf. This unusual behavior triggered Mabel's curiosity even more than normal, and that's when she remembered the photograph and e-mail she'd found in his personal locked files when she'd first come to work for him. The photo was of the senator on a yacht with a beautiful woman. The woman wasn't his wife.

As well, the senator's file held a copy of an e-mail from a woman saying she loved him enough not to wreck his career and his marriage and that the communication would be her last. Attached to that e-mail was his original correspondence, professing his love and asking the woman not to end the affair.

Until a few days ago Mabel had been unable to identify the woman on the boat with the senator. Reasoning there was some grounds for the senator to keep the photo locked away, Mabel had made a copy of it and the letter and had kept them at home in her own locked files ever since. She'd almost forgotten about them until the image of the woman who'd died in the fire appeared in the newspaper and jogged her memory. The woman pictured in the newspaper and the woman in the senator's photos were one and the same—Holly Hanley Everett.

Senator Norton was careful to project to the public the image of a caring Christian, a family man. The documents Mabel held proved the image was a lie. He would be running for re-election in the spring in a conservative state. Mabel smiled to herself with the knowledge she could destroy his political career should he try to cross her. The information was a weapon her friend in California would be very interested in having. Coincidentally, he was in town right now. She intended to pass her information on to him when they met in the next day or two. She knew he would wait until the time was right and use her evidence to his best advantage, and it pleased her to be able to help him achieve his goals any way she could.

Yesterday, upon reading in the papers that Holly Everett's death was a suspected homicide and not the accidental fire from a gas range explosion as first reported, Senator Norton had instructed Mabel to contact Savannah law enforcement and find out all she could about the progress of the case. At first Mabel had been concerned what a probe into Holly Everett's case might bring to light and was reluctant to delve too deeply into it before she passed her information to her friend. However, she'd recently reversed her thinking and come to believe keeping up with the police investigation was to her benefit. With that in mind she performed the task diligently.

On her desk lay some photocopied papers of the latest newspaper articles she'd pulled from the computer and stapled to the police report she'd received that morning. Judging from the report, she had to conclude little had been learned about who set the fire and no connection had been made between

Winds of Fire

Senator Norton and Holly Everett, but Mabel knew enough about investigations to know police omit sensitive information. Her hope was that something of value would inadvertently slip into a report.

She thumbed through the report again, stopping here and there to read comments. She was right. Nowhere was there a hint of who'd been responsible for the crime or even why it had been perpetrated. But today some information had been included in the report that disturbed her. Today's report revealed that Holly Everett had been working on a story about a Ft. Worth gambling ring, something she already knew.

It was just as Mabel feared. The information Holly unearthed about the gambling ring wasn't destroyed in the fire as she'd hoped. The police recovered it, but not all of it, Mabel knew. She decided she needed to find a way to look at what information the police had. She began to think of how she could manipulate the situation to make that happen.

It occurred to her the senator may have kept in contact with Holly in some other manner. If he did, Stanley Everett's gambling wouldn't surprise him. And if he did, would he wonder where Stanley received the kind of money he gambled with? Perhaps he'd even relayed that information and his concerns to the investigators. But could the police link the fire and Stanley's wife's death to the gambling ring?

The thought that Senator Norton might know more than he let on made Mabel nervous, but she wasn't ready to play her ace in the hole. It was too soon.

At the moment the senator was out of the office at an important meeting with Marshal Quinlan, head of Continental Carrying, Inc. and U.S. Senator. Quinlan was in town to discuss the possible expansion of a CC warehouse in Fulton County. The move would mean jobs and a boon for Georgia's economy. Quinlan was also being discussed in the media as a possible replacement for the retiring U.S. Secretary of State or a possible candidate for President of the United States, an important man.

While Senator Norton wasn't supportive of Marshal Quinlan, Mabel thought he'd hear the man's proposal through and didn't expect him to return for another half an hour at least. She decided to take the opportunity to go back into his locked file.

Not surprisingly, this time the file was empty of anything personal.

With her eye on the clock, Mabel shuffled through the other papers on the senator's desk. She wanted to be back in her office before Norton returned. Almost immediately, her attention was caught on a hand-penned envelope that looked to be an invitation; the calligraphy was exceptionally fine. She was surprised to discover the return address read 1600 Pennsylvania Avenue. The White House. Curious, she eased out the invitation and found it to be a request for the senator to attend a ceremony to bestow the Silver Star medal. She was about to replace it, when one of the names of the recipients jumped out at her: On the list was Major Kristopher McTeer.

She froze. The name was well known to her. She clutched her hand across her heart, searching everywhere on the embossed card for the word 'posthumously'. It wasn't there. When she returned the invitation to its envelope her hand was shaking. The invitation must have arrived during the two days last week she missed with the stomach virus, and now her stomach was queasy again. What was the senator's connection to Kristopher McTeer? Was the invitation issued because the senator knew McTeer personally or was he invited on behalf of another beneficiary or merely as a courtesy because McTeer was from Georgia?

Many years ago Mabel had crossed paths with McTeer. Recently she received information that he'd met with a fatal accident. She had been *assured* he was dead. She reached back for the invitation and checked the date it had been mailed, only a week ago, and it had been addressed to Norton's home, not his office. The thought McTeer could still be alive sent a chill down her spine. When she left the senator's office, her hands were moist. She took a moment to walk down the drab yellow hallway to the ladies room to wash them and collect her thoughts before returning to her office.

While she was still mulling over this new information, the senator returned from his meeting and stopped at her desk. "Have you gotten a fax today about the case?"

She didn't need to ask which case. "Yes, sir. It came in a few minutes ago. I was about to put it on your desk." She handed him the report.

He walked into his office, turned around and came back. She braced for the accusation. He had noticed she searched his desk. What could she tell him? But he had something else on his mind, something much more serious. "By the way, did you use my computer this morning?"

She shook her head. "No, is something wrong?"

"Did anyone else?"

She hoped her face looked noncommittal. "I didn't see anyone. I was in the ladies room for a few minutes. I suppose someone could have come in while I was gone." She wanted to ask why again but decided against it.

She watched him return to his office shaking his head as if doubting himself.

She realized she mustn't have left the computer exactly as she found it. Because of her carelessness she'd been forced to lie directly. Not that Mabel Osgood had scruples preventing her from prevarication, but she had an aversion to lying directly when it could so easily be determined as a lie. For her the best course of action had always been subtlety, small fabrications, innuendos, while diligently covering her tracks. If that failed, the next course of action was to eliminate the problem. That second course of action was what Mabel had in mind now when she picked up the phone and punched some numbers.

On the third ring a female voice answered. "Savannah Police Department. Homicide. May I help you?"

Mabel knew caller ID had already identified her call as coming from the senator's office but she identified herself anyway. "I'd like to speak with Detective Joseph Brady, please."

"One moment please, and I'll see if he's at his desk."

A few minutes later another woman came on the phone. "I'm sorry, ma'am, but Detective Brady is away from his desk right now. Perhaps I may be of help to you?"

"Thank you, perhaps you may. This is in regards to the Everett homicide, you know the house fire on Tybee Island that resulted in the death of Holly Everett. Senator Norton was a close friend of the victim's parents, and the police department has kindly been keeping him up-to-date with reports. There are a few matters in this morning's report the senator asked me to inquire about."

"Sergeant Howell has been working with Detective Brady, and I see him just returning to the office right now. Would you like to speak to him?"

Mabel thanked the woman and waited on the line.

After a few minutes of conversation, Mabel hung up.

The final question Mabel posed to the officer was framed as a casual inquiry. It was about one Major Kristopher McTeer whom she described as an acquaintance of the senator's, saying the senator had received an invitation to McTeer's Silver Star award ceremony and heard he was in town. He has the greatest respect for the Major and wondered if his friend were working the case. Sergeant Howell confirmed that as the crime had crossed state lines with Holly Hanley being most recently from Fort Worth, other government agencies had likely been pulled in for information gathering purposes. Then he'd paused for several significant seconds before he said, "As for Major McTeer, I've never heard of him."

Mabel Osgood was sure he was lying. Why?

Mabel had hoped the officer would confirm McTeer was dead. The thought that he was alive once again sent a wave of mild panic down her spine. Had McTeer been able to identify his assailant on the mountain? And of all people, McTeer would recognize the incendiary device used to set the fire at Hanley's house. After that it would just be a matter of time before he traced it to other crimes where that device had been deployed.

She knew what she must do to take care of the problem, lifted her phone, and dialed. When the familiar voice picked up the line, she said. "Where are you?

He told her, and she said she'd like to meet him for dinner the following night. She gave him a time and place, then disconnected without waiting for his answer.

Mabel had nothing if she didn't have a cool head, and as she walked into the senator's office with her pad and pen in answer to his summons, she had the appearance of calm.

But things were slipping out of her control, and Mabel liked to be in control.

Chapter 17

Kip sat on the back porch of Marsh Winds with his computer for company. Yesterday Dylan and his family had left for Pennsylvania, his sister had returned to Atlanta with Barry, and after their all-too-pleasant afternoon together two days ago, he refused to allow himself to call Anna. Without his family around he found the house uncomfortably empty. He'd grown up with his brothers and sister around him and all the companionship and hustle-bustle a large family entailed. He missed it. In California he lived alone, but chasing bad guys didn't give him much home time, and if he did have extra time, he usually stopped in on his shipping business, not so much to oversee it, but to touch base with his very competent manager. He thought he'd gotten used to the solitary life, but after a few weeks at Marsh Winds he realized how much he missed all the family, all the laughter and fun.

He leaned back against the cushion of his wicker chair and listened to the sounds of the old plantation house—the patter of acorns on the tin roof, the rustle of palm fronds and oak leaves in the wind, the birds singing away over the harsh squawks of a few marsh hens—all sounds he loved, but he missed the sounds of Dylan's daughter bustling through the house or interrupting him to attend a tea party she'd set up or show him something she'd made. He missed the sound of Maribel and his sister chatting as they worked with his mother in the kitchen, and he couldn't help but remember back to another time when it was his Marie who'd been the helper, his son who'd been there wanting to play ball. Being here these past weeks had brought back all the old feelings for the family he'd moved away from and his family that was dead.

He drew in a deep breath and stretched out his legs.

And then there was Anna. Once he'd promised to always love her, to protect her and never hurt her. He'd broken all his promises. A relationship with her would necessitate commitment, marriage. He couldn't afford that. Never again. *Anna, Anna, send me away. I don't want to hurt you again.*

He wasn't the monster she suspected him of being. He didn't murder her sister or burn her house, but he wasn't simply the guy she'd fallen for in high school either. He'd seen things, done things that could turn a man inside-out if he dwelled on them. The constant cloud of danger that hung over him wasn't the kind of life he wanted to share with a woman.

He needed her out of his life so he could regain his balance and concentrate on the case. On the other hand, he needed to find her sister's killer. Ironically, in order for him to find the killer he needed to know everything Anna knew. That necessitated he spend time with her. Technically, he thought with a tightening of his jaw, he was what one would describe as being caught between a rock and a hard place.

The kiss had been a mistake. The kiss had only rekindled memories best left forgotten and made him want more. He needed to back off, keep the relationship impersonal. A picnic at Ft. Pulaski—what had he been thinking of?

Hell, he was already in too deep.

When he'd agreed to return to Marsh Winds to recuperate, the investigation had been centered on the west coast and Ft. Worth. He hadn't expected it to follow him, but it had always been a possibility. Stanley Everett's name was on the list of those who worked at the Bureau of Printing and Engraving. Stanley was married to Anna's sister. Col. Harrison had been aware of the connection when he arranged for Kip to return to Savannah. And Kip had been thinking of the connection as well, particularly on the night Anna's home burned.

It was the effect of seeing Anna again that was the something he hadn't anticipated.

"Ah, Kip, there you are." Sarah McTeer stepped through the screened door with an arm-load of packages and caught the door with her shoulder before it banged shut. "I'm glad you're home. I was afraid you might be out on the boat somewhere, and it looks like it's going to rain again."

"Nope, me and my computer are right here—been here since breakfast." He jumped up and took the load from his mother's arms. "Any place in particular you want these?"

"For now the kitchen table will do fine." She followed him inside.

"Looks like you've hit the mall. Any more I can get from the car?"

"Thanks that would be wonderful. I'm afraid there's lots more in the trunk."

He returned with the rest of the bags and stopped inside the kitchen. "Want these upstairs?"

"Just put them on the table there and let's go back and sit on the porch. I need to talk with you a minute."

"Uh-oh. Sounds serious. I'm having coffee. Do I need something stronger?"

"No, oh no," she laughed.

"Can I get you some?"

"Yes, thanks, lots of cream—you know how I like it. And do you mind pouring it over ice?"

When he returned to the porch, she was sitting with her feet on the wicker coffee table. She looked tired. He handed her the iced coffee and sat across from her. He propped his feet on the same table and waited.

"I've been thinking of taking a trip."

"A trip, that's what all this is about. A trip? Of course you should take a trip. You should take lots of trips. In fact, I should have thought to offer and pay for the trip. I'd like to do that now, belatedly. Where are you going?"

"The Greek Isles, and thank you, darling, but there's no need for you to pay for it. Your father left me more than enough to travel. Anyway, there's more to it. I'm going with Evan. He asked me to go months ago. Several of our friends are going. I told him I'd go, then you got injured and Dylan got transferred. What with one thing and another, I backed out. I wouldn't even consider leaving while you were so sick, and Maribel needed me to help her get moved out."

"Oh, Mom, I'm sorry."

"You shouldn't be. I've loved having you around these weeks, and I'm thrilled to see you're nearly recovered. Well anyway, it seems there's still room for me to go. A couple of days before Dylan left, Evan stopped by to let me know that he'd been holding onto a stateroom adjoining his all this while and now that you're ever so much better would I reconsider going with him? I told him I'd think on it, and I think I'd like to go with him. I know I would. I called him back last night. In fact I've bought the mall out, because we'll be leaving for Rome in four days."

Kip went to her and gave her a hug. "Wonderful, Mom. That's wonderful."

"And you don't care that I'm going with Evan?"

He gave her a long look. "Evan's a great guy, and Dad's been dead a long time. You should have done something like this years ago."

"You should, too, son. You should, too. Although I don't exactly know what it is you do besides pretending to run that shipping business of your grandfather's, I worry about you. Why isn't running a shipping business enough to do?"

"I have some unfinished business out there. When it's finished, I'll quit."

"Well, just don't let that unfinished business be the end of you, Kip. Marie and Patrick are dead, and all the bad guys you slay won't bring them back to life. You're a mere mortal, son. Bullets penetrate you like they do every man. Please, be careful. There, I've said my piece, and I'll leave it at that." She rose, wiping a tear from her eye.

He stopped her before she got to the kitchen door and pulled her into his embrace. "I'm listening to you, Mom. Don't let it make you sad. It's just something I have to do. I know it's hard for you to understand, but I couldn't live with myself if I didn't. And now there are some other innocent people who are counting on me. I can't let them down."

"I know, son. I know what kind of man you are, and that's what scares me so. I want you to be careful. Don't let anything happen to you."

Anna added fresh water to the coffeepot and poured it into the coffeemaker. She heard the crunch of soft soles on the wooden stairs coming up from the garage, and her heartbeat stopped, then started again, beating hard under her sweatshirt. She placed the coffeepot in the maker with a clank and turned toward the door. She wasn't expecting anyone and hadn't heard a car drive up.

There was a light tap on the door. "Anna, it's Kip. I've got something for you."

Anna unlocked the door and moved back. He stepped a few feet inside and stopped, the thumb of one hand hooked off his belt. In the other hand he held an oversized black plastic trash bag.

She shoved her hands into to pockets of her jeans. "Thought maybe I'd scared the big, bad, OSI major off."

He gave a mock shudder and looked at her straight-on. "Could be, but if you don't wipe that pretty little smirk off your face right now, I'm going to show you just how afraid this OSI major really is."

She laughed. It surprised her how much she missed seeing him these last two days, how easy it would be for her to slip into his arms, into the ways they'd shared before.

Tenderness suddenly softened the hard lines around his mouth. "A peace offering. Quilts from my mom. The temperatures are supposed to drop into the forties tonight, and she's worried you and Danny might get cold. She insisted I bring them over. We don't need them at the house now that Dylan has gone." He gave the bag a little bounce up and held it out to her. "I think there might be a little something for Danny in there, too."

"How thoughtful of her." Anna crossed over to him to retrieve the bag, closer than was prudent, her heartbeat pounding too hard in her breast. "I just put on a pot of coffee. Why don't you sit down and have a cup?"

She thought she saw a twitch of uncertainty at the corner of his mouth before he spoke. "I haven't eaten lunch yet. Let me take you two out for a bite."

A favorite with natives and tourists alike, the Crab Shack was once a fishing camp with live bait, a boat hoist, and a bar where locals congregated. Wooden tables with holes carved out in the center to accommodate discarded shells were adorned with rolls of paper towels and dime-store salt and pepper shakers. Judging from the noisy crowd, Kip thought the fare must be as good as he remembered.

Danny expressed disappointment that Harlie couldn't join them at their outside table but got over it soon enough when the waitress presented him with some crayons and a page to color. After Anna told him what was available, Danny ordered a hotdog with an ear of corn and slaw.

Studying her sister's son, Anna took a deep breath and closed her eyes, but not before Kip saw the ache in them. He wanted to lean over and take her hands and reassure her. But nothing was sure, so he turned to the waitress and ordered the captain's platter of assorted seafood with boiled potatoes, corn and sausage for him and Anna.

Anna pulled in a breath. "Holly and I had made plans to go to lunch here the day after she died. It was always a favorite place of hers. The lunch was to be a kind of get-together with several of her friends. I never thought to call them and cancel." She wiped a finger under her eye and reached for her water. "You said you found out something about the case."

Kip was stopped from answering, when Danny spoke instead. "I need to go to the potty."

Anna placed her water back on the table and rose. Kip put his hand on her arm. "I'll take him."

Kip was poised to enter the men's room when he became aware of a man in a black leather jacket moving toward the table where he'd left Anna. He was a big man, heavy-set, almost as tall as himself, and he approached from behind so silently Anna didn't appear to notice him until he was upon her. Then she jerked around to face him and seemed to catch her breath as if a sudden jab of fear took it away. With Danny in tow, Kip made a U-turn and was on his way back to the table when he heard the man speak to Anna and slowed his step to listen.

"I'm sorry if I startled you. I saw you across the room and thought I recognized you, but I see you don't recognize me. It's been a long time." He held out his hand. "I'm Carl Goddard. It's good to see you after all these years."

Anna shook it briefly then returned her hand to her lap. She recognized him. How could she not? She'd seen him on the beach in front of her house a few days before Holly was murdered, but she kept the information to herself. "I hope you're doing well."

Halfway across the room with Danny in hand, Kip watched the scene unfold. He wouldn't have recognized Carl Goddard if his name hadn't so recently been brought to mind. Taller than his father by several inches Carl had filled out since high school. Kip didn't think all of it was fat, and he looked like a man who had something on his mind. Whatever it was, it was making Anna uncomfortable.

Carl's hand came down on Anna's shoulder and stayed there. Kip saw her visibly tense. The expression on Carl's face was sly. No doubt he was enjoying seeing Anna's discomfort. Knowing Anna as well as he did, Kip realized she was struggling not to forcibly remove Carl's hand. *Take your hand off her, you snot-nosed bastard. You have exactly ten seconds before I forcibly remove it.*

"I have to go potty," Danny said with a tug on Kip's hand.

"I know. Can you wait just a minute? I need to check on something with Anna first."

Danny said okay, and Kip and Danny rounded the table in time to hear Carl say, "I read in the papers about the fire and wanted to offer my condolences on Holly's death."

"The whole business has been a terrible shock." Anna's voice sounded breathy, like she was having difficulty breathing. She dabbed her mouth with her napkin, though as yet the food hadn't arrived. Kip slid out Danny's chair to lift him into it, but Danny pulled back on Kip's hand, resisting. Kip didn't force the issue but stood behind his own chair with Danny beside him. Carl's hand fell away from Anna's shoulder.

"You remember Kip McTeer," Anna said, "and this is Holly's son, Danny."

In a sudden display of shyness, Danny buried his face against Kip's leg.

Carl straightened and fixed his pale blue eyes on Kip. "McTeer," he said and didn't offer his hand.

Kip met his gaze head-on, then pulled out his chair and sat with Danny on his lap.

With his leather jacket, his hair pulled back at the nape of his neck, and several days growth of stubble on his face, Carl looked like a bad-boy straight off a Hollywood set, except that his eyes were cold, icy cold. Even in high school, Carl Goddard had given him the creeps. Why was he suddenly seeing first his father and then him again?

Oblivious to the tension building at the table, the waitress came with the overflowing platter of seafood and a cheerful smile on her face. She placed plates on the table. "I'll be right back with some lemons and the hotdog."

After the waitress left, Carl leaned closer to Anna. "I read in the newspaper your house was badly burned, so where are you staying these days?"

It was the sort of innocent question anyone might ask, but there was something off about Carl Goddard, enough to make the hackles on the back of Kip's neck stand at attention. That gut feeling or instinct had saved him many times before. He acted on it now, answering for Anna before she could. "She's staying with friends."

"The police are watching my house," Anna added, obviously experiencing the same disquiet as he was.

"It's a shame the police can't watch all the time." His message delivered, Carl smiled and turned to leave. It wasn't a pleasant smile. "See you around."

A dangerous man, Kip thought, noting the bulge under his jacket where he concealed a gun. He would be the type to carry a knife as well. He watched Carl until he left the dining room. He was certain the meeting had been no accident. Carl had followed them. Somehow he'd gotten wind of Kip's inquiries about him at the police department, and he wanted to deliver a warning. Obviously, Carl had connections in places where he shouldn't have any. The thought was chilling.

"A scary man," Anna said behind her hand when he disappeared from sight. "He's changed since high school."

"Maybe we just didn't know him then. We weren't looking for ulterior motives. But I agree. He's a very scary man." Kip moved Danny onto the chair beside him, picked up a crab, pulled out some meat, and took a bite.

"Who's a scary man?" Danny looked at Anna.

"We were talking about someone you don't know, Honey. Have you tried your hotdog yet?"

Danny took a large bite. "Good," he said with his mouth full.

Kip shot Anna a grin over the boy's head that spoke his appreciation of the diversionary tactic.

"Can I go to the potty now?"

"Of course." Kip pushed his chair from the table then bent over to give the boy's wind-blown hair a rub. "Sorry about that, buddy. I forgot."

When they were a few feet from the table, Danny said, "I don't like that man."

Kip paused in mid-step, saddened the child had picked up more of the tension at the table than he'd realized. He gave Danny's hand a squeeze. "I don't like him much, either, but he's gone now."

When they returned to the table moments later, the tension had dissipated and the meal was filled with small talk and laughter. All the while, Kip was aware of Anna sitting across from him, and once in a while their gazes met, a mixing of warmth and apprehension as they cracked shells and devoured the delicious seafood feast. Even Danny shared in some crab and shrimp.

The meal over, a walk along the beach seemed a natural thing. To the strum of the ocean waves rolling against the shore, Kip and Anna walked side-by-side beneath the patchy clouds, not touching but bound nonetheless by the skein of their thoughts and the moments they were sharing. Ahead of them, Danny raced through the incoming tide, his childish giggle music to their ears. Never far from his newfound friend, Harlie, after waiting patiently in the car, bounded in and out of the water in carefree abandon, dutifully fetching whatever Danny found to toss.

Kip stopped to watch Danny throw a piece of driftwood into the waves, reluctant to change the light mood of the afternoon, but there was something he needed to tell Anna. "The Ft. Worth police discovered a bill for a safety deposit box in Holly's mail. The box is registered in her name, but you're listed as having permission to enter into it. You wouldn't by any chance have a key to it?"

Anna turned her head to look at him. She was obviously surprised by the revelation. "She never mentioned the box to me. Stanley's name isn't on it?"

"No. She rented it two months before she came to visit you. I was hoping she might have given you the second key."

"I wish she had. I suppose the police looked through her purse."

Kip shook his head. "They never found her purse. It must have burned or been stolen. You can expect the police to call you about the key."

"If Holly's murderer got it, he's had plenty of time to clean out the contents."

"It depends whether the bank is willing to let someone other than you or Holly into the box…"

Danny raced back to them and tugged Anna's hand. "Come here and see what I found."

Then his small hand found Kip's and tugged him forward as well.

The three of them stood side-by-side with the tide lapping their toes and the sandpipers racing all around them and oohed over the shell of a large horseshoe crab Danny had discovered.

"You live at that big house where I saw you the other time?" Danny asked.

It took Kip a few seconds to pick up on Danny's sudden change of subject. "Some of the time I live at Marsh Winds, yes, but I have a place to stay in California, too."

"Does Harlie go to that California place with you?"

Ah, the dog. "Most of the time she does. But sometimes I have to travel for a long time, so I leave her here with my mom."

"I wish I had a dog."

Chapter 18

Anna watched the clock on her bedside stand flash 4:17 a.m...4:18... She shivered and pulled the thin cotton comforter up under her chin, watching the eerie shadows play across the window screen, imagining they belonged to fingers and the sounds she'd been hearing this past half hour came from someone trying to get inside the apartment. She told herself she was being foolish. She told herself the shadows were nothing more than palm fronds and branches and the noises came from some animal scavenging for food. But it didn't dispel her fears. Something had awakened her.

After a few more minutes flashed off on her clock she forced herself to tip-toe to the window to look outside. For a long time she stared at the moonlit beach, the bright sky, the movement of the trees, straining to identify the source of every little sound. No crickets, no birds, little wind. Everything appeared quite ordinary. Still, she was uneasy. At length she grew weary and chilled and returned to her bed. But sleep was illusive.

Despite her best efforts to keep it at bay, her mind kept replaying the telephone conversation she'd had with Stanley in the wee hours of yesterday morning. In view of what she learned later that afternoon, she was on edge. The call reverberated in her head like a pounding headache.

"For goodness sake, Stanley, it's not even 6:00 AM. I'm not awake yet."

"Don't hang up, Anna. I need to talk to you."

She didn't hang up but sighed in annoyance. "All right. What's on your mind?" On the cot beside her bed, Danny was awake. She propped herself up on her elbows and glanced a reassuring smile at him. He reached for some match box cars and began to run them around the covers.

"Someone's after me."

She thought she heard anxiety in his voice. Whether it was real or feigned, she suddenly was alert and paying attention. She swung her feet over the side of her bed.

She cupped her hand around the receiver and kept her voice low. "Do you think this has anything to do with Holly's death?"

The pause was significant.

Her heartbeat faltered, then raced. You S.O.B.! She bit back apt names and angry words she wanted to shout at him. "Who's after you?" she hissed. "What are you trying to tell me? For goodness sake, you're a cop. Call the police department."

"I have a telephone number I want you to have. Hang on a second while I look for it on my cell. If something happens to me, you get the police to check it out, okay?"

She moved to the chair across the room in search of her purse, a piece of paper, and a pen. "Yes, okay. Give me the number."

He recited it. She said it back to him to be sure she had it right. Then she heard the distinct tones of an unknown male voice before the sound was muffled probably by Stanley's hand over the receiver. Hardly daring to breathe, she sank into the chair and strained to pick up the words. She thought he was alone, alone and afraid.

"What was that? Is someone with you?"

"No. You must have heard the radio. I'll turn it off."

Funny she hadn't noticed the radio earlier. When he was on the line once again, she said with a reasonableness she didn't feel, "Give me a name and address to go with the telephone number. Then call the police."

"Bud. His name was Bud Fields." He paused, and when he spoke again his voice was so low she strained to hear him. "Anna, be careful. I think there's something else this Fields guy wants." He swallowed and went on. His voice had taken on the whinny quality she'd always abhorred about him. "I want you to understand none of this would have happened if Holly..."

An explosion reverberated through the receiver and jerked her to her feet. For an instant she feared something had blown up in her own apartment. Recoiling, she glanced at Danny to be sure he was still playing with his cars, cupped her hand over the receiver, and half ran with the phone into the bathroom.

"What was that?" She closed the door. "Stanley, speak to me! What just happened?"

The phone was dead.

Anna kept the phone in her hand. Her immediate impulse was to call Kip, but she found it way too easy to rely on Kip McTeer. Besides, the last time she relied on him, he disappeared from her life for more than twelve years. She phoned the police department instead and relayed Stanley's call, giving them the telephone number, detailing the sound of what appeared to be an explosion before the sudden disconnect and that Stanley was a police officer at the Ft. Worth department.

Late yesterday afternoon Detective Bill Pennington of the Savannah Police Department showed up at her apartment to confirm that an explosion had occurred in the home owned by Holly and Stanley Everett and at the precise time indicated on her cell phone. A male's body, presumed to be one Stanley Everett had been found inside the house in what was thought to be the kitchen area. A cell phone had been discovered beside him. The preliminary investigation indicated the gas furnace had blown. In view of the recent fire at her home and the death of her sister, the investigation was proceeding on the assumption the explosion was the work of an arsonist.

Anna was still in shock.

Tonight something she couldn't explain had awakened her from a restless sleep. She was afraid, for herself, for Danny. Again she thought of phoning Kip. She glanced at the clock on her cell, 4:21 a.m., way too early to phone anyone, and tried to go back to sleep. When she looked at the time again, only five minutes had passed. She managed to lie there for fifteen more minutes before she gave up. She had to do something.

She grabbed the workout pants and sweatshirt she'd left in the chair the night before and slipped them on over her pajamas. After checking to see that Danny was still sleeping, she made her way to the kitchen in the dark and closed the bedroom door. She made a pot of coffee and tried not to think of what had happened to Stanley yesterday or relive the nightmare night her sister had been murdered. It was no use. Her mind was filled with images she couldn't dispel.

Not quite sure what to do with herself to pass the time until she could fix Danny's breakfast and take him to the kindergarten she'd enrolled him in last week, she picked up some magazines, plopped on the sofa and tried to thumb through them. She couldn't concentrate and tossed the magazines on the coffee table, got up, and went back to the bedroom to check on Danny. He was still sleeping peacefully. For a moment she watched him enviously. Then she walked out and closed the door again. The clock on the microwave flashed a bank of Os at her. She'd forgotten to set it.

The coffeemaker's clock was glowing 2:16. She knew that wasn't correct either, resisted the urge to return to the bedroom, get her purse and cell phone, and check the clock. She filled a mug with steaming coffee before it finished perking. She added some cream, carried it to a chair drawn close to a window overlooking the drive, and sat. She'd been staring out into the dark for several minutes before she realized the security light had gone out. She was pretty certain it had been working the night before.

She was still pondering the light when she became aware of the strange sounds coming from outside her window again, sounds she couldn't convince herself were just the wind in the trees or a neighbor out for an early run or even a raccoon rummaging through her trashcan. *I'm becoming delusional.* She tried to remain calm. When she'd come into the kitchen, she'd turned on several lights. Belatedly, she realized the windows had no shades and if anyone had a mind to take a shot at her, she would be a perfect target. But who would want to take a shot at her? Why? She decided she'd seen too many scary movies. That was all it was. She turned the lights off again anyway and moved back to the window by the light of the microwave.

She'd barely sat back down when she heard a sound that sent chills up her spine. A series of clicks that sounded like they came from the lock on the door to her garage. Had someone just breached her garage? She ran across the room into the bedroom for her cell. On the way she noticed Danny's bat lying in the entrance to the bathroom and picked it up.

She closed the door as quietly as she could, pressed the lock, knowing it wouldn't resist a swift kick, and called Kip's cell, praying he would pick up.

The phone rang and rang again.

Kip hadn't contacted Anna since their lunch together at the Crab Shack two days earlier. He was deliberately keeping his distance. It was better that way, but it was frustrating because she was never far from his thoughts. When he heard the gas heater had blown up Holly and Stanley Everett's house, killing Stanley, he worried Anna and Danny would be next. It was all he could do to resist driving over there and not leaving until the bad guys were dead or in jail. But it was obvious Anna hadn't forgiven him and wanted no part of him, so he stayed away and instead contacted his friend Bill Pennington of the Savannah police to make sure Anna's house was being watched.

No doubt about it, Anna Hanley had become a distraction. It was affecting his sleep. At 4:30 a.m. he was already on the porch putting on his running shoes. He'd been thinking of her, hoping she was safe, and thinking it was going to be a beautiful sunrise, one that would be made more beautiful if he shared it with her, and then berating himself for having such thoughts.

When the cell vibrated in his pocket, Kip frowned and slid his finger across the screen to check the caller ID. Anna. Alarm jolted through him. "Yes?"

"Oh, Kip, thank goodness I reached you. I'm sorry to call you so early."

"I was up. What's wrong?" He pressed his fingers to his eyes, knowing she wouldn't have called unless something was terribly wrong.

"I think someone is trying to get into the apartment."

Damn. He shot to his feet, already running into the house before she could finish her sentence. In the kitchen he pulled his mother's keys from the hook beside the back door then doubled back to his bedroom for his gun. "Where are you?"

"In the apartment, locked in the bedroom."

"Danny with you?" He dashed for the car with Harlie inches behind him. He opened the door for the dog, then jumped in after her.

"Yes, he's still asleep."

"All right. Let him sleep. Grab any weapon you can find, a chair, anything." Slamming the gear into reverse, he backed out then gunned the SUV down Marsh Wind's long drive with oyster shells spewing out behind him.

"I've got Danny's baseball bat."

"Good girl. Now you get behind the door with that bat. If you hear someone fumbling with the lock, wait until the person is inside the room, then hit and hit hard. Don't hesitate. You got that?"

"I won't hesitate."

That wouldn't help her much if there were two of them. "I take it the police aren't parked outside."

"No, once the movers took the salvageable things to storage, they weren't needed to protect from looters. But they're making periodic checks."

"Dammit," Kip hissed under his breath. What about protecting her? Kip felt like smashing a fist into one of them. He kept his thoughts and his anger from his voice. "I'm already on Highway 80. I'll be there in ten minutes."

She took a deep breath. "Did one of your buddies at the police department tell you Stanley was killed?" Her voice caught. "Holly's house burned to the ground."

"I heard." And I should have followed my instincts and gotten you out of there.

She was whispering, and he supposed it was in order not to wake up Danny.

"I haven't heard any more noises in the last few minutes. I'm sorry. I'm afraid hearing about Stanley's death has made me a little uptight. My imagination may have gotten the best of me. I was probably just hearing things—a raccoon or something."

He thought she wasn't a woman given to panic. "Maybe not. Stay put. No problem about the call. Like I said, I was up." Thinking of you, he thought, like I've been doing far too much since I saw you again.

"I was on the phone with Stanley when a blast went off."

She sounded shaken. Anyone would have been.

"So I heard." He'd planned to call her soon as the hour was reasonable.

For a moment she was silent, no doubt gathering herself. He wished there was something he could do to make it all better for her. "The police think the explosion was due to the furnace blowing. It might have been an accident." They both knew it wasn't, but he wanted to take the fear away from her. "Could be. You okay?"

"Yes," she cleared her throat. "Stanley sounded afraid. He said he wanted to give me a telephone number in case anything happened to him."

He knew but kept the information to himself. Pennington had told him last night and that the number Stanley gave her was one of the Walmart limited use phones and no longer in service. Bud Fields, he told him. The name could have belonged to dozens. The police were checking out a page of Fields and Field in the telephone book which could take weeks. And Kip's gut feeling was the name was as fictitious as the telephone number.

Another deep breath. "I wonder why he called me instead of the police."

Kip thought he knew and pressed on the gas. Down the straits across the marshlands Kip kept his mom's car at 90, barely slowing for the traffic lights when he approached the city of Tybee.

She went on, her voice steadier now, and he listened with few interruptions as she relayed the details of the call. "At first I thought he'd called because he was feeling remorse and wanted to apologize, but near the end of the conversation he made it clear he still blamed Holly. To his way of thinking Holly should have kept giving him the money for his gambling debts until he bled her dry. Can you believe him? He never admitted it was his fault. It made me sick. I was about to tell him what I thought of him when I heard the explosion. The phone went dead, and I never told him. He said they were coming after him. Turns out he was right."

"Before the blast did you hear anything unusual? Any suspicious sounds to indicate what was about to go down?"

"No. None. Wait. I did hear something. A few seconds before the blast I'm pretty sure I heard a man's voice. I asked him if someone was there. He said he had the radio on. Then he warned me to be careful. He thought the men he'd dealt with wanted something else."

Kip hadn't heard that. "Did he say what they were after?"

"No, he never did. That's when the explosion happened."

When he got to the end of the island, Kip careened off Highway 80 onto Butler. "I'm about three minutes from your place."

"You must have broken all speed records."

"Not much traffic this time of morning. You should see my headlights in a minute."

Kip heard her sigh of relief. "Anna, that doesn't mean all's clear. Stay put until I tell you to unlock the door. Before I come up I'm going to make a quick walk around the house. I just want to see if that coon you mentioned left any tracks. It may take a few minutes. You all right if I call you back?"

"Yes. Now that I know you're outside, I'll be fine."

Chapter 19

Kip retrieved his flashlight from the car and began his search of the grounds around the garage apartment first. He could see his breath in the damp air. He walked steadily without making a sound, all his senses alert. The flashlight beam led the way, his gun under the flap of his jacket and within easy reach.

The angle of his flashlight made the shadows long, but he well knew coon prints when he saw them and those of most other animals as well. It was the footprints of a man he saw circling the garage apartment that riveted his attention. There was a lot to be read in the prints. The man was wearing running shoes smoothed down from wear. He guessed the size to be 10½, perhaps 11, and the impression was fairly deep in the dew-damp sand. From that he gauged the man to be slightly of above average height and somewhat overweight, the perfect match to fit Carl Goddard, but it also fit millions of others.

The prints could belong to a workman, he surmised as he moved through the shadows, following the prints around the damaged sections of Anna's house where ladders and scaffolding signaled that work had started. The footprints crossed a stack of old boards piled beside the house for reuse, growing wider apart until they indicated a full run. If the man had been there on a clandestine mission, Kip expected he'd long since fled. But he'd seen many false trails, and there were many places to hide, in the trees, in the dunes, under the scaffolding. He didn't let down his guard.

At a footbridge that led to a road where cars were parked, the trail disappeared. Whoever the man was, he'd taken the trouble to park his car half a mile or more from Anna's house. Kip took note of the tag numbers of the two cars parked on the street. Both were local cars. Neither likely belonged to the person who'd been outside Anna's house.

He'd been gone far longer than anticipated. The tracks had been easy to follow. Too easy? Had he been drawn away deliberately? The thought made his stomach turn over. He turned and began to run.

As he ran he dialed Anna's cell. She picked up on the second ring.

"You all right?" he asked, disliking the breathiness of his voice. Six weeks ago he could have made such a short run without pulling a deep breath.

"Yes, where are you? You've been gone close to forty-five minutes."

"On the beach about a block from your house. Worried?" he teased, unable to help himself.

"Of course not. Just wondering. You did say you'd only be a few minutes." Her voice was clipped, sure, but he sensed she was smiling, and it warmed him.

He chuckled under his breath, but he was sure she could hear it. Quickly as it came the mirth drained from him. "No other strange noises? You still locked in the bedroom."

"I'm still in the bedroom. No other noises, but a car made wrong turn down the drive then turned around and left."

It might not be the same man he'd just followed to his car, but Kip didn't like the odds. He kept his tone impersonal, but he was worried more than he cared to admit. "You sure that car left the area?"

"I don't know. Harlie started barking in your car, and it sounded like the car came in a short distance, turned around, and drove away, but I suppose the driver could have turned off his lights and stopped."

That was exactly what he was thinking. "I'll be there in a few minutes."

"Seems like I heard that about forty-five minutes ago."

He didn't like what was going on, but of equal importance, he didn't like that he didn't have a handle on what was going on. Were the explosion in England that killed his wife and son, the attack on Anna's house resulting in her sister's death, and the hijacking and theft of the three hundred million all connected? And now Stanley's apparent murder—was that connected to the other seemingly disjointed events?

Stanley seemed hardly the type to be involved with some radical jihad group which is what his superiors suspected the stolen three hundred million dollars was to be used for. It was becoming clear that the information Holly had pieced together had put her in danger, but what did Anna have to do with any of it? Why was she being watched?

Maybe none of this had anything to do with the gambling ring and Holly and Stanley's murders. Then again maybe it did. Right now it was the only link they had that joined the events.

Kip realized a personal vendetta against him wouldn't be far-fetched. In his line of work he'd made many enemies. Most of them were either dead or behind bars. And he hadn't seen Anna in at least twelve years. There were some important pieces to the puzzle he was missing.

He stopped at the car and let Harlie out then trotted up the steps two at a time with his dog at his heels.

"Okay, you can open up," he said into his phone. "I'm outside your door. By the way, this lock doesn't look like it's been tampered with." When she opened the door to him, she looked up at him with a smile that brightened her eyes and damaged his heart. For a second he couldn't speak. Then he cleared his throat unnecessarily. "Sorry it took me so long."

"I'm just glad you're here."

"Is it all right to let Harlie inside?"

"Of course it is. We love dogs here." She pushed back a wisp of hair from her face and tucked it behind her ear and lowered her voice. "You must have found something."

He gave a nod and took a walk around the counter of her kitchen to collect his thoughts. On the way he spotted Danny who stood half-asleep in the threshold of the bedroom door. He greeted him with a hand ruffling through his sleep-spiked hair. "Hi-ya, buddy."

Kip helped himself to a cup of coffee. "That door over there by the front door—is it a closet or does it connect to the garage?"

"It connects. My grandmother had it cut in when she lived here so she wouldn't have to go outside from the apartment to her car. Why?"

With a glance at Danny who was wrestling with Harlie on the floor, he came up close to Anna and spoke quietly.

"Someone forced the lock to the side door of your garage. I think if we open this door from the apartment to the garage, we'll find the lock jimmied. The downstairs door was cracked open a few inches, when I arrived. I peeked inside with my flashlight but didn't see anyone, then thought I might have a better chance to catch him if I followed his tracks."

Fear flashed in her eyes, and she sank into a chair at the kitchen table, blowing out a long breath. He wondered if he should have thought of a better way to tell her, decided she was strong enough to handle it, but he was sorry for having to frighten her again.

"I feel pretty sure someone was in there and got scared off when he heard my car."

"So he's gone?"

"Long gone. I followed his tracks around the house then on down the beach for about half a mile to a boardwalk leading to a cul-de-sac. A few cars were parked there, but he was gone. I seriously doubt he'll be back as long as he sees a car here, but I think you should call the police."

He took his coffee to the table and sat beside her while she dialed. He could see she was upset. Anyone would be. Still, she hadn't reacted with panic like most women would, and her explanation to the police was concise without any hysteria. When she'd finished talking, he set down his cup. "Why do you think someone is watching you, Anna? Is there something you haven't told me?"

She gave him a level look then shook her head. She was beautiful and her mouth was kissable, but underneath at her core she was strong—strong enough to hold out on him? He wasn't sure. There was no denying there was still a physical attraction between them, but the girl he'd fallen in love with had been in high school. He hadn't seen or heard from her in years.

He rocked his chair back on two legs, his fingers laced on his lap, and waited for her to come forth with something new. When she remained silent, he said, "I think a key piece of evidence must still be here, or at least someone thinks it is. From what you said, Stanley hinted as much. That someone's willing to risk a great deal to see it's not found."

"I can't imagine what it could..." She stopped suddenly and looked across the room at her sister's son who was spelling with "Word Girl" on the public broadcasting channel, then shook her head like the thought that struck her was too preposterous to even consider. He raised one eyebrow and waited for this here-to-forgotten thought to be revealed.

At length she raised her chin heavenward and sucked in a sharp breath. "It just occurred to me that the killer may not be sure I didn't see his face when I ran into the front room. What's more, if his face wasn't covered, Danny probably saw it, too, at the window perhaps, when the murderer made sure my sister was in the room. Oh, my God..." She brought a hand half-way to her mouth, lowered it. "Do you know what that means? The killer may not be a stranger at all. He may be someone Holly knew and Danny and I can identify."

A muscle jumped in Kip's jaw. "It makes perfect sense. If Holly saw him at the window, he had to make sure she didn't expose him. That's why he made sure she was dead and didn't leave her fate to the fire alone."

"That's why he's still hanging around here. To tie up loose ends. What's more, I forgot to tell you that on the phone earlier Stanley said the man who first contacted him told him he had lived in Savannah when he was a child. He told Stanley he knew both Holly and me. He could have been lying, but perhaps not. Then again, the name Stanley gave me, Bud Fields, doesn't ring a bell."

"In all probability it's not his real name."

"Carl Goddard?"

Kip took his coffee and came to sit beside her. "That's the first name that jumps to mind. Or Stanley himself, but now that ol' Stan is gone, only Goddard is left. Neither of them would likely work alone. Neither strikes me as the type to be the brains behind a big operation like what this is beginning to look like. Someone else is behind it all. There are probably several layers protecting the mastermind."

"If it was Carl, why would he come to our table like that?"

"Maybe it was a test to see if either you or Danny showed signs of recognition."

It wasn't that Kip hadn't thought of the possibility the killer thought Anna could identify him, but that she might know the killer was an angle he'd dismissed. The crime seemed against Holly but it sounded like the perp knew both sisters. "Do you recall your sister shouting anything before the explosion?"

"I was broiling crab and had the vent on. She could have shouted, but I didn't hear it. I only heard the explosion and then, after I'd moved from the stove, I heard Danny's crying."

"But your hypothesis is a good one. It puts a new light on something I just now recalled Danny saying at the restaurant the other day. He told me he didn't like 'that guy.' I assumed he meant Carl and chalked it up as him picking up on the tension at our table. Now I have to wonder if Danny recognized Carl."

In his pocket Kip's cell phone vibrated. He pulled it out to check the caller's I.D. It was Barry, so he took the call. "Hang on a minute." Then he spoke to Anna. "Excuse me, Anna, I need to answer this." He said her name clearly and deliberately so Barry wouldn't begin to talk and give away his identity. Then he shoved Anna's laptop across the table toward her. "It may take a few minutes. I think it'd be wise if you wrote out your conversation with Stanley as exactly as you can remember while it's fresh in your mind. Don't spare any details."

He carried the phone outside to the stairway landing. Before he spoke he closed the door.

"You got my message."

"Anna Hanley?"

Kip laughed. "What other Anna do I know in Savannah?" Then he sobered. "Someone's been hanging around her house. The lock to the garage side door was forced..." He briefed him on the recent activities. "I need for you to check out a number for me. The police should already have it, but she just gave it to me. It's the contact number Stanley used. Police say it's a disposable cell, but I'd like you to check it out anyway. He recited the number Anna had given him from memory."

Barry whistled under his breath and repeated the number. "How'd you get that?"

"Stanley gave it to Anna over the phone yesterday morning before he was blown-up. He also warned her she was in danger. I'll fill you in on the details when I have more time."

"Do I hear sirens?"

"Police. Anna called them a few minutes ago."

"I'll get on the number immediately. Anything else?"

"Goddard Financial. I've been checking it out. I sent you a fax earlier this morning with what I dug up. See what you can add to it—financial status, personnel, backgrounds of personnel. By the way, right now Anna's writing down everything she can remember from yesterday's phone conversation before Stanley's house blew. I'll email it to you when she's finished. Might be something we can use in there. And get a report on Stanley's death, everything that's available. Oh, and Carl Goddard, you got any more information on him?"

"I faxed some to you earlier, too. Not a nice guy is your Carl Goddard. He's particularly fond of lighting fires."

"Interesting. I'll get right on what you faxed soon as I get to the house, and Barry, Danny may have recognized the murderer. He's afraid of Carl Goddard, says he's a bad man. Of course, it could be something else."

"Want me to have him picked up for questioning?"

"Not yet. Let's not tip our hand. Maybe he'll lead us to someone else. I'll pull some strings with the local boys here to see about putting a tail on Goddard."

"What about his old man?"

"A slimy fellow, but at this point I don't have any evidence he's involved in this."

The first of two police cars skidded to a stop in the drive. Kip recognized Bill Pennington, a high school football teammate, as he exited his squad car and waved.

"I got to go. Cavalry has arrived."

"Better get Anna and the kid out of there to where you can keep an eye on them."

"That's my plan. Thought I might set them up at Marsh Winds, but I figure it'll be a hard sell. Anna's pretty independent."

"Must be something the women in Savannah are eating..." Barry laughed. "I'll be in touch."

Kip disconnected and held his hand out to Pennington who was trotting up the steps toward him. "Good to see you, Bill."

"Likewise. Nick Howell told me you were in town recovering from a motorcycle accident or something."

"Something like that."

"Glad to see you're up and about. So tell me what's going on here."

"Let me show you something first." Kip ushered Pennington back down the steps, acknowledging the officers who'd accompanied him as Pennington identified them. Then he indicated the tracks he'd found along the side of the house. "I followed these to Palmetto court."

"Ah-ha, that would account for the call we had about a prowler in that area. The guy was in his garage, about to drive to the airport to catch an early flight."

"Did he happen to see a car pull away?"

"He did. It piqued his curiosity because except for himself and his family the other homes on the street are vacant at this time of year. He was curious to find out if it was someone he knew, so apparently he was about to walk out to the street when he noticed a man checking out the cars parked there. Presumably that was you. Anyway, that's when he decided to call 911."

"A cautious man," Kip said as they returned to the back steps. "Did he by chance pick up the make or model of the car?"

"It was still dark, and he couldn't be sure, but he thought it could be a Camry, dark blue or black. He couldn't see to make note of the tag number—he was more interested in what a man was doing checking cars at 4:50 AM. I only talked to him from his cell, but he'll be back in Savannah next week. What's your interest in all this?"

"Anna."

The door opened and Anna stepped onto the deck with Danny tucked under a protective arm. "Hello, Bill," she said, her voice quiet. "I'm sorry you had to travel out here again. It seems you've had to do an awful lot of that these past few weeks, but thanks for coming."

"It's my job, but I'm sorry you've had more trouble again, Anna, and so soon after the fire."

"Not your fault. Come on in. Danny and I have been talking about making some pancakes for breakfast. We hope you all will join us."

"No thanks to the pancakes, but I wouldn't say no to a cup of coffee, if you have any. But first let me take a few photos and make a few impressions of the prints Kip found around your house before someone contaminates them."

Twenty minutes later Bill took a seat across from Anna at her kitchen table and pulled out a small portable recorder from his pocket. "Mind if I record this? Much easier than taking notes or having you make a trip to the station."

While Anna relayed the details of the attempted break-in to Bill, Kip rocked his chair back and tried to focus on the overall picture. Stanley's involvement was becoming clearer, but why Anna's sister was murdered remained a mystery. His mind kept coming back to Holly's notes. What in the notes was so damning it drove someone to want to kill Holly? Was the arsonist after Anna as well? Whatever it was, he hadn't been able to uncover it. What was he missing?

Why didn't the person who ordered Holly hit wait until she returned to Ft. Worth? Did the murderer have a timeframe? Was Holly about to expose something else and him in the process? If so, did the information go to the grave with her? By all accounts, she was a good investigator, thorough, but the information on her computer and in her notes and the few notes she'd left on her computer at the newspaper where she worked didn't appear to be of enough value to precipitate her murder. Why burn the house? Why not simply rob the place?

Maybe Holly's information became too personal so she tucked it away. Maybe it was connected to her affair with Danny's father, maybe not. Right now Kip's only leads rested on Stanley Everett and the ring of gamblers he was associating with, but he suspected Stanley and the other gamblers were the tip of an iceberg. Now that Stanley was dead it looked more and more like Kip was going to have to make a trip to Ft. Worth to check out the contents of the safety deposit box Holly had rented. Something in there might click something else in place.

Thanks to Nick Howell at the Police Department Kip had been able to examine the trigger device of the IED used at Anna's house and determine it was indeed the same make-up as the one that killed Marie and Patrick three summers ago. Since then, to Kip's certain knowledge the same type of device had been discovered and catalogued four other times. One was set off in a post office in broad daylight. In that incident three people were burned, one bad enough to succumb a month later, and oddly, another man who was thought to have been in the post office minutes before the blast was found knifed to death that night on the street not far from there.

A similar device was used to set off an explosion that killed three people in the office of an insurance business in Atlanta, an African American and his girlfriend and a man of Middle Eastern nationality who worked in the office.

On one occasion the device failed. But the explosion prior to the one at Anna's house killed a woman sleeping in her house. The woman was wealthy and had been in the throes of a nasty divorce. There was insufficient evidence to point to the husband's guilt, and no arrest was made. As of yesterday, when Kip made a check, the case remained unsolved as did all the other bombings. So far there appeared to be no connection between all of them except the device which led Kip to speculate the murders could have been perpetrated by a hired assassin.

With the exception of the incident in England all the explosions occurred within the borders of the southern United States. Other than that it occurred in England, what made the murder of his family different was that so many were killed, fourteen, and many others hospitalized. That explosion, possibly the first committed by Holly's killer, was by far the most powerful. Was it a coincidence that this last device was the same as the others? He didn't believe in coincidences. The killer or whoever hired the killer had an ego. He was leaving a trail, but what was his agenda? Who had hired him? How could Holly's death possibly have been connected to the death of his Marie and Patrick? Yet it seemed they might be.

Anna finished her story and Bill's voice broke into Kip's thoughts. "Good to see you again, Kip."

Kip stood and shook the hand Bill held out. "Why don't you and Jenny come on over to the house for a beer on Saturday?" Kip said. "We can catch up. Bring the kids."

"Sounds good to me, but I better check with the wife. I'll give you a call. How long you planning to stick around?"

"A week, maybe two, then I'll head on back to California. However, the business seems to be doing just fine without me." He chuckled.

Bill turned to Anna. "You better see to getting those locks replaced right away. We'll cruise by here regularly, but that's no guarantee the perpetrator won't come back." Outside on the deck, he stopped and glanced at her house. "When did they start reconstruction?"

"Yesterday, well, mostly they've just been hauling away the debris. The insurance man came the day before with the moving crew. They had it all packed up and taken to storage by nightfall. So after all these days of waiting, things are beginning to move."

After Detective Pennington drove away, Kip turned to Anna. "I'll have some of those pancakes, if the offer's still open. Why don't I cook them while you start packing? You and Danny are coming to Marsh Winds."

Anna swung around from pulling the bowl of pancake batter from the refrigerator and slammed it on the counter. "You used to tell me what to do when I was seventeen. I didn't like it then either."

"Yes you did. It was part of the macho-male thing you loved," he said with a grin, enjoying teasing her again.

"Anyway, I'm not leaving."

Kip got still, his eyes narrowing, then he crossed the room with an unhurried pace. "And exactly what do you plan to do when—it's *when* not *if* he comes back? We both know he'll be back. There's something he's looking for, and I can't be much help to you and Danny when I'm fifteen minutes away."

Chapter 20

Carl Goddard worked his way through the plush chairs and contented diners and took a seat at the table overlooking River Street where the boats were moving up and down the Savannah River and where his grandmother waited. In the far corner of the room a woman played soft classical on the piano, fresh flowers adorned all the tables, and the waiters wore black pants and bowties with pressed white shirts and talked in hushed tones.

"You've been hard to reach, Carl. Where have you been these past few days?"

Carl ran a finger around the collar of his new dress shirt and loosened the tie. "Not eating in places like this, let me tell you."

"Once in a while it's good for you to experience the finer things in life," Mabel said, straightening the bodice of her dark purple dress.

"I was in the middle of something."

"You're always in the middle of something. Tell me what is it this time?"

He shook his head. "You don't want to know."

"All right." Mabel turned to the waiter who'd come up to the table and was standing with menus in hand.

"Good evening, may I get you something to drink before dinner?" He placed a menu in front of both of them.

"I'll have a dirty martini, two olives. And I suppose he'll have some sort of beer." Mabel crinkled her nose with distaste. "What would you like?"

"A Bud."

"Very well." The waiter straightened the menus in front of them then recited the specials from memory. "While you look over the menus I'll get your drinks."

Mabel picked up her menu and flipped through the pages. "What exactly was in those papers that was so important, Carl? What did Stanley's wife know?"

"How the hell would I know? I didn't read them. Don't guess I'll ever know what all Holly Everett knew, but she sure as hell recognized me when I bumped into her that afternoon on the beach. I was reconnoitering, so to speak, and she was lying on the beach with her sister, soaking in the rays. She happened to sit up as I walked past."

"Sometimes, you can be a very stupid man, Carl. What happened when she recognized you? Did she say anything?"

"No, not even a hello—always was an uppity piece of you know what. I turned away, and like I said, she was talking with her sister, but it's no big deal she recognized me. We've known each other for a long time."

"So why are you even telling me about it? And what about Anna? Did she see you, too? If she did..."

"No way she saw me. Her back was to me."

"You're sure about that?"

"What is this—the third degree? Yes, I'm sure. I walked on past, and shortly they got up and returned to the house. End of story."

"For all our sakes, let's hope so." The waiter returned with the drinks, and Mabel closed her menu. "In Savannah, one should go with seafood. I think I'll have the salmon with lemon-caper sauce."

Carl ordered a sirloin steak and a baked potato and dug into the hot bread.

Mabel shrugged out of her black shawl and leaned back in her chair, not overly concerned by the attitude of her only grandson. He'd always had a rebellious streak in him, a person with little affection for those around him and too much for himself.

"I've been keeping up with the investigation on the fire at Anna Hanley's place. The police have been providing the senator with the case reports. A messy job, Carl," she said.

"What do you mean messy? I got the job done."

"Not from what I've been reading. Much of the house didn't burn. That means some of Holly Everett's papers may have survived. The man isn't happy."

Carl put his fork down and reared back. "How was I to know Holly's sister would use the hose? Then this guy came along—"

"Loose ends, Carl. Loose ends. They need to be cleaned up. A lot's at stake here. Would you recognize the man if you saw him again—the one who pulled Holly's sister and Holly's son onto the beach?"

Carl shook his head. "He'd be dead if I did."

Mabel looked up from spooning the sauce over her salmon. "By the way, Kip McTeer isn't dead either. Another botched job, Carl."

Carl cut off a large hunk of steak and forked it toward his mouth, stopping inches before putting it in. "Yeah, I know. I was goin' to tell you tonight."

"How would you know?"

"Remember I know him from high school. I was cleaning up some of those loose ends you were talking about and followed him and Holly's sister and Holly's kid to the Crab Shack a few days ago. I stopped by their table to say hello."

Mabel thought Carl didn't have the common sense of a spider that strolls in front of a snake's mouth. What was he thinking exposing himself like that? "You got a death wish, Carl?"

"McTeer doesn't scare me."

"He should scare you, Carl. Don't underestimate him. I've seen him in action, and certainly he scares me." As if to illustrate her point, she shivered and reached for her shawl to pull it over her shoulders. Hearing it confirmed that McTeer wasn't only alive but in town gave her goosebumps.

With insight that surprised Mabel, Carl reached a hand to her forearm and gave it a pat. "It's all right, Gram. I'll take care of him for you."

"Take care of the girl, too. Holly's sister," Mabel snapped, revealing more of her passion than she intended. "Holly may have talked to her before she died." Mabel was thinking of the photograph of Holly and Senator Norton on the yacht. Had Holly told her sister about the affair? How deep had Holly Everett been able to penetrate the layers of protection that covered the man who gave the orders?

In her mind Mabel pictured the man's handsome face and piercing eyes. Only last week he had been on the cover of *Time*. They'd come so far together.

Anna watched Danny and Harlie parade down the steps of Marsh Winds after Kip like he were the Pied Piper, then shut the door to the bedroom behind them, wishing she were indifferent to Special Forces Agent Kip McTeer. If she didn't care for him, if she didn't feel the need to protect Danny, she wouldn't have so easily been convinced to abandon the carriage house apartment to move into Marsh Winds.

Three weeks ago she'd been happily engaged to Dennis Sadler and planning her wedding. Holly had been alive, and her life had been moving along at a comfortable pace. Since then everything had changed. Suddenly she found herself with a four-year-old son in her care and moving into her high school sweetheart's home. Hands clenched at her side, she stared at the closed door. She could still hear Danny's giggles and Kip's low voice as they trotted the steps in happy camaraderie. Damn. She was falling back in love with Kip McTeer.

Anna shook her head. Such thinking wasn't going to get her anywhere. She turned her back to the door and drew in a calming breath. The room was delightful, sunny and fresh with a king-sized bed, fireplace, and a loveseat and coffee table. A breeze was coming through a bank of open windows at the far side of the room. She ignored the packed laundry hamper and suitcase deposited in the middle and headed for the windows. Beneath the soles of her tennis shoes, the heart-of-pine creaked, somehow a friendly sound. She paused to admire the muted blues and greens of the over-sized Oriental rug, loving the colors and thinking they perfectly matched the subtle pattern of the quilted spread and the soft sea green color of the walls. Whoever had decorated the room had given it an air of springtime and openness.

Anna unlatched the cottage shutters of a window, pushed them open, then hitched her hip on the deep recess of the sill. Outside, she could see the long arms of the massive Live Oaks embrace one another above the oyster-shell drive. Swaying from their limbs, Spanish Moss seemed to wave hello to her, and Anna smiled.

She ran her fingertips over the thick paneled sill, noting how stout the walls must be to create such deep window recesses. Marsh Winds, Kip had once told her with pride, had been built in the middle 1700s in the years that General

Oglethorpe had founded the colony of Georgia. For all the years since, the plantation house had welcomed in and bid farewell to generations of McTeers as it housed and protected them all. What memories it carried within its walls. What stories it would tell, if only it could. Anna felt the strength in the house, and unbidden the thought came into her mind the house wasn't unlike its owner Kip McTeer. She breathed, sucking deep into her lungs, into her soul, the peace and quiet the old home offered her, the protection, and she couldn't help but wonder what the end to her story would be. Would the old plantation house be there to witness the end?

Behind her she heard the door open then a suitcase and a box settle onto the floor.

"That's the last of it," Kip said.

Anna turned to see Danny and Kip standing side-by-side inside the doorway with smiles on their faces, looking so much like father and son, she couldn't hold back her own smile. In one of his hands Danny clutched a supermarket shopping bag filled with his toys. A football was tucked through his other arm.

Rising, Anna said, "Good job, men. Thank you." Then she lifted her gaze to Kip. "You know, in all the times I've been in your home, I don't believe I've ever been in this room before. It's beautiful."

"You wouldn't have wanted to see it back when you were last up here. It was Dylan's room and a clutter of posters, trophies and other high school paraphernalia."

"Sounds like what yours looked like."

Kip chuckled. "Pretty much. After Dylan got married and went to work in South Carolina, Mom redecorated it." Kip walked to the far wall of the room where there was an antique armoire between two doors. He bypassed the first door, explaining it was a walk-in closet, and ushered her through the door that stood ajar. "Come here and let me show you the bathroom."

Anna complied, expecting to see a small, attractive bathroom like ones usually found in the older homes of Savannah. She was amazed to see the room was large and modern. Painted off-white, it had twin sinks, a tiled shower, and wondrously, an old-fashioned tub raised on feet that overlooked the same view Anna had just been admiring. "Wow, this is lovely."

"When we kids left the roost, Mom had some time on her hands. When she renovated this room, I think she was planning for the future and grandkids and hoping we'd all come back."

"Where did your mom find the space to enlarge it so much?"

"Originally a room to store trunks and a small bathroom were between this room and the one it connects to. This bedroom and the room next door are the only ones that share a bathroom. All the others have their own."

Anna noted the pride in his voice, and she couldn't blame him. "If your ancestors could only see the place now... I would think you would find it hard to stay away from a place like this."

For a second before he shrugged with practiced indifference, his eyes darkened. "At times it's very hard."

It revealed so much about him, and it hit her afresh exactly what kind of man Kip McTeer really was to sacrifice so much so that others might live in freedom.

"Thank you," she said in a soft voice.

"For what?" He turned to face her, incredulous. "I've done nothing."

Her words had taken him by surprise. She had surprised herself by saying them. Hadn't meant to say them. But she felt them. Had felt them ever since she heard the news that his wife and son were murdered in England. It was too much for a man to have to sacrifice.

"Yes you have—you and the rest of the armed forces. You've done a lot—for our country, for our way of life."

Clearly he was ready with a light retort, but he changed his mind, and looking uncomfortable whispered half under his breath. "Thank you..."

His nostrils distend with the emotion packed inside of him, and she yearned to take him in her arms and hold him, just hold him, like she'd done so many years ago, but they weren't sweethearts anymore.

The sound of a car on the drive broke the tension in the room. He leaned over the tub to look out the window then cleared his throat. "Mom's back. Follow me, and I'll show you the room where Wendy stayed and where Mom thought Danny might like to sleep. Need some help with that bag, buddy?"

"I got it." Danny hefted the bag a little higher from the floor and part carried and part dragged it across the bathroom."

Harlie barged past him and through the door at the other end. Anna followed, pausing to admire the elegant simplicity of the bathroom's décor and to run her fingertips over the plush white towels embroidered with white scallop shells.

When Anna walked into the room to be Danny's, she very nearly sighed. The room was set up perfectly to be a kid's room with its off-white walls, bunk beds covered in bright red, white and blue plaid quilts, bookshelves filled with games and books. One section of the large room had been set up for play with a large round rug, a small table and chairs and an old trunk converted into a toy box.

Over Danny's head, Kip said to Anna. "When I told her you would be coming, she must have run up here and changed the quilts. I think Wendy had Mermaids or Tinkerbell or some such motif on the beds." He laughed.

"That was nice of her. The room is wonderful, but wasn't it Lawton's room?"

"Once it was, but Lawton decided he wanted his room on the third floor so he could have peace and quiet to get away and study when the family got too rowdy."

"And yours? Did you move upstairs by Lawton?"

He shook his head. "No, mine, if you can call it that, when I'm only here so rarely, is still on the river side of the house beside Robyn's. You probably remember it."

"It's not *that* many years ago," she said on an exhalation of breath and looked away from him, suddenly filled with memories of the only time she'd been in his room. Earlier that night he'd been awarded a MVP trophy in football for his high school, not his first, but her first time to attend the banquet with his family. The banquet was over, his parents on to another engagement. They were madly in love. The house was empty, drawing them. She remembered that moonlight streamed through his bedroom window, and they'd almost made love on his bed until the sound of his parent's car cut it short. She remembered the scent of him on his sheets and the jolt of excitement that ran through her when she saw all of him without his clothes. She remembered the crush of disappointment at the sound of tires on the oyster-shell drive and their mad dash to put their clothes back on.

"Of course I remember." So did he, she thought, noting the quiver of mirth around his mouth as he studied his feet.

"I'd like to take you back in there right now and finish what we started." He lifted his gaze to meet hers, a slow grin spreading his lips. "How about it, Anna?"

Already halfway up the ladder to the bunk bed, Danny said, "Can I sleep on the top?" Gazes still locked, Anna and Kip both laughed.

Behind them the door opened and Kip's mother walked through with her arms opened in welcome. "I thought I heard laughter in here. Oh, Anna, I'm so glad Kip persuaded you to come. After what happened to Holly, I worry about you over there all alone until the arsonist is caught." She embraced Anna. "Sorry I didn't get back in time to help you unload."

"I had lots of good help, thanks. Anyway there wasn't much to unload. Now that the police have finally let me back in the house I've been able to rescue some clothes, but mostly those are at the cleaners," Anna laughed. "You're so generous to invite me."

"Purely selfish, I assure you. The house seems empty since Dylan and his family left. I need a little person to play with." She reached up to where Danny was hanging his head over the rail of the top bunk and gave his hair a rub. "How do you like your new room?"

"Cool."

"Good. Now if you folks will excuse me, I'll leave you to get settled in." Sarah turned to her son. "I could use a hand carrying in the groceries."

Chapter 21

Kip sagged down into his favorite chair with a beer, content to leave Anna and his mother finish up preparing the dinner. Danny was stirring up some Brownies for dessert.

He dialed Barry's number. When he answered, Barry asked, "Where are you now?"

"At home."

"Good. Sorry to disrupt your quiet evening, but Col. Harrison wants us both in Ft. Worth posthaste. Yesterday the police at your end identified a mangled key they found in Holly's purse as belonging to a safety deposit box. Previously it had been thought to be a key to a shed and mislabeled. With the help of the banks, they think they've found the box in the First Federal in Ft. Worth."

Kip gave a low whistle. "That was quick."

"They phoned some possible names to the Ft. Worth banks, and late yesterday one called back with a box registered to a H. Hanley, not too hard to find. The colonel thought you'd like to be there when they drilled it. But Harrison emphasized if you aren't feeling up to it, you're not to go."

"I'm fine. What time do we leave?"

"You're booked on Southwestern tonight, the 9:15 flight to Atlanta. We'll meet up at the airport and fly together to Ft. Worth. The colonel briefed me on some other developments. We can go over them on the flight. You're sure, Kip? Anna could be vulnerable."

Kip was thinking the same thing. He wasn't of a mind to let Anna out of his sight. That someone had been prowling around her apartment scared him more than he cared to admit, but he had a job to do. "I figure I should have some time before our arsonist discovers she's staying here." *Unless it's Carl.* Carl would be able to make a good guess pretty fast, knowing his prior relationship with Anna. "Any more information on Stanley?"

"No, the police are checking the DNA of the body they pulled from the fire with some hairs found in Stanley's car. It'll take a few days."

"All right, I'll meet you in Atlanta. Meanwhile, I'll get a tail set up on Carl."

"Good idea. Nick Howell is on his way to your house with the key. By the way, he's the one who figured out it was a safety deposit key. See you tonight."

Kip disconnected. The question was how much time did he have before the arsonist figured out where Anna was staying? Kip made up his mind to ask Nick to keep an eye on her and Danny while he was gone. Harder would be getting Anna to stay around the house until he got back. Hopefully, that would be before his mother left on her cruise.

The doorbell rang, and Sarah called from the kitchen door. "That's probably Evan. I forgot to tell you he was coming for dinner, too. Do you mind getting it, Kip? My hands are full of meatloaf."

Expecting to see Nick Howell or Evan Schroeder, Kip was surprised to see a man he'd never met standing on the doorstep. It took him about ten seconds to recognize him, and he thought it was a measure of how long he'd been out of the field recovering that it took him that long. The last time he'd seen Dennis Sadler was at Holly's funeral. Anna's fiancé had been standing with his arm around her, consoling her in her grief, while Kip had ridden by in a taxi to take some photos. As recognition came, Kip's first thought was to wonder how the hell Dennis Sadler had found Anna at Marsh Winds in such short order. His impulse was to tell him Anna wasn't here and shut the door.

Kip's quiet tone, his easy stance, were meant to mislead. He held out his hand. "I don't believe we've ever met. I'm Kip McTeer."

"Dennis Sadler. You're Robyn's brother. I've heard a lot about you from your sister. It's an honor to meet you."

"Don't believe all you've heard. She tends to exaggerate."

Dennis looked up, smiling, and Kip could see the charm in his smile. "Anyway, I'm sorry to barge in on you like this. If Anna's here, I'd like to talk to her."

"Last I saw Anna was in the kitchen with my mother." Kip closed the door, deciding Dennis Sadler was a far more handsome man up close than in the photos he'd taken. "I'll show you the way."

Laughter greeted them as they approached the kitchen, and Kip wondered if his mother was regaling Anna with stories of some of the infamous McTeers in their past. A fire burned in the raised hearth of the breakfast alcove, and the room had the warm and cheerful feeling Kip remembered as a kid. With its expansive open views of the marsh and river, the kitchen was one of his favorite places in the house.

His mother wore her customary apron. Her cheeks were flushed from laughter and the heat of the fire. She put a meatloaf into the oven and turned to Anna to speak a few words only she was meant to hear. Standing at the sink, Anna snapped some beans into a colander and laughed. She looked so at home in his kitchen with his mother, Kip swallowed down the surge of regret for what could never be.

Kip let Dennis precede him through the doorway. "Anna, you have a visitor..."

Both women turned. Anna gave an involuntary gasp. "Dennis." She dropped a handful of beans into the sink and reached for a dishtowel. "I'm surprised to see you. How did you know I was here?"

Kip rested a shoulder against the door jamb and listened for his answer. Obviously, he needed to plug the leak.

Dennis walked over to give Anna a kiss on her cheek. "A stroke of luck, actually. When you weren't at your place, I phoned a couple of your friends, including Robyn. Robyn told me she'd spoken with your mother not ten minutes earlier and that you were staying at Marsh Winds for a few days. I can't tell you how relieved I was to hear it. When you didn't answer my calls, I worried something happened to you."

Anna opened her mouth and closed it again, swallowing whatever she was going to say. But her mouth tightened with what Kip recognized as annoyance. Kip suppressed his smile. He would have liked to stay there and watch the discourse unfold, but another knock sounded on the front door. As he was the closest to the door he gestured his mom back and went to answer it with Harlie five steps ahead of him.

A surge of pleasure rushed through Kip when he opened the door to Nick Howell. Though they'd talked on the phone or e-mailed on occasion, he hadn't seen him since Nick retired from service five years ago. At six feet four, two hundred forty-five pounds of muscle, except for the different uniform, Nick looked the same. Kip offered his hand then pulled his old friend into a hug.

"Good to see you."

"Same here." Nick's Bronx accent was pronounced despite having lived in the south for the past four years. "If I knew you lived in such a great place I might have come around sooner and not waited until business brought me here. Glad to see you're recovering."

"Better every day. Just don't ask me to arm wrestle. Tell me how you've been. Come on. Let's take a walk down to the dock while we talk."

"Sure, but before I forget, let me give you the key." Nick pulled a Tyvek envelope from his back pocket and handed it to Kip with a chuckle. "Wife would kill me if I forgot to give it to you and had to leave again tonight. It's our daughter's third birthday, and she's having some friends over."

Kip trotted down the steps with Nick on his heel, and they headed around the house with Harlie leading the way. "Three years old. Hard to believe. How many kids you got now?"

"Just the one but another's due in January—a girl, too. Come over and join the celebration tonight. When I told Sheri where I was going, she insisted I ask you to join us. She's anxious to meet you. I got lucky. She's a great gal."

"I figure she must be to nab you. Wish I could take you up on the offer, but I've got orders to go to Ft. Worth in a couple of hours—put that key to good use, I hope. That brings up another reason why I've corralled you out here. I've got a favor to ask. Anna Hanley's here—"

"I noticed the cars. I thought you were having a party."

"Not intentionally."

Nick laughed, and Kip led them out onto the pier where a covered picnic area had been built with benches, table, and a sidebar with a sink for cleaning fish.

Nick chose a bench that faced the river and sagged onto it. "Beautiful place you got here. You ought to retire and come back to live."

"Unfinished business out there, Nick."

Nick leaned back and stretched out his legs with an exhalation of breath. "Ahhh, unfinished business, there's always that. But is it ever really finished? Don't wait too long, Kip. Anyway, what can I do to help?"

Kip put his foot on the bench and rested a forearm over his knee. "Keep an eye on Anna and Danny while I'm in Ft. Worth. It shouldn't be for more than a couple of days."

"Will do. But from what you and Barry have been telling me, I get the impression only the tip of the iceberg is showing in this case."

Kip straightened and walked to the edge of the pier. For several minutes he didn't answer. Then he pulled in a deep breath and blew it out in a long stream. He spoke without turning. "That's my sentiment, too. I've got a gut feeling it might go back to Marie and Patrick's death, maybe before that. The devices used in Anna's house and the one that blew Marie and Patrick are similar, but I haven't figured out exactly how everything's connected. You know anything I don't?"

Nick shook his head. "Wish I did. You may never get all the answers, Kip. You know that."

"I know." He turned. "Here's a name for you. Carl Goddard. Know anything about him?"

"Not much. His father owns Goddard Financial. Oh, and for a while he dated a cop in the department. She invited him to a barbeque the captain had at his home last month. That's how I know."

Kip raised an eyebrow. "Tell me something about the cop."

"I don't know her well, but if you want to know if she might be flattered by his attention, a quick guess is yes she was. I'll look into it. Mind telling me what Goddard has to do with the case?"

"Maybe nothing, but Holly's son is afraid of him for some reason. We're checking all leads. I appreciate the help. And Nick, keep the surveillance on Anna low key. The fewer people who know where she's staying the better. That includes people in your department."

Nick lifted his eyebrows with a curt nod but made no comment.

While the men talked, the tide had come in and the sky had grown dim. Another car arrived at the house, presumably Evan's, Kip thought. The security lights came on. Kip glanced at his watch. "I've kept you too long. Time to go home to your wife and your kid's birthday party." Kip walked beside his friend. "I envy you having that."

Congressman Marshall Quinlan leaned back in his plush leather chair and flipped *Time* magazine over to study the cover. He couldn't help smiling; not the campaign smile that had charmed millions, but the smile of pride rarely seen. On the cover he was pictured at his desk, a distinguish statesman of Pakistani descent. Against the backdrop of an American flag, his sleeves were rolled, his full head of white hair and pale brown skin an arresting contrast to the flag's red, white, and blue. But, he thought in a moment of honesty, it was the promise in his broad smile and not the intelligence in his black eyes that would draw the viewer back for a second look and to the polls to vote.

He swung his chair around toward his office window. Outside the view opened before him, a panorama of Sacramento bathed in white sunlight. The polls had him in the lead. The pieces of Marshall Quinlan's destiny were falling into place in neat order just like he'd always had faith they would. He was pleased. But, he reminded himself, his smile tightening into determination, polls were subject to change. There was still a long way to go. But Marshall Quinlan was a patient man.

Rising, he pitched the magazine onto his desk just as his private cell began to vibrate. He pulled it out, recognized the number as belonging to Mabel Osgood, and his smile returned. He'd last seen Mabel five years ago, when they'd spent an evening together while attending a conference in Hawaii. That was six years after they'd mutually decided to end their affair so he could run for the U.S. Congress. Now he was going to Atlanta for a political rally and would see her in her capacity as State Senator Louis Norton's secretary, and if he could sneak away, they'd share the night together as well.

She was old now, but so was he. Several years his senior, she'd once been a beautiful woman, but it had always been her intelligence that drew him, that and the fact she was without scruples when it came to getting what she wanted. Over the years she had served him well. He relied on her. Without her behind him, he wouldn't have been able to come as far as quickly. If all went according to plan, come November next year they'd have a lot to celebrate. He was looking forward to seeing her again, but faintly disturbed by the rare call.

"Yes?"

"Hello. Have I caught you at a bad time?"

"No, I've got a couple minutes. What's up?"

"I've just finished reading *Time*. I loved the photo on the cover, but I particularly loved the caption, 'Quinlan Ready to Work for America.' Was that your idea?" Mabel said into the cell.

"As a matter of fact it was. I'm glad you like it."

"I do, and the article almost does you justice, but not quite."

"Oh, why is that?"

"Now I've got you worried." She laughed. "I couldn't resist. "No, as you well know, the article is perfect. You couldn't have asked for more if you wrote the article yourself. The woman who wrote it was clearly in sympathy with your positions."

"I thought so. Truth is, much of the article was directly quoted from a document I wrote for her." He laughed, rubbing his hand over his chin and mouth, a gesture he'd developed to keep his feelings concealed. "But that's not why you called."

He heard her intake of breath and stiffened.

"In part it is, but there've been a few complications in getting the funds I promised you. Nothing I can't straighten out, but it's messier and going to take a little longer than I hoped. I just wanted to forewarn you. I'll explain more when I see you. However, before that you may read some things in the paper."

"I'm counting on that money to pay some campaign debts."

"I know, and I have the money, but right now for your sake I want to be completely certain it can't be traced before I get it into your account. But the portion you specified be sent to your charity was deposited in their account yesterday afternoon. You should soon be hearing some news on the overseas front."

"I look forward to that. As for the other problem, whatever it is, take care of it." He didn't like the tension he heard in his voice and tried to warm it. "I count on you."

"I know you do, and I won't let you down."

Senator Louis Norton came into the office with some papers in his hand, and Mabel disconnected, turning to look at her boss. "I was just talking to a friend about the *Time* article on Congressman Quinlan. A great man, don't you think?"

He glanced at her over his glasses. "He's running an impressive campaign, I'll give him that. That said, in my mind Quinlan's policies smack of welfare, unwieldy Federal government, and huge deficits the economy can't withstand. But he is a handsome man, a fine orator, and I agree the article was excellent."

"You don't like him?" Mabel was incredulous.

"And you do, I take it. He's hood-winking you all, Mabel. Mark my words on that. Does your comment have something to do with my upcoming meeting with him? Well, if it does, you may come with me, if that's what you'd like. Now, if you don't mind typing this letter for me before you go home for the evening, I'd appreciate it."

Chapter 22

Inside the spacious lobby of the First Federal, Kip stood, stifling a yawn, and ran his hand over his unshaved chin. Neither he nor Barry had managed more than a few hours of sleep on the plane, arriving in Ft. Worth with only enough time to leave their luggage at their hotel and head for the bank. He poured himself a second cup of coffee and returned to his seat. He didn't want the coffee, but it was something to do while he waited. The key to the safety deposit box had proved too mangled to fit, so under Barry's watchful eye, a lock man was drilling the box right now while Kip battled boredom and fatigue.

From where he sat he could see a uniformed policemen standing guard outside the door. He seemed alert, but the bank was busy with the noon-time crowd. Kip would have preferred to check the box before the bank opened, but the local police were in charge. What looked at first to be a case of arson and the murder of Holly Everett had grown into something else entirely. It was spreading like a cancer, and he didn't have a handle on it. That made him uneasy.

Kip pulled out his cell and punched in Anna's number. She picked up on the second ring.

"Where are you?"

"I might ask the same of you. All right, I'm at the newspaper. Danny's gone to kindergarten, and my boss has me doing busy work around the office. I figure you must have told him to keep me inside."

Kip laughed. "When did your former fiancé leave?"

"Not that it's any business of yours, but he left shortly after you did. I let him stay in my apartment overnight. He should be on his way back to Auburn by now. Happy?"

He was, but he didn't like that he was. Out of the corner of his eye he noticed a heavyset man make his way slowly across the lobby toward the safety deposit boxes with a rolling bucket and mop. Why would someone mop the floors when the bank was full of customers?

"I've got to go. I'll check in later." He made a beeline for the police officer closest to him and spoke close to his ear. "Are the floors normally cleaned at this time of day?"

For a second the officer looked perplexed. "Not that I recall. This morning when I came in I was told the regular janitor was sick. No one mentioned a time change. Is there something wrong?"

"Let's find out. Come with me." With his hand on his revolver hidden behind his back, Kip crossed the marble floor to where the replacement was mopping behind a kiosk that dispensed bank slips. A woman wearing a green flowered blouse was standing at the kiosk and looked up at his approach. Kip kept his voice low when he addressed the man with the bucket. He read the name off the tag on the man's pocket. "Jose, excuse me. I would like to speak with you for a moment."

The man looked up at him. The eyes. Was that fear in them? Because he was an illegal or because of something else?

"This way, please." Kip indicated the office loaned to the police for the morning, noting the man's hair was dark and salted with white, and that he looked very fit, like he was more accustomed to pumping iron than mopping floors.

"I not do wrong."

"And I haven't accused you of doing anything wrong. I just want a word with you. Leave the bucket and please come with me."

The man's hand moved toward his pants' pocket. Kip stopped it short and held on with a steel grip. He resisted the urge to search the pocket then and there only because he was trying to attract as little attention as possible. In case his instincts were wrong. "Keep your hands where I can see them."

The woman at the kiosk was staring at them now. Beside her on the counter was a large, colorful tote of the sort sold to tourists in the towns bordering Mexico.

Kip dialed Barry with his thumb and spoke quietly. "I got a feeling something's going down out here. There's a bucket and mop by the kiosk. Check the bucket. I think you're going to find a bomb in there...yeah, I got the floor-washer here."

Winds of Fire

Kip snapped the phone shut and put a hand on the man's back to urge him forward. No flab there. In front of the cop stationed at the door to the safety deposit boxes Kip paused. "My friend inside will be leaving in a moment. Soon as he does, lock up."

"But the locksmith is still in there."

"Lock him in. Then see that the woman with the large Mexican tote, the one in the green flowered blouse by the kiosk, is prevented from leaving the building."

Kip propelled the man to the office on the other side of the lobby, closed the door, and shoved Jose toward a chair. His stoop was gone and so was the subservient look of earlier. His expression defiant, Jose shifted from foot to foot then reached a hand toward his pocket. Kip was expecting the move and grabbed Jose's arm, twisting it behind his back with a loud crack. The erstwhile floor-washer cried out in pain as a light knock sounded and a cop came through the door. He took the situation in at a glance and drew his weapon.

"Okay, Jose, I'm not telling you again. Stand real still while I take whatever's making you so antsy out of your pocket."

Kip knew what it was even before he eased it out. He handled it gingerly.

"Damn, is that a detonator?" The cop looked startled then angry and wasted no time pulling out his cuffs. "Shall I cuff him?"

"Be my guest. Then evacuate the building, but keep the people nearby for questioning. And send the bank manager in here."

Kip pulled out his cell phone and punched in Barry's. "You find it?"

"Yes, just like you suspected, enough explosive to send the safety deposit boxes to Kingdom Come and kill everyone within fifty yards. The bomb squad is on its way, and the people are already evacuating. You got the detonator?"

"Yes, and the floor-washer. You get the woman?"

"She's in the assistant manager's office arguing with him."

"Don't let her go. Any danger the bomb's about to blow?"

"There's always a possibility, but no, not while you have the detonator. Unless there's a second detonator."

"Search the woman's purse. I'm on my way."

183

Soon as he hung up with Barry his phone began to vibrate. A glance at the screen showed Anna's number. As he moved toward the door Kip spoke to the cop over his shoulder. "Don't let him out of your sight. I've got to take this."

"Kip..."

"Are you and Danny all right?"

"Yes, I just talked to them at the school, but something's happened. The police are here. Last night someone tried to burn down the apartment where Danny and I had been staying."

"Dammit, Anna. Anyone hurt?"

"Dennis's in the hospital. He was staying in my apartment, remember?"

"How bad?"

"He's alive. That's all I know."

"Call Nick Howell. I gave you his number."

"He's already here. Soon as he heard about the fire from the police department, he came."

"Good. I'm in the middle of something here, Anna. Nick will know what to do. I'll call you back soon as I can." With that he severed the connection.

Already, he could hear sirens outside. The patrol cars must have been close. He hurried toward the glassed-in offices. Halfway across the room he came to a stop. The office where the woman had been arguing was empty. It took a moment to locate her walking with a man dressed in a suit and tie toward the exit along with the others being evacuated. The woman's hand was concealed behind her large bag, giving the impression she was holding a gun on him. But something didn't feel right. For such a carefully planned operation, why had the girl drawn attention to herself?

Where was Barry?

He picked up his pace, joining the throng as they moved toward the door in an orderly fashion, then frowned when he realized the law enforcement officer who'd been manning the door earlier was no longer there. He approached the woman from behind and pressed his gun against the back of her neck. He spoke in Spanish. "If you wish to see your friend alive again, do exactly as I say. Turn around slowly and hand over your gun."

"You are mistaken, Señor, I have no gun." She also spoke in Spanish as she turned and showed him her empty hands.

At that same moment the man in the suit accompanying her stepped away from her side and spoke in perfect English. "*I have the gun.*"

But Kip had already figured it out, and before the words were out of the man's mouth, Kip slapped the gun out of his hand. And the orderly exit from the bank turned into blind panic.

Later, when Barry drove him to the precinct in their rented car, the contents of Holly's safety deposit box making the same trip in a squad car ahead of them, Kip took a minute to phone Anna. Assured that she and Danny were fine and well protected and that Dennis's injuries were minor, he turned to Barry.

"Only a big fish has the resources to carry off such operations as we've been seeing."

"Big and far-reaching, too—from Colorado Rockies, to Savannah, to Fort Worth, and no telling where the hell else..." Barry kept his attention on the traffic. "So do you think the departments of both Savannah and Ft. Worth are compromised?"

Kip spent the next couple minutes ruminating over the real possibility before he answered. "How else would the enemy know where Holly Everett's safe deposit box was located at almost the same moment we did or that we were going to be there to open it at this time today?"

"Exactly the way I'm thinking." Barry ran a yellow light to keep up with the squad car ahead.

"Makes me wonder what the common ground is that dirtied the cops in both cities."

"The gambling." Barry sounded unsure.

"That'd only apply to Ft. Worth cops. No, my bet is that there's something else, some other common thread we've missed, something Holly may have unwittingly stumbled across. Stanley didn't strike me as having been a man with a lot of guts. Yet if we're right about him, he was a part of a hijacking, a daring job pulled off in the light of day that necessitated a jump from a plane. Maybe it wasn't only the gambling debt that drew him to take such a course of action.

I'm going to call Anna and have her check the papers again." Kip pulled out his cell and punched in Anna's number.

"You, me, all of us have been over the notes on Holly's computer and those papers a hundred times and nothing showed up. You aren't fooling me. You're just worried about Anna."

"Damn right I am. And one more time over them won't hurt. We had to have overlooked something."

When Anna answered, he got straight to the point. "Can you do me a favor? Please," he added, smiling to himself. "Go through your sister's papers one more time and this time look for something, some activity other than gambling that Stanley might have been involved in."

"Like did he moonlight?"

"Exactly. And organizations—political, religious—did he belong to any organizations? Check all the materials again and see if we missed something. Then get back to me."

"Before I do, tell me, have you heard any more about the fire in Holly and Stanley's house?"

"The house is ashes from what I've been told, but I'll ask. I'll also make it a point of taking a look at the place before I catch the plane back. You got something specific on your mind?"

"No, just wondering...I'll call you back in a minute."

Six minutes later Kip was standing over a table in the evidence room with Barry and a police officer, looking over the contents of Holly's deposit box when Anna called back.

"Stanley did have a second job. I didn't find anything about it in her papers, but I remember Holly telling me he'd recently taken a job with SSI or NSI or something like that to help pay his gambling debt. I think it was some kind of security force, similar to the kind he'd worked for when Holly met him. Hang on, and I'll try and run the name down for you on the computer."

Kip spied a sheaf of papers that had been run directly from a computer website and held his breath. He drew a couple of the pages closer until he could read the heading, MSI, Marshal Security International. "Bingo," he said, half under his breath. "Anna, could it be MSI?"

"MSI, yes, that sounds right. Shall I look it up for you?"

"Not necessary. There's a rundown on MSI in Holly's deposit box. I think you stumbled onto something. This may be the connection we've been looking for. Keep your fingers crossed. Oh, and the police recovered a body inside your sister's house. They are working to ID it as we speak."

Kip perused the papers for a few seconds then handed them to Barry. "Take a look at these. Anna believes her brother-in-law was moonlighting at this Marshal Security International. And take a look at the name Holly highlighted."

Barry whistled under his breath. "Would you look at that? None other than this week's star of *Time* magazine. Owner, founder and sole operator until he put the business in trust to run for Congress ten years ago. Interesting."

"It says here MSI hires cops and retired cops, political scientists, retired military and people who are experts in international terrorism. Stanley would fit into that category, and he needed money. I think we've got another link we were looking for."

"What about Carl Goddard? He had to learn about explosives somewhere."

"Makes sense. We need a list of the employees at MSI. Let's check through the rest of these papers to see if Holly had a list or if there's anything else we can use. We'll make copies of everything before we head back to Savannah. Lots of this stuff Anna will want to look at on her own."

On the way to the airport, Kip filled Anna in on the latest development.

"I'm on my way to pick up Danny," she said into the receiver. "I'll see you at your house when you get back."

"Be careful, Anna. Nothing's different from yesterday except we have a lead. There's a long way to go to prove anything. We don't even know why the crimes were committed, so don't think you're out of danger. Nick's still with you, right?"

"Oh, Kip, he has a family, and his wife's spotting, and she's not due for three weeks. He's worried about her. He needs to attend to his family. I'll be careful."

"You told him to go home, right? Dammit, Anna. The danger isn't over."

"Have a safe flight home. I'll be fine." With that she hung up and left Kip bristling with worry.

Chapter 23

Anna checked to see that Danny was properly strapped into his car seat and got into the car. Immediately her cell rang. It took her a moment to retrieve it from her purse and identify the caller as Nick Howell.

"I'm glad I caught you. Are you still at work?"

"No, I'm picking up Danny from kindergarten. How's your wife doing?"

"Better. The bleeding has quieted substantially, but the doctors want to keep her overnight. I'm still at the hospital. I can't see how I can leave her."

"No, of course you can't." Anna put the key in the ignition but waited to start the car.

"Kip just called. He's on his way to the airport, but he's worried about you and Danny."

"He phoned me, too. We'll be fine. We're headed to Marsh Winds soon as I hang up."

"I've taken the liberty of calling Bill Pennington at Tybee PD. He gets off duty in about twenty minutes and has agreed to meet you at Marsh Winds right after that. I hope that's all right with you."

"Of course. That's nice of him. But I hate for him to go to so much trouble. Kip will be back shortly. Until then we'll be fine. If I see or hear anything worrisome, I promise to call Tybee PD."

"All right, I'll pass that information on to Bill. Let me give you his cell number in case you need to get in touch with him."

She saved the number in her list of contacts. "And, Nick, don't worry about me. Just take care of your wife."

Anna pulled out into the line of cars filled with parents picking up their children. She never noticed the blue sedan pull out behind her. A lone man sat behind the wheel.

It was close to five and the day had turned gray and gloomy, when Anna turned onto the crushed oyster shells of Marsh

Winds' drive. Under the overhang of oaks she was immediately immersed into premature darkness. Apprehension seeped into her. The smell, the sounds, the moss-laden trees were familiar to her. Yet at that moment they had taken on a sinister look. She pulled her sweater closer over her breasts and looked around, suddenly uneasy, and told herself she was being irrational.

It was as though she had stepped into another time. Not one to condone such fantasies, in the back of her mind she knew how far-fetched the notion was. Nevertheless in the eerie twilight under the tree cover she couldn't shake the feeling that something wasn't quite right. Even as she admonished her imagination as silly, she pressed her foot to the pedal, skidding through the last two curves of the long drive.

Marsh Winds appeared. She pulled to a stop as close to the front steps as she could and studied the shadows of the woods that edged right up to the lawn. A lone man or an army of men could easily hide in those trees. Only when she determined it free from any obvious danger did she leave the car, help Danny get unbuckled from his car seat and hurry up the front steps.

Before she could twist the key in the deadbolt, the front door swung open. Anna reeled back, unable to stifle her gasp.

"There you guys are. I was just beginning to worry." Kip's mother was holding a phone.

"Sarah! You startled me. I didn't think anyone was here. I thought you and Dr. Schroeder were driving to Tampa this afternoon."

"That was the original plan. Come in, please. I didn't mean to frighten you." Sarah moved into the front hallway and spoke into the receiver. "Yes, she's just arrived...all right...I'll see you in a few minutes then."

She turned back to Anna. "That was Evan. He's on his way over now. Kip phoned earlier when his flight was delayed in Atlanta. He asked if we could postpone leaving until his buddy Bill Pennington can get here. He didn't get into the reasons with me, but I assume it has to do with your sister's murder. It was evident he didn't want to leave you and Danny alone."

Anna started to tell her that she planned to tell Bill Pennington not to come but stopped herself. Sarah McTeer was her son's mother and wouldn't condone Anna taking unnecessary chances. "You've already done so much for me. Thank you, but I think you should take off soon as Evan gets here. No need for me to interfere with your trip."

"You wouldn't be. We were only going early because there's a restaurant in Jacksonville Evan wanted to take me to. The ship doesn't leave until 3:00 tomorrow afternoon. There's plenty of time to get there in the morning, although we may still go tonight after Bill gets here. I'm leaving that decision up to Evan. He's picked up some steaks to put on the grill. I've got potatoes already baking. Meanwhile the delay gave me a chance to finish up a few things around here, so it's going to work out just fine."

Danny dropped his school backpack in the middle of the hall and made a beeline for the kitchen. Sarah called after him. "There are some fresh baked chocolate chip cookies on the counter, if you're hungry."

"Thank you, Sarah, for everything. I appreciate you offering to stay, but there's honestly no need." Anna picked up Danny's backpack and followed Sarah into the kitchen.

Anna was setting the dinner table, when Bill Pennington arrived in uniform. Evan and Sarah decided to go on to Jacksonville. Bill waited downstairs while Anna monitored Danny's bath and read him some stories before putting him to bed.

She tucked the blankets around him and kissed his forehead. "Night, sweetheart. I love you."

"Night, Aunt Anna. I love you, too."

Anna's heart swelled.

When she reentered the living room where Bill was watching the news, she was still smiling. He had removed his tie and elevated his feet on the hassock, and more closely resembled the boy she'd known in high school. The fanciful apprehension she'd experienced earlier was replaced by a feeling of comfort in this home of Kip's. Whoever attempted to burn her house again last night didn't know where she was staying. The thick stucco walls of Marsh Winds wouldn't succumb to flames so readily as her frame house on the beach. Besides, Kip would be back in a few hours. She was safe at Marsh Winds.

"Thank you for coming, Bill. I'm sure you'd prefer to be home with your wife and kids."

"Glad to. Kids don't have any ballgames tonight, so I'm not missing much. By the way, I took a look around the property while you were upstairs and everything looked good to me. But there're a lot of woods close by. Anyone could hide in those woods."

"I was thinking exactly that when I drove in. Still, I think Kip's just being overly cautious. I don't know why anyone would want to harm me." Anna shuddered at the memory of the fire and her sister's ghastly murder. She hadn't believed anyone would want to harm her sister either.

"Kip seemed pretty worried when he phoned." Bill twisted in his seat.

For the first time Anna noticed the gun strapped under his jacket. She took a deep breath and looked out the French doors that led to the back patio. Beyond the light coming through the windows it was black, no stars, no moon, nothing but black, and her earlier apprehension returned. "Mind if I close the drapes?" She heard the hitch in her voice.

He glanced at his watch then looked up at her. "Yes, please. I meant to do it when I came back inside a few minutes ago. Looks like it's about to storm."

She'd heard a storm was coming on the radio earlier, but so far the rain hadn't started. "Can I get you anything? A beer, coffee, iced tea? We have a couple leftover steaks and potatoes. Are you hungry?"

Bill stood up, stretched. "I wouldn't say no to one of those steaks and some iced tea. I came directly from the department and didn't get the chance to grab a bite."

While Bill poured iced tea Anna walked to the front room and closed the cottage shutters, reassured by the sight of the black and white police car parked out front.

Carl stood in the shadows of the trees. Bill Pennington's arrival surprised him some. It made things a little more complicated but not much. He ducked deeper behind the trees, keeping his gun at ready while Bill made a little walkabout. Not long after Bill's arrival Kip's mother and an older man carried some suitcases to a car and drove away. A few minutes after that, Anna took the boy to a room on the second floor. With the shades not drawn, it was like watching a picture show.

He waited thirty minutes after the upstairs lights went out. By then the mist had thickened into a light rain. Carl left the shelter of the trees and headed for the house.

Kip still hadn't returned home, nor had he called. To Anna it seemed like hours ago the grandfather clock chimed out nine times though by her watch it wasn't quite half an hour. Gripped with her own thoughts and apprehensions, she'd run out of small talk, and except for the low murmur of the television the room had fallen silent. She glanced at Bill. After the large meal and the full day at the office, he was struggling to stay awake.

Harlie got up suddenly and walked to the bottom of the front steps, near the front entry way. What was taking Kip so long? Why didn't he answer her text messages or calls?

"When you last talked with him, did Kip give you a time he thought he'd get home?"

Bill sat up straighter. "No. All he said was the flight had been delayed, and he'd be back soon as he could. He still not answering his phone?"

She shook her head. "I expect he'll call soon as his plane touches down." She stood and listened to Harlie trotting up the hardwood steps to the second floor. "I think I'll go upstairs and check on Danny."

"Want me to do it?"

"No, I want to get out of these shoes anyway."

"All right then if you don't mind, I think I'll get a cup of that coffee. Don't want to be asleep when McTeer gets here."

"Help yourself. The cups are in the cupboard over the pot. Sugar is there, too."

Upstairs she found Harlie standing outside Danny's door, tail wagging. She slipped inside the door, careful to keep out the dog for fear she'd wake Danny. Hand still on the doorknob, she stood at the threshold to watch her sister's son sleep. He was such a beautiful child, so special, and when she looked at him, it hurt her anew that her sister wouldn't be there to witness his growing up.

Harlie began to whimper. Anxious to hush him, she turned to go. The patter of rain on the tile roof reminded her she'd left the window cracked. Halfway back into to the room she noticed the shine of water on the floor beneath the window and grew concerned.

She'd just convinced herself it must have come in on a gust of wind when behind her a floorboard creaked. She whirled. Before she could let out a scream a hand clamped over her mouth and pinned her against a man's chest. She twisted, grabbed the attacker's arm. Her free hand swung around and raked across the assailant's face; fingernails dug into flesh. He recoiled but not enough to give her an opening to break his hold.

"Bitch!" he hissed, and struck her face so hard it lifted her from her feet. Her head reeled backward. Before she could shake off the pain, he jabbed a gun against her ribs and grabbed a handful of her hair. He yanked, tipping her head so far back she feared her neck would snap.

He put his mouth close to her ear. "Try anything like that again and the first bullet drops you; the second goes into the boy." He propelled her toward the window with the tip of his gun. "Out on the roof."

She seethed. "You scumbag! You'll never get away with this."

He jabbed the gun into her ribs hard and kept his voice low. "Shut up and move."

She fought down the urge to try and knock the gun from his hand in hopes Bill would hear the commotion and come to the rescue. But with Carl's gun pressed against her and Danny still asleep on the bed, the time wasn't right. If Carl left Danny behind, it would be a victory of sorts.

By the time she crawled through the window Anna was so angry her hands were shaking. Rain was coming down at a steady pace. The tile roof was slippery with saturated leaves and pine needles. If she hadn't been wearing heeled leather-soled boots made for style rather than practicality, she might not have slipped. As it was, half way across her foot came out from under her and dropped her flat on her stomach. She dropped to all fours and concentrated on backing her way to the edge. She clawed at the tiles, but her fingers slid right over them. With nothing to grab onto she went into a slow, feet-first slide right over the edge and landed with a thud on the ground. Her foot hit awkwardly on a broken branch and rolled. She yelped in pain and crumpled into the leaves.

Carl landed right behind her and pointed his gun at her face.

She grabbed at the riveting pain in her ankle and shivered. "Why are you doing this? What do you want from me?"

The front door opened. Bill must have heard her cry and come to investigate. Carl pushed her deeper into the corner behind a bush where the security light didn't reach and kept the gun leveled at her head. A flashlight beam moved from the right to the left. She willed him to come further around the corner, but he didn't. Instead she heard him mutter an oath. Then he began to shout to Harlie, only he was calling him 'doggie.' Harlie must have run out through the open door, and Bill didn't know his name. Her hopes rose. Harlie could locate them. She could bark and bring Bill to rescue her.

Her fingers closed over a piece of concrete. It had broken from something under the gutter spout preventing the runoff from digging out a crater. She glanced at Carl. The gun hadn't moved. If Harlie could distract Carl so that he lowered his gun, she could hit him in the head and make her escape.

After a short time the calling stopped. The front door closed. Carl's gun was still aimed at her head. Had Bill caught hold of Harlie's collar and brought her back inside or would Kip's dog find them at any moment? The barking resumed, and it came from inside the house.

Carl stood, grabbed her bicep, and half dragged her away from the house, forcing her to limp along at his pace. With each step her ankle buckled from the excruciating pain. She tried to hop. Her best chance for escape had passed. Her hopes sank. How long before Bill wondered what was taking her so much time upstairs or became alarmed at Harlie's barking? Too long, she realized as Carl dragged her off the drive and into the trees.

Carl's car was well concealed at the end of the drive on the Marsh Winds side of a wooden bridge leading onto the county road. She didn't see the car until the last minute. He opened the trunk and forced her to put her hands behind her back. Before he tied her hands she attempted to slip the bit of concrete into her pocket. It missed and fell to the ground.

A glimpse of headlights flashed through the trees. A car was coming on fast like it was in a big hurry as its lights wove in and out of the trees, taking the turns along the marsh edge like the driver knew them all by heart. Kip. Carl guessed it, too. He jammed a rag into her mouth then pushed her into the trunk and shut it. Inside the trunk was pitch dark. The sickening smell of gasoline and mildew attacked her nostrils right away. She tried to remain calm as she struggled to untie the knots at her wrists.

The front door of the car opened and shut, rocking a little from the weight of Carl getting inside, but for a long time the engine didn't start, not until several minutes after she heard the approaching car pass by on the drive. In the distance a dog began to bark. She could tell this time the barking was outside the house. Then Carl started the car and drove it slowly over shrubs and roots that poked and scraped the undercarriage and bounced her against the top of the trunk. When they reached a paved road, Carl put his foot on the gas.

Anna inhaled the nauseating fumes and realized with a surge of panic that the tailpipe must have a leak. Her throat began to burn, reminding her of the fire, and for the first time real fear set in. Her ankle throbbed, and she sensed it was swelling. That was the least of her worries. She'd been kidnapped, and she didn't know why. Where was Carl taking her and for what purpose? Frantically she renewed her efforts to free her hands. The rough hemp chaffed painfully into her wrists. In the cramped quarters of the trunk she couldn't maneuver her legs through her arms to get her hands in front where she might be able to chew at the ropes. She thought of the piece of concrete she'd dropped in the leaves, wishing for its rough edge. The rag stuffed into her mouth made her gag. She tried to spit it out. It was no use. The fumes caused her head to ache, her stomach roiled with nausea. Her thoughts grew foggy until blackness crept in and engulfed her.

Kip you're too late.

Chapter 24

Kip heard the barking before he reached the first curve and felt a knot of apprehension. He hit the gas and fishtailed through the next two turns. The sight of the black and white parked beside Anna's jeep was a relief, but the sense that something was amiss was still there. He skidded to a stop and took the front steps in two long strides.

The door was already ajar.

He pushed it open and anxiously scanned the front rooms. "Anna, Bill..."

The silence chilled him. Behind him came the sound of heavy shoes running up the steps. He whirled around as he reached for his gun.

Harlie darted through the door with Bill right behind her. Bill looked soaked and distressed. "Anna's gone," he said in a breathless rush.

Kip spat an oath under his breath and fired questions. "Danny?"

"Danny's okay. He's asleep."

"When did Anna disappear?"

"Best guess is no longer than thirty minutes ago. That's about that time Harlie charged down the steps and began to bark at the front door. I couldn't make her quiet down so I let her out and walked around the house. Shortly before that Anna had headed upstairs to have a look at Danny. Whoever took her must have been waiting for her up there." Bill shook his head. "I can't figure how he got past me."

Kip took the stairs two at a time. Bill was right on his heels. "Soon as I realized she was missing I called your cell. The line was busy."

"I had a call I had to take." Kip glanced into each of the rooms as he hurried by them toward the room his mother had set up for Danny. He had to see for himself that Danny was safe.

Bill followed. "I've already checked all the rooms, bathrooms, the closets, too."

"Figured you would have."

"Also, I've contacted the department. Some help should be arriving any minute."

"Good. That was my next question."

As they approached the entrance to Danny's room, Kip slowed and lowered his gun out of sight but kept it in hand. The door was ajar. He eased it open, taking the precaution of checking behind it, although he figured whoever had taken Anna was long gone. The kidnapper had an agenda.

His gaze riveted on the empty bottom bunk, and his stomach knotted. "Thought you said Danny was here."

"He was, I swear it. Ten minutes ago he was asleep in his bed. I've been searching the grounds since then." Bill pushed past Kip and pulled the covers back. "The covers are still warm."

"I'm here." Danny peeked his head over the railing of the top bunk. His face was tear-stained, his chin quivering. "I'm up here." His voice broke, and a new shower of tears rolled down the worn tracks.

Kip holstered his gun behind his back and lifted him from the bed. "Come here, son." He hugged his sturdy little body against his chest, absorbing the boy's shaking, cradling his head, rocking him until he felt him breathe easier. "I won't let him get you. I'm here now. Do you know where mommy Anna is?"

In the security of Kip's arms the pent up fear seemed to hiccup out of him. "A man made Anna go with him. He made her go through the window then he came back, and I was afraid he'd make me go in the rain, too. I-I didn't w-want to get my dinosaur jammies wet," he sobbed, and Kip's heart forgot to beat. Sudden tears blurred his vision. He blinked and swallowed and buried his face in Danny's hair. This precious child didn't want the dinosaur pajama's he given him to get wet. He couldn't speak.

After a few moments, Danny raised his head. "I was asleep when Aunt Anna came in. Then I heard noise, and I woke up. Aunt Anna told me shhh." He demonstrated by putting his finger across his mouth. "The bad man was there. I saw him and pretended I was asleep. I saw him hit her..."

Kip sucked in a deep breath through his nose. "You were a brave boy to keep quiet like that. I know you were afraid, but Anna wouldn't want the man to hurt you, so you helped her." He carried Danny into the dimly lighted hallway, sat down on the top step with Danny on his lap, and kissed his brow.

The eyes that stared up at him were bright with tears. Once again Kip pulled him back against his chest and stroked his back. Dear God, how could he question Danny now when he was so vulnerable? But experience had taught him if there was to be any hope of bringing Anna back alive he couldn't wait. Time was of the essence while what just happened was fresh in his mind. Harlie came up behind them and tucked her head through Kip's arm. Danny reached over to pet her. Kip used the distraction to turn to Bill who was standing a little behind them looking like he was thinking about his own kids.

"Do you mind making a concentrated check of the ground under the window before anything that might be there is obliterated or washed away? He may even have had a ladder of some sort."

"No ladder. I'm sure of it, but I'd be glad to take a look around. I was about to do it anyway when I heard your car drive up."

Soon as Bill trotted down the steps Kip turned his attention back to Danny. He used his thumb to wipe the tears from under the boy's eyes. "Danny, if you can answer a few questions for me, it will help me find Anna. Can you do that?"

He nodded, and his little mouth quivered as he sucked in shuddering breath.

"Tell me exactly what happened."

"Mommy Anna tried to get away...she kicked the bad man. He had a gun. I saw it. The man hit her and pushed her. He made her climb out the window into the rain." This seemed to remind him of his pajamas, and he began to pluck at the dinosaurs.

"Danny, this is important. Have you ever seen the man before?"

He darted a glance at Kip before quickly dropping his gaze and nodding.

"Who is he, Danny? Who's the man who took Anna?" Kip held his breath.

"I don't remember."

"Are you saying you don't remember his name?"

Danny smoothed out one of the dinosaurs on his pajamas and nodded again.

"Do you recall where you saw him before tonight?"

"Uh-huh." He looked up at Kip, his mouth down turned. "He's really mean."

"Yes he is. Can you tell me where you saw him before tonight?"

For several moments Danny said nothing, then he buried his face in his hands. "He hurt mommy."

Kip tipped up Danny's chin with his forefinger until he faced him. "Danny, do you mean he hurt your mommy or mommy Anna?"

"He made the house on fire and he stole mommy Anna, too."

Kip's heartbeat raced. "Have you seen him since he hurt your mommy?"

Danny looked away.

"Danny, you've got to trust me. I'm a big strong man, and I promise I'll do my best not to let him hurt you or mommy Anna or me or anyone else. If you tell me where you last saw him, it will do a lot to help me bring mommy Anna back to us."

He drew in a hitching breath. "I saw him at the eating place at the beach."

My God, Carl Goddard.

"Thank you, Danny. That was very helpful." He kissed Danny on the temple, pulled him close to his chest, and reached for his cell.

Moments later he heard the familiar voice of his mother on the other end. "Kip, are you back yet?"

"Got back a few minutes ago. Where are you?"

"We stopped for dinner so we're just on the outskirts of Jacksonville. Something's wrong. I felt it all evening, and now I hear it in your voice."

"I've got a huge favor to ask you, Mom."

"I know you wouldn't ask if it weren't something serious. Just a minute, I want to tell Evan to turn the car around. You need me there, isn't that right?"

"Yes, but I haven't even told you..."

"Go on. He's pulling off I-95 now. We're turning around. Now tell me what's happened."

"I'll fill you in on the details later, but the gist of it is someone has taken Anna and Danny saw it all. I don't want to leave him with a stranger tonight, not after all he's been through."

His mother sighed deeply and her voice was a little unsteady when she next spoke. "Oh, poor Anna. That's terrible, unbelievably terrible. And Danny's all right?"

"He is. He was a brave boy."

"I can't believe someone would kidnap Anna. Who would do a thing like that?"

"Carl Goddard, but that's between us. But Carl's only a chip off an iceberg. I got to go now. And Mom, I can't thank you enough."

There was silence then a soft sigh. "I suppose you're going after Anna."

"Of course. Have a safe trip home, Mom."

"Get some help, Kip. You can't do everything alone. And be safe. I love you."

"Love you, too, and thanks again."

Awareness that she was cold crept slowly into Anna's consciousness. Inside her head was a persistent hammering. She shivered and blinked her eyes open, then moved to rub the throbbing only to discover her wrists were tied behind her back. Instinctively, she struggled to free her hands, twisting against the rough rope until her wrists grew raw, and she was forced to stop.

Even with her eyes wide open she couldn't see a thing, but the rank smell of mildew assaulted her senses. It mingled with the scent of marsh and the sea. She was near the ocean or salt marsh. Rain pounded, and wind howled all round her. The storm hadn't let up. The temperature was cold, bitterly cold, made more so by the fact that she was sitting on a hard surface in what felt like a puddle of water. Her back was against a wall of rock or brick; her blouse and jeans were soaked; her feet were numb, painfully so; her legs were sore and stiff with what she guessed was crusted blood.

She shivered again, and once the shaking started, this time she couldn't make it stop. Tears filled her eyes. She drew in a deep breath, lifting her chin, and ordered herself not to cry. Crying would solve nothing.

A dripping sound somewhere above her head drew her attention. She looked up into pitch black. At least she was inside, sort of. She listened to rain strike and picked up the sound of water lapping. She was definitely close to the sea.

Her instincts told her she was alone, though she realized Carl could be close-by, waiting in the dark. Waiting for what? If he'd wanted to kill her he could easily have done so already. So he wanted something else. What did he want from her?

She mustered her strength and pushed to her feet. That's when she discovered her ankles were bound as well. Her shoes were gone. She hobbled a step, two, wincing each time her bare foot hit the shards of shells that littered the stone. They stabbed into the tender soles of her feet like a series of knives. She sank back down and tried again to rub her throbbing feet and aching ankle, but with her hands bound behind her back it proved impossible. A small cry of anguish emerged from her throat as the full measure of her plight came down on her.

On the next breath she admonished herself for feeling sorry for herself. That's when it hit her like a slap on the face. Carl had taken her in order to get Kip. This was all staged to get Kip. She was the bait in his trap. Her mouth tightened with resolution. If she was going to be able to warn Kip, she had to escape. And she had to do it fast. But what did it all have to do with Holly's murder? She couldn't connect it, none of it.

She renewed her efforts to saw the ropes around her wrists against the brick but quickly realized it would take hours she didn't have. It hit her then that the shells cutting her feet could be used far more effectively, particularly if she could find an oyster shell. Her resolve strong, she curled herself into a ball and began to work her arms under her backside. It wasn't as easy as it had been when she was a kid, but eventually she managed to pull her body and legs through. At last her hands were in front. She wasted no time, but began to crawl along the floor in search of a large oyster shell.

Something jabbed into her face, barely missing her eye. She yelped, pulled back too fast. With no way to catch herself she toppled sideways into a pile of what appeared to be branches. It hurt so much, she uttered a low curse. Disoriented, hurting, she lay where she'd fallen, using her hands to 'see' what was jabbing into her. After a short inspection she concluded she was on the edge of a pile of wood. She tried to calm her frantic breathing, tried to assess whether Carl was about to pounce, before she cautiously moved away from the wood pile, changed directions and once again concentrated on finding the shell she needed.

It didn't take long. With the oyster shell between her fingers, she began to saw on the ropes around her wrists.

There was no time to lose. Kip would come for her as soon as he returned to Marsh Winds and found her missing. In doing so, would he forfeit his life? How much time did she have? She redoubled her efforts.

While she worked she recalled the nauseous smell from the leaky tailpipe of Carl's car, the slow loss of consciousness. She could still smell the scent of gas and thought it must have leaked onto her clothes.

She couldn't recall being taken from the trunk but assumed it had been Carl who moved her because her next memory was of Carl dragging her over a sand and root-filled path through the rain. Shrubs and palmetto palms scraped and slapped her every inch of the way. It had been dark as the inside of a cave, but the brackish scent and the squawk of seagulls told her they hadn't ventured far from the salt marshes. She was still trying to figure out exactly where they were when he pulled her through some water and tossed her inside the place where she was now. But not for long, she thought as the first strand of rope broke.

Somewhere along the path she'd managed to spit out the gag. Sensing there was no one to hear her cries for help, she hadn't called out. She was grateful Carl hadn't noticed the gag was missing and replaced it. The last thing she remembered was that her head hit something hard when he shoved her inside. After that her recollections ended until a few minutes ago.

The creak of ancient hinges stilled her hands. A door opened nearby and someone tossed in another load of wood. Until that moment she'd thought some picnicker had piled the wood for a future rendezvous. Now she knew otherwise. She didn't dare breathe. Carl was back.

Chapter 25

Kip moved quickly. Within ten minutes he'd found tire tracks where they spun from the woods onto the slight incline of the oyster shell drive. He stopped at the edge of the drive and guided the beam of his flashlight along the tracks, over the broken underbrush, and deeper into the woods. He didn't have to search very long before he picked up what looked to him to be muddy depressions from a man's and woman's shoes. He found nothing else, no clue where Carl might have driven the vehicle once he exited the drive. It was as much as he could hope to find.

He was jogging back to the house when the first wave of cops arrived. He retraced his steps and pointed out where the car had turned off the drive then left them to figure out the rest.

On his return to the house, Kip contacted Barry Wesley on his cell and asked him to run an ID on motor vehicles registered to Carl Goddard. Within five minutes Barry returned his call. No cars were registered to Carl Goddard. However, Carl's father had three vehicles in his name: a new Caddy, a Porsche, and a 2004 Ford Taurus. Kip bet on the Taurus but asked the investigator in charge to issue an immediate APB for all three vehicles.

On the front veranda he pulled Bill aside. "I'm leaving this end to you and going to look around a bit. I've got a feeling Carl isn't taking Anna very far."

"What makes you think that?"

Kip trotted down the steps into the rain and pulled open his car door. He tossed his gun and night-vision goggles inside, slid onto the front seat, and sat there without speaking. His mind flashed back to England and the assassination of his wife and son that was meant for him and frowned. "I don't think Anna's his prime target."

"So who is?"

He smiled, and it wasn't a smile of warmth. "He's figuring I'll go after her, and he's right there." Harlie bounded to Kip's side and put her head on his lap. She looked soaked and woebegone. He glanced down and put a hand on her head. "Sorry, girl, this time you have to stay." He motioned for her to return to the house. "Go."

She took a quick look to where he pointed then back to him. Her tail wagged, her big brown eyes pled. "Not this time, girl." Kip held firm and shut the door. After one more pleading look she slowly, slowly, tail between her legs, slunk toward the house. Every few steps she paused and glanced back at him to be sure he hadn't changed his mind. "You stay!" Kip's tone brooked no disobedience.

He shifted into reverse and cracked the window but kept his foot on the brake. "Do you mind grabbing her collar and putting her inside. I don't trust her not to follow me. And you'll see that someone keeps an eye on Danny until my mother gets back."

"No problem."

"Let me know if anyone makes any demands."

Bill nodded. "Of course."

Kip backed up and headed down the drive. As he passed the area where Carl had hidden his car he noticed with satisfaction yellow police tape already marked it as off limits. Too, parts of the ground were covered with plastic sheets to preserve the integrity of any prints. Kip continued on to the end of the drive, turned left, and headed east toward Hwy 80 and Tybee beach. With the rain still pounding and visibility low, he knew there was a better than average chance he'd miss the car even if it was parked in plain sight. He drove well below the speed limit.

The sign designating the turn to Fort Pulaski came into view. The fort itself wasn't visible from the roadway, but Kip pictured the underground bunkers and munitions storages dug into the earth just past the moat that surrounded the walls, perfect places to set up an ambush or hide a captive, and hung a left toward the park's entrance.

When he pulled up close to the gatehouse and stopped in front of the barricade, he didn't expect to find any activity, and he didn't. The park closed at dusk. He got out of the car and looked inside the dark gatehouse, found it empty, and then surveyed the causeway across the south channel of the

Savannah River. It, too, appeared deserted. A yank on the padlock hanging from the metal barricade, confirmed it was locked.

Over his head, rolling booms of thunder cut short his investigations and brought his gaze upward to where lightning spit across the murky black in multiple streaks. Without warning Kip was thrown back into a time long ago when Yankee guns exploded through clouds of gun smoke, breaching walls supposed to be impregnable. Pale light from the lightning flooded the river now as bursting ammunition had done then. Like ghostly mirages marshes appeared and disappeared. His heartbeat quickened with a soldier's fear. His nostrils distended with the stench of gunpowder. He ran a hand over his face to free his mind from the strong images of his forefathers and got back into the car.

How much lead time did Carl have? Where had he taken Anna?

Not two hundred yards past the turnoff a light came through the Oleanders flanking the left side of the roadway. It caught in the corner of Kip's left eye and flickered a time or two before it went out. Someone could be on the water with a flashlight or the lights could belong to a car as it moved behind the trees on the old railroad bed. He pulled over and waited for the light to reappear. Five minutes passed. A vehicle immerged from a dirt road that ran by the boat ramp and turned onto the highway, heading back the way he'd just come. It approached cautiously, its headlights intermittent flashes between the sweeps of his wipers. Kip waited until the road was once again dark before he drove back onto the highway in the direction of Tybee beach.

Her wrists free, Anna tried to ignore the throbbing coming from her head and the aching of her body and concentrated on cutting through the rope around her ankles. A squeak of rusty hinges swung her head to the left then to the right. The sound bounced off the walls and left her confused as to where it had originated. But for certain someone had come in or gone out.

Outside, the patter of rain had lessened; the storm was passing. Without the rain to mask the scrape of the oyster shell against the ropes, the sound grew loud. She slowed her strokes, inching the shell back and forth in tiny motions. Someone was in the room with her, but she couldn't locate him. Not even when lightning intruded from some opening far above did the light reach where she sat or where the person was.

The sound of liquid gurgling stilled her fingers and brought her head up. Before she fully realized the sound's implications, she smelled something that sent fear racing down her spine—gasoline.

No longer caring whether she cut herself or whether she was heard, she sawed at the ropes in earnest, putting all her strength into the motions, praying for the tethers to pop. This was her only chance.

At last, the final strand of rope fell away. She rubbed her throbbing ankle and stood gingerly. It was imperative she locate the door before Carl realized she was free. Hobbling, she quietly circled away from the slosh of gasoline in search of a way out.

It wasn't to be. The beam of a flashlight came on suddenly and picked her out like a spotlight on a stage.

"Ah, bitch, there you are."

Anna froze. Behind the glare of light, she couldn't see his face, but she could see the pile of wood that separated them, the clearly marked gasoline can he'd placed at his feet, and in his hand the gun aimed at her.

He motioned with his gun. "Back up. It seems I underestimated you. You've managed to free yourself from the rope. No matter. You're not going anywhere."

She debated whether to ignore his orders and make a run for it, decided the time wasn't right, and stepped back until the wall stopped her. She shielded her eyes from the blinding beam. "What do you want from me?"

"You? I don't give a shit about you. I intend to kill your boyfriend."

To hear him say it so unequivocally stopped her heart from beating. She turned away.

He doused his beam and the sound of gurgling resumed. She hugged her arms around herself to still the shivering, the fear, and the unremitting frustration of not understanding the events of the past few weeks, her sister's murder, the destruction of her home. None of it made sense to her. The one thing she did know was that she had to get out of here and fast. Her time was running out. She ran her fingertips over the stone behind her to feel for the demarcation of a door then took a few tiny steps along the wall.

A shell crunched under the pressure of her damaged feet.

"Don't move! I told you not to move, bitch!"

She recoiled. He barked a laugh. "Don't even think of making a run for it, or I'll be forced to shoot."

He was in control. She was at his mercy.

Her shoulders slumped an inch before she jerked them upward with a lift of her chin. She wouldn't simply sit around and wait for whatever he intended to do. She needed a weapon, a plan. The shell she'd used to cut the ropes was still in her hand. She twisted it between her fingers behind her back. It was a large oyster shell with sharp edges, a weapon, and he hadn't noticed it.

For the moment it appeared Carl needed her alive. That played into her favor. The door must be somewhere behind him but that was only a guess. To be wrong and have to grope for the door would lead to failure. Carl must have closed it after he came in or the lightning would give it away. Did the door have a latch? Her mind raced. She didn't recall the sounds of a latch, but she could be mistaken.

Distant thunder rumbled the approach of another storm. She waited for the lightning to follow, but when it did, only the faintest light came from the overhead window. The stench of gasoline intensified Anna's headache. She closed her eyes and rubbed her temples, feeling anger rise within her with each throb of her head. She was shocked by the strength of her anger. She swallowed and swallowed again but couldn't tuck away the fury. Her palms sweated, and her insides shook. She had never wished anyone dead in her life, but she was close to wishing it now.

The words came out of her without intention. She didn't shout the words. She didn't snarl them. She didn't pepper the words with the vile language he used. It was the truth of them and the hard, calm of her voice that made them powerful. "You really are a most despicable man, Carl. You were a guest in my parent's home and a friend of Holly's, and yet you slit her throat, and tried to burn her son and me alive."

"Shut up. You don't know nothing." He slammed the gas can against the pile of wood or the wall, she couldn't see which. She heard the crunch of shells breaking under his boots as he approached with short brisk steps, like he was struggling to keep his control, like she'd gotten to him. She waited, anger mixing with fear and coursing through her like molten lava.

When she judged him close, she inched sideways away from the sound. Without warning the ground in front of her exploded. Shards of shells and stone and bits of dirt shredded her jeans and ripped her skin. She jerked back with a cry.

He flicked on his flashlight and she could see the gun. He was holding it out in front of him like he knew what he was doing. Then three-quarters of the way across the room, he stopped and glanced behind him, seemingly unsure. If something had caught his attention back there, she couldn't see it. But for the first time it occurred to her he might not be alone.

"Back up against the wall, bitch, and stay there! Move again and you're dead." He took several more steps until he was directly in front of her and spoke to her like they were having a pleasant conversation. "After all these years in the dark I'm going to make the light shine again."

"What?"

"The light. I'm going to make the beacon shine again. Don't you know where we are? We're in Cockspur Lighthouse, and I'm going to make the light shine just like it did before the war, only better, brighter. It will be quite the spectacle. Too bad you and your boyfriend won't be enjoying the sight."

She should have recognized Cockspur. She regretted she'd never ventured across the oyster beds to explore it. She shielded her eyes from the glare of his flashlight. "You mean you're going to burn it down."

Close by thunder crashed in a barrage of booming explosions and drowned out his answer. The dark flashed with light, and at last Anna had a fleeting look at what she had been searching for. Behind Carl's left shoulder was a door, and it was open. Relief flooded her then fled. In the doorway was the silhouette of another man.

There were two of them.

Chapter 26

The further Kip drove away from the fort the more difficult it became for him to dismiss the flash of light he'd seen. Long ago he'd learned to trust his instincts. He pulled into a boat ramp parking area and waited for the next lightning strike. He didn't have long to wait. In the watery light the low silhouette of the fort and a blimp that was Cockspur Lighthouse stood out. The lighthouse's lanterns had long ago been extinguished, but while Kip stared, a faint beam wavered through the raindrops. It could have come from a small craft but he didn't think so. He made a U-turn. At the Pulaski turnoff he doused his lights and turned in.

A few minutes later he stared at the mangled lock in his hand. He'd pulled it from the barricade on the exit side of the road and failed to notice it on his earlier visit. Disgusted, Kip called Bill Pennington from his car to report his findings. "No sight of Carl's car, but I noticed a light coming from the general area of Cockspur. It could be a small craft heading back to Tybee, but I'm going to check it out. Any new developments there?"

"Your mother called about five minutes ago. She and Dr. Schroeder were only about twenty-three miles from I-16, so they should be here shortly. I'll dispatch backup to Pulaski right away. Be careful."

"Will do. And Bill, have them keep it quiet. No sirens and no lights."

Kip disconnected and drove across the causeway toward the fort. Except for the occasional flash of lightning, visibility was virtually nil so he drove from memory. As he passed the brick walls of the gift shop, museum, and the fort on his right he sensed their presence rather than saw them. The rumble of his tires told him when he'd pulled off the pavement onto the gravel of the parking lot then out again and onto the grass on the far side. There he cut his engine and coasted to a silent stop.

If memory served him, the South Channel and the path to the lighthouse would be straight ahead.

Before he opened the door, he turned off the interior car lights and checked to ensure his gun was loaded. He stuffed a couple spare clips of ammunition into his pockets and reached for his night vision goggles. He closed the door without a sound.

Anna took advantage of the next lightning strike to search the room for a second man. There was no sight of anyone. Maybe she'd imagined him.

Carl came up close to her, so close she could smell the cigarette smoke on his breath. Anna inched away from him toward the door. He struck a match. Anna flinched.

The flame flared then flickered and went out.

Carl laughed. "Thought it was time for the pyrotechnics, did you?"

Carl intended to kill her and Kip, too. She was in a battle for her life. If ever she was going to escape him, it had to be now. She steeled herself. Carl was a tough creep, but he was a man. All men had the same vulnerable parts. She'd seen enough movies, read enough books, to know what to do. With all the strength she could muster she twisted and kicked. Her blow landed between his legs and nearly toppled her backward.

Before she ran, she had the satisfaction of hearing his groan. He sank to a knee. It was the best chance she would have, and she didn't hesitate. Ignoring the shells cutting into her feet and the pain shooting from her ankle, she dashed toward the door. If she could make it outside, she could hide.

She almost got there. Her hand was on the doorframe when a flashlight pinned her in its beam. To the right and left of her she could make out the dark spikes of marsh grass and beyond that the river and freedom. Whoever held the flashlight remained hidden. She considered her chances.

"Don't move. I've got a gun aimed at you."

With a gun pointed at her there was no chance. But it was the voice from the shadows that stopped her cold. Incredulous, she stayed motionless, her mind racing. She knew the voice, but it couldn't be. The voice belonged to a dead man.

He stepped out from outside the doorway and blocked her way. Before she had time to react he grabbed her shoulder, spun her around. Then he slapped the side of her head hard, snapping it back. It felt like a she'd been hit with a rock. She cried out and reeled backward, stumbling. Her legs gave out, and she dropped to the ground. At first she thought her neck was broken. Wobbly, she rubbed the back of her neck and struggled to focus on the man who'd decked her. She couldn't quite believe her eyes. Stanley Everett stood over her with a gun in one hand and his flashlight and what looked to be a pair of goggles in the other. For a dead man he looked very fit.

She gasped.

"I see you're surprised to see me." He regarded her with amusement for several seconds before he seized her arm and jerked her to her feet. "You always were too inquisitive, Anna. You should have backed off when I warned you. Holly's death would have just been an unfortunate accident, but you couldn't leave it alone. You and your sister should have listened to me and stopped probing. Then everything would have been all right."

"You've got to be kidding! To kill Holly was all right? To try and burn Danny and me inside my home was all right?" It was the final straw. Her oyster shell was still in her hand unnoticed. She clutched it and lunged for his face. There was a certain satisfaction when it sliced through flesh. But the damage must have been minimal for he recovered in seconds and swung the butt of his gun at her torso. It connected. She heard the crack of a rib and screamed as she stumbled backward.

From outside the door came the gentle lap of the sea against the shore, the sound of freedom. Staggering, she ran toward the sound.

She never saw who pulled the trigger, but the bullet propelled her through the open doorway. Her knees buckled. The strength drained out of her legs, she dropped to all fours on the stone steps before she toppled face-forward onto the hard-packed sand. She tried to call out to warn Kip. Maybe she did. She couldn't be sure. She lay there in pain.

She was alone and afraid.

Rain came down on her back, blessed, cool. She closed her eyes.

Exposed roots webbed the sand of the trail from the fort to Cockspur Lighthouse, making footing difficult on the best of days. Tonight winds from a recent storm had left the path littered with palm fronds and tree limbs, some limbs as large as trunks themselves. Rain had collected into massive puddles that disguised potholes and snakes. Even wearing night-vision goggles, Kip wasn't able to pick out all the obstacles strewn in his way. Once, his foot landed awkwardly in a hole made by a foraging wild pig. He was lucky to escape with a mild turn of his ankle. Of necessity, he couldn't run as fast he'd hoped.

No longer did he question why Anna had been taken. The shadowy figures that had pursued him for years were after him once again. They'd always been after him. His wife and son had died because of him. The thought that the same fate could befall Anna made his stomach roil with worry. He couldn't let anything happen to her. He wouldn't.

He had almost managed to convince himself Anna wasn't expendable until Carl knew he had Kip in his trap, when the report of a single shot brought him to an abrupt stop. He rocked back in agony, and his breath whooshed out as if he'd taken the hit. Hands braced on his knees, nostrils distended, he sucked air and strengthened his resolve.

He quickened his pace as much as he dared. Moving like a shadow through the cypress and scrub oaks with as little sound as possible, he paid no heed to the palmetto fronds and branches that slapped his face, or to the occasional set of glowing eyes he saw through the shrubs. Carl, he thought, tightening his lips, wasn't the only critter on the prowl tonight.

Normally he could run five miles in under thirty minutes without breaking a sweat. Not now. His muscles felt sluggish, uncooperative. Beads of sweat mingled with the raindrops on his brow and under his arms. He was more afraid than he'd ever been. With each breath he inhaled, he prayed. Not again. Please God not again...not Anna.

On a gust of wind, he thought he heard her voice, a weak cry of his name. His breath caught. He slowed to listen for her to call again. There was nothing more.

The trees began to shrink, barely topping the shrubs and palmetto palms. He ran through them doubled over, conscious of the first whispers of the tide washing through the marsh grasses and the rain falling on the leaves. The lighthouse was close now. On his left, flanked by two clusters of shrubs the outline appeared abruptly, and he picked up a new smell—gasoline. Soon after that the only things remaining between him and the picturesque monument were oyster banks and marsh grass. There was no place to hide. Carl had chosen the site of his ambush well.

Kip dropped to his knees, and cautiously began to move forward again behind spidery blades of marsh grass. Every few minutes he flattened to the ground, his eyes narrowed as he scanned the area. The gallery platform running around the outside of the lantern room of the lighthouse was an obvious spot for a sniper to lie in wait, but the small window and behind the stairs also provided good cover and a view.

The rain slowed to a drizzle. Kip glanced up at the sky then down at the few Sea Oats scattered between him and the water. The urge to charge the lighthouse was strong. But without knowing where his enemy lay, it was a foolish move. He resisted it. In seconds he was on his elbows moving toward the water, inch by inch, expecting the sound of a sniper's bullet to shatter the quiet night at any second.

Like a roach hunkered down in a dark crack, Carl was waiting for him somewhere in that lighthouse. If Carl spotted him now, the game was over. Kip didn't let his mind dwell on Carl or the alligators on the prowl in the shallows along the water's edge. Instead, he concentrated on keeping his elbows and knees away from the oyster shells and keeping his ammunition dry. He slipped feet-first into water with barely a sound and ducked behind a clump of marsh grass. Union prisoners, he recalled from the recent lecture on Ft. Pulaski, had tried to escape by hiding in the marsh grass. All but a couple had been shot dead.

Kip began to work his way through the water around the tiny island.

Anna breathed the sea and the gasoline that Carl had poured on the pile of wood that was to be her death pyre. Maybe she'd passed out or maybe not. But when her eyes opened, she saw Stanley standing over her with a gun in his hand and a pair of night vision goggles strapped on his head. He was looking not at her but across the river in the direction of the fort, looking for Kip no doubt. Carl was nowhere in sight.

Not wanting to draw attention, at first Anna didn't dare move, but her thigh burned like someone held a firecracker to it. She wanted to know how bad it was. When Stanley took a few steps toward the steps and crouched behind them, she gingerly eased a hand to the wound. Blood was oozing from it in a frightening way, but there was little she could do about it. Right now her first priority still was to find a way to escape.

To protect Kip.

Maybe twenty yards away she made out the shape of a boat bobbing off shore. Her hope rose. She lifted up on her elbow and studied the craft, judged it to be maybe ten or twelve feet. With an outboard motor it could easily make the crossing. She looked for signs of Kip then quickly realized her error. By water it would take someone hours to make the trip from Marsh Winds to Ft. Pulaski. Not only would Kip have had to know where Carl had taken her, but he would have had to start about the time he was flying to Savannah from Ft. Worth. Kip hadn't come in that boat. Stanley had. The boat was his and Carl's means of escape. If she could reach it, she could use it for her own getaway instead.

Grimacing, she rose to her knees. If her wounded leg would support her and her bare feet managed to avoid the oyster shells, and if she could get out of their sight long enough to make a run for it in the first place, it was possible. But the prospect didn't look good. Not to mention she was armed only with an oyster shell against their guns. She began to crawl. Her only hope was to get into the sea and swim.

Across the river she could see headlights from the cars on the Tybee road. They would guide her to make the long swim. She was a strong swimmer. She thought she could do it. She crawled a few more inches closer toward the river. The prospect of alligators frightened her, but Stanley and Carl frightened her more.

Once she made it to the river's edge getting into the water presented another huge problem. Cockspur Island was edged with oyster beds. Any attempt to cross the oysters without shoes would slice her feet or knees to ribbons. She just wouldn't think about it, she told herself, thinking about it. She'd managed to inch another foot closer to the water before Stanley turned and cut short her schemes. She flattened to the sand but not quickly enough.

"What the hell do you think you're doing?"

He didn't wait for an answer but crossed over to her, picked up her feet, and dragged her up the steps. The chiseled stone bit into her back and ribs. It was as if he were pounding her with a sharp-edged mallet. Despite herself she yelped. He heaved her into the lighthouse.

Nauseous and beaten, she lay still where he'd dropped her and wondered how many ribs were cracked, not that it really mattered when he set the wood aflame. Something poked into her ribs. Rolling slightly to her left, she retrieved a piece of driftwood. With its water-worn edges, it didn't make for much as far as weapons went. She'd have preferred to have discovered another large oyster shell, but she hid it against her body anyway.

"If you're trying to find Kip, you've made a huge mistake," Anna said, hoping to distract him. "He isn't coming. He's gone to Ft. Worth to check out Holly's safety deposit box."

In the light from the moon she thought she could detect surprise on what she could see of his face below the goggles.

She acted on it. "You didn't know that, did you Stanley? Holly had a safety deposit box in her name only, and the police found the key."

Stanley's lips curled into a sneer, and his voice came out in a hiss. "McTeer'll come. It doesn't matter what information he thinks he has. We've got a score to settle, only he doesn't know it. Sooner or later he'll come for you."

Anna didn't want him to take up a sniper's position so she kept right on talking. "I've got to admit you fooled me, Stanley. I underestimated you."

He smiled. "Nearly everyone does."

She pushed herself so she was sitting. "Holly found out what you were into, didn't she? That's why you killed her. You were there with Carl that night of the fire. She saw you. That's why you slit her throat. You couldn't take a chance she'd escape the flames."

"Your sister was a fool. She could have shared in the riches and power, but she wasn't interested."

"My sister was no fool. The one foolish thing she did is marry you."

He reached out a hand and slapped her in the face. Her head swung back. Tears rushed from her eyes. It wasn't so much from the hurt but from the feeling of helplessness. Before she had the time to collect herself, he hauled his foot back and gave a swift kick to her kidneys. Intense pain radiated through her midsection. She shrieked and kicked at him weakly and shrank into a fetal curl unable to move.

"That's more like it. Scream, and don't stop. That'll attract your boyfriend."

She clamped her mouth shut, but there was no way she could stop tears from running down her cheeks. She understood his true nature now, but if Kip were trying to reach her, she needed to sidetrack Stanley from joining Carl on the lantern gallery atop the lighthouse for as long as she could. Then maybe Kip could work his way to the lighthouse out of sight of their guns.

"And Danny?" Her voice sounded more like a croak than she wanted. She cleared it. "Danny was hiding in his fort of cushions. You didn't see him, and he didn't see you so you let him live. But he saw Carl. You made a mistake there."

Suddenly a bullet hit the wall over her head, whipping by her with a deadly whine. Shards of rock rained down on her.

He spouted a string of vulgarities such as she would expect of a man who ate with the bottom feeders. "Shut up, or the next shot will be into your face. I swear it. We'll get your lover-boy whether you're dead or alive."

She hung her head as if in meek compliance, but in reality she faked it some, mustering her strength, waiting for the right moment. Stanley was mixed up in something more than just the gambling ring. Holly found out what it was and paid for the knowledge with her life. And as soon as Kip showed up, both she and Kip were scheduled to die as well.

Pulling in a shaky breath, she gazed out the doorway. For the moment the rain appeared to have stopped. The moon moved in and out of the clouds providing her limited visibility, but in the distance thunder still rumbled. The rain would be back. The sound of footsteps on stone brought her gaze back inside.

Carl was coming down some steps she hadn't noticed before. Both Carl and Stanley were carrying rifles, straps of ammunition and had hand guns tucked in their belts. Anna thought all they needed were spurs to complete the picture. Stanley crossed the room to meet Carl. She edged toward the door.

At the bottom of the steps Stanley turned and glared at her. "Don't even think about it. I won't warn you again. We've got an excellent panoramic view up there. Try to run, I'll gun you down. Don't doubt my word. I assure you I'm an excellent shot."

She didn't doubt him. In the early years of Holly's marriage, her sister had told her of his marksmanship awards. Halfway up the steps Stanley and Carl met. Heads bowed in close proximity, they exchanged a few words in hushed tones. She tried but failed make out the sense of their conversation.

Then Carl came back down, and Stanley went up. For the moment Carl appeared to have lost interest in her. It was still dark in the interior of the room, but Anna had no trouble keeping tabs on him with the little light that popped in and out of the room. He walked to the wood he'd stacked in the center of the room and flicked his lighter on and off, on and off, like it was a nervous habit. Stunned, Anna stared at him, at the flame of his lighter as it danced higher and higher. Idiot. There were enough fumes in the room to ignite and blow them all to Kingdom Come.

Chapter 27

The smell of gasoline stunk in the air. It didn't take a genius to figure out what Carl had in mind, but Kip hadn't expected it to go down so fast. He'd expected they'd shoot at him first. He had just slipped into the water when a flash of light burst from the lighthouse. Instantly, every small portal was brilliant with light.

Anna was inside there.

Caution gone, Kip burst from the water at a run, zigzagging toward the door. The first shot came from above his head as he expected and hit the sand near his feet. The second was closer, nicking his arm. He was within three feet of the lighthouse steps when Carl staggered through the door, rubbing his eyes and swatting at his burning shirt. Before Carl could get off a shot with his rifle, Kip grabbed it. He swung the butt around at Carl's legs, whipping them out from under him. Carl somersaulted down the steps and landed in a heap at the foot, his bullet spitting harmlessly into the sand a few yards away.

Kip vaulted to the far side of the steps and ripped the pistol free from Carl's other hand. Using the heavy butt, he cracked him across the side of his head. The blow dropped him back to the ground. Kip hoped it was enough to keep him down.

Kip turned back toward the lighthouse entrance. Already the whole room had erupted in fire. He stood in the open doorway and couldn't see through the smoke. "Anna!"

Sucked by the diminishing oxygen, air pushed against his back, rushing inside the lighthouse to feed the fire's thirst. In no time the night air was saturated with smoke. It stung his eyes and caught in his lungs.

Anna was trapped somewhere in there, smothering.

Confined by the cylindrical walls of the lighthouse and fueled by the gasoline, the flames surged upward. Like a cyclone they spiraled, drawn up, up toward the open galley at the top. Moving with the howl of a hungry wolf, the flames burst through the roof.

"Anna. Anna, where are you?"

~*~

The initial explosion had blown Anna half out the door. Struggling, she rose to her knees, only to have Carl slam her back against the doorframe when he bolted to safety. Her head hit the edge of a rock. She gasped and collapsed back inside. How long she lay there she had no idea, but when she became aware again, she heard Kip's voice calling her name.

"Anna! Anna!"

"Here, Kip. I'm here." Only the smallest whisper came from her damaged throat. She twisted around, tried to move toward his voice. The need for air pressed into her chest, shrinking her lungs, crushing them intensely with each of her attempts to draw a breath. Her skin hurt.

Blinded, she fought her way toward the draft of cool air coming from the open door, crawling, dragging her battered body without care to the damage the shells were doing. Then at last, at last her hand touched the doorframe. Clutching it, she heaved herself into the cool of the night and pushed to her feet.

There was no railing on the steps. She remembered it at the last second and stood crouched and swaying on the platform, hesitant to move. Her eyes burned from the smoke, watered, blurry. Her head reeled. She had to escape, but she felt clumsy and disoriented, unsure of the right direction to go. She took a tentative step, winced from the pain in her ankle and nearly fell again. She took another, just managing to stay off her knees. Was Carl waiting at the bottom with his gun?

Distant sirens began to wail, too far away to bring help to her in time.

She misgauged the next step, lost her balance. Just as she began to fall, a hand came out of the smoke, grabbed her shoulder, and pulled her upright.

Kip made a sound as if the breath that had been stopped up inside his lungs had been kicked from within him. "Anna, thank God."

He lifted her from her feet and hurried down the steps, away from the inferno. Safely pressed against Kip's chest, Anna never felt so glad to see anyone in her life.

"I didn't think you were going to get here in time." Her voice shook then suddenly she was sobbing. "I didn't think I'd ever see you again." The tears came pouring from her eyes. She couldn't seem to stop them.

Shots puckered the sand beside him as Kip ran. He waited for one to hit home even as it dawned on him the shots were coming from above. A glance back toward the door of the lighthouse confirmed Carl was still out cold. There were two shooters. Smoke billowed from the entrance. He prayed it was enough cover for him and ran. At the water's edge he crouched behind a clump of marsh grass.

Anna sucked in great, heaving gulps of rain and fresh air. Never had it tasted so sweet. He buried his face in her hair, pulling her hard against him, so tight she could barely breathe. "Oh, Kip, I was so afraid..." She stopped abruptly and her fists gripped the wet lapels of his jacket. "I almost forgot to tell you. Stanley's here." Her voice was raspy, ravaged with pain and fear.

He cupped her face in his hand and rested his lips to her brow. "Sweetheart, Stanley died in the fire at your sister's home. The police found his body. Remember, I told you they'd recovered it on the phone earlier today."

"I remember, but they're wrong. The body isn't his. It couldn't be because he's here. He was upstairs in the lighthouse galley when Carl accidentally set off the blast. I'm sure of it. And he has a boat." She indicated it off shore with her chin.

Kip looked and wasn't all that surprised he hadn't noticed the boat earlier from the other side of the island. If he had, it might have made things easier for him. He scanned the area around them for any signs of movement. With the exception of Carl lying at the foot of the steps the little island appeared deserted. The sirens on the Tybee road had long-since stopped. The only sounds were the tide bumping against the shore and the rain on the water. Even the conflagration seemed to have ebbed to a silent burn.

He tipped back his head to stare at the top of the lighthouse. If Stanley were still up there, either he hadn't seen him or something was preventing him from shooting. "If Stanley was up there when the fire started, he's probably dead." He kept his voice low, keeping a close eye on Carl who was beginning to stir.

"Maybe. But there're stone steps up to the gallery. If Carl who was closest to the blaze got out, and I got out, Stanley might have made it, too."

She was right of course. He slid her half into the water behind a thin clump of marsh grass—not worth much in the way of protection, but his choices of places to hide were slim to none. He had to hope that shooting at something lying fifty yards away in the dark would prove difficult for Stanley, most especially since he would be coming from a fire that could have impaired his vision.

"He was wearing night vision goggles," Anna said, dashing that theory. Of course Stanley would have night goggles. They were readily available if you had a buck and knew the right place to look. Carl had been wearing them as well.

With Anna's hand clasped in his, he brought their joined fingers to his mouth. "Stay right here," he whispered, and crouching low, ran toward the lighthouse.

When Kip reached Carl, the one time classmate turned thug was rubbing his head and struggling to sit. He wasted no words on him but secured flexicuffs around his wrists and jerked them tight. His focus had already shifted to the earlier shots fired at him from the top of the lighthouse. Stanley or someone with a rife and hell-bent on killing them was still out there. Wherever he was hiding, Stanley or a third person would be anxious to deal the death blow to him, then get to his boat and make his escape.

Kip took up a position half in and half out of the water directly in front of the door. He didn't have long to wait before someone appeared. Behind him, the glow from the flames cast a copper tint in the doorway and converted the man into a black silhouette. Kip had a clear shot, but he hesitated and prayed it wouldn't be a fatal mistake. Any minute he expected a barrage of cops to appear. He had never seen Stanley face-to-face, and in the dark with his face half covered in goggles he couldn't be sure he had the right man.

"Freeze. I have you covered," Kip warned. The man failed to heed the warning but began to run toward the boat. That's when Kip saw the guns in his hands. "Drop your weapons and put your hands up!"

Stanley turned toward his voice and fired, getting off two shots in rapid succession. No further ID was needed. But even with the goggles, coming from the brilliance of the flames into the dark put Stanley at a disadvantage. His vision was momentarily impaired. His bullets struck the sand some ten feet to the left and short. His next shots sprayed the beach. Stanley was trying to reach his boat, and he hadn't located Kip.

Kip figured he also was trying to make them give their position away. If Kip's first shot missed, Kip didn't like the odds. He didn't move, barely breathed.

There was a distinct sound on Stanley's right, the sound boots might make crushing shells. Stanley whirled and fired in that direction. Kip used the diversion to roll further away from where he'd left Anna. He kept on rolling until he was a good twenty yards from her and directly between Stanley and his boat. As he moved his gun spit fire, drawing Stanley's bullets. Stanley pivoted, adjusted his aim, but he'd forgotten about the light behind his back. He was a sitting duck.

Kip fired. This time he heard a grunt and saw Stanley stagger. He'd gotten him, but not good enough. Stanley kept right on shooting, a little wildly, Kip thought. Kip slipped into the water and kept moving away from Anna. There were suddenly other noises across the river like boots on the flats, and they were coming on fast. Kip hoped the Calvary had arrived at last.

A swushing sound like something was rising from the water brought Kip's gaze darting to side of the island closest to the fort in search of an alligator. A split-second later a shot rang out. Stanley's body leapt backward before it fell still on the sand. Across the water Sergeant Nick Howell rose from a position behind a driftwood log and stepped into the shallow tidal stream between the mainland and the island.

Kip watched him come for a minute before he, too, rose up. He approached Stanley's prone figure with caution, gun at the ready. He wasn't taking any chances that Stanley didn't have one more trick up his sleeve.

A uniformed policeman materialized from the dark to join him and bent over to take Stanley's pulse. "You can put that piece of yours away. He's not going anywhere. Any more bad guys around here?"

"Not that I know about, but you might have the men take a look in the lighthouse as soon as they safely can just in case."

The officer was one Kip hadn't met before, a big guy who looked like he could take care of himself in a dark alley, the kind you wanted on your side. He jutted his chin at Kip. "You take him down?"

"My bullet's in him," Kip said, turning toward Nick as he came up beside them. "But Sergeant Howell here finished the job." Kip acknowledged his friend with a nod. "Not a bad shot for a has-been," he said with a smile. "Thanks."

"Just like riding a bike. One never forgets. Glad I could help. Anna?"

"She's all right, but she needs a bit of patching up, I'm afraid. She's over there. Looks like a paramedic has found her."

The tiny island was quickly becoming overrun with police, fire brigade and the like. For such a busy scene it was oddly quiet. No sirens blew, not much conversation.

"I didn't expect to see you here," Kip said, and Nick followed when he walked away from the cop.

"I was on my way back from getting some things for Sheri when I picked up the call on my radio. Thought I'd stop by to see if I could be of any assistance. Guess I beat the cops. Does this put an end to it for you, buddy? I hope it does."

"I'm not sure yet, Nick. Maybe. There's still some sharks swimming out there. Carl and Stanley are only little fish. There's work still to do."

"There'll always be sharks out there. You can't get them all. Make it the end, Kip. For your sake, for Anna's."

He nodded, his mouth compressed into a tight smile. "I hope I can."

Kip stood with his friend at the edge of the water where an officer had frozen an alligator in his powerful flashlight beam. At the approach of the two men the alligator backed up a couple of steps into the water. Kip drew his gun but held his fire. Alligators could run fast for a short distance. Though this one looked to be a juvenile, maybe five or six feet long, one whack of its tail could break a leg, or a snap of its jaw could take a big chunk of a man. Once crippled, the gator would drag its prey into the water to drown, even an animal as large as a cow.

"Nasty creatures—" Nick expressed Kip's thoughts—"all brawn and no brain. Not a good combination in man or beast."

Kip tucked his gun in his belt and took a step away from the water. "I take it Sheri is doing all right."

"They got the bleeding to stop. Baby's okay. She's spending the night at the hospital. I'm heading back there right now. When you see Pennington, tell him I'll be a little late coming in tomorrow. If he needs me tonight, he has my cell number." He arched his head up to look over Kip's shoulder. "Looks like they're loading Anna onto a stretcher. Glad she's all right. She's had a rough time of late."

"You could say that. Thanks again."

Chapter 28

The sun was shining the following morning when Kip carried Anna from the car at Marsh Winds. Danny jumped up from the top step of the front veranda where he'd been waiting and raced ahead of them. He was already bouncing on the bed when Kip placed Anna beside him. Kip didn't have the heart to warn Danny to be careful not to hurt her. Danny wrapped his arms around her and hugged.

Anna winced a little before she began to rock him in her arms. "I'm so glad to see you, sweetheart."

Standing at the foot of the bed, Kip looked on at the happy family reunion and felt a pain of longing so powerful he stepped back. While he was away, his high school sweetheart had grown into a beautiful woman, and he loved her still.

Sometime during Anna's short stay in the hospital his mother had managed to bring her fresh clothes. The knit top she was wearing was the pale blue of a morning sky, one leg of her jeans split to accommodate the bandage wrapped around her thigh and revealing a shapely leg. Her hands were dressed with gauze and tape as were her feet. He thought someone must have helped her get into the clothes. He'd like to have been the one, but the nurse had insisted he wait outside the room.

Because of him she'd almost died. He didn't want to think how close he'd come to losing her. But he could think of nothing else.

Her gaze met his over Danny's head, and he managed a smile, but his chest felt tight, his throat raw with all the things he wanted to say. Between them the moment stretched like a living thing, a moment filled with words and dreams and heartaches shared together, and for him the bitter memories of a lost wife and son. He sucked in a deep breath and swallowed hard. The memories they shared were woven into a twine that bound them together, but his own memories made him take a step away. He had no right to involve her in the life he led. This time she had survived his enemies' attack. Next time he might not be so lucky. It was time to break the twine.

He was the first to look away.

Sunshine slanted though the shutters, striping the carpet and hardwood with gold. Through the cracked window a temperate breeze blew into the room with the pledge of a beautiful day. He leaned across Anna and pushed his fingers across Danny's hair. "Bye, buddy, I'll be back to see you soon as I can."

Danny wiggled out of Anna's arms and gave Kip a hug. "I want you to stay."

He wanted to stay, too. "I have to go. While I'm away you take good care of your mommy Anna for me, will you?"

"Yes, sir."

Anna noticed the tense muscles in Kip's arms and the clench of his jaw when he straightened and backed a step away from Danny. His face was haggard with exhaustion and worry. He was running on his last reserves, she thought. Still, his presence filled the room, a big man with broad shoulders, whose convictions and sense of honor were the fuel that kept him going. He had her aching with longings that kept her thinking of him day and night. Soon as he walked out that door, something vital to her life would walk out with him.

Desperately she wanted to tell him not to go, not to leave her. Instinct told her she could never hold him that way. He wasn't a man to quit until the job was done. She turned her head to better see him, but sudden tears blurred his image. All she could think was that she loved him so much. All the days, all the years they were apart, she'd never stopped loving him. If Kip died trying to capture the men or women behind Carl and Stanley, the ones responsible for her sister's death, she never would get the chance to tell him how much she loved him. Let someone else finish the job. Already he'd done more than enough.

She told herself it was his job. She understood that, and that if she was ever to have a chance with him, she had to let him go. But fear gripped her heart so tightly she thought it would break. All the night he'd said nothing about going, but she felt it. Honor and a powerful sense of duty pulled him away. Just as before, he was going to leave her. She lifted a bandaged hand out to him. When he clasped it gently, she held him there and whispered what he needed to know, "I love you, Kip McTeer..."

He wasn't a man given to reveal his feelings, but for an instant before he touched two fingers to her lips, his mouth lifted into a sad smile, and she saw his love naked in his eyes. It was enough, for now. That was all she had.

He let go of her hand then, shaking his head. "This is something I have to do, Anna. I don't know when I can get back."

If ever, he thought, wishing it weren't true, wanting terribly to add that he loved her, too, and hoped she would wait for him. But to make promises he couldn't fulfill was unfair to her, so he kept his words tightly locked up.

Her mouth quivered. A solitary tear spilled down her cheek. It was nearly his undoing.

He backed up a step, and then another. "Take care of yourselves." His voice broke. He turned quickly and walked out the door. In the hallway, he squeezed his eyes shut and took a deep calming breath.

"Kip...you okay?"

He looked up, surprised to see his mother standing at the top of the stairs, an oversized tray filled with bacon, scrambled eggs, grits, blueberry muffins, and a bowl of fresh fruit—his favorites.

"Tired," he intoned, his voice as rough as a three-day-old beard.

"I know, son. I wish you didn't have to go." She put the tray on a hall table and began to fill a plate.

That makes it unanimous he thought and gave her a wry smile. "So do I."

"I thought you might be hungry."

"Starved." He grabbed a blueberry muffin from the tray and bit off half.

"Wait just a minute." She handed him the plate she'd been loading. "You can eat it on the way to the airport."

"Thanks." He leaned over and kissed her on her cheek.

She reached up and hugged him around the neck as if she understood the danger he was walking into. "Evan's waiting out front with the car." Her voice caught. "Be safe."

Kip nodded. *I'll do my best.* He ran down the winding staircase.

The summons had come while he was in the hospital with Anna. It hadn't been a surprise. He'd been ordered back to Ft. Worth by way of Atlanta where Barry was expected to board the plane. In his line of work, postponement wasn't an option. He glanced at his watch. His plane left in an hour and fifteen minutes, barely time enough to get to the airport.

Kip looked back at Marsh Winds where his dog sat on the bottom step, looking bereft. Marsh Winds was the only home he'd ever known, yet in the past ten years he'd hardly been there. He wondered if he'd ever again see it or the family he loved. If the bad guys had their way, he wouldn't.

As Evan sped down Interstate 16, Anna's words whispered over and over again through Kip's mind and in his heart. When he got to the airport, he pushed the thoughts away with stern resolve, but they were back again as soon as he boarded the plane. This was no time for distractions, but when he fell asleep on the plane moments after takeoff, he was smiling. *She loves me...*

Chapter 29

Behind uneasy clouds daylight suffused the slate sky. The faint outlines of mountain peaks appeared. The temperature was cold, bitterly cold. At an elevation of ten thousand feet Kip expected no less and was dressed for it in a down parka over long johns and a wool shirt. A stiff wind blew against his back and brought with it the fresh, earthy smell of last night's storm.

He and Barry Wesley had been working on tying up loose ends of the case for the past couple of months, through Christmas and into the New Year. The information they gathered on this trek up the mountain was one of the last pieces to the puzzle. Their work was almost done. The responders hidden in the handles of the duffels holding the stolen three hundred million had led them to the site of the drop. The duffels had been recovered from beneath the snow and were now secured in their packs. No trace of the money. No one had expected to find it.

What headquarters hoped was that the duffels would reveal latent prints, a hair, or other clues that might help to convict someone, or scare him enough to talk and facilitate a conviction. Even that was a long shot. The end of a long investigative journey was close. It was time to hand everything over to the prosecutors.

Kip pressed his thumb and forefingers against his brow. The ache in his head reminded him how thin the air was. There was a time when altitude didn't bother him much, but on his last two assignments his body had suffered more damage than he cared to admit. Maybe Nick was right. Maybe it was time for him to retire.

The sky was socked in. Clouds had rolled in quickly. As far as Kip could see everything was shades of white and gray and black. For a brief moment he thought of Savannah where the few months of cooler 'winter' temperatures would already have given way to spring. Everything would be green, the azaleas and dogwoods beginning to bloom, the sky brilliant with sunshine and warmth. And Anna was there. He breathed deeply, not quite a sigh, felt the constriction that prevented his lungs from fully filling, and hoisted his pack onto his shoulders.

"We better head back." The last time he'd been on this mountain peak Kip had been ambushed and badly wounded. He would have lost his life but for the man standing on the rock below him. He glanced at Barry Wesley, and a muscle in his jaw twitched. He'd thanked his friend and the others who climbed up the mountain to look for him many times, but there were no adequate words to thank a man for your life.

"Looks like we're going to get more snow." Barry fell in beside him as they started down the mountainside.

The decline was steep, the snow beneath their feet frozen solid, the walking precarious. Their footfalls crunched in the snow, the only sound except for the moan of the wind through the stunted shrubs. February, and winter was full upon the mountains.

After a few minutes Kip took the lead and chose his steps with care, not trusting that the ice-crusted snow didn't camouflage a crevasse, or a deep fracture in the rock of unknown depth. A misstep into a chasm could twist an ankle at the least. Likely it would be much worse.

As he walked, Kip rubbed a hand over the stiff muscles at the base of his neck. He'd not slept well. Besides the gusting forty mile an hour winds and pounding pellets of ice that threatened to blow his tent down the mountainside or tear it to shreds, he tossed the night through thinking of Anna, thinking irrational thoughts about settling down with her and having children, about being a father to Danny. Each time images of Anna suffering the same fate as Marie and Patrick shattered his dreams.

His life was hard, dangerous, and unpredictable. It was the way of life he'd chosen. He wasn't afraid to die, but he was afraid for Anna to die. Loving her as he did was more frightening than the bullets he'd faced in Afghanistan. As overwhelming as the loss of his wife and son had been, losing Anna would be worse. No one else had ever filled his heart and mind as Anna did. Anna, his first love. Recently the risk to Anna had been underscored. In the real world people wanted to murder him. To get to him they wouldn't hesitate to kill those he loved. The thought was sobering, terrifying.

Overhead the clouds grew darker, ominous. Kip studied them as he swallowed several big gulps from the tube connected to his water hydration bladder. Barry came up behind him, hobbling visibly from yesterday's slip on the ice. Not knowing whether the kneecap was cracked or simply bruised, Kip had wrapped it securely for his friend. Though Barry would never admit to it, by the way he dragged the leg along, Kip knew the knee was giving his buddy a great deal of pain. He put his arm around his waist.

"Hang on to me over this stretch. It'll go a little easier on you this way."

Once again they resumed the descent now made more difficult with the necessity of having to walk joined at the hip. The ridge they were cutting across was sparsely forested, the pines stunted and storm ravished, growing sometimes from cracks in the rock. Kip took advantage of them to hold onto. Ever so often he glanced at the clouds, his concern mounting. He was surprised the snow had held off this long. Snow over the ice was going to make walking that much more treacherous, and heavy weather would prevent the helicopter scheduled to pick them up from coming in. He didn't look forward to setting up camp in the middle of a blizzard, but it was beginning to look more and more like they would have to do just that.

Kip's boot lost traction on the ice. He grabbed for a shrub and held on to prevent the two of them from sliding down a particularly icy slope. "I have to admit I never guessed Stanley Everett was Marshall Quinlan's son," he said once they'd gotten off the ice bank, deliberately moving thoughts away from the incoming storm and mounting danger.

"Marshall Quinlan's illegitimate son," Barry corrected, breathing heavily as he eased himself over the ice on his backside. "If it weren't for Holly's report, I doubt we'd have been able to figure that out for a long time, if ever. Holly did a terrific job."

On a flat projection of rock where the wind had swept away most of the snow, the men stopped to take a few more swallows of water. Barry made a point of looking at his watch. "Right about now someone from our team should be in Sacramento to pay a call on Stanley's father, the illustrious Senator Quinlan."

"Cover of *Time* magazine, Chairman of the Armed Services Committee in the Senate, rumored to be a top contender for Democratic presidential candidate. As celebrity fathers go they don't come much more famous than Senator Marshal Quinlan. Hell of it is, knowing it probably is what cost Holly her life," Kip said, recalling the details of the report Holly had hidden in the safety deposit box.

"Stanley was doing all right for himself until he got mixed up in the gambling. That's when things started going bad between him and Holly. That's when she took precautions. Smart girl, just like her sister." Barry winked.

Kip smiled to himself and looked down to where the valley lay hidden under clouds. After studying his GPS for a few moments he pulled a map from his pack and sat on one of the huge rectangular slabs of stone that littered the mountainside, spreading the map across his knees. The wind tore at it, nearly ripping it nearly in half. He folded it smaller and motioned for Barry to sit beside him.

Tapping a spot with a gloved finger, he said, "I think we're here. We have to go to here to reach the valley. There's still maybe ten miles left to go, most all of it steep descent until we get closer to the valley where it eases some. That kind of walking will put a lot of stress on your leg. Maybe we should stop for the night and wait out the storm up here. It's your call. Not likely the chopper's going to make it anywhere near the valley tonight anyway."

Barry's jacket flapped with a snapping sound as he unwrapped a beef jerky and tore it in half. He handed one piece to Kip, bit off a mouthful, and chewed, studying the sky as the first few flakes of snow swirled by. "The leg's okay. I'm more worried about the storm about to slam us. I'm thinking down below under the protection of the trees it should be calmer and a tad warmer. I say let's go on down."

Kip nodded. He was of the same mind.

A gust of wind came out of the valley and whipped against him. His hat lifted from his head. He grabbed for it and tied it more securely. In the last half hour the wind had become a fierce enemy, threatening to unbalance them on the ice. Kip kept a grip on Barry as they maneuvered across the dangerous shelf. On the other side a tree had recently fallen. Kip cut off a branch, fashioned it into a make-shift crutch with his knife, and handed it to his friend.

In less than fifteen minutes the men were moving again. Swinging along on his new crutch, Barry picked up the conversation where they'd left off. "When Stanley didn't show up at Quinlan's doorstep after his mother died, Quinlan must have figured Stanley's mother had kept her secret."

"Mabel Osgood knew Quinlan's secret," Kip said. "She was also quietly investing Quinlan's money for him in Hobart's brokerage Goddard Financial. Carl knew Quinlan, too, from his grandmother. I believe it was by Mabel's design that Carl looked up Stanley. Carl got Stanley to help with the heist to repay his gambling debts. Although there isn't any evidence that supports a relationship between Mabel and Stanley at all. They may never have met. Stanley was always a pawn, easily manipulated. When Stanley landed the job at the Bureau of Engraving and Printing, Mabel and Quinlan came up with the scheme to seize the bills scheduled for demolition. Then they went to work. Like puppets Stanley and Mabel and Carl were on the ends of the strings Quinlan pulled. But Stanley was the key. He had the information and access to BEP they needed."

"Mabel had run the gambling ring for years as a way to garner money that wouldn't be traced for the senator, but that wasn't bringing in enough. Stanley was set up to lose. They figured his wife's money would pay up his debts. Looks like the plan was to pin the heist on Stanley and then eliminate him." Barry pulled his hood up over his cap and tightened the string. The snow was coming down hard, hard enough to make visibility next to nothing. Still the two moved slowly down the slope.

"The explosion and consequent fire at Stanley's house was meant to look like his death pyre," Barry continued. "The whole thing was set up by Carl. But you and Danny were loose ends. Danny recognized him when he set Anna's house on fire, so Danny needed to be eliminated. Mabel Osgood wanted you out of the picture for her own personal reasons."

"I took down her oldest grandson, Carl's brother, years ago. I just happened to be at the right place at the right time. I didn't think much of it, but my name was in the paper. Turned out Carl's brother was part of some underground militia, a nasty guy by all accounts, and with some powerful connections, not the least of whom were his grandmother and her boyfriend Marshall Quinlan. I'm convinced Marie and Patrick's murder was meant for me, revenge for putting Carl's brother away."

"Why do you think Stanley went along to the lighthouse? He'd already staged his own death and was free to go."

"It could be something as simple as Stanley didn't want to look weak in his father's eyes, or maybe it was a matter of money. Whatever Stanley's thoughts were, I expect he planned to disappear after it was over."

Kip's fingers were cold and beginning to get numb. He flexed and unflexed them and put them under his armpits to warm. "Stanley knew his wife was investigating the gambling, and he panicked. He told Carl. Maybe he thought the report would be his insurance policy to save his life. At first neither of them may have realized Mabel Osgood ran the gambling ring, certainly Stanley didn't. Initially the plan was to find Holly's report and destroy it before it got out, but Holly outfoxed them. Then she got in the way. Their schemes began to fall apart. Once the killing started it was hard to stop."

Barry dusted the snow from his face and shoulders. "Quinlan agreed to it because he needed the money. It's expensive business to finance a campaign. And like many in the political arena, Quinlan wanted the power. He believed the flattering articles written about him. He thought he was right. In his mind the country needed him to implement his beliefs. He didn't much care where the money came from as long as it couldn't be traced to him."

Kip ran a hand over his face. When he came upon Anna's house in flames, he hadn't imagined the depths of the plot that took her sister's life and nearly took hers. It still shook him to picture how close she'd come to dying.

Barry blew a breath that turned to vapor and blew away. "If Danny hadn't seen Carl at Anna's house that night, and Carl hadn't been so hell-bent on killing you for putting his brother in jail, with Quinlan's good looks, his Muslim roots, his outgoing personality, and his oratory abilities, he might have made it all the way to the presidency."

"Scary thought," Kip said half under his breath.

Almost an inch of fresh snow had fallen in the past hour. At this rate it would be six inches or more by the time they got to the valley. The new cover of snow made everything look different, unfamiliar, and Kip was relieved when he spotted the blaze he'd slashed on the side of a tree on the way up to help them keep on the right track. He pointed it out to Barry.

"I doubt Stanley ever knew he'd been used," Kip said as they picked up the pace on a short stretch of flat land.

Barry nodded, and tried to make contact with the incoming helicopter. He got nothing but static. Checking their GPS and compasses for direction, the two warriors walked through the snow with only the sound of the wind. Gradually, the trees gained height and became more abundant. The trees kept the wind back; the temperatures rose to just below freezing, but the snow kept coming, harder than ever.

Barry stopped and sat on a fallen pine. "I need to talk to you about something. I've been putting it off, and I don't want you to hear it from someone else first."

Kip joined him on the pine, his attention peaked. "You all right, bud?"

"Yes, it's not that. My enlistment is over in June. I'm thinking of getting out of field work."

Kip paused in the process of pulling a couple of brownies from his pack, lifting his brows in surprise. When he handed one to Barry, he smiled. "I can't say I blame you. You got a reason other than the nature of our work?"

Barry shot his friend a grin. "I do, actually. I'm thinking about marrying your sister and having a passel of kids with her."

Kip chuckled. "Be sure to do it in that order, too."

"You all right with it?"

"Would it matter if I wasn't?"

"Yes, but I'd marry her anyway, if she'd have me. And you ought to marry Anna. Hell, a bedpost can tell you love her."

Kip let loose with a big laugh that rolled down the mountainside like a tapering echo. Then he turned serious. "Funny thing is, Nick Howell told me the same thing the other night."

"And what'd you tell him?"

"That I had unfinished business out there. Now with Senator Quinlan's imminent arrest I'm hoping the buck stops with him. My gut feeling is that it does."

"Then we better nail the S.O.B.," Barry said, his jaw tight, "so we can both sleep easier. But these things never tidy up perfectly. You know that."

He knew. "There's more to the story than even Anna's sister unearthed. But Nick said something else that's been niggling my mind. 'Don't wait too long...' That's what he said. Don't wait too long. I've been thinking about it a lot."

"Good advice, Kip."

Kip clasped a hand on Barry's arm and squeezed. "By the way, just for the record, I can't think of anyone I'd rather have for a brother-in-law."

"She hasn't said yes, yet."

"Trust me, she will." Kip tucked the brownie wrapper into his pack and rose.

Don't wait too long. Don't wait too long... With each step Kip heard the refrain like danger was waiting for him.

Chapter 30

The day was too fine to stay inside. Bypassing the stacks of boxes needing to be unpacked, Anna went directly to the one labeled photos. Ever since she found it hidden away in the back of an upstairs closet, she'd itched to get inside it. A strong smell of smoke clung to the aging cardboard, and she turned her head away as she carried it to the front porch.

Outside the door she stood with her back against the screen and let the fresh scent of the ocean wash over her, filling her senses, cleaning the smoke from the box and the memory of the fire from her lungs. She watched the gulls play and the pelicans dive for dinner, savoring this sight, hers since childhood. The breeze ruffled her hair and danced over her face with a gentle touch. She welcomed the contented feel it brought to her. But all too soon the familiar yearning returned, and the moment was lost.

At length she drew in a deep breath and turned to put the box on an end table. As she passed the new rattan rockers, she paused to appreciate the floral pattern of the seat cushions she'd purchased last week. The bold primary colors were a good choice against the white of the chairs.

In the end the rebuilding of her home had been taken out of her hands. Government regulations demanded the house be built above the flood plain and therefore removed the option of rebuilding it as it had been. The conclusion was reached that it would be cheaper to comply with government regulations by demolishing the rest of her old home and starting from scratch.

In the weeks right after Kip left, Anna passed the majority of her days with an insurance adjuster, sifting through her house, deciding what could be salvaged, what couldn't. At her suggestion, some of the old wood in the back of the house had been carefully removed, pressure-washed then sun dried to remove all traces of the stench from the fire. Now the beautiful weathered gray boards were on the interior walls of her kitchen and breakfast room and chair-rail high in her den, providing a cozy beachy look she loved.

It was the third week of February. Almost two weeks ago she and Danny had left the carriage house and moved into their new home. At first when she watched the old place being torn down, she'd felt a great sense of loss. She'd lived there all her life as her parents had before her. Her home held many wonderful memories as well as the one terrible one. In retrospect she came to understand it was much better to start fresh. When the charred timbers were carted away, the smell of fire disappeared, and the ghoulish nightmares of her sister's murder began to recede. Never again would she walk into the living room and envision it full of flames or see her sister lying on the floor by the window, her throat slit, her eyes lifeless.

The horror of that night would be with her always, but to remember it every time she walked into her front room would have been a different matter altogether. Of her childhood home only the carriage house/garage remained. Once the fire damage had been repaired, except for upgrading the exterior with the same white weather-resistant siding she'd used on the exterior of the house, it was the same.

The architect she'd hired had been a friend of her parents and knew the house. Between them they took the best features of her old home and improved on them. With Danny in mind, she turned the three bedroom house into four, added a couple of bathrooms upstairs, enlarged the front master bedroom, and opened up the downstairs front rooms into a living area rather than the cut-up smaller rooms they'd been before. She'd returned her kitchen to the same as the one she'd recently remodeled. The result was striking. The house was modest but stunning.

Rocking her oak rocker back, Anna wished for the thousandth time Kip had been here to see it grow. He'd been gone now for four months, four months and fifteen days to be precise, not that she was counting, she mused and managed a weak smile. Never was he far from her mind. Her daily texts kept him abreast of her day-to-day activities, but she never knew where he was. Conversations with him were guarded and less than satisfactory, but she was trying to understand he couldn't talk about what he was doing or where he was. That he was alive had to be enough. Most days it was, but the nagging worry whether he would ever make it back to Savannah, to her, was always there.

The sun sank lower in the sky, spilling its rays like gold over the ever-moving water. It shimmered, breathed in peace and tranquility. Anna rocked forward, holding her breath as she enjoyed the ethereal beauty, a treat she never tired of, but she had seen the ocean when it was a violent thing. On a breath it could change, like so many lives had changed on the night Stanley Everett and Carl Goddard burned her house and murdered her sister. Life was fragile. *Oh, Kip, be safe and come back to us.*

A wisp of cloud passed near the sun, the earth tilted, and all too quickly the golden ocean turned to gray. She felt an unbidden punch of emotion and wiped a tear from the corner of her eye.

Three weeks ago all communication from Kip suddenly stopped. No news, no phone calls, no texts, no e-mails. It was as though he'd fallen off the edge of the earth. Until this morning. Anna flipped open her phone and reread the text she'd discovered over morning coffee. It was dated last night 11:00 p.m. and said simply. *C U soon. LK.* Soon as she'd seen it she called Kip's mother to share the good news. Sarah had been as worried as Anna had. She and Evan planned to be married a week from today, and her oft repeated prayer was that Kip was alright and would get back in time to celebrate the occasion with the family as he'd promised. Anna hoped the text meant he would.

She set the cell on the table and slipped the lid off the box of photographs, looked through a few pictures of her and her sister when they were children and stopped. There on the top was a photograph of Holly's kindergarten class. Right away she noticed the face in the second row, a boy of average height and light-colored hair in a striped T-shirt. The handwriting below the child's face was her mother's. It clearly identified the boy as Carl Goddard. For a long time Anna stared at his toothless smile wondering what had made him go so wrong.

The fire in the historic Cockspur Lighthouse monument was the leadoff story in the local nightly television news and on the front page of the Savannah News Press for weeks. The crime had been designated arson. Carl Goddard had been captured and was in jail awaiting trial as the primary suspect. No bond had been set. According to the papers that was the start and end of the story. No hint of a connection to her sister's death or her house fire was ever reported.

Anna knew better. When the police brought her in for questioning, she voiced her opinion. Notations were made of her conviction, but she never heard from them about it again. Frustrated, she did a little digging into Goddard Financial on her own with an eye to writing an editorial. After questioning several employees, Detective Bill Pennington dropped by the carriage house apartment where she and Danny had been staying and politely suggested she back off while the police investigation was ongoing.

She stopped questioning the locals but spent her spare time ferreting out whatever new information she could glean from her sister's notes and from her computer. Everything turned out to be a dead end.

Shortly after Stanley's 'first' death as Anna now referred to it, a story about him ran in the Ft. Worth Star-Telegram; Stanley Everett, local policeman who worked at U.S. Treasury Department's Bureau of Engraving and Printing, died in a fire that consumed his home, etc. The story was never recanted. A few days later a short editorial sited the irony that both Stanley and his wife died in fires in different states. In that article his visit to Savannah to attend his wife's funeral the week prior to his own untimely death was remarked upon. Again, no comment was ever made of Stanley being at Cockspur. No connection was made between the three fires or Holly's murder.

When Carl kidnapped her, Stanley Everett had been very much alive. Of that Anna was certain. But when no mention of his name appeared in the local papers or in the Atlanta Journal Constitution despite extensive coverage of the Cockspur Lighthouse fire Anna began to question what she'd seen. Stanley had fooled her once before. At the lighthouse he seemed to be dead, but she'd not been in a position to draw a certain conclusion.

On several of their periodic telephone conversations she voiced her exasperation to Kip. Each time he told her to hang tight. He was working on it.

And what about Quinlan Marshall, the U.S. Senator from California and presidential aspirant? Where did he fit in? Though since the afternoon before her abduction Kip never again spoke of Quinlan, Anna was privy to his name and that of his company Continental Carrying mentioned in the notes found in Holly's safe deposit box. Beyond that she knew only that he'd resigned his seat in the U.S. Senate. Personal reasons, the dozens of articles she read all stated the same thing. Sketchy background information on him and his wife and bits on his two daughters were often included in the articles, but nothing more to explain what the 'personal' reasons for his resignation were ever elaborated upon.

Then two weeks ago she read in the papers that Hobart Goddard had sold Goddard Financial. No further details were provided, except that his mother-in-law who worked in Georgia Senator Louis Norton's office had left her employment and been indicted for running a gambling ring and extortion. Anna wondered. Were these events connected?

Even with Carl Goddard in jail and Stanley Everett out of the picture, hopefully for good, as far as she knew nothing had really been solved. She suspected Carl and Stanley were just a small part of the entirety. Someone or many were behind it, but she was no closer to solving the problem than she had been before she was kidnapped. She hoped Kip was having better luck.

The setting sun limed the clouds with gold as it sank in the western sky. She sighed, realizing she'd wiled away the day. Holding the box of photos close against her heart, she rose and walked back into the house. She eyed the boxes still stacked in the middle of the room where the movers had left them two weeks ago with a twinge of guilt. Ah well, the kitchen was mostly unpacked. A quick glance at her watch told her it was time to get dinner started. Then she remembered Danny was having supper with a friend, and she wasn't to pick him up until Jimmy's mother called. Suddenly supper didn't seem very important.

That Danny wanted to go for supper pleased her. It was the first time he'd been away from her for that long since her abduction, and she half-expected to get a call to come and pick him up at any moment, almost wished the call would come. She missed him, she realized, worried about him. She smiled sheepishly. After teasing her sister about being a worrywart, now she was becoming one.

How had she ever gotten along before Danny came into her life, his antics, his laughter? Without his sounds close by, how empty the evening ahead suddenly loomed. How completely the little fellow had made his way into her heart.

The ring of her cell gave her a start. Her first thought was Danny then immediately she thought of Kip. He hadn't phoned in over two weeks, and despite this morning's text she couldn't quite tamp down the worry that snowballed as the time lengthened since his last call. She snatched the phone from the counter and saw it was an out-of-state number, not his. Her heart sank. Probably it was telemarketing, but maybe Kip wasn't able to get to his cell. She punched answer and waited a few seconds in anticipation before the recording began it's messaging about some credit card whatever. She disconnected.

Suddenly edgy, she slipped the cell into her pocket and headed for the door. The gust of wind, cool and fragrant with the scents of the ocean and a promise of rain, lifted her hair and her spirits. Breathing deeply, she slipped off her sandals and left them on the top step. The path was a short one between dunes dotted with Sea Oats and strewn with dried seaweed and stinging nettles. She walked gingerly until she got to the packed sand of the beachfront. The gulls and sandpipers took to the air when she appeared but only ventured a few feet away before they came back down and resumed their foraging. She walked on the hard sand at the water's edge, avoiding abandoned castles, drying moats, and tiny sand crab scurrying into their holes. Then, feeling the worry well up in her again, she offered a silent prayer for Kip's well-being as she so often did and began to run.

She ran until she reached the jetties, until the sunlight was nearly gone and clouds had covered over the sky, before she turned back toward home, splashing her feet in the ebbing tide along the way.

Chapter 31

His face haggard from lack of sleep, Kip stepped from his rental car and stood still a moment to savor the rich scent of the sea. It was a warm late afternoon on Tybee beach, a long distance from the blizzard in the Colorado Rockies, but the sky was graying with fretful clouds, and the offshore breeze carried a bite foretelling a cool, rainy evening ahead. With each breath he drew he remembered anew how much he loved that smell, how he missed it while he was away. At length, he shoved his hands in his pockets and tipped his head back to take in the new façade of Anna's house, approving the landscaping and rustic look it still maintained.

The renovations were complete. He knew that. During the months he'd been away, he'd kept up with the progress, but seeing it made him realize the pictures she'd sent hadn't really done it justice.

When no one answered his knock at the kitchen door, he jogged down the steps to the garage and peeked through the side door window. Relieved to see her car inside, he walked around to the porch that spanned the beachside entrance in search of her. Not wanting to disappoint again, he hadn't told her he was coming. Now he wished he had.

The sky had darkened with the threat of rain; beachcombers quickened their steps toward home, mostly couples, a child or two, and a solitary man like the one Anna saw walking toward her. The man's brown hair hung to the collar of his shirt. The jeans he wore were tattered at the knees and faded over muscular legs. He came at her walking with his shoulders broad, his lean hips in a familiar easy, military stride. Anna's breath caught.

Unable to take another step, she stopped, lightheaded, afraid to trust her eyes in the fading daylight, afraid to breathe.

Ten feet from her he slowed his step. The wind came up and tugged at his shirt and hair, and his eyes were as blue as a summer sky. His eyes were smiling, his smile pinned on her, and still she thought she was dreaming. She had dreamed of him so many times before.

She cried out, a shout of joy, and Kip closed the gap in three quick strides. He lifted her from her feet, circling, then let her feet slide to the sand and enfolded both her hands in his. He allowed his gaze to roam over her, and for a moment neither of them said anything, only looked at each other while fierce feelings charged between them.

His eyes intense, he looked down at her and saw right into her soul.

The love she felt for him was so strong it took the breath right out of her. She couldn't resist touching him, running her fingers over his cheekbones, his strong mouth. His face had become beloved in high school, and she understood that it always would be. Loving him was as elemental to her as breathing. Only now that he was back would her life be right again. Whatever terms he could offer, she was his, forever, for always.

"I'm so damn glad to see you," he said, his voice rough as the sands.

Then she was in his arms, snuggling her head against the hard muscle of his chest. "Me, too. I'm so very glad to see you," she breathed, her pulse racing wildly. "No new motorcycle accidents?"

He laughed, shaking his head, and let his chin rest on the top of her head. "No new motorcycle accidents."

She pulled back just enough so she could look at him, and they stood with arms locked around each other, gazes locked, feelings bubbling over. His hand lifted to frame her cheek, his thumb stroking the contour of her jaw. She tipped her head up and let herself be drawn into the promise in his eyes, eyes that burned with a hunger that matched her own.

"Anna," his voice broke, hot and thick. "I've missed you so much... So much..." His head lowered, and his lips brushed hers. He pulled her hard against him. The kiss deepened, and she was consumed by the power of his hunger, and her own.

At length he pulled his gaze from her and looked around for the first time. "Where's Danny?"

"He's having supper with a friend." She was still breathing so heavily it took her a few seconds to catch her breath and assimilate the question. She grinned. "So, where's Harlie?"

"I came here directly from the airport." He kept her hand in his and as of one accord they moved toward the house.

"Then you probably haven't eaten. Come on. I'll show you around the house, and we'll have something to eat."

"So you have the evening free?"

"Well, not the whole evening. But there was mention of watching a video," she laughed, a soft chuckle he'd sorely missed all the years away. "I'll have to pick him up when he calls."

A sudden clap of thunder boomed its warning of the approaching storm. He glanced up at the threatening sky and shouted over the blustering wind, "Come on. We'd better run."

He took her hand, and run they did. Dried seaweed and small shells caught in the wind scurried across the beach ahead of them while the remaining strollers scattered to find shelter. They were still five minutes away from her porch when the first fat drops of rain began to fall. By the time they got to the steps the rain was coming in a full-fledged downpour. When they raced up the last steps, they were both laughing, out-of-breath, and they were drenched.

Still laughing, on the covered deck he pulled her into the cradle of his arms, licking the rain from her cheeks and lips, dropping little kisses where the rain had fallen. He raised his head, breathing hard, and she stared into his eyes.

"Damn," he groaned into her open mouth and rubbed his lips over hers.

"Love me, Kip, just love me... I've waited so long for you to come back to me I don't want to wait a moment longer."

Bending he caught her behind her knees and lifted her in his arms. He carried her across the porch to the front door, impatient while she fumbled with the key. Inside the house, he kicked the door closed with his foot and gripped her shoulders, hauling her against him. Filled with the urgency of all those years without her, the promises he'd made to her and broken, he found her mouth and kissed like he'd never done before.

Never again, he vowed, and pulled her tighter against his thundering chest, drinking in the scent of sunshine and rain in her hair, savoring it.

Longing filled her. He was back. She pulled his lips to hers, and his eyes glowed hot as his tongue plundered her mouth. She wanted him, whatever he could give her. They'd already waited too long.

He tugged at the zipper of her pants, urging them down until they slipped from her feet into a soggy heap. Her panties followed right behind them. She loosened his belt and button and pushed down his jeans. He braced his legs apart, pulling her into the cradle of his hips. And she surrendered to his need, her need.

Their mouths met with a hunger that had been twelve years in the making.

Outside, the wind howled through the palms, whipping off a frond that frolicked across the porch with an ungainly step. He bent over and catching Anna behind her knees and back lifted her off her feet. Upstairs on the bed Anna had waited to share, Kip stretched out his legs, settling over her, and the two high school sweethearts, older and wiser from the years apart, stripped off the rest of their wet clothes and tossed them aside. As the storm outside their window grew wild, so did the passion that surged between them, and they made love as they never had before.

Anna, her face flushed with their love-making, cradled her head on her arm. "So are you home to stay for a while?" She hadn't meant to ask. The words just slipped out, and she wished she could take them back.

He propped his head on his elbow and cupped a hand over hers. Unable to keep the smile from his face, he looked down at their entwined hands and nodded. Then, letting his gaze roam over the woman he loved, he grinned and drew in a deep breath. "Last week I retired from field duty. The Air Force wants me to stay with Special Forces. I told them it would have to be in a capacity that wouldn't take me away from home much, and I'd have to discuss it with you."

When he returned his gaze to her, he was looking at her with such fierce intensity she could feel it like the summer sun burning her face. "Wait here a minute," he said. "I have to get something."

Without another word, he jumped out of bed and dashed from the room. She watched him go, grinning, enjoying the view of his lean, well-muscled naked body, listening to him trot down the steps. Moments later he was back, carrying his wet jeans. From the pocket he pulled out a small black box that was slightly worn around the edges like he'd been carrying it in his pocket for a very long time.

For a moment before he sank to his knees Kip contemplated the ring inside the box. All those years he and Anna had been apart, thoughts of Anna had lived in his heart, comforting him on those lonely nights spent on foreign soil when on special assignments. On those nights when he wasn't sure if he'd live to see the dawn, he relived the memories of Anna at his high school senior prom in her strapless, eyelet gown of blue, her arms around him as they swayed to the music, eyes only for each other; Anna lying on the beach beside him in her bikini on the Sea Oat strewn dune with the stars twinkling above them; Anna on that last day when he'd gone off to the Air Force Academy, kissing him good-bye with tears streaming down her cheeks, and much to his disconcertion his own eyes welling over. The promises they'd made to each other, the promises he'd broken. Despite the foolish mistakes he'd made, his love for her had never died.

"Anna," the sound came out of him rough and filled with yearning. "For a long, long time something has been missing in my life. Until I saw you close to death on the night when your house burned I didn't know the missing part was you." He swallowed hard, and there was sadness in his eyes.

He brushed a thumb across her lips, and at last he spoke the words she'd waited to hear since he left her. "I love you, Anna... I love you..."

"And I love you, Kristopher McTeer. I always have. Seems I'm a one man gal."

God willing, never again would he leave her. "If you'll have me, I'm here to stay with you forever. I love you, and I need you more than I can ever say. I need you in my life for always. Will you marry me, Anna?"

Breathing hard, she leaned over and pressed her open mouth against his lips. "Yes, yes... I will marry you, Kip. I've wanted to marry you since forever. I love you with all my heart." A man of ferocity and exquisite tenderness, a man of contrasts, this man was the man she'd loved since she was seventeen.

"The ring was my grandmother's. I've had it since she died when we were in high school. It was always meant for you. I intended to give it to you that summer after graduation, but then I was going away. The future was uncertain. It didn't seem right to ask you to wait for me. So I kept it in my safety deposit box all these years. While I was at Edwards Air Force base I picked it up." He handed her the ring, a single diamond surrounded by smaller ones in an antique platinum setting and smiled at her, a smile as intimate as a kiss.

He slipped the ring on her finger. She squeezed her eyes shut, trying to keep the tears back. She didn't want to cry, not now when she was so happy her heart was near to bursting. Her hand shook when she swiped at the tears.

"When I heard you'd married someone else, I cried for weeks. I thought you'd stopped loving me."

"I never stopped loving you, Anna, but I was a wild boy. Marie was pregnant with my son. I couldn't just leave her to fend, and neither of us wanted her to have an abortion. And I can never regret our son. Patrick was a joy. I'll miss him every day of my life." He took a deep breath, and something heartbreaking came into his eyes. "It was my fault they were killed. They didn't deserve to die. The assassins were after me. Marie and Patrick were in the wrong place at the wrong time. I can't forgive myself..." He turned away but not before she saw the tears in his eyes.

She slid to the floor beside him and wrapped her arms around him, tucking her head in the hollow beneath his jaw. He smelled of soap and rain and lovemaking, and she'd never loved him more. She'd known since she waved him off for the Air Force Academy that loving him would be hard, even dangerous. She hadn't counted on the heartache. She placed a hand on his cheek and turned his face toward hers. Reaching for his hand, she clasped it between both of hers. "Robyn told me everything.

I've always known. And I know in the end the price you paid was too high."

He moaned into her mouth. "Ah, Anna...so long I've wanted you, wanted to explain all the mistakes I'd made and make them right in your eyes."

She put he finger against his mouth. "Shhhh, you don't need to explain anything."

"I thought I would die before I got the chance to tell you I never stopped loving you. Yet here you are in my arms, and you feel so wonderful. I love you, Anna, I love you. I feel like I'm dreaming."

"If we are dreaming I never want to wake. To be with you has always been my dream, too."

He touched her arms, rubbing his fingers lightly over the bare skin, remembering how sexy she felt then at sixteen, how sexy she felt now.

In his eyes a fire burned, hot as the lightning that streaked across the sky, sizzling, needy. And when he took her again, she felt the heat rush through her like a wind of fire, a fever, searing, forever alight with the love they shared.

Later, when the storm was moving out and his gaze was fastened on her face, his lips soft in a lazy smile of contentment, the shrill ringing of the phone broke into their peace. Kip stretched an arm out for the bedside phone, knowing who it was, grateful for the time alone they'd had, and handed it to Anna.

"Yes, sweetie, I'll be there to get you in a few minutes... And Danny, I have a surprise for you. No, I can't tell you what yet, but you're going to like it."

Kip grinned. He was home.

Now he was really home.

About the Author

Originally from New Jersey, Ann Merritt grew up in Connecticut and the Midwest. After graduating magna cum laude from the University of Wisconsin, she worked as an art teacher, then earned a master's degree at the University of Alabama. She went to live in Savannah with her beloved husband Mac, where she still resides.

Ann is currently working on two stories set in Savannah.

Also available –
A Cry From the Cold

Also, be watching for the upcoming
Marsh Winds

Ann Merritt

Praise for Highland Press Books!

A Cry From the Cold - Ann Merritt has managed to create a beautiful love story that is full of twists and turns that will make it hard for the reader to put it down. The unlikely pairing of the wrongly accused Alaskan recluse and the police officer he rescues from a fatal bush pilot's crash in the middle of the Alaskan winter, sets up what turns out to be one of the most romantic couplings in my memory. Ann writes with a powerful narrative that will translate beautifully into a deeply human love story.
~ *Bart Patton, Amazon*

~ * ~

Revised and Updated! Through its collection of descriptive phrases, ***The Millennium Phrase Book*** by Rebecca Andrews offers writers concrete examples of rich and evocative descriptions. Browsing through its pages offers a jumpstart to the imagination, helping authors deepen the intensity of scenes and enhance their own writing.
~ *Tami Cowden, Author of The Complete Guide to Heroes & Heroines, Sixteen Master Archetypes*

~ * ~

To Woo A Lady – Erin E.M. Hatton has written a series of short stories covering Regency England and the historical standards and expectations that existed then. I especially liked how she made her characters vulnerable, yet strong. There are no wilting wallflowers here. The men are strong, stubborn and even a bit understanding about the women's expectations and the realities of the times and world they live in. The author's storylines are believable, enjoyable to read, and take you to a world of time past, with all its warts and pimples as well as beautiful homes

and good times at public functions. It's not all peaches and cream, but it's real.
~*Aloe, Long and Short Reviews*

~ * ~

Chasing Byron by Molly Zenk is a page turner of a Regency book not only because of the engaging characters, but also by the lovely prose. Reading this book was a jolly fun time all through the eyes of Miss Woodhouse, yet also one that touches the heart.
~ *Orange Blossom, Long and Short Reviews*

~ * ~

Heart's Affections - This isn't a romance in the typical genre fiction sense, but instead it is the true romance of John Keats and Fanny Brawne. Rarely have I ever been brought to tears by a novel as I was after reading this story. Ms. Zenk has produced a shining gem to be proud of for years and years to come. This is one of the most heart-touching stories I've read in a very long time.
~ *Orange Blossom, Long and Short Reviews*

~ * ~

Sweet Salvation by Lis' Anne Harris is a fabulous Georgian romance that will leave readers begging for more.
~ *Virginia Henley, NYT Best-Selling Author*

~ * ~

Sweet Liberation - Adventure, a determined heroine and a handsome hero, what more can you ask for? A recommended read! Lis'Anne Harris is added to my list of favorite Historical romance writers!
~ *Wend Petzler, Amazon*

~ * ~

Timing Is Everything by Annette Louise - A fun Western Romance with a nice dose of suspense. Highly readable, and highly recommended.
~ *Michael Angel, Author*

~ * ~

Ladybugs and Fireflies by Cheryl Alldredge - Simply put, this is a very entertaining story. The backdrop is great—a real

southern small-town flavor. There's a few fun unexpected twists, quips and fun, but readers will want to read this for the wonderful characters and the depth of feelings you'll share as you go.
~Snapdragon, Long and Short Reviews

~ * ~

On The Wild Side - Gerri Bowen is a master at writing Regency romances that really entertain. No boring drawing room drama here. On The Wild Side is a series of six short stories telling of the romantic struggles of men and women who have something special in their blood. Each one has a special gift. And sometimes those gifts get in the way of their finding true love. I found the premise fresh and the paranormal elements (wood nymphs and such) different in this book than any other I've read. I thoroughly enjoyed it.
~Teresa J. Reasor

~ * ~

Audrey's Love by Gerri Bowen - This was a very entertaining read. It made me laugh and cry and kept me on the edge of my seat. The author gave this story an interesting twist in how it played out...you will see what i mean. I recommend this book for any time travel romance fans out there. Enjoy.
~ Amazon.com

~ * ~

For Love of Gwynneth by Gerri Bowen - The author has a gentle winning style and feel for the period that kept me turning pages on this lazy weekend. I thoroughly enjoyed her story. This is my first Bowen book, but it won't be my last. A delightful tale that goes on my keeper shelf.
~ Diane M. Thompson, Amazon

~ * ~

Highland Wishes by Leanne Burroughs. The storyline, set in a time when tension was high between England and Scotland, is a fast-paced tale. This reviewer was easily captivated by the story and was enthralled by it until the end. The reader will laugh and cry, feel all the pain, torment and disillusionment felt by both main characters, but also the joy and love they felt. Ms.

Burroughs has crafted a well-researched story that gives a glimpse into Scotland during a time when there was upheaval and war for independence. This reviewer commends her for a wonderful job done.
~Dawn Roberto, Love Romances
(Also available – the new Christian version –Highland Miracle)

~ * ~

Her Highland Rogue – Laughter, tears and love shine through this wonderful novel. This reviewer was amazed at Leanne Burroughs' depth and perception in this storyline. Her wonderful way with words plays itself through each page like a lyrical note and will captivate the reader till the very end. Read **Her Highland Rogue** and be transported to a time full of mystery and promise of a future. This reviewer is highly recommending this book for those who enjoy an engrossing Scottish tale full of humor, love and laughter.
~Dawn Roberto, Love Romances
(Also available – the new Christian version –
Her Highland Destiny)

~ * ~

Highland Miracle by Leanne Burroughs - Wonderfully written, with vibrant characters, this story is a masterpiece of historical fiction. Readers will be impressed with the amount of research the author has done. She has creatively mixed actual people with fictitious ones, thereby allowing the reader to enter into this momentous period of history. The anguish and adventure of this war becomes very real, as it provides the reasoning behind the characters' words and actions.
~ Joyce Handzo, In the Library Reviews

~ * ~

Her Highland Destiny - Leanne Burroughs continues the fiery tale of Scotland's history with Highlander Duncan MacThomas and his lady wife, Catherine Gillingham of England. Yet, this story shines most brightly through the main characters of Duncan and Catherine. Both have a vibrancy that pulses through these pages. Their personalities are strong and sensual. This author is also extremely skillful with dialogue and was

able to make Duncan's Scottish burr seem almost audible. The mixture of historical and fictional personalities gives the readers a more intimate look at this time period. Readers will sigh, sob and squeal with delight whenever these characters are on the page!
~ *Joyce Handzo, In the Library Reviews*

~ * ~

Heart's Affections by Molly Zenk - This isn't a romance in the typical genre fiction sense, but instead it is the true romance of John Keats and Fanny Brawne. Rarely have I ever been brought to tears by a novel as I was after reading this story. Ms. Zenk has produced a shining gem to be proud of for years and years to come. This is one of the most heart-touching stories I've read in a very long time. A true treasure—this beautifully written narrative has earned a permanent place on my bookshelf. Reading this book is an experience I will never forget.
~ *Orange Blossom, Long and Short Reviews*

~ * ~

Chasing Byron by Molly Zenk- This is a light and entertaining story. Mariah has grand aspirations for someone of her class and the guts to try and follow through. Walter is a sweet man and much stronger than Mariah realizes. She does realize he is very attractive and a good kisser, but has to work through her infatuation to really see him. The storyline is easy to follow and the characters are well written and likable. I enjoyed this one.
~ *Maura, Coffee Time Romance*

~ * ~

Almost Taken by Isabel Mere takes the reader on an exciting adventure. Ava Fychon, who is highly spirited and stubborn, will win the respect of the readers for her courage and determination. Deran Morissey, the Earl of Atherton, who is rumored in the beginning to be an ice king, not caring about anyone, will prove how wrong people's perceptions can be. ***Almost Taken*** is an emotionally moving historical romance that I highly recommend.
~ *Anita, The Romance Studio*

~ * ~

Isabel Mere's skill with words and the turn of a phrase makes ***Almost Guilty*** a joy to read. Her characters reach out and pull the reader into the trials, tribulations, simple pleasures, and sensual joy that they enjoy. Ms. Mere unravels the tangled web of murder, smuggling, kidnapping, hatred and faithless friends, while weaving a web of caring, sensual love that leaves a special joy and hope in the reader's heart.
~ *Camellia, Long and Short Reviews*

~ * ~

Almost Silenced by Isabel Mere - Interesting romance. Both main characters are of European heritage, not usual leads for an historical romance set in England. Adding to this mix a deaf child gives a depth not always present in romances. An enjoyable read that I gladly recommend to others.
~ *L. Shirley, Amazon*

~ * ~

Almost Forsaken - Saved of sure death by another servant of the royal family, Mei resents being a servant in the royal household and dreams of escaping. Her savior, Hayden, has been a servant for years and also yearns for freedom. She is a spitfire and he's falling in love with her. Will they survive to escape? A villain, a hero and plenty of action. I loved this book and the way Isabel Mere wove the threads together to create a page turning story that I couldn't put down!
~ *Jackie Loehr, Amazon*

~ * ~

Court of Love by Cynthia Breeding - This delicious anthology of convention-bucking heroines in three separate time periods will delight anyone who likes Jane Austen, but wishes to peek under Mr. Darcy's clothes. Although the historical accuracy of this collection is a bit suspect and the plotlines are wrapped up with slightly alarming speed, each story features a woman with a unique personality and an independent soul, not to mention some very sexy men in breeches. Perfect bedtime reading for lovers of spicy historical romance.
~ *Jaysen Scott, Romantic Times*

~ * ~

In **Fate of Camelot**, Cynthia Breeding develops the Arthur-Lancelot-Gwenhwyfar relationship. She does not gloss over the difficulties of Gwenhwyfar's role as queen and as woman, but rather develops them to give the reader a vision of a woman who lives her role as queen and lover with all that she is.
~ Merri, Merrimon Books

~ * ~

Cynthia Breeding's **Prelude to Camelot** is a lovely and fascinating read, a book worthy of being shelved with my Arthuriana fiction and non-fiction. (*Second book in Breeding's Camelot series.*)
~ Brenda Thatcher, Mystique Books

~ * ~

Camelot's Enchantment by Cynthia Breeding is a highly original and captivating tale! (*Third book in Breeding's Camelot series.*)
~ Joy Nash, USA Today Best Seller

~ * ~

All I Want for Christmas Is You (*Anthology*) - A warm cup of romance is just the thing for a chill winter evening... This is a compulsively readable anthology of short romance. Highly recommended.
~Michael Angel, author of Three Curses

~ * ~

I loved it! Curl up with three dashing, sexy pirates and three daring women in three delightful romances. **The Last Pirates** makes for great reading. You'll be wanting more from Cynthia Breeding—I know I will!
~ Sandra Madden, Best Selling Author

~ * ~

From betrayal, to broken hearts, to finding love again, **Second Time Around** has a story for just about anyone. These fine ladies created stories that will always stay fresh in my heart; ones I will treasure forever.
~ Cherokee, Coffee Time Romance & More

~ * ~

If you want original medieval romance, captivating heroines, sexy heroes, stories of adventure, fantasy, and poignant love, Cynthia Breeding's ***Lochs and Lasses*** has it all!
~ *Ann Major, USA Today Bestselling Author*

~ * ~

Madrigal: A Novel of Gaston LeRoux's The Phantom of the Opera - Ms. Linforth has written a love story sure to please Phantom fans old and new alike.
~ *Amanda Ashley, NYT Best-selling author*

~ * ~

Abendlied: A Novel of Gaston LeRoux's The Phantom of the Opera – Madrigal continues. Jennifer Linforth has written another noteworthy tale about the Phantom. I enjoyed how the author takes the reader back to Erik's life below the opera house to unfold a new tale with the Phantom's friendship with Comte Philippe de Chagny.
~ *Karen Michelle Nutt, PRN Reviews*

~ * ~

Rondeau: A Novel of Gaston LeRoux's The Phantom of the Opera - *Rondeau* is the stunning end to a wonderfully penned trilogy by Jennifer Linforth. Each book had me remembering why I empathized with and loved Erik so much over the years, despised Christine for not being able to see behind the Phantom's mask to Erik, and hated Raoul for destroying Erik's chances for happiness. Ms. Linforth has done a superb job of staying true to Leroux's original madman of a Phantom while showing the heartbroken man who lay behind the mask.
~ *Night Owl Romance*

~ * ~

In Sunshine or In Shadow by Cynthia Owens - If you adore the stormy heroes of 'Wuthering Heights' and 'Jane Eyre' (and who doesn't?) you'll be entranced by Owens' passionate story of Ireland after the Great Famine, and David Burke - a man from America with a hidden past and a secret name. Only one woman, the fiery, luscious Siobhan, can unlock the bonds that imprison him. Highly recommended for those who love classic romance and an action-packed story.

~ Best Selling Author, Maggie Davis, AKA Katherine Deauxville

~ * ~

Coming Home by Cynthia Owens - A heartwarming visit to a nineteenth century Irish village filled with memorable characters, post-famine intrigue, and bittersweet romance. (*Sequel to In Sunshine or In Shadow*)
~ Pat McDermott, author of A Band of Roses

~ * ~

I just finished reading **Playing for Keeps** and I have to tell you I think this just may be Cynthia Owen's best book to date. I am a big fan of her Claddagh series books. It was a great romance, a lively story and very well-written.
~ Liz, Amazon.com

~ * ~

Cave of Terror by Amber Dawn Bell - Highly entertaining and fun, **Cave of Terror** was impossible to put down. Delightfully funny with a true sense of teenagers, Cheyenne is believable and her emotional struggles are on par with most teens. The author gave just enough background to understand the workings of her vampires. Ms. Bell has done an admirable job of telling a story suitable for young adults.
~ Dawnie, Fallen Angel Reviews

~ * ~

Like the Lion, the Witch, and the Wardrobe, **Dark Well of Decision** is a grand adventure with a likable girl who is a little like all of us. Zoe's insecurities are realistically drawn and her struggle with both her faith and the new direction her life will take is poignant. The references to the Bible and the teachings presented are appropriately captured. Author Anne Kimberly is an author to watch; her gift for penning a grand childhood adventure is a great one. This one is well worth the time and money spent.
~ Lettetia, Coffee Time Romance

~ * ~

Into the Woods by R.R. Smythe - This Young Adult Fantasy will send chills down your spine. I, as the reader, followed

Callum and witnessed everything he and his friends went through as they attempted to decipher the messages. Each time Callum deciphered one of the four messages, some villagers awakened. Through the eyes of Ellsbeth, I saw the other sleepers wander, make mistakes, and be released from the Netherwood, leaving Ellsbeth alone. Excellent reading for any age of fantasy fans!
~ *Detra Fitch, Huntress Reviews*

~ * ~

Brynn Chapman will captivate the reader with intricate details, a mystery that ensnares the reader and characters that will touch their hearts. By the end of the first chapter, this reviewer was enthralled with **Bride of Blackbeard.** *It*'s a compelling tale of sorrow, pain, love, and hate. Each of the people Costanza encounters on her journey has an experience to share, drawing in the reader more. Ms. Chapman sketches a story that tugs at the heartstrings. I believe many will be touched in some way by this extraordinary book that leaves much thought.
~ *Cherokee, Coffee Time Romance*

~ * ~

Brynn Chapman makes you question how far science should take humanity. **Project Mendel** blurs the distinction between genetics and horror and merges them in a reality all too plausible. A gripping read.
~ *Jennifer Linforth, Author, Historical Fiction and Romance*

~ * ~

Saving Tampa - What if you knew something horrible was going to happen but you could prevent it? Would you tell someone? What if you saw it in a vision and had no proof? Would you risk your credibility to come forward? These are the questions at the heart of *Saving Tampa*, an on-the-edge-of-your-seat thriller from Jo Webnar.
~ *Mairead Walpole, Reviews by Crystal*

~ * ~

Hidden Death - If you're looking for a good mystery with a twist of romance, this book just might be what you're wanting. With some books, it's easy to figure out who did it. Not this

book! Jo Webnar kept me on the edge of my seat, not sure who was the bad guy and needing to find out. Loved it.
~ *Long and Short Reviews*

~ * ~

The Necklace - I don't read historicals that often but am glad I picked this one up. Be ready for a lot of dry wit and humor. Ms. Corwin gives you a generous dose. This is an interesting mix of history, romance and mystery in which the hero finds himself knee-deep in trouble and a growing affection for a woman who thinks she has given up on men.
~*Bobbye R. Terry, Amazon*

~ * ~

Moon of the Falling Leaves is an incredible read. The characters are not only believable, but the blending in of how Swift Eagle shows Jessica and her children the acts of survival is remarkably done. Diane Davis White pens a poignant tale that really grabbed this reader. She tells a descriptive story of discipline, trust and love in a time where hatred and prejudice abounded among many. This rich tale offers vivid imagery of the beautiful scenery and landscape, and brings in the tribal customs of each person, as Jessica and Swift Eagle search their heart.
~*Cherokee, Coffee Time Romance*

~ * ~

I adore this Scottish historical romance! ***Blood on the Tartan*** by Chris Holmes has more history than some historical romances—but never dry history! Readers will find themselves completely immersed in the scene, the history and the characters. This intricate historical detail emanates from the story itself, heightening the suspense and the reader's understanding of the history in a vivid manner as if it were current and present. ***Blood On The Tartan*** is a must read for romance and historical fiction lovers of Scottish heritage.
~*Merri, Merrimon Reviews*

~ * ~

The Mosquito Tapes - Nobody tells a bio-terror story better than Chris Holmes. And like all of Chris Holmes' books, this

one begins well—when San Diego County Chief Medical Examiner Jack Youngblood discovers a strange mosquito in the pocket of a murder victim. Taut, tingly, and downright scary, *The Mosquito Tapes* will keep you reading well into the night.
~ *Ben F. Small, author of Alibi On Ice and The Olive Horseshoe*
~ * ~

Binary Bingo by Chris Holmes is a quick-read science fiction story that explores an extra-terrestrial encounter within the realm of possibilities. The scenario is quite plausible given what we know and don't know about the universe. Set in San Diego and the Tucson desert, streets and neighborhoods are very familiar. One can visualize the offices and laboratories mentioned in the story.
~ *Thomas Franci, Amazon*
~ * ~

The Garden of Evil - Chris Holmes's novel is a modern day cat and mouse, no...cobra and mongoose investigation...with the stakes more personal and deadly as the adversaries find themselves continually within striking distance. The weapon – food – is one of man's most basic needs.
~ *John Sylvester, FBI Agent (Ret.)*
~ * ~

The Medusa Strain by Chris Holmes - Race with government and civilian virus chasers as they trace how the plague disease travels from Iraq throughout the United States. This thriller incorporates the very best of military, government and civilian disease centers, and political knowledge. The author takes the time to leave your teeth on edge in parting with his knowledgeable reassurances in the epilogue that this bio-weapon technology is with us today. *The Medusa Strain* really could happen!
~*The Heartland Review*
~ * ~

Spores, Plagues and History – The Story of Anthrax – With this (non-fiction) book, Dr. Chris Holmes traces the known history of anthrax, from Moses to Saddam Hussein. He shows us how it has caused problems for millennia and tracks its

beginnings as a weapon. He caps the past with frightening accounts of the very recent uses of anthrax, even leaving us with several unknowns about where we will go next, and if we can or will be able to handle the next outbreak.
~ *Journal of Emergency Medicine*

~ * ~

In the Lion's Mouth by Jean Harrington - Impressive! In this sequel to *The Barefoot Queen*, Harrington delights with an evocative tale sure to please. A strong heroine, intense emotion, and a vivid setting make *In the Lion's Mouth* a breathtaking romance. Well done!
~ *Sue-Ellen Welfonder, USA Today Bestselling Author*

~ * ~

Ah, the memories that ***Operation: L.O.V.E.*** brings to mind. As an Air Force nurse who married an Air Force fighter pilot, I relived the days of glory through each and every story. While covering all the military branches, each story holds a special spark of its own that readers will love!
~ *Lori Avocato, Best Selling Author*

~ * ~

An anthology by amazing women with character and grace— incredible writers, wonderful stories about our US Military! ***For Your Heart Only*** is not to be missed!
~ *Heather Graham, NYT Best Seller*

~ * ~

Rape of the Soul - Dawn Thompson's characters are unforgettable. Deep, promising and suspenseful. Around every corner was something you didn't know was going to happen. If you love a sense of history in a book, then I suggest reading this book!
~ *Paranormal Romance Reviews*

~ * ~

Static Resistance and Rose - An enticing, fresh voice. Lee Roland knows how to capture your heart.
~ *Kelley St. John, National Readers Choice Award Winner*

~ * ~

Eyes of Love by Katherine Deauxville - A Romantic Times Best Historical Fantasy - I read this book when it came out, then lost my copy. So delighted to find this again. It's funny, it's romantic, it's a really great read!
~ *Victoria Devlin, Amazon*

~ * ~

The Crystal Heart by Katherine Deauxville brims with ribald humor and authentic historical detail. Enjoy!
~ *Virginia Henley, NY Times bestselling author*

~ * ~

Southern Fried Trouble - Katherine Deauxville is at the top of her form with mayhem, sizzle and murder.
~ *Nan Ryan, NY Times Best-Selling Author*

~ * ~

When the Vow Breaks by Judith Leigh - This book is about a woman who fights breast cancer. The storyline dealt with the commitment between a man and a woman, with a true belief of God. The intrigue was that of finding a rock to lean upon through faith in God. Not only did she learn to lean on her relationship with Him, but she also learned how to forgive her husband. This is a great look at not only a breast cancer survivor, but also a couple whose commitment to each other through their faith grew stronger. It is an easy read and one I highly recommend.
~ *Brenda Talley, The Romance Studio*

~ * ~

Romance on Route 66 by Judith Leigh and Cheryl Norman - Norman and Leigh break the romance speed limit on America's historic roadway.
~ *Anne Krist, Ecataromance, Reviewers' Choice Award Winner*

~ * ~

A Heated Romance by Candace Gold - A fascinating romantic suspense tells the story of Marcie O'Dwyer, a female firefighter who has had to struggle to prove herself. While the first part of the book seems to focus on the romance and Marcie's daily life, the second part transitions into a suspense novel as Marcie witnesses something suspicious at one of the fires. Her life is

endangered by what she possibly knows and I found myself anticipating the outcome almost as much as Marcie.
~ *Lilac, Long and Short Reviews*

~ * ~

Beats A Wild Heart - In the ancient, Celtic land of Cornwall, Emma Hayward searched for a myth and found truth. The legend of the black cat of Bodmin Moor is a well known Cornish legend. Jean Adams has merged the essence of myth and romance into a fascinating story which catches the imagination. I enjoyed the way the story unfolded at a smooth and steady pace with Emma and Seth appearing as real people who feel an instant attraction for one another. At first the story appears to be straightforward, but as it evolves mystery, love and intrigue intervene to make a vibrant story with hidden depths. Once you start reading you won't be able to put this book down.
~ *Orchid, Long and Short Reviews*

~ * ~

Down Home Ever Lovin' Mule Blues by Jacquie Rogers - How can true love fail when everyone and their mule, cat, and skunk know that Brody and Rita belong together, even if Rita is engaged to another man? This is a fabulous roll on the floor while laughing out loud story. Rarely do I locate a story with as much humor, joy, and downright lust spread so thickly on the pages that I am surprised I could turn the pages. A treasure not to be missed.
~*Suziq2, Single Titles.com*

~ * ~

Rebel Heart - Jannine Corti Petska used a myriad of emotions to tell this story and the reader quickly becomes entranced in the ways Courtney's stubborn attitude works to her advantage in surviving this disastrous beginning to her new life. This is a wonderful rendition of a different type which is a welcome addition to the historical romance genre. I believe that you will enjoy this story; I know I did!
~ *Brenda Talley, The Romance Studio*

~ * ~

Brides of the West by Michèle Ann Young, Kimberly Ivey, and Billie Warren Chai - All three of the stories in this wonderful anthology are based on women who gambled their future in blindly accepting complete strangers for husbands. It was a different era when a woman must have a husband to survive and all three authors wrote exceptional stories featuring fascinating and gutsy heroines and the men who loved them. For an engrossing read with splendid original stories I highly encourage readers to pick up a copy of this marvelous anthology.
~ *Marilyn Rondeau, Reviewers International Organization*

~ * ~

Cat O' Nine Tales by Deborah MacGillivray. Enchanting tales from the most wicked, award-winning author today. Spellbinding! A treat for all.
~ *Detra Fitch, Huntress Reviews*

~ * ~

Within every heart lies a flame of hope, a dream of true love, a glimmering thought that the goodness of life is far, far larger than the challenges and adversities arriving in every life. In **Flames of Gold** lie five short stories wrapping characters into that mysterious, poignant mixture of pain and pleasure, sorrow and joy, stony apathy and resurrected hope. Deftly plotted, paced precisely to hold interest and delightfully unfolding, **Flames of Gold** deserves to be enjoyed in any season, guaranteeing that real holiday spirit endures within the gifts of faith, hope and love personified in these engaging, spirited stories!
~ *Viviane Crystal, Crystal Reviews*

~ * ~

Romance Upon A Midnight Clear *(Anthology)* - Each of these stories is well-written; when grouped together, they pack a powerful punch. Each author shares exceptional characters and a multitude of emotions ranging from grief to elation. You cannot help being able to relate to these stories that touch your heart and will entertain you at any time of year, not just the holidays.

~Matilda, Coffee Time Romance

~ * ~

Christmas is a magical time and these talented authors answer the question of what happens when **Christmas Wishes** come true in this incredible anthology. What a joy to read such splendid stories!
~ Debbie, CK2S Kwips and Kritiques
(Revised e-book now available online.)

~ * ~

I don't think the reader will find a better compilation of mouth watering short romantic love stories than in **Recipe for Love**! This is a highly recommended volume—perfect for beaches, doctor's offices, or anywhere you've a few minutes to read.
~ *Marilyn Rondeau, Reviewers International Organization*
(Revised e-book now available online)

~ * ~

Holiday in the Heart *(Anthology)* - Stories that would put even Scrooge into the Christmas spirit. It does not matter what *type* of romance genre you prefer. This book has a little bit of everything. The stories are set in the U.S.A. and Europe. Some take place in the past, some in the present, and one story takes place in both! I strongly suggest you put on something comfortable, brew up something hot (tea, coffee or cocoa will do), light up a fire, settle down somewhere quiet and begin reading this anthology.
~ Detra Fitch, Huntress Reviews
(Revised e-book now available online.)

~ * ~

Legend says that if you wish with all your heart upon the rare blue moon, your wishes were sure to come true. Angels may help, ancient spells may be broken. Even vampires will find their perfect mate with the power of the blue moon. **Blue Moon Magic** is a perfect read for late at night or during your commute to work. It offers historicals, contemporaries, time travel, paranormal, and futuristic narratives to tempt your heart. If you do not have the time to finish a full-length novel, and hate

stopping in the middle of a loving tale, I highly recommend grabbing this book.
~ *Kim Swiderski, Writers Unlimited Reviewer*
(Revised e-book now available online.)
~ * ~

Legend has it that a blue moon is enchanted. What happens when talented authors utilize this theme to create enthralling stories of love? Readers will find a wide variety of time periods and styles showcased in this superb anthology. **Blue Moon Enchantment** is sure to offer a little bit of something for everyone!
~ *Debbie, CK²S Kwips and Kritiques*
(Revised e-book now available online.)
~ * ~

Love Under the Mistletoe is a fun anthology that infuses the beauty of the season with fun characters and unforgettable situations. This is one of those books you can read year round and still derive great pleasure from each of the charming stories. A wonderful compilation of holiday stories.
~ *Chrissy Dionne, Romance Junkies*
~ * ~

Love and Silver Bells - I really enjoyed this heartwarming anthology. The characters are heart-wrenchingly human and hurting and simply looking for a little bit of peace on earth. Luckily they all eventually find it, although not without some strife. But we always appreciate the gifts we receive when we have to work a little harder to keep them. I recommend these warm holiday tales be read by the light of a well-lit tree, with a lovely fire in the fireplace and a nice cup of hot cocoa. All will warm you through and through.
~ *Angi, Night Owl Romance*
~ * ~

Love on a Harley is an amazing romantic anthology. Each story was heartwarming, tear jerking, and so perfect. Lost love, rekindling love, and learning to love are all expressed within these pages beautifully. I couldn't ask for a better romance

anthology; each author brings that sensual, longing sort of love that every woman dreams of.
~ *Crystal, Crystal Book Reviews*

~ * ~

No Law Against Love *(Anthology)* - If you have ever found yourself rolling your eyes at some of the more stupid laws, then you are going to adore this novel. A stellar anthology that had me laughing, sighing in pleasure, believing in magic, and left me begging for more! This is one novel that will go directly to my 'Keeper' shelf, to be read over and over again. Very highly recommended!
~ *Detra Fitch, Huntress Reviews*
(Revised e-book now available online.)

~ * ~

No Law Against Love 2 - I'm sure you've heard about some of those silly laws, right? Well, this anthology shows us that sometimes those silly laws can bring just the right people together. I highly recommend this anthology. Each story is a gem and each author has certainly given their readers value for money.
~ *Valerie, Love Romances and More*

Be sure to check Highland Press Publishing's website often to see the newest available books, eBooks, and single short stories/novellas

http://highlandpress.org